One of *Booklist*'s Top Ten SF/Fantasy Books of 2007

"A fierce and stout narrative that echoes certain other fantasy classics even more so than it does the canonical authors Milton and Dante, while retaining a splendid novelty of conception . . . given all these inflowing currents into the mighty river of Barlowe's own imagination, the book attains a weighty magnificence."

—*Sci Fi Weekly*

"Hell's denizens struggle for redemption in this evocative epic fantasy. . . . [Barlowe] succeeds; at some points, his depictions of both the grandeur and the horror of Hell even surpass his original paintings and drawings. . . . A vivid travelogue of a place we'd all like to avoid."

—*Kirkus Reviews*

"Best known for extraordinarily imaginative fantasy art, Barlowe now sets his talents to writing equally compelling speculative fiction. . . . A compelling view of Hell and of a demon who seeks redemption."

—*Publishers Weekly*

"An electrifying, chilling trip through the netherworld. The landscape is so well depicted, you can smell the brimstone and feel the despair."

—*Romantic Times BOOKreviews* (Top Pick)

"*God's Demon* is the closest thing we have to a modern-day version of Milton's *Paradise Lost,* which served as inspiration for Barlowe's latest work of genius."

—*Bookgasm*

"[Barlowe] earns himself a shining star in the dark fantasy fiction firmament with this beautifully horrifying novel of Heaven and Hell engaged in the ultimate war between good and evil. . . . Brilliantly conceived and written, Mr. Barlowe has created a sweeping dark fantasy epic that is terrifying, exciting and quite moving."
—*The Tomb of Dark Delights*

"An extraordinary fantasy novel . . . a tremendously compelling epic that will satisfy fantasy readers many times over, it is also a startling artistic accomplishment."
—*Fantasy Book Critic*

"There are abundant political intrigues, philosophical discussions aplenty, and actual romance, too. . . . With sex, romance, blood, redemption, and vengeance on the table, I am 100 percent sure that everyone can find what they are looking for in this book."
—*Dorkgasm*

GOD'S DEMON

Wayne Barlowe

TOR ®
fantasy

A TOM DOHERTY ASSOCIATES BOOK
NEW YORK

This is a work of fiction. All of the characters, organizations, and events portrayed in this novel are either products of the author's imagination or are used fictitiously.

GOD'S DEMON

A Tor Book
Published by Tom Doherty Associates, LLC
175 Fifth Avenue
New York, NY 10010

www.tor-forge.com

Tor® is a registered trademark of Tom Doherty Associates, LLC.

ISBN-13: 978-0-7653-4865-4
ISBN-10: 0-7653-4865-9

First Edition: October 2007
First Mass Market Edition: January 2009

Printed in the United States of America

0 9 8 7 6 5 4 3 2 1

For Shawna

Acknowledgments

This book was, by any measure, an ambitious undertaking for me. There was not one moment during its creation that I was not certain I had made a terrible mistake in breaking away from painting and drawing to attempt it. During the arduous process of writing, however, I was bolstered by people both alive and dead, without whom I could never have finished the task. First and foremost among them was my wife, Shawna McCarthy, who told me more times than I can count that this was a journey that I was capable of completing. This book could never have been finished without her wisdom and unflagging encouragement, and my gratitude to her is total.

I must also thank my wonderful agent and friend, Russell Galen, for his continued support and valuable comments. Thanks must also go to my editor, Pat Lo-Brutto, who understood this project from the start and whose humor and insights into matters both heavenly and infernal were always welcome.

Thanks also to my great friend, TyRuben Ellingson, for his deep understanding of the labyrinth that is my creative mind.

God's Demon would not exist but for the inspiration provided me by John Milton's *Paradise Lost*. That work of genius, arguably the greatest poem written in the

English language, set me on the path to first visualize Hell in artwork and then in writing. Like Dante's Virgil, Milton's spirit was a constant, guiding companion.

John Dee's *Complete Enochian Dictionary* provided me with the basis for the language used throughout this book in both the pure "angelic" form and the somewhat corrupted "demonic" form. Dr. Dee's unique work was derived from conversations he had in 1581 with two angels and, therefore, seemed to me authoritative.

To enrich your reading of *God's Demon* with many of the images of Hell that I have created, please visit www.godsdemon.com.

"Is this the Region, this the Soil, the Clime,"
Said then the Lost Archangel, "this the seat
That we must change for Heav'n, this mournful gloom
For that celestial light?"

JOHN MILTON
Paradise Lost

Awake, arise, or be for ever fall'n.

JOHN MILTON
Paradise Lost

GOD'S
DEMON

PROLOGUE

Ash fell from a sky of umber darkness, softening the jagged chaos of the world below his open window. It obscured his vision so that he could barely discern the distant, broken towers he knew to be there. Only the star Algol, ever burning, ever watchful, managed to pierce the dark clouds and tint his room with a subtle ruddy glow. Eligor sat motionless, as he could for hours, watching the flakes drift down, and thought it fitting that they should come so heavily. He watched the tiny laborers far below, as they tirelessly rebuilt the shattered city of Adamantinarx. The ash fell peacefully; no burning wind played upon its slow descent and so Eligor could write without having to clear his desk every few minutes.

He wrote in ferocious bursts, punctuated only by his countless interviews and his moments of reverie. He wrote because he felt that he had to, and when he wrote it was in the script of angels. Because now it was permitted. The script had come fitfully, at first; it had been so long since he had written in it. The long strokes of his precious quill pen had been just a little too precise, the terminating circles a little too crabbed. But eventually he loosened up, remembering his way, and the letters flew from his pen like lightning. Soon the events of the not-so-distant past were flowing freely and the story of the last days of his lord, Sargatanas, took shape.

Eligor barely remembered the flight from the battlefield back to the palace. He had only the vague impression of passing through the shredded clouds of war with *his troops, an elite squadron of Flying Guards, and of being so weary that he could barely stay aloft. There was too much to say between them, and therefore no one said anything.*

Beneath him the clouds had parted to reveal the dark landscape. From their altitude the world looked as it always had. Vast olive-brown plains, like sheets of skin, rended and folded, were cut by flowing, incandescent rivers of lava and pocked by scattered outposts, pincushioned with fiery-tipped towers. The fires of Hell still blazed, at least, and Eligor had tried to convince himself that all was as it had been.

On they flew, their spirits beginning to lift, but when they entered Sargatanas' wards all their fantasies vanished. There were virtually no intact buildings to be seen, so complete had been the need for the city's bricks, for its souls. Where once had been laid out a vast and bustling city there now was a dismal grid of tumbled blocks and foundations. Like some newly excavated ruin, the city of Adamantinarx lay exposed and broken, its empty streets only discernible with the greatest effort. Colossal statues stood tilted upon pillaged pedestals, ornamental columns were strewn like broken bones across avenues, and the once-active river harbor was submerged for many blocks in the absence of its former embankment.

Sargatanas' palace had fared little better. Looming up from the mount in the city's center, it looked dark and ominous. The immense, domed building was pierced in a thousand places, its walls ravaged for their bricks, allowing the wind, cinders, and ash to move freely within. Eligor closed his eyes when he first saw the palace. Here was the home of his lord, abandoned and subject to the fury of Hell's fierce elements. Empty.

Eligor and his traveling companions alighted upon the rim of the dome's oculus and, wings folded, peered down into the once-great Audience Chamber. Nothing could be seen.

They descended into the darkness, silently. As they dropped down, the only light came from the fires guttering atop the Guards' heads, reflected as tiny pinpricks of flame that gleamed back from the innumerable distant gold columns that ringed the space. It took many minutes to fall to the floor and, once there, many more for them to cross the space to the exit, so great was the chamber's size. In the flickering flame-light they could see only portions of the silver-white sigil—his sigil—that was inlaid into the soot-covered floor. Sorrow once again washed over them as they looked at one another.

The party entered the wide corridors, and here the pierced walls allowed enough light from outside to penetrate, creating an irregular patchwork across the floor. Their muffled footsteps echoed around them as they walked away from the Audience Chamber. They did not bother to light the torches that lined the walls, mostly because to do so would reveal even more of the disarray. The sighing wind from outside, they agreed, would have extinguished them anyway.

They picked their way through the palace, stepping around tipped-over cases, torn tapestries, smashed friezes and tiles, and the rich furnishings that had given their lord his little pleasure. All were covered in mounds of ash, which, when kicked up, suffused the hallways with a dense, choking fog.

Eligor was the first to enter the Library and all could hear his sharp intake of breath upon seeing the devastation. He had spent so much of his time there, most of it with his lord. They wended their way through the giant piles of enormous, heavy books pulled from the shelves and left in moldering tumuli. The wind whistled over them, rustling the pages back and forth, blowing ash and bits of parchment in small whirlwinds around them like swirling motes of memories.

Eventually the party split up. One by one each Flying Guardsdemon broke away to descend deeper, on his own, into the palace, seeking their chambers and, per-haps, their lost purpose. Eligor wondered what they must have thought upon reaching their rooms, each find-ing his own personal chaos.

After clearing away a mound of debris, Eligor en-tered his own chambers, high atop the main tower, and found them to be ankle deep in ash. His desk, still firmly growing from the floor, was an island in a sea of cinders. His books and papers were barely visible, scattered on the floor by the winds that came freely in through a new and gaping hole in the wall. Oddly, the obsidian-glassed window was intact, banging open and closed in the same hot wind. He pulled it shut and latched it, feeling odd that this was his first act upon entering his personal world. The hole yawned just next to the window and he stood at its verge, his cloaks and folded wings flapping, looking down at the ground so far below. He would be-gin the reconstruction of his life immediately, fill the hole, clear the floor, tidy the shelves, and set his desk in order. He had a mission now. He had to reveal every-thing. He had to tell his lord's story.

I

ADAMANTINARX–UPON–THE–ACHERON

There was the Fall. And no one was permitted to speak of it, or of the time before or of the Above. But it was the Fall that established many things in Hell, not the least of which was the distribution of territory. The future wards of Hell were randomly determined as each Demon Major, on his own sizzling trajectory from the Above, plunged headlong, meteoric, into the unknown wilds of the Inferno. Some impacted far apart, setting up their realms in relative seclusion and safety, while others, less fortunate, found themselves in close proximity, able to see the rising smoke of their neighbor's arrival. These close arrivals began plotting and campaigning as soon as they could gather about them enough minor demons to form a court. The fratricidal wars that erupted lingered for millennia, occasionally flaring up into major conflagrations. These were the volatile times of Settlement and they were never forgotten by the survivors. Many of Lucifer's original Host were lost, but those that remained, the strong and the cunning, established powerful kingdoms that would grow and prosper.

When Eligor Fell he found himself upon a smoking plain cratered with the barely moving bodies of a thousand fallen demons. They lay, as he did, stunned, twisted by their furious descents, and glowing from myriad tiny embers. Eligor had been a foot soldier in the celestial Host, attached to the seraph Sargatanas' legions, and could remember nothing of his final moments Above.

Somehow, as he Fell, he had managed to stay near his general's flaming smoke-plume.

Eligor came upon Sargatanas as he stood upon a wind-whipped bluff, unsteady, the steam of his descent wreathing him. Transformed from luminous seraph to Demon Major, he had lost all of his heavenly trappings and none of his dignity. A corona of embers flitted away from his massive head and Eligor saw it form into a great and complicated sigil for the first time. Sargatanas had been one of the fortunate ones, a demon who had Fallen, uncontested, in an infernal region harsh and inhospitable, albeit rich in minerals and perfect for city-building. Glowing milky white upon a flat plain before them, and bending around a tall central mount, oxbowed a slow-flowing river that would be named Acheron. Here, Eligor somehow knew, a great city would rise.

They stood silently, watching the shower of fiery contrails, the paths of slower descents as they approached their new, unwelcoming home. Eligor glanced over at his lord. He saw Sargatanas looking up, beyond the contrails and beyond the clouds, and saw him close his burning eyes.

A great number of demons gathered about Sargatanas as he set about the founding of his city. The earliest, mostly unknown to him, were those who had descended nearby and, after meeting with him, agreed to join his van. Others traveling from afar, more often than not, had known him from before the Fall and wanted to be by his side, perhaps for comfort, in the new world.

Eligor's intuition had proven correct; Sargatanas had seen the same potential in the land near where he had Fallen. The boundaries of Sargatanas' future city were vast, yet the Demon Major had walked them himself, pointing out to Eligor the specific features of the landscape that had provoked his interest in this particular spot. The great river, especially, had won Sargatanas over. As he and Eligor approached its steep banks, they smelled a distinct saltiness carried upon the thick air.

They peered down into the languorously flowing Acheron and both of them could see tiny forms, indistinct and writhing, in the thick water. An unaccountable deep sadness filled them as their lungs filled with the mist-laden air that rose up, and, after a moment, Sargatanas shook his great head and spun away. The gesture surprised Eligor, breaking the odd reverie that had fallen about him.

They left the river and ascended the gradual rise to the projected city's periphery where, standing assembled in a seemingly endless line twenty ranks deep, were countless souls. They were a miserable, deformed crowd, crying and trembling, as yet unaware of what was going to befall them. Sargatanas drew himself up, smoothing his robes as he walked toward them, deaf to the echoing pleas that filled the air. Eligor, too, ignored them, grown accustomed, as he was, to the souls' ways.

They were the first arrivals, souls who had been sent as the vanguard of humanities' effluvia, the damned. A steady stream of them had been arriving since shortly after the demons' Fall, and while he was repulsed by them and their ways, Eligor found himself fascinated nonetheless.

Their appearance was as grotesque as their croaking chorus; they were as varied and individual as the capricious laws of the demons could create. Somewhere in Hell, somewhere Eligor would never visit, a veritable army of lesser demons had their way with the endless flood of souls as they entered the realm. Legless, headless, corkscrewed, folded, torn, and pierced, each soul wore but the thinnest mask of mankind. No two were alike. And pushed, as if into gray clay by a giant's hand, into each soul was a black sphere, heavy and dull. Sargatanas told Eligor that the Demons Major had fashioned these globes, filled with the essence of the souls' transgressions, to serve not only as reminders of their punishment but also as a means for the demons' control. Beyond that he did not say, but Eligor marveled at the simplicity of it. As he and Sargatanas passed them, Eligor looked into their fog-white eyes and wondered what they knew, whether there was any remnant at all of their previous lives to be found in the gray husks.

Sargatanas approached his new Architect General, greeting him warmly. The Demon Major Halphas, thin and flamboyantly spined, was bedecked in layers of clacking, bone-ornamented robes while above his head blazed his new sigil, an elaborate device that now incorporated the sigil of his liege, Sargatanas, as well. Halphas was smiling as his lord approached. Around him were a half-dozen other demons, his assistants, each of whom looked at their lord with anticipatory pleasure.

"My lord," Halphas said dramatically, his smile revealing through his destroyed cheeks myriad tiny teeth, "we await but your command and the walls' foundations will be laid."

Sargatanas examined the deep trench and took the maps from Halphas, comparing what he could see with the glyph-dense diagrams that appeared on the chart. He nodded and handed them over to Eligor, who studied them briefly.

"You have done a flawless job, Lord Halphas. It is obvious to me how much effort went into your careful plans. And I checked the city limits; they are just as I laid out without the slightest deviation. Excellent!"

"Lord, I am pleased," Halphas said modestly in his scratchy voice. "The Overseers only await your command."

"We cannot begin soon enough," said Sargatanas. He raised his faintly steaming hand and with a small gesture, a flick of his hand, created a simple fiery glyph that immediately fractured and sped off to the many attending demons. They, in their turn, dutifully produced their own glyphs that rose into the sky, and these, flying along the outline of the wall, galvanized the distant demons who began the process of converting souls into bricks. The wailing grew in intensity, but none of the demons paid it any attention. Conscious of their lord's presence, they were too intent upon beginning the job at hand, as the wall's foundation started to take form around them.

Eligor watched in amazement; this was the first time he had witnessed any real construction in Hell. The techniques, he knew, were relatively untried. As each glittering glyph touched a selected soul upon its black sphere it would instantly transform from a solid globe into a thick, black liquid that flowed down into the ground. And even as the liquid began to pool, the glyph's true meaning impacted upon the soul, hammering it, compressing it into a brick, wringing out what little blood there might be, and then sending it tumbling into position in the wall. Silencing its cries forever. And upon each brick, stamped in relief into its wrinkled surface, was the sigil of its lord, Sargatanas.

Black and oily Scourges, demon-tamed Abyssals that flapped their short wings and cracked their cranium-mounted whips, darted about keeping the quavering souls in line. Eligor loathed the Scourges but had to admit their effectiveness. Pressed closely together, the clay-colored souls reacted to the commencement of construction in various ways. Some collapsed, some knelt sobbing, while others, wide-eyed, looked stunned and seemed unable to move. Most stood and pleaded at the top of their voices while a few desperate individuals attempted to run, though Eligor, who was watching all this intently, could not imagine where they thought they would go. Time and again, he would watch the well-trained Scourges fly away in short pursuits, mindlessly flailing the fleeing souls until they collapsed. Once they were still, the souls were hooked and brought back to the trench's edge. None ever escaped.

The Overseers, arms outstretched, repeatedly created

their conversion-glyphs with such rapidity that the over-all impression of the growing wall was one of a luminous ribbon of twinkling fire, a radiant necklace set upon the dark bosom of Hell.

The Overseers were, under Halphas' able tutelage, extremely skilled; it took enormous concentration to create, size, and shape the bricks and set them in place quickly, and some of the demons openly competed with their neighbors, racing to complete their sections.

The broad trench filled smoothly and efficiently. Huge gaps were left for the seven massive gates that would be built. Halphas' calculations were perfection; Sargatanas had said many times that he thought him the best archi-tect in Hell. As a raw material the souls were malleable and—best of all—plentiful. A hundred souls every foot created the beginnings of a wall twenty feet thick and ten feet high—nothing compared to what the finished wall would be, but a start nonetheless.

Eventually, as the numbers of standing souls dimin-ished, the wailing tapered off to be replaced by the low moan of the hot winds. Algol was setting; the long day's work was done. More souls would be collected, more wall would be created, and eventually this moment would become nothing but a distant memory for demon and brick alike.

When all was done for the day, Sargatanas walked along the fresh foundation for some distance, hands be-hind his back, inspecting the site. He was smiling broadly. His city would be built, and this ceremony was its har-binger. His elation was unmistakable, and Eligor and the others could not help but be swept up in it.

Eligor watched with growing wonder and enthusiasm as Adamantinarx-upon-the-Acheron rose, layer by layer, like a dark, growing crystal from the fleshy ground. As a moon is to a sun, so was Adamantinarx to the cities of Heaven. Under the guiding hand of Sargatanas, the city's planners did their best with the materials at hand to emulate the splendor of the Above. Eligor suspected that those similarities in architecture were born merely out of the desire of the demon planners to live as they had and not meant to be a cynical parody of a lost world. At times, as he walked the growing streets, Eligor felt at ease, even at home. But at other moments, moments when the memories of his former life came to him, the dark evocation made him sad.

The great hunts that Sargatanas organized to rid the nearby Wastes of the Abyssal fauna and the Primordial natives would help cheer Eligor at these times. It was impossible for him to not share the wild exhilaration that everyone felt, charging through the chaotic landscape after the fearless wildlife, and he would soon forget his sadness. The indigenous creatures of Hell posed a continuing threat to the construction of Adamantinarx, and it was challenging, even for former angels, to run them down and destroy them.

The city grew quickly and was populated just as quickly. There was no shortage of ready inhabitants. Hell, Eligor thought often, would never have a problem filling its cities. Soon not only demon workers but demons of all description as well as gray, twisted souls by the hundreds of thousands strode the broad avenues dwarfed by the enormous buildings; the only requirement to existing within the city's boundaries was fealty to Sargatanas' bidding.

And when Adamantinarx had grown for ten thousand years, the two demons had found themselves together, surveying the great city from one of its lofty towers. Eligor, in a moment of sincere enthusiasm, had turned to Sargatanas and said, "This exile, my lord, has not been nearly as grievous as we had, at first, thought. So much has been achieved!"

Sargatanas looked at him and said, "But Eligor, this is only the beginning of the beginning."

Sargatanas' voice, all harmonics and rumbles like the woody intake of some giant pipe organ, had sounded sardonic. Eligor had no reply for his lord. They had spent so much time in Hell already. Eligor would always look back at that small conversation as the moment when the enormity of their banishment—of their shared eternity—crystallized.

Perhaps, Eligor had thought during this early period, *this is why there is such frenetic building.* Like beasts who groom themselves when confronted with the insoluble, the demons, confronted with the eternity of their damnation, built. What else could they do but attempt to make this place their own? If they had to live in this place forever, they would try to tame it first, make it their own. But he knew that Hell could not be brought to heel. It was a living place, a place with its own will.

Sargatanas went about his tasks with a preternatural intensity that bordered on the obsessive. He never tired of directing the large and small matters of state. It was, Eligor guessed, his way of not thinking about the reality of their situation. He seemed, too, to be preoccupied with the affairs of his neighboring fiefdoms. The lands of his mentor from before the Fall, Lord Astaroth, bordered his largest ward, and this pleased him. Astaroth was old, genial, perhaps a little inept in his governing, and Sargatanas looked with some dismay at his old teacher's failures. But, in those early days, he posed no threat to Sargatanas or his realm and peace reigned.

Adamantinarx was not dissimilar, in its composition, from many of the cities of Hell; its flagstoned streets ran red with the blood of its souls, its soul-bricks sighed and blinked as one passed them, and its countless low buildings groaned and shuddered like any others in any other infernal city. But it was also the least tortured of Hell's cities, and its underlying openness was due solely to Sargatanas' will. Just as Hell's capital, Dis, was a horrific reflection of its creator, Beelzebub, Adamantinarx seemed, to its demonic inhabitants, as tolerant as its lord. There was a difference, a nobility, to this demon. Eligor could see it, as could any who entered Sargatanas' court. When he laid the foundations, high atop the center mount, for his many-bastioned palace, he consulted not only with Halphas but also with each of his chief underlings. Eligor saw how this openhandedness affected the court, how it served not only to bring together each demon but also to make them loyal to Sargatanas.

During one such consultation, high atop the windswept crag, Sargatanas had convened a general meeting to discuss the number of tiers the palace would have. The hot, ember-laden wind whipped Halphas' plans about, making it hard for all to see, and Sargatanas bent down to gather a few rocks to anchor them. When he had arisen, a newcomer had joined the party, having climbed the steep ascent unseen by all. Eligor's hand went to his sword, as did a half-dozen other demons'.

"Do you not know me?" the shrouded figure asked, putting down a long, narrow box and looking directly at Sargatanas. A long, bony needle pierced the flesh of the newcomer's hood, holding the heavy folds closed save for a gathered hole left for speech.

Sargatanas was a full head and a half taller than all assembled. It was a habit of his, when confronted or challenged, to fold his arms and straighten up to his imposing full height. The bony plates of his face began to shift subtly while the flame that crowned him grew more brilliant. The gathered demons knew the signs when he grew impatient and each looked at one another with anticipatory relish.

"How can I possibly know you, cloaked as you are? Your sigil is not lit."

"Surely you must remember me . . . from before the Fall. My voice, at least, must be familiar."

And of course, Eligor thought, that was the most absurd thing he had heard in a very long time. No one's voice had remained the same. The bells of the Above had left their throats long ago, burned away by the fire and the screams. The newcomer was playing a foolish, dangerous game.

Nonetheless, there was something compelling about the words that made Sargatanas look more intently at the enigmatic figure. Sargatanas' personal Art was to divine the hidden, but, strangely, in this case he seemed unable.

"Draw aside your hood." The rumble in his voice was unmistakable.

"Perhaps—if you were to ask me in the Old Tongue . . ."

"My old tongue is gone. Only this sharp one remains."

"Well then, perhaps your ears and eyes are as they were Above." The figure slowly reached up with a skin-covered, gloved hand and withdrew the bone needle from his hood. "Micama! Adoianu Valefar!"

"*Valefar!*" exclaimed Sargatanas, and rushed to embrace him.

Eligor and the others watched in wide-eyed astonishment as their lord released the Demon Major, the purest joy pouring forth from him. Here, Eligor knew, was Sargatanas' dearest friend from before the Fall, the loss of whom had been spoken of only briefly, and to only a select few, for all the long millennia. Valefar's absence had been a great blow to Sargatanas, as if more than just his great heart had been torn from him by the victorious seraphim.

"Where have you been all this time?"

"I was in Dis," Valefar said, dropping his chin. "I lingered there much longer than I would have liked. It is not an easy place to leave, once one enters."

Sargatanas put his clawed hand upon his friend's shoulder. "Ah, Valefar, all that is behind you. You are here now and here you will stay."

Picking up the long metal box, Valefar swung it easily over his shoulder, the charred plates of his face shifting into a broad grin.

Together they descended the mount. As Sargatanas passed, he nodded to Halphas, who began to roll the plans into a tube; the palace could wait.

Eligor saw how Valefar's arrival seemed to complete his lord. Though both figures were physically greatly transformed by the Fall, it was easy to see how they might have been before the great battle. Sargatanas carried his looming flesh-cloaked form more lightly. And Valefar, who knew his somewhat secondary role perfectly, also knew exactly how to prize his lord away from his dark moods. Valefar's was a lighter spirit that seemed, to Eligor, totally out of place in Hell.

II

DIS

Lucifer was gone.

By all accounts, his had been the most spectacular descent of all. Those who were able to remember said that the entire sky had lit up with his passing, that the entire surface of Hell had glowed and rippled when he Fell, yet no one could remember any one site for his impact.

Where? Where could he be? Adramalik wondered. It was a frequent thought, one that he indulged most often when he was alone, traversing the dank corridors deep within the immense pile that was Beelzebub's citadel. Adramalik would stop at a tower window, peer out nearly two hundred spans above the tallest rooftop of Dis, and focus on the city and that question. It was a question that his master, the great Prince Beelzebub, allowed no one to utter.

When his duties did not prevent it, Adramalik would linger at that same window staring out through the oily columns of smoke, the intermittent lightning, and the clouds at all that was Dis. The city was a paradigm for all that was Hell. As the First City, its layers went back to the Fall; its founding had been almost immediate. Its growth never stopped and the sheer profusion of cube-like buildings, twisted alleys, and clotted avenues was beyond count. Adramalik could stare at it for hours, spreading, he imagined, like a cancer upon the necrotic surface of Hell. As he peered downward, toward the base of the fortress, he could see in great detail the lower hovels, squeezed in among bigger, grander governmental buildings. All seemed to be tilted and angled, straining to shrink away from Beelzebub's towering citadel. Which, in fact, they were. Adramalik liked that. It spoke of fear and power. Power. *Where is Lucifer?*

Lucifer was absent and so, by default, his greatest general had assumed the scepter of rulership over Hell. Beelzebub was, some said and Adramalik agreed, an aggregate, a being who had added to his physicality the tattered remains of those fallen angels who had not arrived intact. These he had folded into himself, focusing and shaping and transforming their pain into the tens of thousands of flies that comprised his body. He was unique in Hell, and many wondered if his assumption to power had not been part of Lucifer's plan. Beelzebub's motives and inclinations, so unlike those of any of the other Demons Major, were never questioned. And his abilities were never challenged.

Adramalik moved around the labyrinth of arteries within the city-sized fortress unerringly. Most of the buildings were completely submerged in the thick mantle of cold flesh that completely covered the upper surface of the fortress. He saw the outside only rarely, when on the uppermost tiers or when he was sent on some mission of state, but this was of little concern to him. Adramalik took his role as Chancellor General of the Order to heart, and he saw his surroundings only in the context of his lord's needs. His Order served as bodyguard to the Fly, and they enjoyed privileges that were unheard of in Hell. In exchange they were his eyes and ears in Dis and the fortress.

Beelzebub's palace was a place of dark recesses and hidden culverts, a breeding ground of intrigue and apprehension that made Adramalik's job that much more difficult—and interesting. The twisting halls were dim, constricted, and damp and were fashioned not of Hell's customary soul-bricks but of enlarged veins and stretched arteries. These opened into small, stark, murky cells like the interiors of giant organs. Their floors were frequently pooled with fluids, and the furnishings, minimal and bleak, were often slick as well. The vast court, which navigated the fleshy tunnels murmuring among themselves, knew that these privations were the price they paid for the privilege of proximity to the Ruler of Hell.

As he made his way toward the Fly's Rotunda, Adramalik entered the Order's quarters. The corridor emptied into a huge basilica-like interior with hundreds of doorways cut into the tegument of the walls. This was the Order's barracks, a chamber within the Priory so deep inside the mountain of flesh that the unstirred air was thick and cool. As he passed room after room he could hear the muffled sounds of his Knights enjoying the pleasures of the court succubi. *They deserve their entertainment. I use them like a knife, to flense away the layers of deceit. And like a knife, they need to be kept sharp edged.*

He smiled as he passed each closed door. A blazing

sigil—each Knight's personal emblem—floated outside the occupied rooms. Moans and sighs mixed with growls and short panting shrieks, not all the sounds of harmless release. The succubi knew how to please, whether it was through their pleasure or their willing pain.

Adramalik, himself, rarely indulged. He could not afford to have any attachments to compromise his office, least of all the fire-laced loose lips of some highly placed, utterly tempting courtesan.

He moved purposefully, crossing the barracks floor quickly. The floor was moist and dotted with random puddles of reddish liquid that flecked his long skin robes. The feared Chancellor of the Order splashed ingloriously toward the far rear exit, where he ascended a wide staircase and passed beneath a carved archway, the final threshold before the Rotunda's narrowing artery.

Beelzebub's infamous domed Rotunda sat atop his fortress, embedded in the topmost folds of its rotting mantle. It was the single largest building in Hell, as much grown as it was built. Adramalik remembered standing on the foundation's edge, the empty socket yawning, as the vast, archiorganic foundation had been laid and the dome had been blocked. A foul updraft continuously blew stinking air from the crater into his face and he would turn away frequently, gritting his teeth. He saw the first soul-bricks being conjured into place by Mulciber, Beelzebub's architect-genius, the force behind this vast project. Adramalik remembered the endless lines of souls, kept in place by an army of winged Scourges, as they awaited their eternal fate. He could still hear their plaintive wailings as they were enfolded, layer by layer, into the great edifice. And he remembered how their cries had creased his master's face with delight.

Adramalik made his way down the final tubular corridor toward the Rotunda, stooping as he approached the clenched doorway. By design, no attack on his lord could possibly have been launched from such a position of forced supplication. Adramalik was nearly on his knees as he scribed in midair the fiery glyph that would gain him entry. It was ironic, he thought, that the most powerful demon in Hell should be thus approached. It spoke volumes about Beelzebub's paranoia.

As the sphincterlike door expanded, Adramalik saw the gathered demons only vaguely, distant and diffused by the dense atmosphere. The fires of their heads were bright sparks that flickered in the shifting skeins of airborne detritus. This was to be an Induction into the Order, an event as rare as it was important.

He entered, stood up, and the door constricted behind him. The twilight of Beelzebub's chamber took a moment to adjust to, and Adramalik tried to see whether any significant changes had been made to the vast, circular room. Eons of attendances had imbued him with a familiarity and practiced eye that missed very little.

He was used to the suffocating closeness of the place but always thought it ironic that the largest building in Hell was also one of its most cramped. Few standing in the Rotunda's center would have guessed at its monumentality. As he looked about, all looked as it should.

Adramalik slowly made his way toward the gathered demons, careful not to trip over the chunks of raw-looking meat that floated in the ankle-deep puddles of blood. He was used to this as well. *One had to get used to everything one saw in this chamber*, he reflected, *or one would go insane and find himself cast out naked upon the Wastes*. He enjoyed watching demons from outside of Dis when they entered this chamber. They would look forward, never down, rarely up, and focus upon the distant, towering throne. Their eyes would adopt a haunted look, and their jaws would clench. Their loathing was as clear as it was amusing to him, and their need to leave as quickly as possible was just as evident. *No*, he thought, *those Outlander demons could never get used to this environment as he had.* That always gave him a wonderful sense of pride.

He stepped up to the gathered demons. There were about twenty of them—petitioners mostly—and Adramalik noted that not only was his lord not seated upon the throne but that the Prime Minister Agares, a great duke and personal advisor to Beelzebub, was also absent. *What could he be doing that is more important than this?* Adramalik looked at the gathered demons and then focused on the initiate.

Adramalik knew everything about this fellow. Lord Agaliarept and he had left no stone unturned in their investigation of him. His had been a truly remarkable journey, beginning with an impact in Hell that put him far from every other demon who had landed. He had landed so far out on Hell's fringe that, after wandering alone for millennia, he had taken up with the enigmatic Salamandrine Men. There he had learned to survive in the Wastes, to hunt Abyssals of all description, to adorn himself with their glowing stalks and pelts, and to use them as a native would. His weapons skills, which drew heavily on patterns and moves from the Waste dwellers' craft, would be far beyond those of the other Knights. And he had a look to him that was intelligent and more than a little wild, due in part to a single, glowing Abyssal stalk that he'd thrust into his smooth skull. He was highly adaptable and had learned the ways of the court quickly and was quiet at the right times. Adramalik, who thought of him as something of a personal protégé, knew that he would serve the Order well.

Coinciding with Adramalik's arrival, the gathered demons began to hear a faint buzzing that seemed to emanate from between the thousands of skins that hung from the domed ceiling. These skins hung from an intricate webwork of sinew, swaying as if caught in a gentle breeze, but no breeze, no cleansing balm, had ever filtered through the windowless chamber. The movement was created by the soul-skins themselves, rippling and contorting and trying futilely to free themselves from their captivity. Adramalik had sometimes come upon Beelzebub as he sat gazing up at their rustling dance and giggling softly, unaware that he was being watched.

The buzzing grew louder; in moments Beelzebub would assume his throne. Some of the demons shifted uneasily, but the initiate looked upward without a trace of apprehension. Adramalik thought again that he had chosen well.

III

ADAMANTINARX-UPON-THE-ACHERON

There could be no day or night in Hell. What was regarded as day would have been as twilight in any other place. Only red Algol, which some regarded as the Above's Watchdog, could be used as any true measure of Time. It scratched its lonely path through the blackness at intervals regular enough to be measured and useful, and it was the wan star's pallid rise that heralded the day. Its light affected nothing.

When Algol finally rose over Sargatanas' finished palace, many millennia had passed. Its spire-ringed dome, now empty of the thousand winged workers, reared up over the city like a mighty mountain peak. The Audience Chamber within had no rival for its dark architectural beauty. Sargatanas' aesthetic had been so sublime and its execution by Halphas so deft that when he first entered the chamber Eligor nearly forgot that he was in

Hell. Mineral resources from all over Hell had been brought together, floated on barges down the Acheron, and used with such craft and subtlety as to strike dumb all who saw the chamber for the first time.

It was a hundred spans wide and the domed, pale-obsidian ceiling above soared half again more than that. Sargatanas took each visiting demon dignitary around himself, pointing out details, like the carved smoked-crystal capitals atop each of the five hundred gold columns or a particularly eloquent vein in the polished bloodstone floor. While the palace's shell was built traditionally of bricks, there was not a soul-brick to be found in its core; all the materials used in the arcade, the Audience Chamber, and the dome had been painstakingly quarried from veins of native rock. That, alone, made the edifice unique. Sargatanas had had no desire to incorporate the suffering of souls into the heart of his great building-of-state. Some might have called it a monument to ego, but Eligor knew that it was a sincere attempt to keep the memory of the Above close at hand.

He, Valefar, and sometimes Valefar's lieutenant, the Demon Minor Zoray, were frequent guides to the sights of the palace. When the great Earl and Demon Major Bifrons arrived with his large entourage, his three eyes widened with the sheer size of the chamber. As befit Sargatanas' Prime Minister, Valefar took the lead, showing them the splendors of the new palace. Gasps came from the corpulent earl—gasps of admiration, Eligor was sure, and not due to the demon's bulk.

"My lord," Eligor said, dropping back with Sargatanas, "if Earl Bifrons, whom none could call abstemious, is impressed, everyone who enters here will be awed. You will be known across all of Hell for this marvel."

Sargatanas stopped and cast his gaze up toward the distant oculus. Dark clouds slid above it. "I am sure you are right, Eligor. But what he will not realize is that I built this place as a symbol for Them—so that They can see that some of us still have our . . . dignity. Even now."

Eligor was joined by Valefar, who had broken away from the visitors. He looked intent.

"It always seemed to me, my lord, that we were doing the best we could given our circumstances," Valefar said. "I never considered that They cared at all about us since the Fall."

"They care, I am sure, enough to watch us, if for no other reason than to guard against our return. Which means that They are paying us some attention." Sargatanas' face was shifting. Gaps were opening and closing; tiny eyes or teeth appeared and disappeared again. He looked at Valefar and shook his head. "Look at us, Valefar; look at what we have become. Perhaps we deserve all of this," he said, indicating his steaming form. "Certainly most of us do. But I will not allow Hell to change me more than it must."

"Lord, I agree," said Valefar, "but our stance will do little to endear us to the vast majority of demons. They, in their anger and bitterness, have happily made peace with their transformations. To them, it stands as a symbol, a badge of their hatred for the Above."

"I know," said Sargatanas. "I have been to Beelzebub's court too many times, met with too many demons, not to have seen that. I do not care. This is my court and this is how I would have it."

"Your court is unlike any other in all of Hell, Lord," said Eligor. "It attracts those who share your enlightened beliefs." Suddenly a fork-shaped sigil appeared before him glowing insistently. "See? Even as we speak," he said, indicating the floating mark, "yet another stranger begs an audience. This one, too, hails from the Wastes. The storms seem to be driving them all to our doorstep. Should I send him away as I have the others?"

"No. I have a palace to fill now, Eligor." Sargatanas

looked at the sigil. "He is a high-ranking fellow and I will meet him. There," he said, nodding toward the immense pyramidal dais that rose from the center of the chamber. "Bifrons may stay, if he likes."

Valefar raised his hand and the stranger's sigil was augmented by two smaller glyphs, which whisked it away. He, Eligor, and Sargatanas made their way to the dais, crossing over Sargatanas' enormous circular sigil that was inlaid into the floor. It was complex and made of poured silver that gleamed against the polished stone.

Even as they began to ascend the stairs to the pyramid's flat top, they could see the stranger, having just reached the far columns, begin to cross the floor. A contingent of Eligor's Flying Guard, Sargatanas' personal bodyguard, was already landing atop the dais. As Sargatanas settled into his throne and his two aides took their positions on either side, the Guard moved in to flank them. The newcomer could be seen energetically striding toward them; he was quick and his movements were oddly clipped. *Perhaps too quick,* thought Eligor, *too eager.*

They waited as the newcomer began to climb the stairs. The many-layered garments of skin he was swathed in were covered in the convoluted patterns of tiny perpetually lit embers characteristic of a Waste dweller. Steam poured off him in thin clouds, billowing with his precise movements. When he reached them he respectfully knelt, undoing the muffler of skin that had covered his face.

He was bluish in hue, and what the trio of demons could see of his hard, chiseled face was outlined in a linear tracery of small glowing spots. Whether these were his own or acquired and applied from Abyssals they could not tell.

Sargatanas gestured for him to rise, and when he did, his mantle opened somewhat, revealing a strong body, carapaced in articulated bone strips and covered with many ossified scars. The Wastes had written their dis-

tinctive signature upon his body; the fierce conditions
and denizens encountered far from the cities rarely destroyed demons, but one could always spot a Wanderer
by their many scars. And he had another Waste dweller
trait that would mark him to a knowledgeable demon—
he moved with an almost jerky deliberateness, which
some of the Fallen found inelegant and distasteful.

"Tell us about yourself," said Sargatanas. "What is
your name?"

"I am called Faraii, Lord. I fell far from here, well
past the Flaming Cut, out beyond the Fifth Gate of
Seven. I did not fall intact but spent much time searching for my burned-off arm. After I recovered it and had
it set back upon me, I wandered the Wastes and many of
the outlying frontier-encampments. I have lived alone,
mostly, and with some of the Waste dwellers, occasionally."

"Really. Your survival skills must be extraordinary."

"Perhaps, my lord," said Faraii with great humility.
"By necessity. I explored, hunted Abyssals for provi-
sions, and made many notes on the indigenous dwellers
and their culture, Lord." Faraii seemed to Eligor at ease
and yet respectful. He also seemed a little stiff, something that Eligor put down to his having been away from
the cities for so long.

"Well then, you and Eligor, here, will have many
things to discuss. He thinks of himself as something of
an ethnographer and spends much of his free time com-
piling material on the creatures of the wilds, as well as
what the souls can remember of their civilizations."

Faraii's expression did not change. He bowed his
head slightly in acquiescence.

Sargatanas was silent for a long moment. "You
haven't mentioned that you are a baron," he said unexpectedly. Valefar looked at him for a moment and back
at the newcomer.

"I was a Seraph Minor in the court of Iuvart before

the Fall, Lord. Forgive me; no guile was intended. I do not like to think of my prior life." He looked away for a moment, the pain evident upon his face.

"It hurts all of us who choose to remember, Faraii. Myself included," said Sargatanas after a moment. "The War . . . the War had to be fought. We lost and we paid for it dearly." He looked at Valefar and Eligor and both nodded. "Well," Sargatanas said more brightly, "I think that you will be a fine addition to our court. With your knowledge and experience we will be able to more confidently traverse the outlying regions with little fear of running afoul. Welcome."

A glyph appeared from Sargatanas' chest, a duplicate of one that hovered near where his heart had been torn out. It floated toward Faraii's burning sigil, where it intertwined with it, becoming one. The pact of a new alliance had been sealed.

Sargatanas rose, patted Faraii on the shoulder briefly, and strode down the stairs. "Get him settled in, Valefar," he said over his shoulder. "It is time the Baron had someplace to call home."

As Sargatanas strode from the chamber, Faraii looked relieved, if not outwardly pleased. But when Valefar and Eligor approached him with outstretched hands he readily took them, clasping them in a grip that surprised both demons. Valefar said, "Welcome to Adamantinarx, Baron Faraii. Whether you chose this city by chance or not, this is the best of all cities in Hell. You will see."

Faraii smiled faintly. His eyes shone brightly.

Eligor studied the newcomer with interest, wondering what lay behind his laconic stoicism. This demon of the Wastes might well be worth further study.

Valefar, however, seemed more reserved in his interaction with Faraii, walking a pace behind him as they left the chamber, watching his peculiar movements closely and taking in every detail of this newest member of the court. Eligor realized that this was as it should be, that Valefar was dutifully performing one of the most important functions of his office—that of appraising those who might aspire to Sargatanas' inner circle. This exotic figure, clad in burning skins and moving in his odd, angular way, was, in fact, a baron, not some untitled itinerant, and he deserved a respectful but thorough evaluation.

The three demons exited the huge chamber, and at its main threshold guards handed Faraii his bundled traveling kit. This included a rolled protective hide, worn cooking utensils, and a strangely wrought blade that did not go unnoticed by either Eligor or Valefar. It was black and very long, with a grip ample enough to have been used with two hands. Unlike most weapons, it seemed to have been fashioned from the sharpened spine of an Abyssal and had teeth, small bells, and dried eyes dangling from short cords tied into its hilt.

"An interesting weapon, Faraii," Valefar said.

"Acquired in an interesting way, Lord Prime Minister," Faraii said, handing him the blade. "As part of a ritual of acceptance into one of the local Waste tribes I had to hunt and kill what they call a Great Gouger, and take its skull-spine for a weapon. They are regarded as the tribe's totem and are formidable creatures standing nearly thirty feet high." Faraii seemed very matter-of-fact.

"Did you use an Art Martial to kill it?" asked Eligor, who found this mysterious figure more fascinating by the moment.

"That would not have been acceptable," said Faraii. "The tribes are neither demon nor soul but, as you know, were here before us. They live an austere life out there, and rely on nothing but their cunning and traditional skills to combat the elements. As a sign of respect to their culture, I killed it with their simplest weapon—a heavy sling."

Valefar hefted the weapon for a moment, then handed it back to Faraii.

"If you like, Captain Eligor, at some future time I will show you some of the traditional fighting forms that the tribespeople taught me," Faraii said, shoving the sword back into his bundle.

"I would very much like that, Baron."

They walked through one of the axial arcades that led out of the palace complex and exited out onto the center mount's parade ground. The ragged clouds had parted and a high-altitude firestorm burnished the city's tiny buildings below a coppery orange. They continued around to the court residences. These massive plain-facaded buildings were set into the mountainside, their large quartz-glazed windows commanding an unobstructed view of Adamantinarx.

Unlike the palace, the residences were constructed of massive soul-blocks, each one comprised of at least fifty compacted souls. They had been intentionally finished and laid down so that their many eyes were exposed, blinking constantly in the ashy wind.

Eligor and Valefar left Faraii at the entrance to his suite of rooms. He bowed slightly but did not say any words of thanks as they turned away. It was, Eligor was sure, simply his way.

IV

DIS

She lay naked, facedown on her bed upon a pile of bleached skin covers, their tangy odor filling her nostrils. She was as white as the clouds Above, and the soft curves of her undulating body, the smooth angles of her shoulders as they swept into her back and on to the rounded rise of her buttocks, were a landscape of undiluted sensuality. She glistened in the half-light, tiny stars of perspiration forming on her pale skin from the slow, half-conscious gathering movements of her hips.

Eyes closed, she clutched the skins with strong, trembling hands and ground herself into the bed, filling the room with her soft gasps. Her nails tore through the blankets, scraping on the pallet beneath as her movements became more urgent, her gasps became cries. And when she had finished she rolled slowly over, cloud-white breasts rising and falling, as she tried to focus on the barely discernible patterns on the ceiling of her world.

She had once been given a true world of her own, but that had ended badly and this, this was anything but what she had had in mind. Six rooms sheathed in flattened and polished bone with only one door and no windows. It was her world, which was situated in the center of his, *its,* world. Which was all of Hell.

She had had many names to many peoples, but with the passage of eons she had come to think of herself as Lilith. Especially because her lord had difficulty enunciating it. A tiny victory, perhaps, but even the smallest gesture helped her swallow her unending disgust with finding herself bound for eternity to the Fly. She shuddered and shook her head violently, trying futilely to clear it of unpleasant memories. It was her special punishment, no matter where she existed, to belong to another. She accepted it because she had no other choice, but her soul rebelled at the reality of it.

Lilith heard a rustling in the next room. It was, she knew, Ardat Lili, her devoted handmaiden, removing her traveling Abyssal-skins after her long journey back from Adamantinarx. She had been away for some time, but it had been an opportunity not to be missed. Lilith swung her body upright and dropped one of her feet to the floor. The four thick claws, stained reddish-brown from blood, scraped on the tiles.

Will I ever get used to seeing them? Despite the changes to her feet, she had, she knew, been more than lucky when she Fell. Her body had been unscathed; even her heart—the only one in Hell—was left within her. She sometimes felt, though, that that might have been her worst punishment. *No one should have to have a heart in Hell.* Perhaps Lucifer had done it somehow, to preserve her when he had thought she would be by his side. She did not know.

"Ardat Lili?" said Lilith, standing. Her nude white body, voluptuous in its curves, almost disappeared against the whiteness of the room.

"Yes, my lady," came the reply from behind the closed door.

"Come in and tell me how you fared. Did we manage to put a few of them into good hands?"

The handmaiden entered, still removing her outer garments. Ash fell from the folds onto the white floor, and she looked down in dismay.

"Yes, my lady. That city is so different from ours . . . so much easier to walk about in. All of them are gone. Each and every little statue," Ardat Lili said enthusiastically. She knelt and began to neatly pile the ash. "One soul looked at his and even said that he thought it was you. He said that he'd seen you; can you imagine that?"

"Yes, I can," Lilith said, softly drawing on a robe. She walked over to a small bone table. Upon it were some carving tools and a half-finished bone statuette. The resemblance to its maker was uncanny; even the clawed feet were perfect in their detail.

Ardat Lili had mounded up a handful of the black ash and was sweeping it into the hem of her skin skirt.

Lilith picked up a small chisel, blowing bone dust off its tip. "That would be a hundred or so that we have sent out into the population, true?" she said, rolling the tool absently between her long fingers.

"Yes, Mistress, one hundred and fifteen tiny missionaries."

"And neither Lord Agaliarept nor Chancellor Adramalik knows anything about them, right?"

Ardat Lili looked up, nearly spilling the ash. "I have been so careful. You *know* how much I love you, my lady, how long I have been by your side. I would be destroyed before they would find out!"

"I do know. And I love you as well. You know that. I am just nervous every time you go out. The slightest things make those two suspicious. And one never wants to be the object of their suspicion," Lilith said with conviction. She turned to the polished bone wall—the source of her raw materials—and looked for a moment at it. There were small pits scattered upon its surface. She ran her hand across it, and then she tapped on a particular subtle twist of bone and said to herself, "This bit would make a fine figure. Larger than most. I must remember this." And with the tip of the tool she etched a small glyph upon the surface.

She turned back to Ardat Lili. The slim handmaiden had done her best to clean the ash. Lilith smiled as she watched her leave the room.

Lilith sat down and began carving the half-finished piece. With clever fingers wielding a variety of tools, she peeled away the harder striations of bone, refining the likeness, smoothing and then polishing the gleaming surface. When the little idol was done she put the tools aside and sat back for a moment turning it in her hand. She never varied the poses from one piece to the next but kept them iconic, like altarpieces. She put it down and closed her eyes, and as she did a tiny fiery sigil appeared—the secret sigil that she had devised for herself, for, not being a demon, she had not received one when she Fell. It lingered for a moment and then she willed it onto the sculpture's surface, where it sank slowly within. It was her signature, but more than that, it was her message.

Lilith opened her red eyes, satisfied, as she looked at the piece. "My message," she said in a barely audible whisper. "Will you ever find the right soul?"

She stood and brushed the white dust from her thighs. Then she picked up the finished idol and, walking to the now-slashed bedcovers, tucked it deep beneath them.

V

ADAMANTINARX–UPON–THE–ACHERON

Eligor wandered into the palace Library exhausted. He removed his heavy cloak and piled into a huge chair that already had a comforting clutter of books surrounding it. Now that the palace's construction was complete, life had settled down to a routine that Eligor found to be demanding and predictable. As Captain of the Flying

Guard, he found himself ceaselessly occupied reviewing the various weak points of Adamantinarx. Outside
threats, mostly in the form of spies, were an unending
problem.

His thoughts, though, were never far from the palace
Library. Here, in the company of his friends—the countless ancient tomes that had been written and collected
over the ages—he could try to understand the world that
he had left and the newer world to which he now belonged. Many of the volumes were reference works,
books that contained elaborate formulas for arcane spells
or incantations. Much had been lost by the demons' separation from their angelic counterparts, and these books
were often sad attempts at reconstructing the elusive,
vaguely remembered rituals.

Here, too, were the innumerable Books of Gamigin,
the Books of the Dead Souls. Stretching for bookcase
after dusty bookcase, these incredible books, many of
which were yet to be cataloged, compiled an accounting
of every soul who had ever descended to Hell and his or
her sins. And more fantastically, every soul who ever
would arrive, a concept that even Eligor had trouble
wrestling with. Reading even one of those immense
books was tiresome work. The books of the souls were
interesting, but the books that Eligor found most en-
grossing were the memoirs, written shortly after the Fall
by so many demons trying, as best they could, to come
to grips with what had befallen them.

All of the books, their vellum pages made of souls,
were capable of mindlessly reciting their contents in their
many droning voices but had been prudently silenced
by a glyph from the Librarian, an equally quiet demon
named Eintsaras. When he was alone, Eligor found ways
of countering the glyph and would sit, listening to some
ancient soul quietly recounting a life lived long ago.
Eligor suspected that Eintsaras knew his secret, but the
two never brought the issue up.

Eligor enjoyed all of his time in the Library, but he truly enjoyed the moments, as today, when he would encounter his lord buried behind a stack of enormous volumes, slowly turning the thick gray pages and poring over some forgotten passage. He kept his powers sharp and Eligor watched him occasionally scribing an old glyph in the air repeatedly, incorporating its essence into himself.

Eligor picked up the nearest book and began to read, taking notes as he did, but it was not long before the low and measured intonations of his master's voice distracted him. The Demon Major was focused and Eligor studied him, trying to view him objectively. Eligor was so used to the towering demon that it seemed he never pulled back to actually look at him.

In the uneven light of the candles Sargatanas was an imposing figure, dark and potent, with thin coils of steam rising from him. After the Fall, many demons had faces that seemed in keeping with their true being—tortured, prideful, and violent. Sargatanas was not among them. His massive head was deeply sculpted, bony, and strangely handsome. Even without its nose, the long face in repose still bore much of what had made it angelic, noble. Floating a few inches above his head were the three small horns of his rank. These, Eligor knew, could be withdrawn for protection and were considered a great prize if taken in combat. Over the eons Sargatanas had filled a small cabinet with those of his enemies.

He was clothed in his ruddy flesh-robes, his customary raiments when he went about the palace. The glare from his fiery pectoral sigils highlighted the prominent veins and creases of the thick garments that crossed his upper torso and flowed into the wide cloak that trailed him. Beneath them the fused rib-carapace bore a hole, ragged and sharp edged, where the demon's huge heart had once been. A slowly pulsing glow, not unlike that of a cooling furnace, illuminated the terrible wound, and like the persistent flames that played upon his head, this inner fire, like that of all Demons Major, was slave to Sargatanas' temperament, gathering in brilliance when he was angry. Such was not the case, now, as Eligor studied him. The studious Lord of Adamantinarx, book splayed before him, was at ease.

This was the Sargatanas that Eligor was most accustomed to. But he had seen that other side of his lord, the fierce, turbulent personality that none in Adamantinarx, and only a relatively small number in all of Hell, could withstand. His fury could be immeasurable, and the changes it wrought on him physically were astounding. Eligor remembered sudden, organic metamorphoses that rendered his lord utterly unrecognizable. The more agitated he became, the more rapid were the shifts. Such was the fearsome power of a Demon Major. They were changes that a Demon Minor could not fully comprehend, and, to be sure, Eligor himself sometimes found them frightening.

"If you like, I will stand up so that you can get a better view," Sargatanas said, looking up, a twinkle in his silvered eyes. He rose up from his seat, enormous. "But I will turn away so that you can continue staring surreptitiously."

Eligor laughed. "I am sorry, Lord. I was trying to look at you as if I had never met you before. I wondered what Faraii and all the others must have thought upon meeting you."

"Why, they are supposed to be completely awed, Eligor," he said, a hint of mockery in his tone. "I am not so different than any other Demon Major, am I? Surely you have better things to do than to sit about in such 'deep' thought. How is the northern border these days?"

"Secure as always. To be truthful, Lord, I was also trying to remember you as you were. I only saw you in the Above a few times, and those were from afar."

"That is strange, Eligor. I was trying to remember that, myself, a while back. I almost could. Much time has passed." Sargatanas sat back down. An unidentifiable expression clouded his features.

Eligor closed his book. He could see some deep emotion working at his lord.

"Tell me, my lord, if you would. What was he like?" Eligor asked. "I was just a lance-wing in the War. I never met him. And you were so . . . close to him."

"Him. Him I can remember. After all this time. I can see him just as he was. Lucifer," said Sargatanas. "I have not said his name aloud in millennia." The Demon Major paused, looking up toward the vaulted ceiling. "He was the best of us, Eligor. Something truly special among us. He shone with . . . with a ferocity that made us pale by comparison."

"Everyone I have spoken with, or read, says the same of him," said Eligor.

"He was beloved by the Throne and he knew it. But that was not enough," Sargatanas said as if he had not heard Eligor. "He was not content. There was something that he had to fulfill. He called it . . . his restless vision."

Eligor looked quizzically at Sargatanas.

"He could not understand the purpose behind the creation of humanity. They seemed, he said, like a new and unthinking child, suddenly thrust into the world and loved just as much as the old. Because of this he felt they were a threat and Lucifer wanted the Throne and all of us to see their potential flaws. Many of us agreed with him. Too many."

"Or not enough, depending on one's point of view," said Eligor. But his attempt at vague levity fell on deaf ears.

"Eligor, what we did was wrong. Catastrophically wrong. Of that I am now certain. Lucifer's truest gift—no, his greatest curse—was his ability to convince us to follow him. Of course, there were far too many of us who needed no excuse to go to War. The rhetoric, the very words were like shards of ice; once plunged into you they melted and flowed deep within, permeating your soul with their coldness. It was impossible not to hear them again and again, even in moments of rest. It seems never to have occurred to us what we might lose if we heeded them. I, for one, was entirely seduced."

Sargatanas was silent, his head bowed.

"My lord, it all made sense at the time."

"And now?" Sargatanas' voice was a husky whisper. Embers floated languorously from his head.

Eligor shrugged.

"Now we must try to be what we are, not what we were," said Sargatanas. "That, at least, is the theory."

"And what of humanity?"

Sargatanas slowly shook his head.

"Look around us—look at them, at what 'knowledge' has granted them. They are the saddest casualty of our War. They have become everything Lucifer might have hoped for. A triumph of disappointment to those Above."

Eintsaras walked to their table and, with a curious look upon his face, placed an old, heavy book atop the stack before Sargatanas. A small cloud of its dust puffed up and dissipated after a moment.

Eligor nodded. It was true; whether he had been prophetic or hopeful, Lucifer's world had come to pass. Could he have dreamt that it would have failed so spectacularly?

Eligor picked up the sheet of vellum he had been taking notes on. It twitched in his hand.

" 'He Fell, and it was like the stars torn down . . . the entire sky was afire with his descent,' " read Eligor. " 'I saw him, like a bolt of lightning, streak down toward Hell . . . ,' and, 'Lord Lucifer Fell, slow and deliberately, a trail of fire behind him . . . ' " He put the page down and looked directly at Sargatanas. "Which of these is true? They cannot all be."

"I do not know," said Sargatanas, shaking his head. "My feeling is that there is probably some truth to all of them. Perhaps at various points in his descent it appeared differently. We all saw things when we Fell. The agony did things to all of us."

"Where do you think he is, my lord? In hiding—ashamed? Or waiting? Or when he Fell, was he destroyed outright for his efforts?"

"I could not begin to say. Our very first Council of Majors addressed that question. I, like all the others of my rank, sent out countless parties to search for him. Some never returned. We found nothing. Not even a hint of where he might have Fallen."

Eligor picked up a carved jet book-weight and rotated it, considering what he had just heard. It still seemed impossible to him that Lucifer had simply vanished.

Sargatanas stood, straightening the heavy folds of his robes. The charred seraphic wing-stumps that floated behind his shoulder blades flexed and relaxed. He picked up the book Eintsaras had just laid down and put a hand on his captain's shoulder.

"We can manage without him and his gilded words. This is no place for them. Hell rages around us and we have risen to its challenge and, in so doing, we have tempered ourselves against sentimentality. Against nostalgia, against the memories. And that is how it should be, Eligor," Sargatanas said, standing. "That is how it has to be."

Eligor smiled and his chest filled with devotion to his master. He was truly privileged to be in Sargatanas' company.

As Sargatanas swept past him, Eligor caught a glimpse of the title of the book his lord was taking back to his rooms. It was an ancient book, as old as any Eligor had ever seen in the Library, and carved into its wrinkled and liver-spotted cover were the words "The Secret and Blessed Recollections of the Above."

Time flowed past in blood and fire, and Eligor watched Adamantinarx-upon-the-Acheron grow into the most enlightened metropolis in Hell. Sargatanas not only encouraged a degree of leniency toward the souls in his keeping that followed the letter of Beelzebub's law, if not its spirit, but also promoted the growth of the Arts, both Dark and Light, among the demons. Souls with any recollection of craftsmanship were given the chance by patron demons to ornament buildings, tile floors, and sculpt the myriad statuary that dotted the plazas. It was, Eligor thought, a dark renaissance—an echo of what had been lost.

Adamantinarx blossomed into an Infernal anomaly. The city could never be confused with its counterparts Above, but there was enough of a resonance to lessen the demons' burden somewhat. The palace, indeed the whole city, was an amazing mélange of architecture. Eligor saw not only buildings nearly identical to those of the Above but also wonderful human architecture gleaned, he knew from his research, from the memories and skills of the worker-souls. Huge basilicas flanked pagoda-like towers, which sprouted up from between the souls' densely packed quarters. All were, with the exception of the palace complex on the central mount, a uniform gray-olive color, which somehow made the odd juxtapositions less jarring.

Surrounded by the howling wilds of Hell, populated by the countless twisted human penitents, and governed by the most learned of demons, Adamantinarx became the bitter envy of all of Sargatanas' rivals. They neither understood nor tolerated his goals, and a gnawing resentment began to grow in the provinces around him.

Sargatanas and his court sensed their growing animosity. Visitors from afar became less frequent and forthcoming, bringing fewer gifts and even less news from abroad. Demons Major, other than true friends of the court, stopped coming altogether, sending in their place minor officials. Eligor saw this as not only insulting to his lord but ominous as well. Why, he wondered, was Adamantinarx not seen as the best model of a city but the worst?

It was with a sense of urgency that he met with Sargatanas and Valefar, and after very little discussion it was agreed that the borders should be made less porous and that entry into Sargatanas' wards would only be by special permission. Eligor applied himself happily; it was good to have a specific and important task at hand. And to his delight, he was invited to participate in the conjuring sessions with which Sargatanas bolstered the borders. Acting as second to his lord, Eligor watched with profound admiration as a variety of complicated guardian-glyphs, abstract and beautiful, were created, only to speed off by the hundreds to the farthest corners of Sargatanas' wards. There, Eligor knew, they would take up position, hovering and expanding to hundreds of feet in height, fiery warning-beacons in the ashy gloom.

Even with such insurances the wards were not entirely safe from spies. They could take nearly any form that a Demon Major could imagine, and Eligor always brought the more baroque infiltrators before Sargatanas or Valefar to show them their enemies' ingenuity. All manner of walking, crawling, tunneling, and flying creatures were interrogated, examined, cataloged, and then summarily destroyed. They were much too dangerous to keep imprisoned.

The Great Lord Astaroth, in particular, began a persistent campaign of espionage and theft, flooding the fringes of Sargatanas' wards with innumerable stealthy flyers.

"His capital and wards are a shambles," said Valefar
in his chambers late one day. Quartz-paned cases filled
with odd curios lined his rooms, reflecting the dim light
of Algol, which was sinking behind the horizon. "I cannot understand how one so venerable could have let this
happen. Who are his advisors?"

"Deceitful puppets standing firmly with Beelzebub,"
Sargatanas said. "I do not believe that the Fly ever really wanted him as a vassal. He has never had much use
for Astaroth and regards him more as an antiquated curiosity than as a noble ally. His interest in Astaroth has
always been nominal."

"We could always lend him support, my lord . . . ,"
said Eligor.

"We have been, unbeknownst to the Prince, for the
last two millennia," interrupted Valefar. "But we cannot
support his wards as well as our own. We are going to
have to cut him off and he knows it. Times to come will
not be easy for him."

"I see."

Valefar looked at Sargatanas, who sat, fingers steepled,
and said evenly, "It might also create problems for us."

Sargatanas rose and crossed the room to the large
leaded-obsidian windows. He unlatched one and gazed
out toward Astaroth's ward. The wind was strong at this
height; heavy parchments on Valefar's desk began to
stir.

"You, old proctor, are going to cause me a great deal
of trouble," Sargatanas said quietly, staring out into the
distant clouds. A roiling storm was punishing the Wastes;
red lightning scratched at the horizon. And then, re-
signedly, Sargatanas said, "Valefar, we must go to Dis. To
discuss this in person with the Fly. It is too important to
delegate to a messenger. We will leave Adamantinarx in
the capable hands of Zoray. Along the way we can hunt
a bit and bring some great trophy to the Prince as a token

of our enormous high esteem. And you will come as well, Eligor. It has been too long since you were in the capital."

"I am sure you missed it, eh?" smirked Valefar.

Eligor's wide eyes rolled.

VI

ADAMANTINARX–UPON–THE–ACHERON

The soul who called himself Hani groaned as he tugged the sinew rope. It was tied to a giant block that scratched its way up the flagstoned dockside causeway, and Hani could see, past the dozens of souls who were, like him, straining against the rope, that it had moved only a few yards. They had been pulling for about an hour and their progress had been slower than usual.

The work-gang was shorthanded due to sudden attrition; at the last moment, as the inclined causeway was being completed, the demons had run out of bricks and had had to resort to incorporating some of the gang itself into the ramp.

Hani had knelt, eyes down, as he watched the grumbling demon Overseer's sparking feet pass him by. Fear had bubbled up into his throat as he had contemplated the awful fate of being transformed; it was every soul's worst fear. But he had been lucky; the demon moved away, selecting the soul two down from Hani instead. When there were some twenty souls assembled, the demons had taken them away, leaving Hani kneeling on the filthy flagstones, still not looking up but able to breathe again.

It was not the first time Hani had been lucky. He was tall and strong, sharp-eyed, clever, and not too ravaged by the Change. Lucky, he thought, but just how lucky could one stay in Hell?

Work resumed, but it was now staggeringly difficult. The twenty souls had made a huge difference, and Hani's agonized limbs began to tremble uncontrollably. He tried to distract himself by focusing out toward the ghostly river with its sprinkling of barges. Once, he knew, the Acheron had been choked with heavy supply barges laden with exotic materials from the far-off quarries destined for the palace-mount. But that time had passed and now the building projects were more functional and pedestrian.

His tactic did Hani little good. The pain in his arms and hands only increased with every step; the tremors became more obvious. Then, as his continuing luck would have it, a great cloud of ash descended and obscured the work site. Hani groaned with relief as he let the rope slip from his shredded hands. The gang, as well as the incensed demons, was forced to stumble to shelter, the souls with their hands upon one another's shoulders for guidance. He could just begin to feel the tattered flesh mend itself the way all small wounds did upon the souls. It might take an hour or two to completely heal if they had that much time to wait it out. The pain was enormous, but, Hani reflected as he had a million times, that *was* why he was here.

At the growled command of their Overseer the work-gang gathered in the lee-side of a monumental brazier so tall that neither its heat nor its light could be perceived through the blinding ash. Only the modicum of shelter that its plinth provided and the sound of its giant flame crackling and billowing gave proof of its existence. Through slitted eyes Hani tried to take stock of his fellow souls, trying to identify who had been taken. Those who remained were a ragged group, squatting on their haunches and huddled against the densely falling particles. There was Chaw, the swollen hedonist for whom work of any sort was torture. There, lying on her side, was La, the powerful female who only had one-half of a face, the other side having been rubbed completely smooth in some ancient construction mishap. She was always sharp-tongued and malicious. And next to her, kneeling on the branching limbs he called legs, was Div, a quiet, brooding male who liked watching the others get punished. Beyond them Hani could see only indistinct forms.

Hani looked back toward the Overseer; he, too, was crouched down, leaning on his whip-staff. He was facing away from the wind but also from the souls, and Hani felt safe enough to converse with his fellow workers. Infractions of any sort were always punishable by conversion into bricks. That ultimate threat, alone, was enough to maintain discipline among the most fractious of souls.

"Bad one," Hani said, looking at Div, indicating the ashy wind with a quick shake of his head.

"Yes, but it'll be over sooner than we'd like," Div said fatalistically, picking a small piece of pumice from between his misshapen toes. "Aah, that's better!"

"We need some new recruits. It'll take us a year just to get that block up there."

"Do I care?" Div was rubbing his foot.

"Not any more than me," said Hani. "But *they* have a schedule to meet. Too many rest periods won't sit well. And we would bear the brunt. . . ."

They both knew what that meant. Hani ran his hand over the black orb they called the Burden that jutted, for the moment, from his left side. As they had been straining, the Overseer's impatience could be measured by its increased stinging.

"So be it," said Div, but Hani knew that was nothing more than idle bravado.

Hani debated opening the next topic. It was dangerous to let anyone else in on his secret, dangerous and
unpredictable. But something was compelling him to
share it, to bring others the message that had been
brought to him.

"Do you remember me mentioning the visions I've
been having?"

"It's hard not to remember. Everyone knows when
you're having them. And they're becoming more frequent, aren't they?"

That disturbed him. If it was so apparent to the souls,
was it equally obvious to the Overseers?

"Maybe." He paused. "I think I know what is causing
them."

Hani brushed the ash off his hands as best he could,
reached into a slit in his right side just under his ribs
where a small pocket of flesh had formed. He looked
nervously at the Overseer and back at Div. Revealing
anything to either had its risks. The soul was not the
brightest individual, nor the stupidest. In Hell, intelligence was a rare and true curse. It served as a lens to focus all of the pain and loss and misery upon its bearer in
a way that the more mindless souls could not begin to
understand. Most souls, Hani had long ago concluded,
seemed in a trance, their minds skinned over by a veil
of dullness. It was his mixed fortune not to be among
them. Or maybe he simply was not as lucky as he
thought.

He withdrew his hand from the cleft and he stared at
the small, precious object for a moment, remembering
how he had come by it. He and the work-gang had been
walking up the congested Avenue of Fiery Tears, trying
to stay together as they marched through the shuffling
crowds. She had been walking toward him, alone, clad
in unusually pale and hairless traveling skins, and, as he
walked toward her, they had made eye contact. This had
not been broken, even when she intentionally bumped

into him, placing the object in his hand. His first reaction had been shock, followed nearly immediately by fear. He looked furtively around, making sure that no one had seen the transfer.

Hani walked on for some distance without daring to look at what was in his clenched hand. When he finally had a moment to study it he had sworn under his breath. It was beautiful in every way: an exquisitely carved bone statue of a voluptuous woman with clawed feet. The finely chiseled features, the perfect, polished breasts, and even the tiny scales on its feet were depicted with incredible attention. But who was it? And why did he now possess it?

Those questions were only heightened by the onset of strange waking visions—he thought of them as the mysteries—that began to wisp through his mind while he labored. They started as brief image-skeins of her bone-white face, beautiful and placid in repose, the slightest hint of a smile traced upon her lips. These momentary glimpses had blossomed into longer day-visions, dangerous in their distracting duration. Hani saw, through a miasma, the woman he had named the White Mistress, seated in a strange, vast room, flanked by two fierce eyeless creatures and surrounded by countless kneeling souls. Where was she and what were those beasts? And all those souls, why were they prostrating themselves before her? And why was he merely standing amidst them, not kneeling as they were? He wanted to kneel; the ineffable adoration he felt for her was nearly overwhelming. But something kept him from genuflecting, from giving himself over to her completely. That disturbed him so he had taken to secretly moistening his fingertips with his tears and rubbing them into the figurine, his silent libation.

And there was something else about the visions that he could not explain, something beyond their obvious message of hopefulness. After he experienced them he felt inexplicably . . . self-assured. He wondered if it was possible to have a more inappropriate emotion in Hell. All of these gnawing emotions he traced directly to the acquisition of the tiny figure. After so many centuries of mind-numbing sameness, the new feelings excited him.

That had been weeks ago, and the visions had, if anything, grown in potency. Now, squatting in the ash storm, figurine in hand, Hani wondered if he was doing the right thing bringing the others into his private world. They were an intolerant, self-absorbed group, steeped in their own miseries, and the chance that they would try to curry some small favor from the Overseer by revealing Hani's secret was high. And yet there seemed some purpose to showing them.

Div was looking at him. "Well?"

He handed the figurine over to the soul.

Div took it in his rough, spatulate fingers, rolling it, examining it. He looked up at Hani and back at the statuette.

"You're telling me that this is what gave you your visions—this thing?"

"Yes, they started when I got it." Hani was already defensive.

Div's face looked blank for a moment. He shuddered and then pushed the object back at Hani.

"It has power; I saw . . . something. A woman . . . a white woman for just a second."

"It's her," said Hani, "the White Mistress! She is out there somewhere; I know it." And then he took the next step, the step he was not sure that he should take. "I think . . . I think we are meant to worship her."

Div looked away, obviously thinking. A cargo barge, only half-filled with stone, caught his attention as it slid slowly up the Acheron. Sargatanas' large, fiery sigil hung low over the square bow, and surrounding it, obeying a timeworn invocation, shifting navigational glyphs steered the craft.

By now, La and Chaw had edged in to hear the exchange.

La reached out and Div, first looking to Hani for permission, handed the figurine to her. She looked at it with disdain, weighing it in her twisted hand, and then passed it right to Chaw. The obese soul smiled lasciviously when he saw it, rubbing his finger over its breasts stupidly. Hani had expected that.

"Where did you get that?" La said stiffly. She thought of herself as the workers' leader, but Hani suspected he knew how the others regarded her.

"It was given to me."

"More likely you found it. Probably belonged to one of them," she said, nodding in the Overseer's direction. "It will have us all turned to brick if they find it on you. Get rid of it!"

"No, La, I won't," Hani said evenly. "No one's found it yet and no one will. Unless one of you tell them. And, as you said, we all know the repercussions of that."

The small group was staring at him.

"Tell La and Chaw what you told me," Div said seriously.

Hani hesitated. There was ash in his mouth and he took the moment to spit it out. The others took it as a sign of disrespect.

"I've been seeing her," he said, pointing at the figure, "in my mind. Ever since I was given it, these visions have been growing clearer, stronger. I don't know who she is but I think that she has given that little idol the ability to speak for her. And I think she wants me—us—to pray to her."

Hani could not believe what he had just said.

La snatched the figurine away from Chaw's gross attentions and flung it to the ground. It disappeared into the ash.

"Souls are not meant to own anything!" La spat. "Except their pain!"

Hani rose, shaking with rage. "Pick it up!"

"Turn to brick!"

He struck her sharply, and though she was larger and more powerful than him, she reeled and fell, sending up a dense cloud of ash. She rose again, eyes blazing, but Hani was ready for her. He was about to strike her again when he saw the Overseer rise and turn toward them, whip in hand. Hani sat down quickly trying to conceal his anger. The demon flicked his whip ominously and approached, trying, Hani thought, to analyze the situation.

"Get up! Work again!" the demon barked in their language, and the souls slowly scrabbled to their feet. The storm was abating and Hani, still in a rage, looked down at the ground frantically. He could not leave the little idol; it was all he had. Everything. When the demon prodded them forward Hani lifted his gaze and focused on the back of La's head. He would never forgive her. He would find a way to have her turned.

As they marched back toward the work area, Div sidled up and cautiously held his hand out, and, to Hani's utter relief, he saw the little white figure in the soul's calloused palm.

"It was in the ash right by my feet," he said, looking oddly at Hani. "Take it, but I wondered if I could borrow it sometime soon. I will give it back; I swear."

Hani sensed the sincerity and urgency from Div. And something else that might have been respect. The idol was working on him as well, just as Hani guessed it was supposed to. He looked at Div and smiled.

"Keep it for now. Tell me what you see, later. But tell no one else. Something must be taken care of before we can talk of this again."

"Be careful of her, Hani," the soul said, jerking his head toward La.

Hani picked up the sinew rope; his hands were only partially healed, but he felt strong, even confident. As he and the others strained to tug the reluctant block up the causeway, Hani's eyes narrowed as he studied and gauged the heavy female.

It had not been hard, after all, Hani thought, to deal with La. He had been right to assume that most of them would either help to remove her or stay back. Hani found that stepping into the role of leader, even while she was present, was somehow natural. He had waited a week for the right moment, and when it came he had found that his strongest ally came, not surprisingly, in the form of Div. It was easy, with his help, to maneuver her into a position so that she could be crushed by a huge block. She had been so badly flattened that, with little thought, the demons unceremoniously added her to the pile of bricks that the workers drew upon. Hani, himself, helped haul her to the pile, tossing her high atop the stack, a grim smile upon his lips. As the work progressed, whenever Hani passed her, he could feel the hatred emanating from her. Once, when no one could see him, he even spat on her and watched his spittle sizzle off from the heat. La glared angrily back at him but could do little more than blink. It was, he thought, good practice for when she would be a brick.

Div told Hani of his many visions; they were, for the most part, the same as Hani's own, but with one difference. Div's visions seemed more supplicatory, more servile. It was a difference that was not lost on Hani.

VII

ADAMANTINARX–UPON–THE–ACHERON

The small party left the palace and headed down the center mount to one of the many stables. On their way they followed the edge of the Acheron, descending the newly finished causeway, passing the endless work-parties that stopped their labors to turn and kneel as they passed.

Eligor led them into the sprawling square walled-in stables that covered acres. There, like the many similar paddocks that dotted his wards, were a hundred long, low buildings that housed a full regiment of Sargatanas' mounted troops. Eligor liked the stables, liked the bustle of activity and the look of the soul-beasts that hunkered in their individual cells.

They were souls that had been manipulated into steeds, giant, solid chargers that could bear heavily armored cavalry quickly over the infernal battlefield. This was a Household regiment, which meant that they were bulkier, better trained, and that their trappings were more ornate. Their mahouts, usually former Waste dwellers, silently went about their rigorous training programs leaching the last of all the enlarged souls' reticence from them until they responded with complete obedience.

Eligor entered one of the stables and before long had arranged for a small caravan of soul-steeds as well as a contingent of his Foot Guards.

They all watched as the huge embroidered carpetlike blankets were tossed over the rough-skinned backs of the steeds, which shifted from hand to hand, rolled their fogged eyes, and made deep sounds in their throats. Intricately worked, solid copper saddles were cinched in place, and reins were first passed through the huge single nail that penetrated each of the steeds' broad foreheads and then fastened to the light bridle-rings that pierced the souls' lips. Eligor shook his head with disgust as long streamers of gelatinous foam drooled from their slack mouths as they each took their bridles. Careful not to step in the puddles, each of the demons donned traveling skins, mounted their souls, and gathered in the stable courtyard.

Waiting for them were twenty of Eligor's summoned Foot Guard, tall warriors dressed for the Wastes in long silvery-black Abyssal skins, scaled and dotted with tiny glowing lights. About a dozen more travelers bound for Dis waited to join the trek on foot. All lesser demons, they had come from many parts of Adamantinarx and waited to travel, hoping for the much-needed protection of the Demons Major and Minor and their Guard to survive the treacherous Wastes. They stood about, a group varied in rank and occupation, all pulling on their hooded skins and adjusting the straps of their heavy satchels and pole-mounted sacks. For them, the weeks-long trip to Dis would be an arduous journey that tested their endurance. *Truly,* Eligor thought, *they do not make this trip to Dis lightly.* And, as far as he was concerned, the destination was worse than any of the potential hardships of getting there.

Half of the Guard preceded the ranking mounted demons and led them out of the courtyard. The demons on foot were followed by the remaining Guard, who balanced their pole-axes on their spiny-armored shoulders. The caravan proceeded down the Avenue of Sorrow, easily cleaving through the crowds, passed beneath a huge arch commemorating the War, and headed for the river. As they crossed one of the Acheron's many bridges,

Eligor stole a wistful glance back toward the city and clenched his jaw.

Adamantinarx's massive fifty-storied Eastern Gate rose before them, giant banners flapping in the wind. Sargatanas' sigil floated above it, throwing its upper parapets into stark silhouette. Eligor stared up, trying hard to find the tiny figures that he knew looked out past the city's walls. They were soldiers of the gate-garrison, Zoray's archers, each of whom bore a long bow that Eligor knew was composed of a single stretched, shaped, and bent soul. His friend Zoray, who was a marvelous archer himself, had told Eligor that the final step in becoming one of these prestigious archers—each risen from the Foot Guard—was the fashioning of these bows, a task that each candidate performed in a solitary ritual somewhere out in the Wastes. The bow-souls were picked carefully, the demons' Art being in the ability to find a soul upon the streets to match the specialized task. Only then could the marksmanship training begin. Many demons never found their weapon and walked the streets, seeking the right candidate, for years, finally giving up only to fade back into the Foot Guard or, discouraged, reenlist in a less demanding, less elite part of Sargatanas' army. Eligor could barely see them high atop the gate and resolved to actually visit them when he came back. It was a mind-trick, he knew, to focus on the return; it helped get him past the feeling of dread that always accompanied a trip to Dis.

They descended from the gate into the rough terrain that bordered the city. Much of it was covered with thick veins and arteries that fed the city, burrowing down under the city's wall and rising up again from beneath the streets to snake upward, crisscrossing the facades of the archiorganic buildings. It brought the yellowish lymph-fluids that kept the bricks of the buildings, as well as the organs that provided other functions, supple in the searing heat.

As they marched, the veins became less prominent and the countryside subsided into its characteristic gray-olive layered sheets of flesh. Huge, swaying arterial trees would spring up farther out, tough survivors that relieved the barrenness of the horizon but offered little shelter. Prominences and karsts of native stones rose, jagged, tearing up from beneath both the black matrix and the laminate of skin sheets that overlaid it. Eligor saw rookeries of many-headed winged Abyssals dotting the prominences' upper surfaces and could hear their distant shrieks, even above the wail of the wind, as the caravan passed.

In contrast to himself, Sargatanas sat swaying upon his steed, relaxed, swathed in his skins, reading some thick tome he had snatched from the Library. Of all the party he was the least affected by the landscape of Hell. *And why should he care?* thought Eligor a little enviously. *There is very little here that can harm him.*

The soul-beasts' heavy padding footfalls blended together with the rhythmic jingling of the creatures' harnesses. When Adamantinarx had dwindled to little more than a glow on the dark horizon and then to nothing at all, the caravan picked up a flock of skewers. They dropped in from the dark clouded sky and hovered a hundred feet above, circling and diving. These opportunistic flyers were common travel companions that usually kept their distance, only swooping in on membranous wings when they sensed that someone might be in distress. Eligor, like most demons, knew he would tolerate them until they became either too annoying or too aggressive, whereupon, with simple glyph-darts, they would then become challenging targets to while away the tedium.

Despite the sometimes difficult terrain, the soul-steeds kept up a steady, quick pace, and Eligor marveled at how those on foot kept up. Occasionally he would twist around in his saddle to watch them as they picked their way between the folds, pocks, and fissures that blemished the ground. He reasoned that apprehension kept their steps quick and constant.

Three days of travel found them nearly to the Flaming Cut, a massive lava flow that cleft the mountains and signaled a change in the landscape. The air grew thicker and smelled burnt. Through the smoke and heat-haze the Cut looked surreal, like a column of fire that reached into the sky. Around them the fleshy ground had given way to ugly clumps of convoluted, hardened lava, which assumed bizarre and unimaginable forms. Eligor liked this region even less than the oppressive flesh-fields. *Why did Sargatanas and Valefar not simply fly to Dis? I could have remained in Adamantinarx and kept an eye on security.* And then he remembered that Sargatanas specifically wanted him to go, and speculated that perhaps his lord, like the mentor that he was, felt he needed the perspective, needed to be reminded of the darkness of Dis and Hell's monarch in contrast to life in Adamantinarx. Eligor did not agree; the simple thought of going to Dis was reminder enough.

Into the third week of their journey the caravan marched past the famed twin cities known as the Molars of Leviathan, and set up camp on an outcrop. The Demons Major needed neither sleep nor food, but the soul-steeds were fatigued, as were the lesser demons. Eligor, only slightly weary, walked to the edge of the cliff. The cities were situated at the foot of a mountain, built into a vast pocket cut in its side. There one city hung above the other, each mirroring its twin in size and shape. They were both in an advanced state of construction, and the scaffolding from each, barely visible from this distance, nearly touched. Surely, Eligor thought, the workers at the apex of each city's scaffolds could even pass one another their tools, and yet Valefar said it was forbidden. Since the cities' founding eons ago they had become terrible rivals and it had been decided that neither city could have any exchange with the other; nothing was to aid either in their progress. As Eligor knew, when both cities reached completion, great destructive bolts of lightning would flicker between them and then the roof of the mountainside pocket would descend to the rise below, grinding the city and its countless inhabitants beneath as if between unthinkably massive jaws. And then, when the ceiling had lifted and the dust had cleared, the construction would begin anew. This event seemed not to be too far off, but Eligor would not be present to witness it. Their trip was too important to linger, and he regretted that he would miss the catastrophe. *Perhaps on another trip,* he thought with a ripple of misery.

Algol had just finished its monthly circuit and the party began to describe its long arc to skirt the Plain of Nagrasagriel, home of the numberless and legendary Soul Puppeteers. This was Eligor's first visit to the Plain, and that may have been why his lord chose the route; prior journeys to Dis had used other passages. It was widely known that Sargatanas enjoyed the exploration of Hell, especially on foot, feeling that every bit that he learned firsthand about the Inferno might prove useful someday. On the other side of this field of creatures, Eligor was told, lay the final marches to the capital, but he remembered that on foot the region's circumnavigation would take another three weeks. To achieve a variety of goals, his lord had determined how long he wished to be traveling, the urgency of the mission notwithstanding. And this spectacle was something he wanted his pupil to see.

Eligor heard them before he clearly saw them. The din of the Soul Puppeteers, the Sag-hrim, was an exoskeletal symphony of percussions, a sound so jarring that it set Eligor's nerves on edge. The closer they approached, the more unbearable the sound became.

Sargatanas sidled up his soul-beast next to Eligor's.

"They are amazing," Sargatanas shouted, reading Eligor's expression. "They are as old as Hell itself. When Beelzebub discovered them he knew at once what he could use them for. He tinkered with them, adjusted their minds to focus upon humanity, and then set them upon their Task. Do you know what it is that they do, Eligor? What that Task might be?"

"No, my lord. I have heard rumors that they have something to do with humans, before they arrive here."

"That is true. The Sag-hrim have the ability to connect with them and, more important, to *influence* them. Humans are flawed, weak; they only need that extra push to enable them to choose the path that leads here. The Sag-hrim provide that . . . incentive."

"How?"

"Trained attendants, Psychemancers, conjure a single human's psyche and then guide the Sag-hrim according to Beelzebub's plans. Each individual creature is equipped with manipulators—those long fingers that you can see—that can alter the abstract design that represents that psyche. These designs encompass an entire lifetime. Every human has one, or really two—one that is spiritual and one that is physical. Both are represented and both can be altered. When you look closely, the spiritual design is the glowing tracery; the physical is the floating collection of boneshards. All psyches are subtly different from one another, some tougher than others. At first they may seem perfect, but there is almost always a flaw. Once found, that flaw in the design is pulled, twisted, severed, or even added to, and the Sag-hrim achieves its goal. When they have succeeded with a soul they discard the psyche's physical shards onto the pile they sit upon. And then, eventually, that soul arrives in Hell. But remember, Eligor, the humans are not being forced; they are being tempted. That is much harder. And much more satisfying to us, for they cannot blame anyone but themselves for being here."

Sargatanas looked out at the Plain for some moments and then slowly shook his fiery head. "One has to admit that it was brilliant to see the potential in the Sag-hrim, that it was genius to exploit them so well."

Eligor looked at Sargatanas, surprised at the admiration in his booming voice, at the expansive credit he was giving Beelzebub. He looked back at the creatures. He had not noticed the relatively frail Psychemancers before. They seemed roughly his own height but were dwarfed by their charges. Seated, the seemingly headless Sag-hrim appeared to be nearly six times his height, covered in chitinous armor with odd organs bulging from their swaying torsos and massive multifingered arms swinging slowly as they performed their tasks. Hanging in the air before them were the glowing psyches, and Eligor watched carefully as the creatures pulled and adjusted and wove the designs with their wandlike fingers and flickering ribbons of fire. It was fascinating to watch, nearly hypnotic, and even more wondrous when Eligor thought about what they were achieving. These Sag-hrim, so distant from their human subjects, were actually coaxing them, tempting them to sin. From the smallest sins to the largest. Entire patterns of human culture were shifted, wars were begun, atrocities committed, murders, rapes—human evil in all its manifold forms—all because of the machinations of these beings. And all according to the grand strategy of Beelzebub. It was almost more than Eligor could grasp.

"It almost seems unfair. I mean, with humans as frail as they are. Who among them could withstand these?" Eligor said almost to himself.

"Not many," Sargatanas agreed. "Not many at all." He turned away and Eligor, gaze fixed on the Sag-hrim, only barely heard him walk off.

Eligor would study them for as long as the caravan halted; he knew it might be some time before he passed this way again. So absorbed was he, so in awe, that he was surprised to turn away eventually and see Sargatanas and Valefar deep in conversation with a winged newcomer.

Eligor approached them and recognized the messenger. He was a lesser demon of the Flying Guard named Murup-i, a good lance-wing as Eligor remembered. Murup-i knelt before his lord, undoubtedly grateful for the brief rest; his flight from Adamantinarx had to have been long and arduous.

"Eligor," Sargatanas shouted over the cacophony of the working Sag-hrim, "your centurion here has been sent on Zoray's urgings. It seems that, while we have been away, our old friend Astaroth has finally summoned enough courage to mobilize very nearly all of his troops and he has started to send them toward our border. Zoray says that they are establishing huge camps but not actually crossing into our wards yet. Valefar and I have agreed that we three should abandon the caravan and make all speed to Dis."

Eligor nodded and stole a glance at the others in the party. Without the Demons Major their survival was suddenly in question, but this was his lord's order and Eligor supposed the travelers would have to take their chances. As he watched them, they got to their feet, sensing, perhaps, that something had changed.

"It looks like the old fellow has finally run out of bricks," said Valefar, smiling.

"And options. So now he looks to us for more. Not very grateful, is he?" said Sargatanas.

"We should never have bothered to help him," ventured Eligor.

"We do what we are told," said Valefar. "That is why we are heading to Dis."

Eligor stretched his wings; they were stiff from inactivity and he flexed them to work the muscles. He slung his packs and watched as the two Demons Major, whose wings were only just beginning to appear, readied themselves, donning flight skins. Theirs was a complete transformation; unlike Eligor, they no longer possessed functional wings after the Fall and had to manufacture them from tissue and bone. It was a drastic process, and after their bodies had attenuated and flattened and enormous scarlet wings and spines had fanned out they bore little resemblance to their former selves. Only their faces, which peered out from within hoods of flesh, remained untouched. *Another miracle associated with Demons Major*, thought Eligor. *How amazing it must be to have that kind of power.*

They arose into the air in unison and Eligor watched the caravan shrink beneath him. The Guard would undoubtedly see them through to Dis; of that he was reasonably sure. As the demons gained altitude, he looked down over the Plain at the dark mosaic of the Sag-hrim, their flickering adjustments to the fate of mankind twinkling now like the stars of the Above and yet as unlike them as they could be.

Eligor looked ahead of Sargatanas and, through the ragged clouds, could just see an orange glow upon the horizon that he knew was the fires of Dis.

VIII

DIS

Adramalik watched the white figure pick its way across the Rotunda floor toward the empty throne. She was still some distance off, and, as she approached, she faded from view behind the irregular clumped piles of flesh and bones that dotted the floor. Her pure white body, undraped the way Beelzebub insisted, contrasted starkly with the deep reds of the surroundings. She stepped so lightly upon her bloodstained bird-feet that she avoided touching any of the disarticulated bones that littered the floor.

He wanted her just as did nearly all the demons of the court. As a sexual plaything, as a possession. She was, he thought, at turns beautiful and terrifying, sensuous and cold, fragile and strong, and, perhaps, because of these intimidating, unfathomable contradictions, almost irresistible. But, like all the demons, Adramalik knew what the penalty would be if Beelzebub even thought there was any competition. His paranoia was matched only by his wrath.

The buzzing started as she drew nearer.

Adramalik did not bother to look for the origin of the sound. He knew from past experience that this was futile; even if he could pierce the gloom, the sound's pervasiveness told him that there was no single point of its origin. His master was up there, he knew. Up there amidst the densely packed hanging skins and floating chunks of meat, watching Adramalik and Lilith as she crossed the Rotunda. Navigating the moist columns and islands of rotten flesh was slow work.

The buzzing grew more intense, more localized. Now, if he concentrated, Adramalik was sure he could see movement, see them take wing, the first of the tens of thousands of flies that he knew were coming. He had long ago grown used to Beelzebub's entrances. But in that Adramalik was somewhat unique.

Lilith was close; he could see the red sclera of her eyes, the tiny nostrils, the thick, tight curls of her snowy mane. And, brought on perhaps by the stagnant, hot air, the thin sheen of perspiration that glazed her perfectly sculpted body.

Above them a wavering dark cloud of flies was growing

and coalescing, rotating like a slow tornado in the debris-laden air. The buzzing rose and fell arrhythmically, an insectile threnody that almost sounded like words. Beelzebub's Voice never failed to bring a crooked smile to Adramalik's hard features.

He thought of it as a miracle, a miracle that only Lucifer could explain, for solid rumor had it that it had been he who had created Beelzebub. Adramalik had heard that Lucifer, just before the War, had wanted a fearless and unquestioning lieutenant, a being so different from his angels as to answer to none but himself. Secretly, and against the will of the Throne, he had created such a being, had dipped into the stuff of the Above and imbued the motes he found there with a loyal soul. It was not called Beelzebub then; no one but Lucifer knew its original name, and that was now lost.

After the Fall and after Lucifer's disappearance, Beelzebub, in a hate-filled rage, had crushed those original motes that were himself into rapacious flies. Upon them he impressed grotesque caricatures of the faces of those seraphim still in the Above. His transformation was a grand gesture of self-mutilation, an event so incomprehensible that Demons Major still spoke of it with whispered awe.

This was all nearly forgotten history to Adramalik. His thoughts were almost always of the here and now and rarely of those chaotic days immediately after the Fall.

Above the persistent buzzing he heard the faint delicate splash of Lilith's footsteps as she crossed the final few puddles of blood. She stopped at the base of the throne, head down.

Above her the flies swarmed, winged atoms of her master's body. From what court-spies had related, he was sure that she wished she could tread upon each one, crushing them until he no longer existed. He was also sure that she would willingly sacrifice nearly everything just to accomplish this.

When he spoke it was in the Voice of the flies, a layered and droning Voice that emanated from a thousand tiny throats.

"Fleurety tells me of a growing cult among the souls. A cult of . . . you?" The ambient Voice paused, but a buzzing wheeze continued for a moment. "What do you know of this, dear Lilith?"

Adramalik thought, from where he stood, that he saw Lilith wince when her name was pronounced.

"I have heard rumors, but nothing more, my Prince," she said, still looking down. Her voice was strong, husky. And not particularly contrite.

"You are mine, Consort. Not Hell's at large. I would find it most distressing if Fleurety's tales about you proved true. He is convinced that you are, in some way, fostering these cults. Just as you once did with the living humans."

"The Duke has his own designs, my Prince," she said plainly. "Perhaps you might ask him why he takes any interest in me at all."

"I have. For once, his suspicions outweigh his obvious urges toward you."

The Chancellor General reflected on that with mild amusement. Duke Fleurety's carnal interests were extraordinary, his imagination nearly unmatched, his resources boundless. *He must be very sure indeed,* thought Adramalik.

Lilith tilted her head up.

"He suggested that I have Lord Agaliarept minister to you—that, perhaps, only *he* is capable of gaining the truth from you. I found that suggestion . . . disagreeable. What are your feelings about this?"

That had an effect, thought Adramalik, pleased. Her slight movement backward had been unmistakable. She was too proud, too unaffected by the Prince's presence.

Ten thousand faceted eyes were fixed upon her.

"*My* feelings?" Her voice broke ever so slightly. "I . . . I have done nothing." Adramalik saw a tear well up and glisten down her ivory cheek. It stopped for a moment on her jaw and then dropped onto her clawed foot where a few black and green flies had gathered. One sizzled briefly from the moisture and vanished, and Adramalik could not be sure that he had heard a momentary sigh mingled with the low buzz of Beelzebub's breath.

"Nothing. That is good, Lilith," the Voice buzzed with no inflection. "I will not share you, not with Fleurety, not with Agaliarept, and certainly not with the dirt of humanity."

There it is again, thought Adramalik, *that incredible possessiveness. And who can blame him?*

"Thank you, my Prince," Lilith said quietly.

"And keep that handmaiden of yours at heel. Her many trips away are at an end." His Voice trailed off into a prolonged buzz, losing all semblance to language. The faintest whirring of wings could be heard from atop the throne, growing in volume as more and more of the flies of his body grew agitated. Lilith stood her ground, her red eyes focused somewhere beyond him, somewhere in the dark recesses of the dome, searching the gloom above for the first signs of movement.

The buzzing increased and Lilith's eyes betrayed her. The Chancellor General could see the weight of her resignation in how she held her head, the way her hands hung by her sides.

Adramalik always wondered if when Beelzebub broke apart or came together it started with a single fly, one who gathered all the rest about himself. One with that particular spark that was Beelzebub. He would never know. As the Prince took wing, his garments tumbled and floated toward the ground and Adramalik caught them with practiced hands.

He watched, fascinated, every time his master approached. The already-thick air around the throne grew dense with a shimmering cloud of flies, each trailing a tiny flame of green. They circled the dome's interior, fading in and out of the murky light, growing in numbers and density until it seemed that an almost solid, fluid body twisted between the hanging skins. After a few sinuous, blurred revolutions the swarm finally coalesced yards from Lilith into a dark, roughly humanoid shape. There, a few feet from the ground, it floated, its surface alive with the settling movement of the flies. Suddenly each fly purposefully inlaid itself like a tiny fierce tile in some living mosaic resolving its form, smoothing itself, and when it finally extended a taloned foot to step upon the floor it was transformed into the Prince of Hell.

Adramalik hastened forward to help drape the fine skin tunic, the sumptuous crimson and gold cloak, and then the heavy necklaces of state upon his Prince's form. He took special care, as he did so, not to touch the huge iridescent wings that hung, trembling ever so slightly, from Beelzebub's back. As the Chancellor General stepped back, Beelzebub's ornate sigils flared to life upon his chest, fiery filigrees that cast a dull light upon the Fly's face.

Unincorporated flies still swarmed, like the eager pets they were, around him and then made their way to Lilith. She ignored them, staring fixedly at the charnel-house floor.

Adramalik stepped a few paces back. He took a deep breath and looked, once again, with pleased reverence upon his Prince's face. It had been weeks since he had been in the Rotunda.

"Ah, Lilith . . . ," the Prince said.

She looked up, then, into his face. It was a beautiful face, Adramalik thought, an uneven split of human and fly, the greater influence leaning toward the insect. This time, he noted, Beelzebub had fifteen eyes; it was a number that changed every time he appeared.

Adramalik could guess what Lilith thought when she

looked into that face, softened, as it was, with the unfor-
givable love its owner felt for her. Personally, the Chancellor General could not fathom that emotion. Lust, no
matter what the form, he understood, but not the additional embellishment; that he regarded as a sign of
weakness and vulnerability. Not that he would have ever
explained that to Beelzebub.

Adramalik watched Beelzebub, as he had so many
times before, reach out a clawed, bristled hand, palm up
and coaxing. She took it, unhesitatingly, unflinchingly.
She had learned, Adramalik thought, smiling approvingly, remembering all the hard lessons. The millennia
had taught her. That and the Scourges.

The Prince drew his Consort close. He towered over
her and it was only after the flies at his joints separated
somewhat that he could bend to reach her. And when he
had, he tenderly held her head in his hands, guiding it
toward the long proboscis that depended from the center
of his face.

Lilith closed her eyes. She had learned that, too.

He kissed her, the long, thick tongue reaching downward, its hundreds of glistening black flies dancing in
her throat.

Throughout the long embrace Lilith held herself
rigidly still; Beelzebub either did not notice or enjoyed
her resistance. Adramalik found himself unable to look
away.

He knew that, somehow, she had found ways to ignore
Beelzebub's paranoia, his strict authoritarianism, his
delusions, his rages. These things, Adramalik reasoned,
she could forgive. But, he knew, she would never forgive Beelzebub his affections.

Adramalik continued to watch; he found her unwillingness beyond exciting.

IX

DIS

Eligor's spirits sank with every step he took. He, Sargatanas, and Valefar had landed before the Western Gate—the so-called Porta Viscera—and stood, for a moment, at its foot. It, like its four counterparts, was an angular edifice reaching up five hundred feet, constructed of slate-gray native-stone towers, each linked by broad, blank walls. Imposing as they were, there was an additional feature upon its surface that made Eligor's mouth open in amazement. Protruding from the stone, every foot or so, was an L-shaped iron spike, each adorned with withered, impaled human organs. Most were hearts—that most superfluous of organs in Hell—but there were other bits and pieces of forsaken human detritus. Entrails, sexual organs, even eyes decorated the walls, all buffeted in the stiff wind and giving the impression of a vertical carpet of moving life. Among these gruesome trophies scuttled a variety of small climbing Abyssals whose sole purpose, it seemed, was to pick at the remnants. As Sargatanas, Valefar, and Eligor passed under the gate's arch, he watched as waves of the many-legged creatures ebbed and flowed across the wall's surface, plucking, pinching, and tugging on the shredded flesh. As they passed beneath the gate's arch, fragments skittered down the wall narrowly missing them, clumping in the wide passageway only to be swept up by attendant souls.

They exited the gate onto the broad Avenue of the Nine Hierarchies that dipped down a few miles distant, offering a wide, panoramic vista of the ancient city. Valefar led the small party's progress, guiding them around the foul detritus that littered the streets. Everywhere, in sharp contrast to Adamantinarx, lay bones and discarded chunks of humanity. These were wrestled over by the wrist-thick worms that slithered through the back alleys and boldly emerged from the gloom when food appeared. Once found, a meal was hotly contested, and hundreds of the hook-headed creatures converged, twisting and coiling among themselves for even a tiny morsel. Any soul caught in this frenzy was reduced very quickly to even more morsels; most knew to shrink into the shadows. Eligor, who was used to Abyssals of every description, was repelled by these, intentionally crushing many under his bony foot when he had an opportunity.

The city's chaotic sprawl reached to the distant horizon, where it faded into the smoky haze that hung low in the air. Only the twinkling fires and the columns of smoke in the far distance belied the true extent of Dis' margins. It was a vast city, many times the size of Adamantinarx, with many times the population. From his vantage point he could easily see a dozen or more huge personal glyphs hanging above various city-sections, indicators of entire large neighborhoods governed by powerful deputy-mayors within Dis.

At its center, dominating the Plain of Dis, was Beelzebub's Keep, a structure nearly two miles high that looked all the more lofty for the flatness of the surrounding terrain. Mulciber's Miracle, some called it. Eligor thought it the perfect symbol of its owner—overblown beyond any reality. It rose improbably toward the cloudy sky, an archiorganic mountain, polyhedral in plan with each side slanting, flat, and smooth save for the gigantic sustaining organs that broke the surfaces. The thick, heavy mantle of flesh on its upper surface was cleft by numerous black spires and domes, one of which, far to the right of the famed Rotunda dome—the Black Dome—was alight. Piercing its narrowest section was an immense arch through which flowed a lava stream—part of the glowing moat that encircled the entire artificial mount. At the base of that arch was the great portal that led into the Keep from a single gargantuan bridge. Eligor knew from the past that this was their immediate destination. Once there they were to be met by one of Prime Minister Agares' secretaries, who would guide them through the vertical labyrinth that was the Keep's interior.

Eligor trod heavily through the streets. He wondered, hopefully, when Sargatanas would tire of the endless rows of sullen buildings, when they would again take wing and truncate the unpleasant journey to the base of the citadel. Both of his companions were silent, each bearing an expression of distaste, Eligor suspected, for their surroundings.

Valefar guessed his line of thought. "When I left here," he offered, "I wished I would never return. And now I am back, wishing precisely the same thing. Perhaps, in the future, I should wish for the opposite and see what happens." He laughed, but Eligor felt the strain. He knew, from experience, not to ask the Prime Minister under what circumstances he had left Dis. No one, with the possible exception of his lord, knew that story.

Eligor nodded. He, too, had made a similar wish. "Will the Prince recognize you?"

"I was never important enough for him to know of when I was here. I doubt that he would."

"Just as well," Eligor said with conviction.

The buildings on the city's edge were low, leaning, and dried-blood red. Created eons ago from slabbed and chunked souls, topped by ruffling tufts of hair, they looked hollow eyed with their gaping windows. Half-attached souls protruding from walls or roofs flailed their arms spastically as the demons passed, uttering garbled sounds from afflicted throats. While Adamantinarx's single-soul buildings were used for the same purposes, as solitary places of punishment, their equivalents in Dis were almost primitive in their crudity; they were considerably older and built in a time when the process was not yet perfected. Eligor recognized the various forms of the dwellings, noting that they reflected the earliest types of buildings that humanity had constructed.

He looked into a few open windows as they passed. The buildings' inhabitants, melded to wall or floor in their personal punishments, were not too dissimilar from their counterparts in his own city. These were the unusually corrupt and depraved, those who deserved special attention. Seated, standing, or hanging, they rolled their eyes frantically, silently, the racking pain obvious in their minimal movements. That much, he thought, was familiar. But that familiarity brought him little comfort.

As the party descended toward the distant Keep, the avenue grew more populous. Souls kept mostly to the sides, huddled against the buildings. Small contingents of Beelzebub's troops passed them, and even though Sargatanas was an obvious, imposing presence, the soldiers never once acknowledged him. Instead they respectfully gave him wide berth, eyes averted. This was the way of the capital, a city so much under the heel of the Prince of Hell that obeisance to any other Demon Major might be construed as disloyalty.

Only a squadron of Order Knights, swathed in scarlet-dyed skin, looked directly at the trio, and Eligor could feel something—was it arrogance?—pouring from their hidden eyes.

Suddenly a piercing wail rent the sky, an ululating scream so anguished that Eligor stiffened when he heard it.

Valefar turned back and wordlessly grinned at him even while the prolonged sound continued. It was a reassuring gesture, but Eligor remained wide-eyed. He had been to Dis many times but had never gotten used to the unpredictable Cry of Semjaza. According to common knowledge, this giant Watcher, whom few had ever seen, was one of only a very few survivors of a Fall that predated the War. Like its brethren it was flung down into Hell and shackled so as never to rise again. The anguish of Semjaza, imprisoned deep beneath the Keep, was extreme, its torment unending. Days, weeks, or years might pass without a sound emanating from its hidden chamber, but when Semjaza did give voice all of Dis reverberated.

Sargatanas strode on, outwardly oblivious to all around him. But the small bone plates of his face were ceaselessly shifting, agitated and angry.

"By now, my friends, you must be wondering why we walk these streets rather than take wing." He paused. "It serves to remind me. Hell is punishment. Punishment is why we are here. Ours and theirs," he said, nodding toward some souls. "But I see no reason to surround myself with filth and decay in Adamantinarx. We are on foot because we three must remember the differences between our own city and nearly every other city in Hell. Especially this city. Too many centuries have passed since we were last here. I, for one, had lost touch with the place, with its character. That character is a reflection of the demons in charge. It says as much about them as it does about us."

Valefar suddenly looked puzzled. "Does it, my lord? I ask because I do think, after all these centuries, Eligor is warming to this place. Just last month he told me that he missed his trips here. He said that he really could not wait to come back."

Eligor's mouth opened.

"Perhaps we should make this an annual pilgrimage then, eh, Eligor?" Sargatanas said earnestly.

Eligor was so surprised that the most he could do was

vehemently shake his head. Sargatanas and Valefar looked at each other and smiled.

The streets around them broadened, though the conditions in them hardly improved. Monumental statues commemorating the fallen heroes of the War rose from ornate pedestals too thickly, Eligor thought, to connote anything more than insecurity and forced patriotism. They entered a district of larger, more imposing buildings. These were part of the mayoral complex of this ward, and hanging high above them was the unfamiliar aerial sigil, Valefar told them, of the general Moloch.

"He is never in residence at these palaces; he favors the Keep," Valefar said, and added, "so that he can be at his master's feet at all times."

"Bitter, Valefar?" asked Sargatanas.

"No, my lord, simply aware."

"I think it is time for us to take flight and meet the Prime Minister. I am feeling well enough grounded in this place."

They opened their wings and in moments were flying over the city. Eligor was grateful to be up and out of the streets. The hot air was refreshing compared to the clammy, close air of the city.

Hours later, as they drew close to the Keep, Eligor could see activity; the sky was filled with demons swarming around the towers and spires, while in the flat courtyards other administrative clerks and court functionaries bustled to and fro.

The three demons dipped down, sweeping low over the wide, incandescent lava moat known as Lucifer's Belt. It was an artificial defense, and Eligor saw the open mouths of the conduits lining the far embankment that carried the magma up from the depths and poured it into the surrounding channel. Mulciber's genius again. Eligor could feel the shimmering heat when they landed at the foot of the Keep, and it barely diminished as they climbed the long steps to the gate itself.

Valefar, in his capacity as Sargatanas' Prime Minister, approached the captain of the sentries and made the formal announcement of their arrival. The demons waited briefly until a small door in the great gate opened and the many-horned secretary to Prime Minister Agares ushered them inside.

It was strange, Adramalik reflected, strange that suddenly so much should turn on Astaroth's faltering wards. Agares had been informed weeks ago of the departure of Sargatanas and his caravan. That was unusual; it had been six hundred years since his last journey to Dis. So long, in fact, that Beelzebub had grown petulant about the unorthodox, charismatic Demon Major and his evident lack of respect.

And now waiting with him and Agares in the Rotunda was a messenger from Astaroth. Spies in Adamantinarx had been informed of Sargatanas' intentions, and when news had reached Astaroth in his crumbling capital, Askad, the messenger had been hastily dispatched. He had flown the entire trip without pause and was still trembling from the effort. His wings were shredded and Adramalik saw tiny smoking pits upon his skin from embers that had buffeted him; he had apparently taken the most direct and perilous route.

When he landed he had been brought straightaway into Agares' chamber and met almost immediately by the Prime Minister. There they had spoken for some time, and even though Adramalik could not hear the conversation, he knew, afterward, that the messenger was here to strengthen his lord's alliance with Beelzebub and weaken Sargatanas'.

And now all three stood in the Prince's Rotunda awaiting him. Adramalik knew he was up amidst the hangings, watching them with his thousand wary, calculating eyes. He also knew that the messenger's journey was not to have been in vain. Beelzebub's jealousy-born indifference to Sargatanas was no secret among those in his court; the Demon Major's ways were appealing to many who still thought of themselves as Fallen angels and not as demons. For the Prince, who had watched the slow rise of Sargatanas as a potential rival with suspicion, it was a delicate yet irresistible moment to exploit. And for Astaroth, whether it ended as he wished or not, a moment that would bear the sanguinary rewards of war.

No one saw the slight smile that crossed Adramalik's face. Dis had grown boring of late, he thought. A war of some significance would certainly make it more interesting.

The steep ascent through the Keep to Agares' tower took nearly a day. Adjacent to the Black Dome and protruding through the flesh-mantle, it was a many-spired and buttressed claw tearing at the clouds that tried so hard to conceal it. From the long, vertical windows that ran the height of the building the small party caught breathtaking glimpses of the city. When they arrived in its vaulted reception hall adjacent to the Prime Minister's chambers, the secretary indicated a long row of bloodstone benches and then disappeared hurriedly into one of the smaller adjoining rooms.

None of them sat. Valefar paced while Sargatanas stood at a window, gazing down at the soaring thousand-foot-high Arch of Lost Wings. Eligor studied a dingy fresco of some long-forgotten battle that must have been applied millennia past.

When Agares finally did appear he seemed preoccupied and distant. He ushered the three demons into his opulent chamber of state and indicated some heavy chairs. A pallid greenish light streamed through the windows in broad, dusty shafts. Tall and gaunt, Agares had a brittle, bureaucratic air, and his movements were almost nervous. While Valefar had never said anything in favor of the Prime Minister, Eligor remembered, neither had he said anything too condemning.

"The Prince has asked me, in his stead, to discuss your situation. He is, at the moment, with his Consort and has asked not to be interrupted." The Prime Minister's clipped, scratchy voice seemed grave but oddly tentative to Eligor's ears.

"We can wait," said Valefar evenly. A frown had worked its way onto his features.

"I am afraid that will not be necessary, Prime Minister. The Prince has fully briefed me on his views regarding the situation on your border." The Prime Minister folded his arms and Eligor could see the large gold fly-shaped ring of rank on his thin finger. It was clearly an intentional gesture.

Eligor saw Sargatanas tilt his head. Agares was neither looking at him nor addressing him but speaking instead to Valefar while adjusting his floor-length robes. *An insult to be sure*, Eligor thought. *Had things degenerated this far between the Prince and his lord?*

"Lord Astaroth is poised on our border," Valefar said. "We are simply asking what the Prince's reaction will be if we engage Astaroth."

"You will not engage him on the field of battle and, therefore, there is no reaction to anticipate. We will assure you that he pulls his troops back. And we will attempt to revive his failing economy as well."

"And if he strikes at us first? Should we not defend ourselves?" Valefar's tone was sharper, edgier.

"He will not," Agares said, finally turning to Sargatanas. "Lord Astaroth is desperate. You know the state of his wards. If he were to launch an attack he would lose everything, and he knows it. This is merely a posture to gain attention. *Our* attention, not yours."

Sargatanas slowly rose. The hornlets that floated above his head were encircled by orbiting jets of flame. "You do know, Prime Minister, that I will do what I must to protect my wards. I have spent far too much energy building them into what they are to let them be jeopardized. I may not have been waging incessant war on my neighbors, but trust me, I remember how it is done."

Agares glared at him.

"And you may tell Prince Beelzebub that he is always welcome to visit Adamantinarx." The remark was a direct challenge; Eligor knew the Prince had never visited the city.

With that, Sargatanas drew his cloak in, turned, and headed for the door. Valefar and Eligor, taking their cue from their lord, dispensed with any formalities and, without another word to Agares, followed. What he was thinking Eligor could only guess, but when he walked past Agares he saw the Prime Minister's jaw clenched and trembling slightly.

Sargatanas crossed the chamber, opened the thick, pressed-soul door, and burst into the hall beyond, nearly knocking down a diminutive passerby. Eligor, close behind, hastily sidestepped the pair, noticing that the figure, adjusting its white raiments, was female.

Sargatanas pulled back, steadying her in his huge, clawed hands, keeping her from falling.

She had apparently come from Beelzebub's Rotunda; the hall led only there. Her face was set, eyes wide, nostrils flared, jaw tight. It was an expression of some fierce emotion barely contained. The skin of her face, normally white as bone, was mottled with slight bluish-gray spots, and she was somewhat disheveled.

And yet even so, Eligor thought, not since the Above had he seen anyone as beautiful as the startled creature that stood before them.

Valefar closed the heavy door behind them, breaking the silence.

"I . . . I did not see you," she said after a moment. Her voice was calm. Her deep-set eyes were locked on Sargatanas' face. Whatever emotion was at play, it was not leveled at him.

"Nor I you . . . Consort Lilith." His voice was low.

"You know me?"

"I would hardly say that I know you." Sargatanas suddenly seemed to realize that he was still grasping her and let go. "I saw you from afar at the opening of the Wargate. That was . . . nearly five thousand years ago."

"And still, you remember me."

Sargatanas looked down. Eligor saw something ineffable in his lord's manner that he had never seen before. Only the barest wisps of purple flame wavered upon Sargatanas' head.

"Yes."

With that, Eligor thought, Lilith's face seemed to brighten. She put her hand on Sargatanas' arm for an instant and then pulled her white skin mantle tighter. She turned to Valefar and smiled.

"It is good to see you again, Valefar. It is Prime Minister, is it not?"

Valefar bowed and nodded. "It is, Consort. Thank you for remembering me. It has been a long time since I was in Dis."

"Before you left, there were some who thought of you very highly, Val—Prime Minister. Your differences with the court were not universally rejected. But you were fortunate that they did not engender more anger than they did."

"Of that I am aware."

She clasped both of his hands tightly and Valefar looked pleased and then a little puzzled. She pivoted to greet Eligor.

"My name is Eligor," he blurted. And when she laughed, it was so immeasurably unexpected and so pleasant a sound to his ears that he was sure that he betrayed his surprise. He had never heard anything close to genuine laughter in Hell. Sargatanas and Valefar looked nearly as startled as Eligor felt but recovered more quickly.

"I am sorry, Eligor. I meant no offense. It was just . . . Eligor?" She knit her brow and looked at him strangely.

Eligor, head tilted and mouth slightly agape, was focused on a small fly that had walked from beneath the fold of her skins and was slowly creeping up her thin neck. It was black and the closer he looked the more he was sure that he could see a face—a distorted angelic face—peering back at him.

A giant hand shot past him and plucked the fly from her neck, crushing it into greasy slime between clawed thumb and forefinger. Sargatanas wiped his fingers on the wall, leaving two short, dark streaks. The rasp of his claws echoed in the hall.

Lilith looked startled and then, almost immediately, her face returned to the expression Eligor had first seen. He read it, then read the emotion that had eluded him. It was hatred, veiled but deep, and he saw the weight of it descend like a heavy shadow across her perfect features.

"I must be going. Ardat Lili is waiting. . . . I told her . . . I must go now. Safe journey back, to you."

She walked away, quickening her pace, hastening down the corridor without a backward glance. The three demons, shocked, saw her pale form recede into the shadows and vanish. They knew not to follow her; this was her realm, her prison, and no one knew the ways of it better than her.

They looked silently, solemnly, at one another as they began to move down the hall. A few paces away, Eligor thought he heard the door open, and when he looked back he saw Agares' head poke out, craning around the doorjamb to examine the short, black smears upon the bricks.

When they were outside the Keep once again, the demons took wing without exchanging a word. Only when they had flown the breadth of Dis, landed, and approached its gate did they speak.

Valefar looked as downcast as Eligor felt, but Sargatanas seemed strangely in good spirits. Eligor shrugged when Valefar glanced at him; both demons had thought their lord would have been filled with anger over their aborted meeting.

Valefar shook his head, a wry look of incredulity written upon his face.

"What is it, my lord?" he said. "Does Hell's firmament suddenly have a second star?"

"Not a second star, Valefar, but a new moon, pale and beautiful and luminous." His eyes seemed fixed inward.

And Eligor realized what had happened. Lilith had had an effect far greater upon the Demon Major than either of his companions could have guessed. That distant look spoke volumes.

All three walked in their own astonished silences until they had cleared the Porta Viscera. They stopped just outside the gate.

"We should make all haste back to Adamantinarx," Sargatanas said, narrowing his eyes as he looked out at the fires on the horizon. "I know Astaroth; he will not wait long to attack."

"His desperation is like a gnawing beast at his throat," said Valefar, momentarily distracted. Eligor saw that he was looking at something white in his palm. Before Eligor could get close enough to see it, Valefar had tucked whatever it was into his traveling skins.

Without a backward glance at Dis, the three ascended into the air and banked toward Adamantinarx.

X

ADAMANTINARX–UPON–THE–ACHERON

The long journey back to Adamantinarx taxed Eligor more than he thought possible; he never thought the trip could be made so rapidly. If anything, the two Demons Major had held back because of him.

The approach to the city was obscure; an eruption to the west had created a vast front of dark ash clouds, and the city was just beginning to feel its arrival.

When Sargatanas, Valefar, and Eligor alighted on a rise outside the city, Adamantinarx was already on a war footing. Zoray had seen to that. Protocol dictated that they be met at the Eastern Gate by an escort contingent of Zoray's Foot Guard, and the party could see them gathered beyond the wall.

These were the very best of the Household Guard, each stone-gray soldier bearing two curved lava-tempered swords that grew, instead of hands, from his thick wrists.

Zoray's First Centurion of the Foot Guard stepped forward carrying Sargatanas' robes of state and bladed scepter, and following him was an imposing line of standard-bearers, each carrying a stretched demon skin upon a pole. Some of the skins retained their owner's bones, and they clacked together in the hot breeze.

When Sargatanas was before them, adjusting his robes, the assembled soldiers knelt in unison, fists to the ground.

"Are these what I think they are, centurion?" asked Sargatanas, silvered eyes sweeping across their number. The skins' empty eye sockets gaped back at him.

"Yes, my lord," he said, kneeling. "The Baron expressed his hope that this display of Astaroth's spies would please you. It was Zoray's idea to let him handle the problem. Apparently the skins were removed in ways that—"

"Faraii has been very busy, I can see. As has our venerable neighbor," Sargatanas interrupted, smiling slightly to Valefar. "Thank the Baron for his diligence and good work, centurion, and have these displayed prominently at each gate."

"Sire!"

As the centurion departed, three giant soul-beasts were brought up by their white-masked mahouts and the weary demons were helped into their howdahs. From his high vantage Eligor watched as the clay-colored throngs of foot-dragging souls, most of them work-gangs whipped aside by Scourges, crouched against the sides of buildings. The streets were, if anything, more crowded with the additional flow of legionaries streaming out to assembly points outside the city.

There were many more soldiers now in Adamantinarx than when the three demons had left. In his mind's eye, Eligor could easily picture the raising of additional legions in the fertile lava-fields not so far south of the Acheron. Dispatched from the palace, dozens of decurions bearing Sargatanas' conjuring glyphs, Eligor imagined, were coursing over the lava incunabula, carefully choosing the best sites. A fertile lava pit could easily yield a thousand legionaries, but finding one was a challenge; successful decurions were often rewarded with citations and sometimes promotion.

Long ago, Eligor, curious as always, had accompanied one such decorated decurion, had seen him expertly select just the right spot, where he cast the fiery glyph high into the ashy air and watched it plunge into the bubbling lava. Almost immediately, Eligor had marveled, the tips of halberds, the spikes of helmets, and the fingers of reaching hands broke the surface, parting the slowly swirling, incandescent flow of the lava. He had never forgotten the thrill of watching a battle-ready legion pull themselves from the very stuff of Hell, opening their eyes for the first time and lining up by the hundreds before him, steaming and tempering as they cooled. All this, Sargatanas had told him, was happening even as they entered the city.

The soul-beasts' lumbering progress was steady through the congested streets. Carrying Sargatanas' sigil-topped vertical banners before them, the Foot Guard and Scourges pushed through the milling souls, Overseers, municipal street-worm hunters, legionaries, and officials, widening a broad path for the three mounted demons.

Halfway to the center mount, Sargatanas had the other beasts draw up next to him and stop.

"Before we rest, I would visit the site of the ridiculous statue Beelzebub insisted be built. From here I can see that it is very nearly finished."

And, indeed, when Eligor peered into the cloudy distance he, too, could see the dark head of a colossal statue. The three demons turned their beasts, following the redirected troops down a long, gradually descending street toward the work site.

DIS

Adramalik followed Prime Minister Agares along a narrow dim corridor, like the fleshy, dank inside of a worm, that sank sharply beneath the Prince's Rotunda. They were nearly as powerful as each other in their own spheres, nearly as influential, and their mutual suspicions kept them silent as they walked, a not uncommon occurrence when the two were together. Adramalik distrusted the Prime Minister, and in the paranoid world of the Keep distrust kept demons alive.

The corridor terminated into the entrance to Lord Agaliarept's Conjuring Chamber. Beelzebub had ordered them to attend him here, and, having no other choice, they dutifully agreed. If anything bound the two demons together, it was their sense of incomprehension and distaste for the Prince's Conjuror General. Sequestered deep beneath his master's Rotunda, he never left his circular chamber, never interacted with other demons until they visited him, and never spoke unless it was in the course of a conjuring. His was an obsessive world of ancient spells, muttered incantations, and bricks. In many ways, bricks were Agaliarept's primary focus, for it was through the combined and varying energies of specially selected bricks—souls of particular darkness—and through their kinship with other bricks throughout Hell that his powers played out. Endless deliveries of bricks, sought and found across Hell, made their way to his chamber and found themselves stacked everywhere.

Agares and Adramalik entered the wide kettledrum-shaped chamber and were immediately confronted with the sight of a thousand soul-bricks floating through a shredded mist at various heights. They moved in ceaseless concentric rings, hovering over the concave floor, out from which Adramalik could see complex branching patterns of brickwork radiating. At the Conjuring Chamber's center, barely visible for all of the circling bricks, was Lord Agaliarept, illuminated only by the chains of glyphs that hung in the air before him.

The bricks, some of which narrowed their eyes as Agares and Adramalik passed, parted like a school of the Abyssal flyers they had seen many times in the Wastes. Agares pushed those that did not move quickly enough aside, and Adramalik heard them sigh or sputter or swear. As the pair moved downward they were careful to avoid the occasional gaps in the brick floor. Adramalik knew that the floor acted as a kind of abstract map of Hell itself and that the gaps, or the simple placement of brick into them, affected those that Beelzebub chose to influence.

As Adramalik and Agares drew near him, the Conjuror General swung toward them. In his spindly arms Adramalik saw a single brick, a mouth visible upon its folded surface.

He is so different from us, thought Adramalik, jarred as he always was when confronted with the Prince's chief sorcerer. Agaliarept stood, an ill-defined, robed figure, countless arms jutting from his torso like the spines on an Ash-burrower. These wandlike arms were constantly moving, seemingly tasting the air or feeling the ever-drifting currents of events. What little head protruded was cowled deep within a collar of skin-enfolded eyes, each tiny orb a different color. Disconcertingly, Adramalik never knew if he was being watched or, more irritatingly, perhaps, whether he always was. He regarded Agaliarept as a dark tool of his master's and little more; the distance both Beelzebub and the strange being had created to keep him obscure also served to keep him relatively unapproachable.

Agares and the Chancellor General took up a position yards away from Agaliarept but close enough to discern the ember-lit flies that circled him. Without a word, the Conjuror raised a dozen of his thin arms and began weaving ghostly glyphs from tissues of misty air, drawing toward him selected bricks from the vast floating catalog and gesturing them into specific holes in the floor. The single brick that he held began to whine piteously and glow from within, and when the dozen or so summoned bricks were firmly in place Agaliarept laid it gingerly into a space at his feet.

The mouth on the brick snapped open. A flattened black tongue poked out for a moment, failing to moisten its cracked lips.

A susurration gradually filled the demons' ears as the chamber came alive, the faintest of whispers growing as the myriad dry mouths of countless bricks gave voice.

The two demons unconsciously stepped back as the brick at the Conjuror's feet coughed. For a moment it was silent, working its lips as if to speak. And then it retched up a fine mist of blackish blood that reached eight or ten feet into the air, spattering Agaliarept. Burst after burst of the mist hung before them until they saw a shape appear within it, the motionless, congealing form of a Demon Major.

A low buzz, Adramalik imagined of approval, emanated from the flies around the Conjuror.

The blood-formed demon, an avatar only, raised his head and looked at the demons present. Adramalik recognized the Grand Duke Astaroth, his sigils palely lit against his dripping chest, his sagging shoulders creating an impression of age and weariness.

The buzz of the circling flies became a Voice.

"Your spies have not returned, Astaroth. They were intercepted through the efforts of a Baron Faraii, I believe. Sargatanas' Guard are very well trained."

The conjured demon hesitated. Two tiny glyphs of sight blazed in his blood-filled eye sockets.

"Indeed. I taught him their drills." Astaroth's voice was distorted, gurgling.

"Their leadership is quite good as well. Of this," the buzzing Voice said, "I am sure you are also aware.

"My six legions," it continued, "are marching into your wretched wards as we speak. They will be held back until they are needed. They will reinforce yours, if yours falter. There must not be the perception in Adamantinarx that we are leading the attack on his wards."

Astaroth's chin sank. "It will be as you say, my Prince."

Adramalik knew that the old demon had hoped for more, that he wanted Beelzebub's alliance to be known to all in Hell.

"Are your troops in readiness?"

"No, my Prince, but we are close."

"While you may have superior numbers on your side, Astaroth, do not be fooled. Sargatanas has managed his wards brilliantly . . . far better than you . . . and he is cunning. This is a second chance. Be clever and what is his will be yours. And mine."

Astaroth's chin rose and he nodded.

"Victory to you, Astaroth!"

The distant Demon Major bowed and was gone in a shower of descending blood. Agaliarept, spattered from head to toe, bent and plucked the brick from the floor.

The Voice returned.

"Agares, see to it that Duke Fleurety's legions in the field do not engage Sargatanas' armies. They will remain after the battle. Also, Adramalik, have your Knights and Nergar's agents round up all of Astaroth's emissaries here in Dis and have them destroyed. That weak fool Astaroth's time in Hell is at an end." And with that the Voice trailed off into a barely audible wheeze and then nothing at all.

Adramalik and Agares bowed and turned to ascend out of the Conjuring Chamber. Before he was too far from its center the Chancellor turned, for a moment, and caught a glimpse of Agaliarept, his many long tongues extended. The Conjuror General was cleaning himself, lapping the blood from his darkly glistening robes. Adramalik shook his head and followed Agares.

ADAMANTINARX-UPON-THE-ACHERON

Hani was pushed up against the giant plinth along with the hundreds of other brick workers. After the quayside ramp had been completed he and the remaining souls were shunted to a new location—the site of a towering figure of Sargatanas that loomed over the Forum of Halphas.

It was a colossus among colossi. Cruciform, with its arms and six wings outstretched, the black statue stood nearly five hundred feet tall. Built upon a natural rise in Adamantinarx, it faced the river, chin down, eyes closed in the tragic, court-sanctioned idiom of nearly all monumental statuary in Hell. During breaks, Hani looked at it, trying to fathom the emotion that must go through the demonic mind when it regarded such works. It was impossible; not having been an angel, he could only guess.

Work had finished on the statue itself. Hani and his gang had been called in at the very last days of construction. Only the last step of the plinth remained unfinished, and as the demon engineers and architects gathered at its base he could see that some sort of ceremony was about to take place.

Overseers prodded him and Div and the others into a long line that paralleled the plinth. There Hani stood waiting, watching.

The demons assembled in what he could plainly see were hierarchical ranks, anticipating the arrival of some official. Hani tried to hear any name, but the moaning of some of the workers was too loud to penetrate. It was amazing, he thought, how much sound some of the mouthless souls could make.

After standing for a short time, he saw the vanguard of the approaching party—standard-bearers carrying their narrow, vertical banners with the ubiquitous sigil of Lord of Adamantinarx Sargatanas blazing above. A thrill of fear washed over Hani; it would be his first close-hand glimpse of a Demon Major and he did not know what to expect. Whatever a high demon's appearance, it was the awareness of his dreadful capriciousness when it came to souls that terrified Hani.

Scourges set about the throng of souls, whipping them into silence. For that he was almost grateful.

Looming behind the phalanx of skin-cloaked standard-bearers were three enormous soul-beasts, creatures that

Hani had seen before but never so close. He had heard that these souls were special, that in their Lives they had been prominent but corrupt religious leaders from many sects and that their transgressions had been deemed even more punishable than most. Because of this the demons had taken an unusual and heightened interest in them. Hani thought it showed.

As the small procession approached, he could hear the dull thud of the heavy beasts' feet, the scraping of their unshorn nails upon the flagstones, the grunting exhalations of their breath. A dozen harness-spikes were driven into each of their heads, through which their jingling bridles and reins were strung. They were so near as they passed him that he felt the air move from the swaying blankets that hung upon their rough-hided bodies. He could not help but be amazed at their size. One of them rolled its giant head and its bloodshot eye fixed upon him. A strange ripple of some distant memory, of creatures nearly as ponderous and eyes nearly as intelligent, flashed before his mind's eye. He closed his eyes to try to grasp it, to analyze it, but it was too fleeting and vanished altogether.

He was so distracted by the beasts that he almost neglected to look upon their riders. And when he did he was thoroughly, breathtakingly impressed. These were dark, godlike beings, terrible to look at, yet fascinating in every detail of their appearance. When their creatures came to a halt before the plinth, they dismounted, light upon their feet for creatures more than twice his height, and his stomach churned as they came toward the line of souls.

Sargatanas, for it must have been him, led the trio, and he was all that Hani would have expected of the Lord of Adamantinarx. Huge legs covered in skins and bone greaves and as thick as Hani's torso carried him easily toward the assembled demons. Tiny sparks sprayed when he walked. His steaming body was cov-

ered in layers of deep-crimson trailing robes, finely decorated with his sigils picked out in gold thread, and
adorned with long garlandlike strands of organs picked
out from choice souls. A gaping hole, jagged and seemingly ember filled, glowed from his medal-decorated
chest, but it was nothing next to the fires that crowned
his bone-plated head. Hani stared at his face, aquiline,
broken, animated, and fierce. He saw tiny, wholly non-
human bones shifting as unfathomable emotions played
upon its surface. It was a face that, even in its frightful,
degraded state, suggested something lost long ago—an
alien grace, perhaps. Hani knew what Sargatanas had
been—the colossus showed him that—and now knew
what he had become. Stealing a closer look, craning his
head up, he saw the silvered eyes that glittered and
darted, veiled, armored eyes, he imagined, to look upon
the sights of Hell.

Sargatanas stood mere yards from Hani and he felt
his knees buckle slightly. For all his observations, the
physical presence of the Demon Major was overwhelming; there was, it seemed, a tremendous, supernatural
power to his proximity. Hani did not know if it was
some studied force of intimidation that the demons used
to enforce servitude or merely some innate part of their
being. And Hani was not alone in its influence; some
souls actually fell before the demon, unable to stand,
whimpering without control. The demon engineers, architects, and Overseers, too, seemed as if they were
holding their breath. Only the banners flapping loudly
in the hot wind fought the silence.

Hani watched as one of Sargatanas' two companions
leaned in to his lord. This demon, too, was impressive
but, if appearance was any gauge, was the Demon Major's inferior by reason of his less elaborate decorations.

"I know that you never wanted this, Lord," Hani overheard. His eyes widened in amazement. While he had
understood the Overseers' infrequent guttural commands,

he had never imagined that the higher demons' speech would be intelligible. Their accent was strange and hard to penetrate and their voices many layered, but with some effort he could understand them!

"Here it stands, Valefar. I accept that. But I do not accept why Beelzebub insists on these hollow gestures. I do not like this *thing* any more than I like his motives."

Sargatanas' voice sent a chill down Hani's spine. It was a terrible voice, resonant, and almost hoarse to the soul's ears. He tried not to imagine what it would be like angry.

"My lord," the demon called Valefar said, "this was not a battle worth fighting. Just accept it. Anyway," he said, looking up at the figure, "it looks good here."

Sargatanas shook his head. "I have never been good at blind acceptance."

Hani saw some more workers collapse.

"Enough," said Sargatanas to Valefar, taking a thick, glyph-dotted scepter from him. "Let us finish this pretense and go back to the palace." He beckoned the Chief Engineer, a beast-headed demon whom Hani had rarely seen, who nearly fell in his haste to obey his lord.

"Yes, my lord," the engineer said, saluting, covering the hole in his chest.

"You have done a splendid job, Abbeladdur. And you have left the last step for me to finish."

"Thank you, my lord." Abbeladdur's eyes never met Sargatanas'.

Hani quailed. He realized that he and his small group of workers were very close to the unfinished step. Overseers edged in, prodding and compacting the line so that he was even closer. Dangerously close.

He turned back to Sargatanas, who had his scepter in hand.

More souls tumbled to the ground, begging not to be turned to bricks.

"No, please. My only crime," a soul waving his forked

flipper-hands cried out, "was to steal bread for my family. Please, please don't do this to me."

Another soul with half a jaw shrieked, "Please, Lord, please. This is forever; please, no." This he repeated over and over.

Hani clenched his jaws and tried to close his eyes but could not.

As he raised the scepter, Sargatanas stopped. Hani saw him staring at a single soul who, it appeared, was unafraid to stare back at him.

Hani had seen her earlier, as they worked; she was hard to ignore. Tall and striking with unusually piercing, blue eyes, she, like himself, was relatively unscathed by the Change. He had almost thought her attractive, a thought so ludicrous in Hell he had smiled inwardly. Souls around her had called her Bo-ad and given her some breadth for her fierceness. Now, she stood proudly at the moment of her ultimate punishment.

But the Lord of Adamantinarx was not about to suffer the insolence of a soul lightly. He moved a pace, which brought him toweringly before her.

Hani saw her trembling, saw how she resisted sobbing or simply collapsing as the others had done. Instead, she looked up at Sargatanas, shaking, and Hani, himself shaking, swore under his breath in incredulity. Looking closely at her, he saw that she was wearing a necklace upon her well-formed bosom, a necklace from which hung a tiny white figure, the sister of his own!

"Why," she asked, "why am I here? I killed, it is true, but I fought justly against a ruler who neither understood nor cared for me. Is *that* any reason to spend eternity here? Is it?"

Again Hani swore, but this time in admiration. The passion and forcefulness of her words carried Sargatanas back half a step. For a few seconds he stared at her and then, incredibly, he turned away, brows knit, jaw set. Valefar stepped toward Sargatanas. The two demons stood looking at each other for a moment.

"What is it, my lord?" the demon named Valefar asked.

"It is the same reason *I* am here," Hani thought he heard Sargatanas say. Walking past Valefar, the Demon Major placed the scepter in his companion's extended hand, and the Prime Minister spun, glaring at Bo-ad.

With an uttered command, Valefar sent a bolt of luminous writing forth from the baton touching the female's forehead and imploding her in a horrific instant. The glyphs flickered outward to each side of where she now lay, a steaming, rectangular brick. Vengefully, it seemed, the glyphs jumped from soul to soul converting each of them into a brick and stopping only two souls short of Hani.

The step, smoking from the heat of its creation, was complete.

Sargatanas turned, like one who had forgotten something. He moved slowly back to where Bo-ad had stood and knelt down, his robes falling in a wide arc around him. Hani, who could see what no one else could because of his position, watched the demon probe with his clawed fingers in the brick, poking into the folds of what had been the woman. He saw Sargatanas pause for a moment and then, tugging lightly, withdraw the necklace, sinew strand first and followed by the amulet. The demon rubbed its polished surface, thoughtfully, and then clenched it tightly in his fist. And then, without any warning, an eye opened on the brick's uppermost surface, a piercing blue, pain-filled eye that looked up accusingly at Sargatanas. The Demon Major started and then stared back. Hani could just see a tear welling in the eye, unable to free itself, pooling. Amazed, he watched Sargatanas carefully dip a claw into the welled tear and, after a moment's hesitation, inexplicably smear it upon the little white statue's surface.

The demon rose, a mountain of flesh and bone and fire, majestic and menacing again. And yet, the soul thought, he seemed somehow shaken. Hani had seen something no one, let alone a soul, was meant to see, and it had given him a great deal to wrestle over.

"Valefar," said Sargatanas, his voice low, "bring up the mounts and let us go back to the palace. I am very tired."

XI

DIS

Ardat Lili was late. She had insisted upon going out with the half-dozen new statues, and Lilith, remembering the Prince's words, had come very close to ordering her to remain in the chambers. Instead, seeing her resolve, Lilith had warned her to be extra careful leaving and entering the palace, to take special precautions to avoid any detection. *Perhaps that was it,* Lilith thought. *Perhaps even now she is carefully sneaking past the guards at the Keep's entrance.* As much as Lilith cared for her handmaiden and feared for her safety, she still needed Ardat to spread the statues throughout Hell's cities.

Work, Lilith decided, would be the ideal distraction while she waited for her handmaiden to return.

The marked piece of bone had freed itself from the wall easily, almost as if it wanted to be prized away, and when it lay upon Lilith's small table she had been even more pleased with its shape than before. It was special and she knew exactly what she would do with it. And to whom it would be given. She had found Sargatanas' charisma undeniable.

A shaggy pile of curled bone shavings lay around the piece's base. She watched, almost like an onlooker, as the fine chisels seemed to move almost by themselves, so light and deft was her touch, so inspired was she. Even so, this piece would take some time before it was finished; not only was it larger, but it also demanded more of her than she fretted she was capable of.

Her little Liliths were easy now; the formula for them was so clear that she could sculpt one in two sittings. Ardat was so impressed with that and so eager to take them out, Lilith thought, stinging herself with the reminder of her absence.

It had been good to see Valefar again, good to know that the influence she had exerted had succeeded in saving him. He had been so reluctant to leave. But it comforted her to know that he had been smart enough to settle in the only city in Hell remotely worth living in. Lord Sargatanas' city, Adamantinarx-upon-the-Acheron. It seemed like a dream, to her.

She had been in Hell a long time when that city was founded, alone and bitter, wandering through the darkness with only her hatred of the Throne growing in her belly. That, she had repeated for millennia, was not how it was supposed to be.

At times, she thought her ceaseless tears could have put out the very fires of Hell. Through the darkness she wandered and wept and brooded. And then came the Fall and Lucifer. She remembered staring up at the perpetual night sky, a mixture of fear and awe in her breast, as she watched the fiery descents. And then, somehow, Lucifer had found her and her world of isolation was changed.

She and he were alone together, far away from the others. Traversing the blasted landscape, sharing their

rage and sorrow, they were almost happy to have been
given each other. As she sat carving, she remembered
the day she turned away from him and the moment
when she turned back to see that he was gone. She knew
where he was and knew, too, how and why he had left.
These things he had sworn her to secrecy on, a secret
she had faithfully kept. She had been his consort, his almost willing possession, for days only. But it had been
time enough, she thought, chipping and shaving away at
the statue, time enough to see the beauty and the base-
ness in him. The nobility and the deceit.

Lilith put the chisel down. *That was it,* she thought.
*That was what I saw in him. In Sargatanas. The same
churning emotions, the same compelling look in his eyes.*
But was he the same? From everything she had heard,
the Demon Major was fierce but fair. He ruled through
wisdom, not butchery.

"Oh, where is she?" Lilith muttered, and almost as
the words died on her lips she heard scuffing sounds
outside her chamber. She rose, relieved, and walked
quickly to the door.

The Chancellor General of the Order stood in the
open doorway, cloaked in an ember-flecked and smoking traveling skin, a clear sign that he had just returned
from outside the Keep. Eyes slitted, a smirk jagging his
mouth, Adramalik signaled two flanking Knights to take
up positions on either side of her. Without a word she
followed him, the red-swathed Knights looming so large
on either side that she felt smothered by their robes.

They traveled the corridors in silence, heading, she
realized, toward the Rotunda. *An audience with him? At
this hour?* Lilith always needed some kind of advance
notice to put her mind in the right state for Beelzebub.
That had been their agreement. This was unprecedented
and with each step, though her fears were inchoate,
Lilith grew more apprehensive.

They halted at the Rotunda's entrance and Lilith

stooped over the narrow threshold, followed by Adramalik. The buzzing was loud, louder than she had heard it in some time.

She hated the long walk through the fetid gloom to the throne; there was too much time for her to undo the emotional armor that she ordinarily layered on. She looked up and saw that the hanging skins were unusually active, moving as if a strong wind was daring to disturb them. She was nearly to the throne; a single thick pillar of chewed flesh rose before her obscuring the view. The obscene buzzing was almost unbearable and now that she was so close another sound was also barely audible—a moaning that sent a blade of terror into her heart. She saw Agares in the shadows, chin down, arms stiffly at his sides, and heard something—a sound of rending. And then, passing the pillar, she looked up and, struck as if by a hammer, fell to her knees.

Twenty feet above the puddled floor, suspended by her wrists from a sinew and bone hanger, was Ardat Lili. Lilith saw her traveling skins lying in a heap far beneath her feet and saw, too, the six tiny statues arranged carefully, ludicrously, upon them. With a chuckle, Adramalik picked up Lilith by her neck and tossed her easily to the floor at her handmaiden's feet. Lilith landed upon her back and with flailing arms and legs scrabbled upright. Spattered with splashed blood, she looked up and saw her handmaiden's dangling body, alive with the rippling subdermal movement of hundreds of flies. Lilith knew what he was doing. Beelzebub was feeding, consuming everything within and liberating Ardat's skin just as he had done to all the other undead skins above.

Ardat Lili sighed and somehow Lilith heard it above the buzzing, above her own screams. The Prime Minister turned to her, and the haunted look in his eyes made his feelings clear.

"Nergar's police took her just as she was exiting the Keep," said Adramalik crisply. "The Prince warned you,

Consort, warned you to keep your affairs . . . simple. Instead you involved her."

Lilith's breath came in huge gulping gasps. Time passed and stood still. Somewhere in her mind, between the terror and the anguish, a horror was unfettered—the guilty understanding that, as much as she had cared about Ardat, she had used her zealous, trusting handmaiden and was solely responsible for her miserable end.

Lilith looked up. The Prince—her Prince—was almost done. What had been Ardat Lili was little more than a flapping skin-sack, hollow and empty, yet aware. Exiting flies issued from her mouth, swarming around her flaccid skin, examining their handiwork.

As Lilith watched, the rack begin to ascend, carrying the pathetic skin up into the gloom of the dome, and she heard Adramalik's soft laughter and splashing footsteps fade away. Only the Prime Minister remained with her and the Prince. He stood over her and reached down, putting his hands under her arms and legs and lifting her carefully.

Agares carried her through the Rotunda, and when he brought her back to her chambers and laid her gently upon her skin-covered pallet the only thing circling erratically through her mind like a fly was the droning sound of the Voice that had oscillated through the dome.

"Remember this, dear Lilith. *She* will."

ADAMANTINARX–UPON–THE–ACHERON

Eligor studied him as he sat motionless upon his throne. Far away, deep beneath the Audience Chamber floor, he thought, he could hear the distant sounds of new construction. The barely audible, muffled clink of hammers upon stone was all that disturbed the stillness of the enormous chamber. He knew that the faraway hammering had to be of native stone being worked; the flesh-bricks always cried out when they were being cut and placed.

Sargatanas, too, seemed far away. He had returned to his palace in silence and had remained there, not leaving his throne and speaking only briefly to Halphas and then to no one for days. Eligor and the dozen Guard troopers stood some paces from Sargatanas like a frozen tableau. Once a day, for some hours, a dim shaft of Algol's red light would enter through the oculus and pirouette upon the floor, marking time, only to fade away as if it were sad to be ignored.

Sargatanas sat, only occasionally lifting or lowering his flaming head. A few times he raised a finger to his lips as if he were about to speak but then changed his mind. Through the night he did not stir, the only sign of life being the guttering sparks from his knit brow. His form shifted frequently, sometimes subtly, sometimes drastically. For one night he had no head at all, only concentric multicolored rings of flames with rotating horns at their center.

It is strange, Eligor thought, *to see my lord like this. So deep in thought and yet not exactly brooding.* Eligor's mind wandered back to the events of recent days and he realized that Sargatanas had more than enough upon which to reflect. Certainly their treatment in Dis was disappointing and redolent of darker implications. But Dis had brought unexpected rewards as well; Lilith had surprised them all. The imminent war with Astaroth, too, was something to address, something that always took much planning, albeit with the general staff. And then there was that soul, Eligor remembered, that insolent female soul. What had she stirred up? She had obviously affected his lord, though why Eligor could not be sure. Never had he been so happy to see a soul so transformed.

Sargatanas shifted his torso and Eligor saw him trace Valefar's sigil in the air. It was the first real action the

Demon Major had taken in days, and Eligor felt something ineffable in the pit of his stomach. There was a decisiveness in the movement that contrasted with Sargatanas' earlier seeming lethargy.

Whether he had been concerned for his master and waiting outside the vast chamber or he had used other occult means, Valefar appeared at the arcades startlingly quickly. Walking briskly, resplendent in tissue-thin embroidered skins, he climbed the steps to the dais three at a time and bowed deeply, formally, before Sargatanas. He, too, seemed to sense something.

Eligor stood closer to the throne than the Guard and always heard his lord's conversations. He thought of it as a privilege of rank.

"Prime Minister," Sargatanas said, staring fixedly into Valefar's eyes, "I have no stomach for it anymore."

"I know, Lord," said Valefar softly. "It was that soul, was it not?"

"She made me see them all as . . . people."

Valefar was silent.

"Before that moment, Valefar, they were nothing. I resented them and, because of that, I used them. As we all did. But now, when I pull back after all of these many eons, I see with clarity what this place is . . . and how I cannot endure it, as I see it now, any longer." He paused. "It is time for change, time to make a stand. Time to do instead of dream."

"My lord?"

"The incessant wars. Old Astaroth upon our border, hungry and desperate. What will happen when we destroy his legions as we surely will? Nothing. We will appropriate his broken wards, rebuild them with uncounted souls, and return to our complacency. Hell will not change. And neither will we; we will still be here, exiled, punished . . . rejected."

"Rejected?"

"By Those Above."

"That is our lot."

"For how long? Eternity? When will the Fallen have had enough punishment?"

There was silence and Eligor worked at the question in his own mind.

"For some," Valefar said with no irony, "there can never be enough punishment."

"And what of us? We are not like the others—like Beelzebub and the rest. Must we share *their* fate forever?"

Valefar returned Sargatanas' gaze and for a moment said nothing. Eligor held his breath.

"What you are suggesting cannot be done. We cannot go back."

"I would try," Sargatanas said evenly. "I do not know if we can or not—if accepting our responsibility in the War is enough. Or if pleading our remorse can absolve us. I do not know, Valefar. I do know that I cannot live in this place, as it is—under the Fly—and that I would destroy all this, this palace, this city, this world, and myself as well, if only to look upon His Face again for an instant."

Sargatanas rose. He described the sigils of the Barons Zoray and Faraii in the air before him, sending them on their way with a dismissive twitch of his hand.

Valefar approached him and, to Eligor's surprise, embraced the Demon Major. He then dropped to one knee.

"My lord, my friend, let me be your fiery right hand, your burning torch to light your way back. And to flame the very streets of Dis, if need be."

"I would have it no other way, Valefar."

Eligor walked before the two demons and sank to his knees as well.

"Lord, I, too, have heard all that you have said. I would be your left hand and, in it, the uncleavable shield that protects you."

Sargatanas, smiling, bade them both stand.

"We have many preparations. As of this moment, we

must regard ourselves as a state apart in this world. A renegade state. Therefore, Prime Minister, I need you to go quietly and quickly to the Lesser Lords Andromalius and Bifrons and bring them here. As my clients they will have no choice but to come. And no choice but to support me."

And to Eligor he said, "Henceforth, in this new time, you and your Guard will have to add secret police to your list of many tasks. I must know of the shifting thoughts of those closest to my throne. As seemingly unimpeachable as my inner circle is, no one is safe from corruption."

Valefar bowed and withdrew, and Eligor nodded, resuming his station just behind Sargatanas. As Eligor watched the figure of the Prime Minister diminish across the wide floor, he saw the distant, fiery-headed forms of the demons Faraii and Zoray emerge from the arcades. *It would be interesting,* Eligor thought, *to watch their reactions to his master's plans. As it would all of Hell's.*

XII

DIS

For the first time that any demon could remember, Algol could be seen during the day in Hell's troubled sky, blazing bright and luminous. *Like a blood-filmed eye,* Adramalik thought, staring out from his window in the uppermost level of the Keep. What did the Watchdog look down upon that engendered such anger?

The Chancellor General looked out at his city far below. Normally dark and lit only by patches of spontaneous random fires, it now looked painted with blood. Algol's furious brush had daubed the roofs, the streets, the statues, the many-spired, huge edifices, and even the Keep itself in red. A world bathed in the blood of its souls. That, he thought, would be a more perfect world.

He found the vivid light beautiful, evocative, an artifact of the star so compelling that he sat on the window-ledge until Algol set. The city returned to its former self, dark and mysterious, its shades of black cloaking the horrors that he had helped create.

ADAMANTINARX–UPON–THE–ACHERON

Eligor, too, watched the star set as he waited for Baron Faraii to join him. Its remarkable fading light turned the Acheron into a shimmering red snake sinuously meandering through the city. He looked down at the bricks of the dome's parapet upon which he sat and saw a half-dozen souls' eyes staring out, the ruddy light reflected sharply in their glassy surface. What were they thinking?

Eligor heard the distant flapping of wings and saw one of his patrols circling high above him. Evidence of what Sargatanas had called a heightened readiness. He turned and cast his eyes up at the enormous dome behind him. Giant braziers were inset into its curving, otherwise smooth wall, spaced evenly around and reminiscent of the flaming coronet that sometimes encircled Sargatanas' head. At the moment, Eligor noted, they were an ineffective light source against the last rays of Algol.

The Baron was late, something that had been happening more and more frequently in the course of their meetings. Eligor wondered if there was some significance to this, whether it indicated a growing unwillingness on the Baron's part to continue their discussions about his travels. He valued the talks, realizing at that moment just how much he would miss them if they ended. The Baron was a vivid storyteller and his wanderings made for compelling listening, but more than that, Eligor found the demon's enigmatic personality fascinating. Faraii had proven himself time and again in the hundreds of wars he had fought in for Sargatanas; his weapons-skill and ferocity were unmatched and did not go unnoticed. Eventually, because of his indisputable prowess, his lord had seen fit to commission Faraii to create a special unit of shock troops composed of the most intimidating of Sargatanas' newly fashioned legionaries. But, even with this honor, Faraii rarely spoke of his battlefield exploits, and this only lent more luster to Eligor's opinion of him. Unconsciously Eligor clutched his vellum notebook and bone pen a bit tighter, as if they, too, might cease to be, along with the meetings.

He sat in a rare state of anticipation; this was the first time since Sargatanas' amazing decision that Eligor would be alone with Faraii, and he was eager to hear the Baron's thoughts away from the constraints of the court. The Baron was more than forthcoming about his journeys, but it was rare that he spoke of his own feelings.

Algol had just set when Eligor heard the light scrape of the Baron's footsteps as he climbed the stairs that led to the balcony. Wearing his black Abyssal-spine sword on a decorated baldric, he was armored as commander of the Shock Troops. Broad, thick pieces of blackened and tempered bone overlay his segmented torso, each skillfully fit piece inlaid with obsidian and jet. Special vents edged the cuirass, allowing flames to lick outward in the heat of battle. Though Faraii's was a lighter version of the armor his troops possessed, Eligor had seen how intimidating the effect could be.

"Eligor, I am sorry to have kept you waiting," Faraii said. "I was drilling my troopers and time got away from me."

"They are, without a doubt, the best trained of any troops in Hell," Eligor said enthusiastically, "solely for their commander's diligence."

"Thank you. Coming from the Captain of the Flying Guard, that is high praise."

Eligor smiled. He knew that his Guard was drilled as well, if not as often, but coming from Faraii the compliment was gratifying. Eligor also knew that while his winged Guard relied on speed and precision, Faraii's heavy legionaries were a bludgeon, a nearly irresistible force upon the battlefield. Where the Guard was a lance, sharp and swift, the Shock Troops were Sargatanas' hammer, prized and pampered for their brutality.

Eligor looked closely at Faraii's breast-armor. "There is ash upon your chest. Are you injured?"

Faraii looked down and, indeed, a wide, dull pattern of ash clouded the high, black gloss of the armor.

"It is not mine, Eligor. One of the troopers got a bit too excited. I had to . . . correct him."

Faraii unstrapped the long sword and, setting it beside him, sat down heavily on the parapet's low wall. He looked out at the remaining sliver of Algol's light as it sank behind the horizon. Eligor saw the weariness in his actions, the angle at which he held his hard, gaunt head.

"Our lord has chosen to place a heavy burden upon us all," Faraii said, not taking his gaze from the city.

"We are at the start of something great, Faraii," Eligor countered. "All great endeavors are a challenge."

Faraii did not respond immediately but instead looked at his feet.

"I wonder if our lord truly knows what forces he may unleash."

Eligor looked at the Baron.

"I am sure he knows exactly what he is starting," Eligor said earnestly. "His powers and influence have never been greater. Believe me, this was not a decision that came easily. I stood beside him for days and

nights while he considered it. He is certain the time is
right."

"What he is certain of, Eligor, is that he cannot stand
another moment of this place and his subservient standing here. And this reminds me of someone else."

"Really, Faraii, you cannot seriously compare—"

"Why not? From what I have heard there were few
Demons Major as zealous as Sargatanas when it came
to supporting Lucifer. And like him, our lord aches for
something he cannot have."

Eligor put the notebook and pen down beside him.

"We were all caught up in Lucifer's rhetoric," he said
plainly. Something was clearly troubling the Baron.
"Look around you, Faraii. We are all defined by this
place, by the fire and the flesh. And the pain. We, like
the souls, are Hell's inmates. But we are also their jail-
ers. Is this how you would choose to spend Eternity? As
little more than an embittered jailer?"

"Perhaps," Faraii said quietly, gloomily. "Is Sargatanas' rhetoric all that different?"

"I thought that I knew you better than this, Baron."

"I have seen enough of the Above."

"Surely you have also seen enough of Hell."

Faraii turned slowly to Eligor; his face, limned in
faint, pulsing fire, was cast in deep shadow. Only the
mask of tiny lights defined it. His metallic eyes glittered
and Eligor, for just a moment, saw something in them
just beneath the surface, something repressed. He felt an
inexplicable sense of menace.

"More than you can imagine." A tiny spark flew from
Faraii's nostril. The Baron closed his eyes and said, "I
am sorry, my friend. I am tired and I would be lying to
you if I said that I did not have doubts. I do, but I am
also confident that Lord Sargatanas has matters well in
hand."

Relieved, Eligor sat back. He picked up his pen and
notebook.

Faraii, seeing this, reached for his sword and stood up.

"I am sorry, Eligor, not tonight. I would just like to retire to my chambers. It has been a tiring day. Tomorrow,
perhaps?"

"Of course, Faraii," Eligor said, hoping that he had
managed to conceal his disappointment.

Eligor returned his gaze out over Adamantinarx. When
he looked back, a moment later, to where Faraii had
stood, the Baron was gone.

A light storm blew embers down upon the streets before
him. It was night and Hani took full advantage of the
greater darkness to slip down the crowded streets unnoticed. The thoroughfares were only slightly less congested with souls than during the day, and he made an
effort to blend in, to seem as though he were a member
of the various bustling work-gangs.

Hani felt the solid weight of the Burden, which was,
for now, fortunately, embedded in the small of his back.
Had it been jutting from one of his legs or, worse, in a
foot, he might not have been as reckless. Just one of the
many things, he reflected, that had fallen into place,
compelling him to break away, to attempt the utterly unthinkable.

A plan had begun to form while he had watched the
demon lord. Div and the others had all seen Sargatanas
kneel, but no one had seen why. They had listened intently, hours later, when Hani had told them what he
had seen. And when he had sketched out his plan as
best he could they looked at one another without expression. He could not discern whether they understood or merely thought him raving. Either way, he was
going to leave; there simply was no point in trying to
explain to them what he could not fully explain to himself; his inner vision was cloudy at best. He would attempt to confront the demon with the statue, if even for
a moment, to simply ask him who he had once been. If

it failed, he would be destroyed or worse, but he would have tried.

A few days after Sargatanas had left the construction site, the demons had lit the colossus' head like a giant torch, scattering the Scourges who had been perched upon it. Gauging this as the perfect distraction, Hani had faded away into the crowd. Even he was amazed that it had worked.

Now, as he walked, he felt a raging frustration at having to match his pace to the slower, stumbling souls around him. Far up ahead, through the darkness and smoke and blowing embers, he saw the dim silhouette of the palace dome high atop the center mount, its pinpoints of flame marking its countless levels, and realized that it would take many hours to reach the palace. He did not have any idea what he would do once he was near its towering gates, but he trusted that he would find some way in.

When will the Overseers notice my absence? he thought, with a stab of fear, for the thousandth time since he had left. *And when will my Burden betray me?* He had seen what happened to souls when the black orb had been triggered, how they had dropped to the ground and, screaming, been incinerated from within by a single fiery glyph. Only gray ash had remained. *It won't happen to me . . . it won't.*

He moved on, looking into the faces of the souls as he passed them. Rended, twisted, cleft, pierced, or severed. Eyeless, jawless, noseless, or even entirely faceless. This was humanity. Or most of it. Thrust into Hell by their own hand, by their irresistible weaknesses. This was what they had made of themselves. He felt neither sympathy nor disdain. Just an odd belonging that he was not sure felt very good.

War, it had been whispered, was again looming. Long files of legionaries and officers were everywhere, but he passed them confidently; they had no reason, as yet, to be looking for him. Once they knew he was missing it would not matter that he was surrounded by millions of souls just like him. The Burden would betray him. That was its purpose.

Hani pushed on in what he came to think of as an exercise not of stealth or speed but of patience. The milky Acheron vanished behind the blocks of low buildings as he walked farther up toward the city's center. With all his walking, though, he was amazed at how the center mount never seemed any closer.

Sounds of torment emanated from within most of the low, featureless buildings along the avenue, sounds that Hani barely heard anymore. Most of the meaty exteriors were punctured by a window, and, as he passed these, everything from sobs to screams reached out onto the street. None of it shocked him; his work-gangs had labored in proximity to buildings like these frequently, and his own curiosity about their inhabitants had long ago been satisfied. These were simply the places where the worst souls were kept and punished, their torments in many cases gruesomely tailored to their crimes.

Hani looked ahead, trying to penetrate the clots of souls and legionaries and Scourges, and saw a contingent of demon phalangites some hundred feet away. Larger and more solid than most demons, they strode slowly through the crowds, long hand-pikes shouldered, intentionally trampling any hapless soul too slow to avoid them. In fact, Hani thought, it appeared that they were going out of their way to inflict damage on the crowd.

Hani decided to duck into the first open doorway that he could find; demons rarely entered domiciles. A procession of odd foreigners stumbled past him, eyeless, beating hand-drums and in some kind of chanting trance. Were they souls? He could not tell, but he used them to hunker behind nonetheless, entering the nearest building unseen.

Within the dimly lit cell the air was thick and foul,

redolent of smoking flesh. Burning embers, the odor's source, provided the only faint light. In the room's center was a solitary seated figure. Oversized and gangrenous entrails spilled from within him, forming the seatlike pedestal to which he was forever affixed. A long stream of saliva descended from his mouth and onto his glistening, embedded arms.

He was moaning and it took a few moments for him to realize he was not alone.

"Who's there?" the soul whispered, his voice strained and filled with pain. He tried to move his head, but large growths, arranged like a grotesque necklace, inhibited him. "I know you're there . . . who are you?"

Hani ignored him.

"Why won't you say something?" The soul began to sob, his body convulsing. The organs wobbled and Hani looked away.

"Shut up!"

"Ha," he wheezed, "you're in my cell and you tell me to shut up!"

Hani peered cautiously around the door frame. The phalangites were nearer, and he could clearly hear the cries of the pedestrians and their bones snapping underfoot. He pulled his head back in and turned to face the soul.

"There is a problem out on the street. I'll be gone when it's passed."

"You're a soul. What are you doing running around on your own?"

"That's my business."

The phalangites must be very close, Hani thought. Like waves breaking before the bow of a barge on the Acheron, he saw the crowd just outside begin to part, falling and crashing into one another in an effort to avoid being trampled.

Hani caught a glimpse of the phalangites' armored thighs as they passed the low doorway.

"What's happening out there?" the soul asked.

"A cohort of phala—"

"No, no, I don't mean just now. I mean . . . I am hearing soldiers—lots of soldiers—passing."

"There will be a war," Hani said plainly.

"There is always war."

"This is different. More troop movement. More urgency to it all. It all seems familiar, somehow."

The soul's sudden, snapping cough sent a chill down Hani's spine. "Familiar?" he finally gasped weakly.

"The urgency, the excitement of war. I know this feeling. And seeing all those troops . . ." Hani's voice trailed off. The stirrings of his Life were tantalizing, and their wisps were never to be ignored. A series of the most fleeting impressions passed through his mind: a vast, blue sea of water dotted with strange ships, men—not souls—in burnished cuirasses holding swords and spears, and then a field of death with red-washed bodies piled eye high. What it meant Hani could not imagine. But he tucked the memories away, next to the others he had made a mental catalog of. Next to the little statue, they were his most treasured possessions.

"Are you still there?" Hani heard the desperation, the plaintiveness, in the soul's voice; he might have been the soul's first visitor in millennia. The loneliness was incomprehensible.

"Yes."

"Who are you?"

"I don't know."

"Please don't leave. Talk with me for a bit. It's been so long. Hello? Hello? Are you still there?"

Hani backed silently toward the door and then turned and looked out. The street, uncharacteristically silent save for the moans, was painted in fresh, slick blood and crushed souls, many of whom were dragging themselves toward the doorways. Long, wet footprints, like brushstrokes, trailed off in the direction the phalangites had taken.

As he crossed the threshold and walked away from the domicile he could feel the soul's fading, whispered entreaties clawing at his conscience, compelling him to stay. He set his jaw, looked up at the palace, and picked his way through the sliding bodies.

Some miles later, the avenue regained its former aspect, the crowds merely stepping over any residue from the phalangites' passing. The thoroughfare dipped down and Hani faded behind a caravan of lumbering soulbeasts draped in billowing concealing blankets and laden with goods, led by robed guides and destined for the palace. And once again, walking alongside the enormous creatures, he felt that strange stirring of memory. He knew that he had lived before, but as with all souls, that Life and its memories were still opaque. A mystery. As he hid amidst the shuffling creatures' legs, an ember of optimism brightened, fanned by the awareness that he might actually recover his memories, that he might come to know who he had been. He did not know what forces were at play or whether any of these new feelings were due to his possessing the tiny statue. Before he had acquired it there been no such sudden flashes. With a pang of awareness, Hani realized that something had changed, that he was regaining a sense of self that had been forcibly taken from him and that the memories might be a part of some regrowth. It was a brightening thought that he almost dared not to contemplate, but, despite himself, it drove him onward with a growing sense of expectation.

XIII

ADAMANTINARX–UPON–THE–ACHERON

Two weeks after Sargatanas' momentous decision Eligor and Valefar descended the long, arcing causeway to the palace gate in uncustomary silence. Both demons were deep in thought, wrestling with the implications of recent events, and when they stopped just outside the gate to await the arrival of Bifrons and Andromalius they remained silent. Much had been accomplished in the brief time since that decision, but much more needed to be done. The two immense shallow-bowled braziers, mounted atop building-sized pedestals that flanked the causeway gate, cast a fluctuating orange glow and deep, wavering shadows upon the guards and the milling crowd below. Their seventy-foot flames reached into the sky with the roar of a dozen furnaces.

As he waited, Eligor surveyed the dense crowd that seemed to always gather around the gate. Mostly lesser demons seeking audiences with administrative officials, there was the odd sprinkling of Waste travelers, shepherded work-gangs and exotic soul-beast caravans newly arrived from distant cities. The confusion of noise that Eligor knew must arise from them could barely be heard against the sound of the angry flames from high above.

Finally, he spotted the floating sigils and then the tall, vertical banners of the two approaching demon lords. Both had apparently met up before reaching the gate, and their file of soul-beasts and escort-guards snaked well behind and down into the darkness of the city streets below.

The crowd parted at the prodding of the gate-guard, and two especially large military Behemoths trudged into view. Three times the size of the average soul-beast and powerfully muscled, they were former human kings designated for special use because of their lost rank. Each was ornately caparisoned in rich robes, festooned with elaborately threaded harnesses, pierced in a hundred different ways with jeweled nails and rings, and bearing smoking incense burners that trailed long, twisting lines of bluish smoke. Beneath the robes, and reflecting the new political footing, Eligor saw the dull sheen of black, volcanic armor.

Valefar stepped forward and greeted each Demon Minor as they dismounted their Behemoths. His was an affable manner, and Bifrons and Andromalius both responded in kind. One could not have imagined, Eligor mused, that Adamantinarx was on the brink of the most divisive war Hell had ever seen.

Both visitors flanked the Prime Minister as they headed up the causeway with Eligor in tow. The contrast between Valefar and the two demons was striking. They, having traveled in comfort, were swathed in their finery and sprinkled with gold and jewels, while Valefar's dark, unadorned skins were drab by comparison. It was, Eligor thought, emblematic of this regime that its wealth was not worn for all to see.

When they reached the main palace Valefar led the party into the great entry hall. It was a large, basilica-like area, well lit, and filled with officials and guards ebbing and flowing, paying the newcomers no heed. There, in the middle of the floor and seemingly waiting for him, was a single hovering glyph of golden fire that, when he raised his hand, quickly sank into his palm. When Valefar turned to them a look of mild surprise was written upon his features. His gaze lasted for only a moment and then he led the group down a series of corridors, which grew more and more unfamiliar to Eligor with every turn. They were gradually descending; that much was clear. But the palace was so vast, so filled with administrative levels, that it came as no real surprise to him that they might be in an area that he had not traversed. As they proceeded, the number of chambers diminished until they found themselves heading down an ill-lit and doorless passageway.

The realization that he was completely lost came at nearly the same moment that they arrived at their destination. They reached the end of the corridor and stopped in an anteroom adorned only with a semicircular stone bench facing a single closed door. While the others sat at the urging of Valefar, Eligor looked at the tall door before him, framed oddly with the rarest white native rock, and noticed that there was still stone dust on the flagstones before it. Large footprints were still visible, as if recently made. And looking up, over the lintel, Eligor saw Sargatanas' elaborate circular sigil subtly inlaid in the finest flowing silver.

Eligor suddenly realized that not a soul-brick was anywhere to be seen, that the anteroom was built entirely of stone, and that their degree of dressing was of the highest order. Fresh, white dust stuck to his dark fingers when he ran them over the stones' surfaces.

They waited for some time and then, without fanfare, the door opened noiselessly and Sargatanas emerged. The two earls stood and obediently knelt before their patron. For a moment their fiery sigils separated, intertwined with their lord's, and then returned, resuming their positions above each demon's head.

"Welcome, Brothers. It is good to see my two closest neighbors again after so many centuries. I understand that you both prosper, and for that I am pleased," Sargatanas said plainly. "However, I am sure you are both aware that your wards, sharing common borders with my own, are threatened by Lord Astaroth's intentions. As are mine."

Both Demons Minor nodded.

"For the hundredth time we are going to have to defend ourselves against one of our brethren—be it Astaroth or one of Beelzebub's clients—who thinks it necessary to upset the balance among us. It is a cycle seemingly without end. A cycle that has its origins in the First Infernal Bull issued so long ago during the first Council of Majors—that we may never attack a sovereign capital. 'We may wage war to gain territory, only as it does not jeopardize another demon's existence.' So says the Bull and so said I until of late. Now, however, I cannot subscribe to this law any longer," said Sargatanas, pausing, waiting for the statement to sink in. "Bifrons . . . Andromalius, I am about to shake the very foundations of Hell. With your aid, I am going to challenge everything that this world stands for. Brothers, I am Heaven bound."

Eligor saw the shock written upon their faces. They sat transfixed by their lord, looking at him with mouths partially agape.

Andromalius regained himself and said, "Lord, you do not really think that engaging in a war such as you envision can—"

"I do," Sargatanas said, his voice resonant. "It is naive to think that what transpires here is not being watched from Above. Would we miss an opportunity to watch Them if we could? What have we shown Them after these countless eons here in Hell? We have fulfilled every one of Their claims against us, proven ourselves to be anything but the angels we once were, and denied ourselves any consideration for return. We must show that after all of these grim millennia, after all the pain and punishment, we *are* capable of change. I am convinced that if our intentions and actions are clear— that our opposition to Beelzebub and his government is in earnest—They will take notice. And that is the first step to regaining our lost grace."

Bifrons stood. He looked agitated. Eligor almost felt sorry for them. They had no choice but to go along with their patron, but they did not have to accept his precepts.

"You are talking about total war," Bifrons said, shaking his spined head in disbelief, "a war that would engulf all of Hell. No demon would be able to remain neutral. And to what end?"

"No demon *should* remain neutral," said Sargatanas acidly. "As to what end . . . the end of all this. And a beginning—the beginning of our Ascent."

"You do not really think—"

"I do think and I do dream, but I do not really know, Bifrons. What I do know is that I cannot shake my memories. Nor, I suspect, can anyone else present."

Without waiting for an answer, Sargatanas turned and put a steaming hand upon the door latch. "Yours has been a long and tiring journey and I will send you on to your chambers shortly. But first it is important for you to understand what lies beneath my decision."

He opened the door and Eligor could only see darkness beyond.

"We are directly below the throne in the Audience Chamber," said Sargatanas. "I had construction begin on this . . . shrine when I decided my course."

The others followed him, a dark silhouette outlined in a scalloped tracery of steaming embers, into the narrow vestibule, and the only faint illumination was from their flickering heads. Eligor could see, between the shadows of their passing and then only dimly, pale walls covered with neat lines of incised angelic inscriptions. He found that provocative, curious. It was a small heresy to write in the old style; it was a much larger one to commit that writing to stone.

The walls fell away on either side as they entered a larger, circular room. The hollowness of their footsteps echoed through the unseen reaches, making the group sound larger than it was. Sargatanas uttered a word and suddenly the room was suffused in pale light. The dark, cloaked figures of the five demons contrasted starkly with the luminosity of the space. Eligor's jaw dropped and Valefar audibly released his breath, while the two visiting earls looked as if they might turn and run at any moment. All this Sargatanas measured as he stood back and watched the demons.

Eligor squinted, his eyes adjusting to the brightness. He took in the lambent room and realized that for all this to have been completed in such a short time—a matter of weeks—his lord must have driven Halphas and his laborers very hard. And then Eligor remembered the sounds of masons ringing through the long nights.

The joinery of the stones, their perfect dressing, and the care with which they were chosen all bespoke a level of craft that Eligor thought must have been augmented by an Art. Only the fairest, palest stones, laced with delicate veins of gold and silver, had been employed. The walls were punctuated at regular intervals with columned niches, each home, Eligor could discern, to a miraculous lifelike statue of a many-winged figure. The low-domed ceiling, hewn from an unimaginably huge pale-blue opal, flickered with flecks of inner fire, a perfect evocation, Eligor remembered, of the coruscating sky of the Above. Such a room, he knew, was not meant to exist in Hell.

But it was not the walls, nor the beautiful ceiling, nor even the heretical statuary that stirred the demons most. It was the running mosaics with tiles so small that Eligor could barely see them and the nearly floor-to-ceiling friezes and their incredible imagery that took the demons and wrenched them and pulled them in. And reminded them.

Each of the demons approached these shimmering murals and each walked slowly, silently, transfixed. Eligor found himself not looking at the friezes but into them, so rich was their execution, so vivid their portrayals. They began, at both sides of the room, with simple renderings of the Above, of the clear and glowing air, of the lambent clouds and the jeweled ground and the vast sparkling sea. And farther on, the great gold and crimson Tree of Life, heavy with its ripe, swollen fruit set amidst broad and sheltering leaves. Eligor saw, looking closely, the fabulous serpentine chalkadri flying through its boughs, their twelve wings picked out in rainbow jewels. He remembered their mellifluous calls and the Tree's sweet fragrance and could not imagine how he might have forgotten them.

Eligor paused to look at his fellow demons. Thin wisps of steam, barely visible in the light, streamed from their eyes. The two earls had given themselves over to the images and were breathlessly sidling along the walls, murmuring to themselves and each other. Valefar walked a few paces unsteadily, occasionally putting a tentative hand out upon the wall for support. And at the room's center, standing by a raised altar and watching them all with his intent, silvered eyes, was the fallen seraph, a dark figure as immobile as the angelic statues that surrounded him.

Eligor turned back to the wall and saw the twelve radiant gates of the sun and the twelve pearlescent gates of the moon and the treasuries that housed the clouds and dew, the snow and the ice. There he saw the first depicted angels who guarded those storehouses, and it was a shock to see them, for he had tried very hard to forget their gracefulness.

Valefar, who was ahead of the other three demons, reached the farthest tableau, and something there that Eligor could not yet see caused him to cry out. He reeled backward, as if struck, nearly colliding with his lord. Sargatanas put out a hand and steadied his friend.

As if he were clinging to the side of a cliff with his hands, Eligor guided himself tentatively along the curving

wall, examining its images, pausing to remember. The
mosaic-bordered bas-reliefs showed more and more of the
glittering hosts and their cities of light. Eligor knew what
would follow: the ten greatest cities of creation, tiered like
enormous steps upon the flank of the celestial mount, ascending toward the Throne.

These spired cities, crystalline and pure, filled with
their multitudes of seraphim and cherubim, seemed, to
his pained eyes, alive with the angels' comings and go-
ings. He was sure that he even recognized some of the
angels, so great was the craft of the sculptors. In stone
and jewels and metals the angels marched and sang and
toiled, and as he looked at them Eligor recalled doing
all of those things.

When he reached the foot of the Throne in all its
soaring radiance he saw that it was surrounded by the
six-winged archangels, swords in hand, singing praises
as he had seen them do. The echoes of their celestial
harmonies were so loud and the vision of them so real
that he stumbled upon Andromalius, who, along with
Bifrons, had reached the spot ahead of him. They were
both upon their knees, gasping, hands outstretched
against the wall. Eligor caught himself and, with pounding trepidation, looked upon the sublime Face of God.
Its evocation was so glorious and terrible, so threatening and full of love, that he, too, exclaimed aloud. *How
did I forget?* He found that he could not look away. Its
beauty burned fiercely into his mind like a brand, like
sparking iron—but not nearly as powerfully as when he
had been in its presence so long ago. He could not control his shaking and, with steam blurring his vision,
staggered away to where his lord and Valefar stood.

Sargatanas, his chest rising and falling, appeared
moved by their reactions; Eligor heard his breath, deep
and rhythmic like a bellows. He had not strayed from
the room's center, but in his hand, drawn from some hidden sheath, Eligor now saw a new-forged and unfamiliar

sword, downward bent and vicious, wreathed in vapor and glyphs. A new sword—a Falcata—consecrated for a new war. Sargatanas held it up before him, and all of the demons' eyes were drawn to it.

Looking at each of them in turn, the Demon Major said coldly, "Brothers, we will look upon that Face again."

DIS

Lilith rocked on her heels, balled up, like something empty and windblown and discarded, cast into the corner of her bedchamber. It was dark and she wore the darkness like an old, comforting friend. Once, for a short time, she had been very much a creature of the night, and she still could see quite well in the blackness. Her precious carving tools were strewn about on the floor; she could see them and the torn and broken furnishings and the holes she had punched into the bone walls. She could see, too, the broken room partition, evidence of where the Order Knights, angered by her furious struggling, had thrown her. She did not need to see the bruises; they were obvious enough. She crouched in near darkness, the only light filtering in from a crack she had kicked into the door.

It had been weeks since Ardat Lili had been taken from her. Weeks of confusion and pain and darkness. She had determined to give the Fly nothing willingly. His attempts at what he considered sex, while growing less frequent, were also growing more violent. Lilith feared that it was only a matter of time before she, too, swung high above his throne. *Could he actually do that to me? What would he tell Lucifer?*

Her shaking subsided and she rose, unsteadily. Her clawed feet trod upon the bits and pieces of her few possessions as she crossed the room to the upended little table she had done her carving on. It was oddly unbroken—a survivor like her. She righted it and then went about searching for the few items she would need to summon her familiar. She had not done that since she had come to Hell and worried that perhaps she might not remember how. But try she would. The time of tears was over. Now was the time of action.

She had to get out, away from Dis. That much was clear. This last encounter had been too . . . invasive. And even as she had that thought, Lilith felt a small stirring and looked down. An errant spark-backed fly, having made its way from within her, was walking down her thigh. For an instant her eyes grew wide, and then, with a blindingly fast motion, she scooped it into her hand and then into a small metal urn that lay on the floor nearby. She narrowed her eyes and smiled. Fortune had given her that fly.

She resumed her search, finding some shards of bone, some torn skin from her bedclothes, the gold threads from a rent robe, and a needle. Carefully wrapping the skin around the bone armature, she stitched together a zoomorphic form, winged and clawed and with huge, empty eye sockets. She was a proficient sculptor, and when she had finished the small maquette she sat back and nodded approvingly.

Without hesitating she took up the needle and stabbed her palm until black blood, thick and hissing, dripped freely down her wrist. She picked up the assembled figure and caressed the blood into its wrinkled surface.

"Draw from me my pain, my little one," Lilith whispered. "Draw from me my boundless sorrow and my timeless hatred. And take these things of mine, I adjure you, and lay them before the Lord of Adamantinarx."

The small figure, its naked white skin smeared black, twitched and stretched. It jumped up and onto feet not unlike her own, gracelessly at first, and as its dangling, shriveled wings began to expand and flap it hopped toward her. A pinched mouth yawned open and then snapped shut. Lilith took up the urn and violently shook the angry fly out into her hand. She plucked its wings and held it in front of the night-creature's beak. The familiar plucked it greedily from her fingers and gulped down its first meal. It cocked its oversized head and stared at her with its empty sockets, as if waiting for more.

"Good, good," she purred menacingly. "You liked that. That was the taste of him."

Lilith gestured a glyph into existence, blew it into the familiar, repeated the act, and then put the creature on her wrist. She walked to the broken door, peered out cautiously, and, seeing no one near, carefully squeezed the familiar through the widest part of the crack. It stood there on the flagstones just beyond, looking in at her inquiringly.

"Go now. Stay in the shadows and find the nearest window. Go to Adamantinarx; tell Sargatanas of my suffering. Give him that fly. And tell him I am coming."

The familiar turned obediently and took wing and, just as she had ordered, disappeared silently into the gloom of the arched ceiling.

ADAMANTINARX-UPON-THE-ACHERON

The palace gates loomed large and imposing before Hani, their twin braziers creating enough deep shadows upon the surrounding buildings to conceal him. As he had predicted, it had been slow and tedious work gaining the palace entrance, and, now that he had, he could hang back, affording him an opportunity to rest and survey the area. He realized that actually getting through the gate might not be as hard as he had feared; so many workers passed within and so improbable was any threat from a soul that he was relatively sure no demon would question him, let alone look twice at him. He only needed to wait for a group of workers who were walking between soul-beast caravans. He waited for what seemed like hours and, marking that time, the Burden crept relentlessly upward through his torso. His fear was that he would find himself impaired, that the Burden would settle for a time in his head and make it impossible for him to accomplish anything for some while.

The jostling crowds flowed slowly through the gates like oozing lava, breaking sullenly around any obstacles that did not move quickly enough. But the soul's patience was rewarded when he saw the giant bobbing heads of two soul-beasts, the vanguard of a pair of columns of similar creatures heading toward him. And between them was a mélange of souls bound for work farther up the mount. Inwardly excited, Hani emerged from the shadows, his aquiline features set in an imitation of the dull, ravaged look worn by most souls. His gait, once again, matched the shambling stride of the workers. It was the best disguise—the only disguise— he could employ.

Passage through the gates went smoothly—no guards even looked at him. Armed warrior demons were everywhere, their officers hissing out commands and glyphs with what Hani thought was more urgency than normal. Between the lumbering bodies he saw guards stationed outside all of the residences and official buildings, ever watchful, he guessed, for spies.

He continued up the steep incline, the warm flagstones under his scuffing feet growing cooler as the winds grew. Looking up, he saw the enormous breast-like swell of the palace dome. At this distance its size took his breath away. Again the poison of self-doubt seeped into his veins. *I can't do this. What was I thinking?* Secretly he pulled the little idol out of his side and ran his thumb over it for comfort. *Look at what this thing has compelled me to do. I've risked everything on a dream. I don't regret it, though.* Fearing he might drop the idol amidst all of the shuffling feet, Hani pushed it back within himself.

The caravan threaded its way up toward the palace itself. The huge souls, spurred on by their cudgel-wielding mahouts, were burdened down with Abyssal hides, rolls of soul-vellum, and other luxury products from the remote towns of the Wastes. Palace bound, Hani suspected. He needed to actually enter the palace before separating from them and hoped he was right about their destination.

When they passed through the threshold, plodded to a halt in the great entry hall, and began unstrapping the cargo, Hani felt a mixture of satisfaction, relief, and then apprehension. He was inside Sargatanas' palace! Hani was surprised at the feel of its interior; he had been prepared for something much darker, more oppressive. Instead, its bustling interior, brightly illuminated by fluorescing minerals set in sconces, conveyed a sense only of purposeful power, infernal bureaucracy untainted by true evil. Despite the building's outwardly benign atmosphere, he knew that the hardest part of his journey still lay ahead; his goal to kneel before the feet of Lord Sargatanas might truly be impossible. Hani reached for a huge bundle of dark-scaled hides, and, hefting it up with some difficulty, he began to follow a string of souls who seemed to be heading deep into the building. An Overseer glanced at Hani, his wary, reflective eyes probing deeply but apparently finding nothing unusual. With a flick of the demon's whip and the touch of it still stinging Hani's back, he moved on, walking through a succession of long corridors until, in the distance, he saw a high, curving wall, its tiled surface broken at long, regular intervals by tall, column-framed entrances. Beyond them, he suspected, was the audience hall, but what lay between remained a mystery. Quite soon, he was going to have to break away from the workers and the security of numbers they afforded. As careful as he was, he could not help but wonder how far he could get before inevitably being spotted.

DIS

Lilith awoke to a quiet knock upon her broken door. She waited in the darkness, hoping she had only dreamt the sound, but when it came again she slowly went to the door and paused. She was emotionally exhausted; the idea of another encounter with Beelzebub and the resulting struggle was enough to make her numb. But something within told her that the knock had not come from one of the Order Knights; it had not been forceful enough.

"Consort, please open the door," came the voice from the corridor. "It is I, Agares."

"So the Prince is now using his Prime Minister to fetch his plaything? You must be proud of your new position."

"You misunderstand, Consort. Open the door, at least, so that we can talk."

She knew that if he was not alone the door would not keep them from her. With a shrug she opened the door, expecting it to burst inward with the weight of Agares' accomplices.

The Prime Minister, Lilith saw, was alone. He entered, bowed, and, closing the door behind him, stood back. In his arms was a bundle of clothes.

"I have come to get you out of here," he said with quiet urgency.

"Why?"

"Because the Prince grows tired of you. And I will not be able to serve him with you up there . . . up above the throne."

Lilith looked at him with some disdain. "So this is about you, then? You would not be happy with me dangling above you for eternity, looking down upon you, as I most assuredly would."

"I am sorry, Consort; that was not quite how I meant it. Yes, I would be disturbed. But to survive I must be able to serve him without any . . . ah, impediment. And while I have no love for the Prince or his ways, I do recognize him as our regent pro tem. Until, that is, Lucifer should ever return."

Lilith turned from him. "The hope still burns, eh?"

"Yes, Consort, it does."

"And, perhaps, if he does return . . . and I do survive, why then, whoever was instrumental in my survival . . . ," she said. She nodded, smiling faintly. "I think I understand."

Agares held out the traveling skins.

"I will tell the Prince, when he next summons you, that you are ill, that you have asked not to be disturbed. Given his feelings toward you, at the moment, I think he will welcome that. For a while, at least. I have arranged for a caravan to escort you—incognito of course—to virtually anywhere in Hell that you choose. Your destination is your own affair and how you dispose of the demons of the caravan, too, is your own business; I do not want to know. That is my parting gift to you; if I should be found out to have helped you escape . . . well, I will not be able to betray you at my . . . last moments."

"Very noble. I will try to remember that, if Lucifer should ever return."

"Thank you."

Lilith took the heavy, hooded garments that smelled faintly of smoke. Agares turned to leave.

"Just one thing, Prime Minister," she said. "How did you know that I would not tell the Prince of your betrayal?"

"By chance, I saw your familiar fly away into the night. It really was nothing more than a coincidence that I happened to be on a balcony. I heard something and looked up. I knew the moment I saw it what it was and what it represented. A plea for help."

"Answered by you," she said with a tinge of irony. But she reconsidered and said, "Thank you, Prime Minister."

He bowed slightly and left.

Lilith put the skins down and began to assemble some of her possessions from the scattered debris of her life in Dis.

ADAMANTINARX–UPON–THE–ACHERON

The game of subterfuge was over. Hani zigzagged as quickly as he dared between the myriad pillars of the arcade, always heading, he hoped, toward the dome's central chamber. The arcade, one of dozens radially arranged, was like an artificial gorge, narrow, with a fan-vaulted ceiling three hundred feet above and steep walls only occasionally interrupted by floor-level doorways. Fifty-foot columns, each bearing a lit sconce that faced the main passage, supported overhanging offices, and while the effect was airy, the fans of shadow they provided were welcome to Hani. He knew, though, that his discovery was only a matter of time.

Streams of legionaries filed through the stone forest of tall columns, pole arms upon their shoulders, the heavy scuffing of their bone-shod feet filling the space. They, too, were heading toward the great chamber, a fact that did nothing to comfort the soul but did convince him of his insanity. While they marched, without combat orders, they were not the real threat to his detection; their metallic eyes never seemed to stray from the soldier ahead of them. Hani knew that their heads were scooped, empty, and that they were nearly unable to think for themselves. But the centurions Hani watched carefully. Nearly ten feet tall, armored and wielding two sword hands, each proudly bore two upward-curving pectoral bars of flattened bone—prized signs of their rank. With experienced eyes ever gauging their surroundings, the centurions' vigilance sharply contrasted with their soldiers' indifference. Their battle-scarred faces bore the same two mouths—one for speaking, the other for feeding—that typified all lower demons, but, due to their rank, there was a slightly more refined quality to them. They were, the soul knew, imbued with a greater intelligence and, complimenting it, a greater sense of awareness. And they could, with a simple command-glyph, turn the mindless marching infantry into the irresistible tool of Hani's destruction. He could not help but compare them to the Overseers that he was so used to obeying and knew that the military demons' ferocity far outstripped them.

For all his care, he never saw the officer that raised the alarm, or the glyph that he knew, as he started to run, must have followed it. He only heard the echoing bark of command and the clatter of dozens of troops in the distance wheeling to pursue him.

The legionaries ran heavily in their tempered stone armor, and while they may have been comparatively fast upon the battlefield, they were gaining only slowly on Hani. For the first time in Hell, he ran, stretching his legs, stumbling a bit at first, but gaining in confidence as he raced between the columns. *I might be able to elude this detachment, but if they send flying troops after me I'm finished.* So far he had not seen any command-glyphs flash ahead of him. Probably the centurion felt he could handle one renegade soul. Maybe, Hani thought, just maybe, he was wrong.

Ten thousand lava-gray troops gathered in Sargatanas' Audience Chamber and stood at attention before the central pyramidal dais. The air was hazy with the steam that arose from the gathered army. Each Demon Minor, accompanied by his senior officers, stood beside his gaudy standard-bearer. The effect of all of the massed vertical banners, topped as they were with their incandescent regimental glyphs, was like a shifting sea of lava, hardened gray and spangled with myriad specks of magma. The sound of kettledrums, arrayed around the chamber's periphery, was muffled and distant, providing a marching cadence familiar to the entering legions.

Eligor, standing near his lord, looked on from his higher vantage upon the dais, taking in the spectacle of the massed troops. Great wedges of soldiers, each separated by broad aisles, faced him, the sea of officers and their newly risen troops motionless and attentive. Before him, Sargatanas waited, head lowered and aflame in a blazing coronet of leaping fire. The top of his head had broadened out to accommodate six lidless and staring eyes. He carried, unsheathed, the new sword, which, Eligor had found out, had been forged of some of the most powerful souls, folded countless times, beaten into shape and tempered, and then sharpened. A strong shaft of Algol's light played down upon the dark blade, its shimmering red reflection briefly flashing upon Valefar and Eligor and Faraii, Bifrons, and Andromalius as they watched the last of the soldiers filter in. Finally the enormous room was filled.

Sargatanas, the focal point of thousands of eyes, raised his sword overhead and the drums grew silent. Glancing from side to side, he stepped forward until he stood at the top of the stairs, a dark, fiery figure, eyes intense with an inner fervor, flexing wing-stumps describing a vee. His sigil blossomed above his head, a full span across, a circular signet of fire.

"Demons Minor!" Sargatanas' voice boomed out through the chamber. "Brothers in exile! You know what we lost so long ago and why you have been mobilized. For too long you and I have accepted our Fall, the terrible result of Lucifer's flawed dreams and leadership. We have accepted, too, the laws that have been imposed upon us regarding how we are to govern in Hell. We have adapted to the worst imaginable conditions, and somehow . . . somehow we have thrived. But we have also paid a steep price for that adaptation . . . a price paid in the currency of our consciences. I need not tell you how staying true to our inner selves while doing our mandated duty has taxed us. I will not say that we were cast down here unjustly. But I will say that we have served here long enough . . . that we have paid for our transgression. Now I say . . . enough!"

Eligor saw him pause and saw, too, the effect his words were having on the assembled demons.

"What we are about to attempt is something that no one in Hell's long history has ever dared. We are about to embark upon a journey of redemption and reawakening . . . a journey Heavenward . . . a journey Home!"

The gathered demons' murmuring grew in volume.

"Brother demons, this will be a war of remembrance. A war wherein we Fallen try to reattain the grace that we once shared. Our enemy, content to wallow in the corruption of Hell, is mighty and outnumbers us many to one. But if we fight like the warrior-angels we once were, with that same, almost-forgotten, inner fire of purity, we *will* prevail. Yesterday you were an army of Hell. Today you are my Army of Ascension! *Tomorrow, Heaven!*"

With that, Eligor saw his lord's giant sigil break apart into a thousand glowing comets that darted outward, each alighting above the regimental glyph of a different banner, each transforming into Sargatanas' iconic battle emblem.

A great cheer rang up and Eligor tingled with the auspiciousness of it all. He knew what this ceremony, this charging of the banners, meant. They were at war.

Amidst the clamor, Sargatanas descended the great flight of stairs followed by Eligor and the others. He would review his new army and make what last-minute suggestions to Faraii and Valefar might be appropriate.

At the base of the stairs stood five of Sargatanas' most trusted generals. Backs straight, heads held high, they looked upon their lord with a near-religious zeal.

"Generals," Sargatanas said so that only they could hear. "What I am ordering is nothing short of open rebellion. To free ourselves we will, if need be, storm the gate of Beelzebub's Keep itself! I tell you now: this rebellion will either break us or free us forever. Either way, we will be done with Hell.

"Through the course of this campaign we will be facing a superior force composed of those Demons Major and Minor who have willingly taken up with Beelzebub. Astaroth—the first—is little more than a puppet; his destruction will be a prelude only. Our legions are the best conjured in Hell, led by the best officers in Hell. They are obedient, disciplined, and, at your hands, brilliantly trained. Use them recklessly and we will be at an end before we start. Use them wisely and we will achieve something unimaginable for all these long eons. This campaign will be your last, the final demonstration of all you have learned. Be bold; be creative; be ruthless upon the field of battle. I, and my Guard, will be with you every step of the way. We will prevail because we share a single vision . . . the vision of the Light that we once cherished.

"Generals, Heaven awaits!"

The generals knelt as one, and with a vast clattering

the entire gathered army followed them to their knees. The generals were smiling and Eligor saw the fervor flooding through them. He watched Sargatanas reach down and clasp each by the arm and as he did they, too, received a small token from his sigil.

The small party moved on past the general staff, on to Faraii's Shock Troopers, big, brutish, and very heavily armored. Each of their arms ended in a variety of crudely conjured cleaverlike blades, thick enough to easily split a legionary's torso agape. Their oversized, scarred heads were squat, and their feeding mouths were lined with thick, pointed teeth. When Sargatanas approached them, they turned to Faraii, almost as if looking to him for guidance as to how to behave before their lord. Unseen by all but Eligor, he quickly bowed his head—a signal meant to be imitated—and the troopers followed his cue. It was an odd moment, Eligor thought, odd that they would not immediately have saluted their lord, odd that they would look to the Waste wanderer for guidance. Eligor put it down to their obvious mental deficiencies; they were, after all, dim but effective fighting creatures, not reasoning demons.

Without warning a glyph soared from the arcades overhead. Eligor's keen eyes spotted the tiny running figure just as it burst from one of the arcades and was hooked by the closely pursuing squad of his Guard that flew above it. At that distance he could not see the web of chains that dragged what appeared to be a soul into the air, but as they approached, he did see the flailing soul tugging futilely at them. Eligor turned to see Sargatanas staring intently at the scene but, with some anxiety, could not imagine what the Demon Major was thinking or what the consequences would be of such a flagrant security breach.

Pain and terror and a sudden sinking feeling of disappointment filled Hani as he felt himself jerked into the air. He was used to pain and almost welcomed it. Its infliction meant, at least, that all of the questions—how his quest would end—were answered. It had been an amazing journey, the journey, as it turned out, toward the end of his conventional existence. For surely his punishment would be unthinkable. But still, he had gotten as far as he had hoped. Farther than he dreamt. Even now, twisting in numbing pain at the end of a dozen hooked chains, he was sure that he saw in the distance his true goal, the large form of Sargatanas as he walked amidst his troops.

Above Hani, the six flying demons were dipping and rising, expertly keeping their chains taut. The barbed hooks were deeply embedded all over his body and he finally gave up struggling. What really was the point? If he fell, it would only be atop a waiting legionary's halberd.

He saw the ranks of legionaries looking up at him, expressionless; they were weapons to be wielded, mindless and dangerous. He saw them in an agonized blur, each nearly identical to its brother, focusing only upon a face, or a scooped-out cranium, or a thick carapace with its distinctive chest-horns. They were all alike, all cruel and efficient.

They flew on toward the central flat-topped mountain of stone. He saw a great throne atop it. At its foot he saw the nearing dark figure of the Lord of Adamantinarx staring up at him, unmoving, waiting, and fear added itself to the pain that bled through his limp body.

Through tear-veiled eyes he saw the figure grow larger as the flying demons dropped down. He saw the coronal eyes encircled by flame and then, beneath them, the intense, metallic eyes that reached up toward him with a penetrating intensity. A few moments later he was hanging mere feet from Sargatanas, dangled like a lifeless puppet by the hovering demons.

Hani hung there, transfixed by the eight eyes of the

demon, convinced, in his delirium of pain, that they were what held him aloft rather than the chains. The gigantic chamber dimmed and swirled and blazed before him as he drifted in and out of consciousness, but each time he opened his eyes the demon's were always, unblinkingly, upon him. Was it for seconds or minutes? Time, as he perceived it, could only be marked by the uneven rhythm of pain, the artificial night and day of his tenuous awareness.

"Why are you here, larva?" Hani heard, and his eyelids fluttered open.

"I sinned," he said foggily.

"Why are you *here* before me?" the rumbling accented voice said.

"I had to come," he said, his voice cinder dry. "I have something . . . you would value."

He saw a demon step forward and, because the memory was still so sharp, remembered that he was named Valefar.

"Lord, there is nothing this larva can offer us. Shall I have it dispo—"

"No, Valefar. You do not find it remarkable that this *soul* is here . . . now? I cannot remember this ever happening before. And that, alone, interests me."

Hani saw Sargatanas turn back to him.

"What do you want from us . . . from me?"

And even through his haze of agony Hani realized that this was his opportunity, *the* opportunity.

"I want only to know who I was. And what I did to get here."

Sargatanas stared at him, cocking his head slightly to one side. Hani saw the demon close his many eyes, saw the flames about his head gutter, and saw, too, the very slight trembling of one clawed finger.

And then Hani felt it. It began as a sharp, hot breeze upon his mind, strong and persistent, and gathered quickly into a rushing, searing gale that surpassed the hottest winds he could remember, the roaring Tophet blasts from the child-sacrifices in his home city.

He shut his eyes and the memories of his Life began to cascade back into him like the most precious, sweetest wine being poured into an amphora. He knew then that the bits of memory that he had experienced in Hell had been like some barely fragrant residue clinging to the inside of his mind, the stubborn dregs that been left in a vessel when it was emptied.

The fleeting images of a wide, sun-kissed sea had been the Central Sea, the huge wall-encircled city his beloved Qart Hadasht—the New City—and he knew now that the soul-beasts had evoked nothing less than his prized war elephants. Had he not made this fateful journey he could have wrestled with those images' meaning for all eternity.

Hani opened his eyes, but he was Hani no longer. And he was no longer hanging by the hooks. Instead he was lying upon the warm flagstones, the six flying demons behind with their lances tipped toward him. Sargatanas was watching him carefully, as were the five attending demons.

"Your name was Hannibal, son of Hamilcar of the House of Barca. Does that mean anything to you?"

"Yes . . . everything."

"You were, among your kind, quite remarkable; your hatred ran deeper than most," the demon said.

"I had much to hate."

Sargatanas appeared not to have heard him. "What is it that you bring to me?"

And in that moment, with the awareness of his past achieved, the plan that had begun with the small statue became something else.

"I know that a great war is imminent," Hannibal said, rubbing the puncture-wounds on his shoulders. The pain was still enormous. "I can give you an army. An army of souls."

Valefar snorted and threw up his hands.

"Look around you," Sargatanas said with a sweep of his hand. "Does it look to you as if I need another army?"

Hannibal knelt, head bowed. Just as he had feared, the Burden was approaching his head, sliding through him inexorably. Wincing from his wounds, and with some effort, he shook his head. "Your legions are beyond impressive, Lord. Their capability is so far beyond any army I ever led that I cannot imagine withstanding them.

"However, like pieces set upon a board, they are predictable once seen. The army I offer you can be that board, unseen until you need them, and therefore unpredictable. No one knows better than you, I am sure, the advantage gained by the careful manipulation of the battlefield, the very buildings and streets under your enemies' feet. Of course you could do it on your own or delegate it to one of your generals, but even that would take your attention away from your pieces . . . your demon legions. Nor do I think you could find a demon happy with the task of leading . . . us.

"Given the . . . authority, I could lead them as I've led others . . . before."

"What makes you so sure that they will follow you?"

Hannibal hesitated and then reached into the cavity in his side. His fingers closed upon the small statue, feeling its familiar, comforting shape. He pulled it out and held it up before the demon lord.

"She has led me this far. I must believe that she will help me lead my kind."

Sargatanas' eyes widened. To the amazement of Valefar and the other demons, he reached under his fleshy robe and brought forth a statue nearly identical to the one in the soul's hand. Only Hannibal seemed unsurprised, having witnessed the moment of its discovery.

"I have seen her visions. They are glimpses of the Light . . . of Heaven regained."

"Mine are visions of freedom," Hannibal said. "If freedom begets redemption, then I can't complain. If not, we'll take it anyway. And stay right here."

"You are quite the opportunist," said Sargatanas. He regarded the statue in his bone-covered hand, weighing it. "I have been told that others like these are out there, but only you have understood its implications, have shown yourself able to do the exceptional by bringing it to me. Perhaps you can be exceptional, as well, upon my fields of battle and under my banners. I *will* give you your army, Hannibal Barca. And, with it, someone to accompany you, to watch over you, to mold the souls you need however you see fit. Go and gather your host. When you are ready you may join my legions."

"Thank you, my lord." Hannibal bowed with some difficulty, top-heavy as he was with the weight of the Burden.

"You will truly thank me in a moment," the Demon Major said, raising a hand. It glowed with a small but intricate glyph that shot out and touched Hannibal upon the Burden. For an instant, more pain seared through his already-weakened body, but it subsided quickly, replaced by a growing feeling of lightness, and when he looked down, shaking, he saw that his chest was covered with a thick, black liquid that flowed more profusely as the orb began to dissolve. Moments later a large deforming cavity was the only evidence of the cumbersome Burden he had carried. His collapsed head tilted unnaturally until the flesh and bone began to fill in, and when he was completely mended, Hannibal, mouth agape, eyes round, knelt before the demon lord almost as one reborn. At Hannibal's feet a large puddle of malignant blackness had pooled and begun to congeal.

Valefar stepped forward, turned to one of the attending winged demons, and indicated the pool that had once been Hani's Burden. Light-headed, Hannibal heard him say, "Have that jarred and returned to the Wastes with the proper ceremony."

Sargatanas lowered his hand and silently looked the trembling soul up and down. Satisfied, he turned quickly to resume his review, his burning robes trailing a thin, rising vortex of steam. A messenger approached him, and Hannibal could not help but hear their conversation.

"Lord," the trooper said breathlessly, "I have just now come from the border. Lord Astaroth has launched a massive attack on our western margin."

"Is there any evidence of support from the Prince?"

"No, Lord."

"Our losses, so far?"

"Demolishers are eating away at the buildings on the edge of Zoray's Thirty-fourth Ward. Lord Astaroth's reconnaissance was good; with no true resistance there he has made substantial gains."

Sargatanas waved the trooper away and then turned to the massed soldiers.

"Legions," he shouted, his voice like a pure trumpet, "the first move in our campaign has been made for us! We are at war!"

And Hannibal heard a martial cheer spring from thousands of inhuman throats and rise to the heavens, a cheer as he had never heard before.

After conferring for a moment, Valefar turned away from his lord and looked back at the soul. The Prime Minister was shaking his head, an expression upon his bone-plated face that seemed amazed.

"The fruits of your boldness come sooner than you could have imagined, soul!" he shouted through the cheers. "Hannibal Barca, you are now a general in the active service of his lord Sargatanas, Brigadier-Major of the Armies of Hell, Lord of Adamantinarx!"

XV

ZORAY'S THIRTY-FOURTH WARD

The flight to the border with Sargatanas, Faraii, and
Valefar had been quick and easy. War had been imminent for some time, and Sargatanas had had his chosen
troops in place long enough for their camp to be well
dug in. Upon landing, Faraii headed off to join his Shock
Troopers, while Sargatanas and Valefar joined the staff
that had gathered beside a conjuring pit. Eligor, wings
twitching in anticipation, volunteered to reconnoiter and
chose six flyers from the Flying Corps. They took to the
air and, after a few dozen wing beats, Eligor realized
just how much he enjoyed being in his lord's service at a
time as important as this.

Looking down through a heavy mist upon the remnants of the border outpost, Eligor saw Astaroth's Demolishers chewing their way through the remaining low
buildings. Broad-backed and flattened, each slow-moving
creature was, in reality, hundreds of souls compressed
together to form nothing more than a giant mobile di-
gestive tract. Myriad enlarged mouths bit off large sections of soul-brick wall and masticated them into pulp.
Eligor saw the ruddy haze kicked up by the destruction
and the long, straight reddish mounds that trailed behind them, the excreted remains of processed souls. The
mounds extended for hundreds of spans, all the way back,
he guessed, to the edge of the ward. The slickened ground
they left behind was scoured and bloody, smooth and
featureless.

The lower he and his half-dozen lightly armed scouts

flew, the more distinctly he could see the buildings twisting upon their foundations in a futile effort to protect themselves and hear them crying out. When he had witnessed Demolishers in the past, Eligor had felt a sort of pity for those soul-bricks, mostly, he thought, based upon their complete defenselessness. The wailing only heightened this.

He flew on until he spotted the carpet of slowly marching soldiers that was Astaroth's army. Glyph-commands sprang up from its officers, guiding the Demolishers, opening the front so the legions could advance. Eligor counted twelve full legions but due to the mist could not find any evidence of Astaroth's Flying Corps. The more Eligor peered into the concealing clouds, though, the more convinced he was of their presence.

Eligor turned his flight back toward the massed legions of Sargatanas' advance army. A virtual legion of fleet mounted decurions had been dispatched with utmost haste to the region's lava-fields to conjure an army as quickly as possible in immediate defense of the distant ward. They had been marvelously successful; arrayed like a vast checkerboard, they only awaited orders to march on the invaders. Eligor knew that, once engaged, these few legions would serve as a delaying force until Sargatanas could bring his approaching ground army to bear.

Eligor descended and swooped in low over the legions, seeking his master's personal sigil amidst the many glowing unit commanders' emblems. He found the glowing emblem and, beneath it, his lord standing next to his mount discussing the terrain with the Decurion Primus, a scarred, battle-hardened commander named Gurgat. The one-armed veteran seemed just as interested in Eligor's findings as his lord.

"It is just as you thought, my lord," the Captain of the Guard said. "The town of Maraak-of-the-Margins is almost gone. Its inhabitants are scattered. A full dozen

Demolishers have seen to that. Behind them is Astaroth's entire army; he is gambling everything on this move."

"He feels he has nothing to lose," Sargatanas said gravely, shaking his head. "We must show him that, in fact, he has everything to lose. Gurgat, rouse the legions. I have orders to issue. It is finally time for this to begin."

The Decurion Primus mounted a waiting soul-beast and trotted off. Already shrill horns could be heard. Sargatanas turned to Eligor. "I want my old friend Astaroth taken alive, Eligor. I have said as much to Valefar and Faraii as well. It is the least I can do for him. But as for his army, it must be annihilated to a demon."

"I understand, Lord."

A red, permeating blood-haze from the Demolishers hung low and heavy above the glistening rubble, making it difficult to see their looming forms as well as their relentless progress. Only Astaroth's protective guiding seals hovering over them could be seen easily, each slowly growing as they drew nearer. Eligor could hear the siege creatures masticating their way through buildings and streets alike, the cacophony of their thousand jaws mingling with the sound of crumbling walls and the diminishing cries of the bricks. The metallic tang of the pulverized souls' blood upon the hot air reached Eligor's nose. The winds were, largely, heading obliquely to them; otherwise they, like the landscape before them, would have been stained red from the mists.

Eligor looked at Sargatanas, who stood, impassive, as if rooted to the ground. His unblinking eyes were fixed upon the vaguely seen Demolishers. The plates of his face shifted, reconfiguring his visage into a rigid series of bony planes, barbed and heavily textured. Where there had been eight eyes only three remained, and these were mostly hidden behind protective sclerotic armor.

"Enough of this," he said softly, almost to himself. "They are close enough."

Sargatanas raised both hands and a blue effulgence grew between the floating horns above his head. It drew together, growing brighter, and became a quickly rotating ball composed of a dozen tiny repeated glyphs. Eligor could not discern their meaning, but in moments it became clear. The ball split apart and each twisted symbol sped away like a blue-flamed arrow shot at the center of each Demolisher's glyph. With a crackle of electricity audible even from where they stood, Sargatanas and his legion watched the short but fierce struggle for control that ensued. One by one the blue glyphs disassembled the great fiery-orange seals of Astaroth, casting aside and extinguishing the component glyphs until nothing remained to protect the lumbering Demolishers. Eligor saw the first tendrils of jagged blue lightning scratch at their backs, setting them aflame. It took only a few seconds before all of them were burning. Then, nearly simultaneously, they arched their backs in spasms of pain and burst apart, ripped into glowing chunks that tumbled into the few standing buildings, causing them, in turn, to explode.

A roar of approval rose from behind Eligor and Sargatanas as the front lines of the legions saw the empty expanse of terrain that now lay before them.

Sargatanas mounted his soul-beast and unsheathed the sword named *Lukiftias-pe-Ripesol,* Light of Heaven. With a flourish of the blade, he and the legions behind began to advance. Eligor and his chosen Guards spread their wings and took up position above him, measuring their wing beats so as not to outpace their lord.

Eligor saw Faraii and his troopers running to create a wedge in front of their lord. As big as they were, they ran easily, powerfully, their thick ax-hands swinging low at their sides. Eligor, remembering Faraii's ceaseless training, now admired their discipline and their merciless teacher for it.

The legions' steady tramp could be heard—almost felt—as high as Eligor flew. He banked to the left, coming around until he was over the left wing cavalry, a full brigade of troops who referred to themselves as the Spirits. Eligor had been told, long ago, that this name was out of deference to the souls they rode and bonded with. Now, led by Valefar on the one side and his tribune, Karcefuge, on the other, those expertly ridden souls were walking slowly, matching pace with the center legions. Eligor knew, even without flying there himself, that on the right wing an identical brigade was advancing, lance-hands seated, in a similar fashion.

Returning to the center of the line, he saw Sargatanas issue the command-glyph to halt, a great glyph that rose high, vertically like a banner, so that all could see it; his army was more than halfway to where Eligor knew Astaroth's many legions waited. Eligor circled lower, keeping his eyes fixed on his lord, watching him prepare for the battle to come. Seated upon his plodding war steed, Sargatanas composed himself, chin down, hands upon the flexing sword that lay atop his saddle, his back straight. He seemed relaxed and Eligor saw him fade into a state with which he could not identify, a state that, undoubtedly, balanced the phantom armies in his mind that needed his commands and the physical armies in the field that needed his sword arm.

Sudden puffs of hot, spark-laden vapor vented from Sargatanas' flared nostrils, blown out in short, sharp exhalations; some decision had been reached. A few small glyphs appeared above him, blossoming larger and heading off toward the troops. Dozens of horns, made hollow and eerie from the distance, acknowledged their receipt. These were just the beginning of a fountain of glyphs, a fiery cascade of orders that Eligor knew would flow from his master as long as the battle lasted, whether he was engaged in combat or not. Such were the manifold powers of a Demon Major that he could split his awareness, enabling him to wield the legions as he did his own sword. As the armies converged and the glyphs came more rapidly, Eligor grasped his lance more tightly, grateful that he had only to fight.

Much to his disgust, Adramalik found himself accompanying the Duke Fleurety and his ten legions well to the rear of Astaroth's army, there, he knew, more as a symbol of support than a perceived weapon of final resort in the event that things went badly. Marching behind the ragtag legions, he mused that it was more than likely that he would not see action, that Astaroth's army would be obliterated quickly, leaving the demons of Dis to simply fade away to do the Prince's bidding. Adramalik could see that this army of Astaroth's was as poorly trained as it was ill equipped. Most would undoubtedly perish against one of Sargatanas' relatively small but well-trained border armies. Fleurety, empowered with a seal from the Prince, would step in and assume control in the Prince's name of the old demon's wards while Astaroth would be offered exile in Dis—a choice even he could not be foolish enough to dismiss. And after Astraroth had been escorted back to Dis, after he had fulfilled his master's misbegotten sense of honor, Adramalik vowed to ask Beelzebub to send someone else on these kinds of official missions. His place was with his Knights, not serving as escort to an impotent lord. For now, Adramalik rode next to the Duke and off in the distance Astaroth and his army etched their fate upon the ash-gray ground with each footstep.

The two lines met with a thunderous impact, like that of many massive stones colliding. Eligor saw the long, continuous point of contact flicker with the incessant sparking of tempered-stone weapons upon tempered-stone armor.

Sargatanas, Eligor saw, was keeping his troops' line taut, neither advancing nor falling back. The demon lord, protected by Faraii and his enormous Shock Troops, had moved slowly toward the front line of his legions while Valefar and Karcefuge were keeping the Spirits in place.

A shroud of smoky ash began to ascend where the two armies met, blanketing their frenzied ferocity in gray and muffling, somewhat, the clash of arms. Astaroth's legions fought with an urgency born, Eligor suspected, of the awareness that uncompromising annihilation lay in defeat. There would be no prisoners, no demons left standing to swear allegiance to a new lord. Astaroth had removed that conjured element—that possibility of shifting allegiances—from their seals of obedience. He had committed them that completely in his final cast of the die.

Eligor saw the distant Great Seal of Astaroth dimly through the pall and knew that beneath it that lord was guiding his army. And for the thousandth time, he wondered how one as great as he could have let his realm sink so far. Turning his gaze behind Sargatanas, he saw his own Guard, lances and shields in hand. Five hundred strong, they awaited his orders with eyes trained upon him, gleaming eagerly.

Sargatanas broke Eligor's momentary reverie. "I do not trust the air to my next command, Eligor. I must be beyond careful when facing Astaroth; he taught me so many of my command-glyphs. Fly to Valefar then, and to Karcefuge as well, and tell them to advance, to draw up the ends of our line."

With a nod, Eligor took wing and sped over the five legions between the center and Valefar. He hovered beside the bone-armored Prime Minister, momentarily admiring his effortless handling of the giant soul-steed.

"Valefar, Sargatanas wishes you to begin drawing up the wings."

"Is Astaroth where we want him?"

"Yes, if he does not alter his position at his army's center he will be enfolded." Eligor paused, looking out at the chaos of the battlefield ahead. "It will be sad to see him under these circumstances, Valefar."

"True, but he will survive. I am to escort him back to Adamantinarx on Sargatanas' orders."

"It will be a quiet journey."

Valefar looked down, frowning. "I had not thought of that."

He shook his head and then, unseating his pike, spurred his mount with the two large spikes on the insides of his boots, and beast and rider leaped forward. Eligor raised his hand and waved Valefar on. The Spirits around him were whining, straining to break into a gallop, and in a few short strides got their wish.

They are advancing too fast, too far. Reckless. What is he thinking?

Adramalik could barely see the rear guard of Astaroth's army as it disappeared across the gray-olive skin of the field and into the haze, and while Duke Fleurety could have issued an order to keep up, he seemed disinclined. So began the betrayal. Just as well, reasoned Adramalik. There was no place for fat upon the bones of Hell. Astaroth, and what was left of his army, would be absorbed by the urban body of Dis.

Reports had been coming in since the two armies had engaged each other. Sargatanas' destruction of his own town—a bold move after the Demolishers' elimination—had been a surprise, his ruthlessness commendable. And now, when he could have dashed into the unknown and attempted to overrun Astaroth, Sargatanas' restraint was proving admirable. It would be interesting to watch him perform upon this field. The

Chancellor General smiled inwardly; Sargatanas could
be an enjoyable opponent if it ever came to it. But for
now, at least, Adramalik knew the Prince had no interest
in confronting him.

As he flew back, after conveying his lord's message to
Karcefuge, Eligor saw that the air had grown thick with
the gyrating bodies of fighting demons. Both forces had
waited until the sky was heavy with smoke to throw
their flyers up into the air, an effort to conceal their true
numbers. In Astaroth's case it was a prudent measure; it
seemed he could not field more than a legion of the
winged soldiers, and this he broke up to create the illusion of greater numbers. But it was this very tactic that
spelled their destruction as Sargatanas' flyers chopped
them into even smaller groups until they were no more,
raining their crumbling limbs down upon the combatants below.

Nearing Sargatanas' position, Eligor saw three winged
forms drop down around him. He pulled up and saw that
it was an officer—a Demon Minor—and his aides. They
were in a grievous state, their wings tattered and weapons
notched, but Eligor knew better than to think of them as
anything but a serious threat. Even with his many battle-
earned wounds, the officer—whose sigil proclaimed him
as Scrofur—was an imposing demon bearing massive
horns upon his shoulders and dozens of tiny, luminous
eyes that spattered his face like blood-drops.

Eligor cowled the two small neck-wings about his
head protectively and slitted his eyes, studying the two
aides for a brief instant. They would have to be dealt
with first and quickly.

He grasped his lance and threw it vertically as hard as
he could. The three demons, jaws agape, stared up at it
for just long enough for Eligor to raise his hands and
create two destructive glyphs—glyphs that Sargatanas
had taught him—which he fired into the bony torsos of

the flanking aides. They each looked down in amazement as a livid fiery script from within burst them apart. With a snarl, Scrofur leveled his halberd and attacked, and Eligor, with the deftness and assurance of one well practiced, reached out and felt his descending lance slide into his waiting hand. Dodging sideways, he parried, evaded the other's strike, and lashed out, feeling his jagged blade tear satisfyingly at the officer's wings. It was not a painful wound, but it was a telling one. The Demon Minor lurched and spun as his wings tried to compensate for their sudden loss of effectiveness. He stabbed out desperately and caught Eligor under his cowl and behind the ear-hole, chipping the bone and causing him to wince and pull back.

Shaking his head, Eligor twisted back in and determinedly focused on his opponent's wings, slicing and tearing while evading the hurricane of blows that Scrofur was dealing. As they fought they both dropped lower and lower toward the battling legionaries below, who reached up with their pole arms in a vain effort to hook the demons. Ribbons of slashed wing-flesh gathered and swirled around Astaroth's officer as he tried to stay out of Eligor's lance's reach, but the inevitability of the fight must have been apparent to him. Wings beating twice as hard as his opponent's, Scrofur's breath came out in great, stentorian coughs.

With a move as graceful as it was deadly, Eligor whirled and severed one of Scrofur's wings at the elbow-joint. Pulling his lance free, he stabbed again at the reeling demon, thrusting unerringly and deeply into the demon's gaping heart-hole. Amidst a blaze of ruby light Scrofur began to collapse into himself, shrinking and compacting until he was nothing more than a hand-sized flattened disk adorned with his frozen face and glowing sigil. Teeth bared in a smile, Eligor snatched at the tumbling trophy and, holding it tightly to his breast, watched as it fused to his bone breastplate—a permanent phalera imbued with the powers that had been Scrofur's.

Eligor paused, wings beating slowly, and breathed in deeply. A palpable ripple of pleasure warmed him, causing him to relax momentarily. As he dropped even farther, three heavy, hooked pole arms came up to greet him from Astaroth's legionaries waiting below and he immediately flapped his wings hard, shooting upward.

Dodging knots of winged combatants, he flew back to his lord. The front line had slowly bowed backward, not, he knew, because of Astaroth's legions' ferocity but because Sargatanas had ordered it so. The mounted Spirits had curved around behind the enormous force of enemy legions and were driving them in upon themselves. Pushed irresistibly together, their formations mingled, losing cohesion. And facing them in the now-inflexible shield-wall of Sargatanas' army, poised like an arrow at their breast, were Faraii's troops, honing their ax-hands upon their rough greaves and bellowing in anticipation of the slaughter to come.

From a few hundred feet away Eligor spotted Sargatanas, falcata in hand, a dark form limned in the fiery light of his Great Seal, standing against a backdrop of fluttering banners. Watching with unwavering attentiveness the battle unfolding and without turning toward him, the Demon Major issued Eligor his flying orders.

He assumed his place at the head of a giant wedge of his Flying Guard and ordered them to drop down. The five hundred closely packed flying demons swooped over the middle of Astaroth's confused legions, harrying them with their long lances from above. Eligor heard the shrill whine of arrows passing close to him. He saw a wavering sheet of another flight, poorly arrayed, arc up from behind the enemy legions only to bounce ineffectively off his and his demons' shields. He could not

tell if they had been aimed at his troops or Sargatanas'
but saw few gaps in his lord's legions below.

Diving headlong, Eligor led his troops into a slashing
attack designed to help the Spirits gut the rear forces of
Astaroth's middle legion. Stabbing lances and weighted
sinew nets reached up from the enemy troops in a vain
attempt to claw his demons from the sky, but the Guard
was far too well trained to fall victim to these tactics
and, with wings flapping furiously, darted into their midst.
His lance connected with both a standard-bearer and a legionary with a satisfying jolt, impaling and lifting them as
one, and he watched them crumble away into falling piles
of rubble that tumbled onto their comrades. He hovered,
seeing how the ash blown up from his wings, and the
Guard's behind him, disoriented the enemy legionaries,
and taking advantage of their confusion, he proceeded
to spear one after another. The smoking rubble grew in
mounds, making the footing treacherous for the enemy
troops.

Eligor felt that long-missed exhilaration—the Passion, he called it—come over him; it had been a millen-
nium, at least, since he had been in full combat. With
the Passion brought on by the cumulative brutal physicality of it all, he smiled as he thrust and jabbed and lost
all sense of time. The battle-change was common
enough—every demon he had ever spoken with had experienced it in some way, called it something. And
every one had spoken of it with open yearning. Had the
Fall changed them that much? He had often tried to remember if he had felt the same Passion during the War,
fighting the Cherubim, the Seraphim, but found that he
could not.

Eligor pulled back and up and watched his Guard
slice into the legionaries again and again. Directly beneath him he saw a centurion's head explode from the
impact of a lance driven through his eye socket. And

then, seconds later, one of Eligor's own was pulled down and ripped apart. It was the give-and-take of war, something he was used to, but in this battle, he knew, there would be far more taking of life than giving. He watched rank after rank fall beneath the Guard's lances, leaving a trail of rock worthy of a mountainside. As he had hoped, the enemy beneath him began to waver, with small clots of soldiers trying to protect their backs, milling in tight clumps or striking out blindly. And better than that, some began to run forward pell-mell, trampling their comrades, pushing into the already-crowded legions ahead of them. It would take little time; the panic they had created in the rear of Astaroth's formation would affect the entire army's cohesion.

Still thrusting and parrying, Eligor made his way to his lieutenant, Metaphrax Argastos, a former cherub whose laconic demeanor was counterpoint to his exuberant bravery upon the battlefield. Like himself, the wiry many-tailed demon was caked in dark, smoking ash and was grinning as his wings beat furiously and his lance flashed.

"Metaphrax, assume command!" Eligor shouted. "I am going to return to Lord Sargatanas."

Metaphrax, never losing concentration, nodded as Eligor's superior glyph-of-command blended into his own. Eligor then picked two dozen demons to accompany him across the battlefield. Soaring fast and low away from his Guard, he plunged through the columns of smoke and ash that rose skyward from the line of battle, the clashing of arms below mixing with the ferocious bellowing of the combatants and filling the Captain of the Guard's ears like a cantata of chaos.

For an instant he had seen, through the billowing ash, Lord Astaroth's blue and shimmering Great Seal. Faraii's troops, with orders to capture the enemy lord, had finally entered the fray, and Eligor, with his lord's approval, had vowed that he would not miss that eventuality.

Eligor had never seen the Baron's sword-work so eloquent, so deadly upon the battlefield. He had seen Faraii practice many times, even witnessed him in battle before, but this was something special. The Waste-wanderer's black blade flitted from victim to victim fluidly, wielded by an artist of death with an eye trained like no other's in Hell. And in contrast, behind him, his Shock Troopers' axes hacked a wide avenue of destruction that left nothing but mounded stone and powder. They were as artless in their killing as Faraii was talented—his tutelage could never give them his elegance. Astaroth's legionaries were chopped and tossed up above them as cleaved limbs and heads and torsos, only to bounce down upon their dark armor as rock to be crushed into black gravel beneath their heavy feet.

Did Astaroth know what fate was fast approaching? Eligor wondered. Surely he must. Or, seeing Sargatanas' line bending, did Astaroth think he was winning the day? Anything was imaginable in the confusion of battle, especially when one was losing.

Eligor and his cohort of demons hung above Faraii, watching his progress as he carved his way toward Astaroth's position upon a folded and veined rise. The Baron was always easy to find, the train of flames that licked out from his breastplate-vents lit all around him. From where he hovered, Eligor could actually see the tightening periphery, the noose of Sargatanas' encircling army drawing tighter and leaving nothing alive outside of its confines. And, with grim fascination, Eligor watched Faraii's demons stab deep into the body of the remaining enemy troops, plunging toward the heart that was Astaroth.

Eligor felt a hot wind gathering up from the south. Unimpeded upon the barren, now rock-strewn plain, it was gaining strength, and he saw in the distance that it brought with it heavy, dark clouds. He hoped that the battle would be over by the time they arrived; he would have to ground his flyers when the storm passed over.

The airborne demons passed through a broad, dense plume of smoke and were enshrouded in disorienting darkness. Command-glyphs sizzled past him, fiery arrows pointing his way out, and when Eligor burst into clear air it was only to realize just how close he was to the battle's center.

The fighting had reached an intensity that he had rarely seen; Astaroth's demons, true to their orders, were yielding only in death. Looking with admiration at Faraii, at the maelstrom he was within, Eligor excitedly realized that the battle's end was nearly at hand. Hanging in the air no more than a hundred yards before him and his flyers was Astaroth's blue-fire Seal, crackling with intensity, while, lit by its cool glow, the Baron and his demons were engaged with the Demon Major's last defense, his implacable bodyguard. Dressed in their characteristic patterned and dyed skins, they fought to protect their lord with tiring sword arms, valiantly, grimly, and they fell where they stood, one after another, before the terrible onslaught.

Small pockets of demons fighting desperately in knee-high ash dotted the battlefield, but to all intents and purposes the battle was won; Sargatanas had easily carried the day.

A glyph sped into Faraii and Eligor read it; Sargatanas was on his way. Almost simultaneously the last of Astaroth's bodyguards fell beneath Faraii's sword and the Baron contemptuously lifted his iron-shod foot and crushed the upturned cleft face. The bodyguard crumpled inward, providing the Baron with yet another phalera that she applied to his breast, even as she shook the dust from his foot. And there stood the Great Lord Astaroth along with his sole remaining field marshal,

Nebiros. The panting troopers, ax-hands hanging, surrounded them, creating a huge wall of dull, dark armor that contrasted with the pair's tempered-topaz armor. Ash and grit were all that remained of Astaroth's army, and it eddied around him in sere winds like a vortex of dark, disappointed ghosts.

He stood unbowed, head high, but to Eligor's eyes the Great Lord looked hollow and tired. Ribbons of protective glyphs twined and wove about his body, and his face morphed continuously, uncontrollably. Only momentarily did Eligor see the old demon's face as he remembered it, and it looked withered and gaunt. Astaroth looked at Nebiros and then down at the baton of command in his hands and, with the slightest shake of his head, knelt and proffered it to Faraii. Nebiros followed suit and remained kneeling, looking up at the Baron with undisguised resentment.

"A most remarkable performance, Baron Faraii," Astaroth said, his voice dry and quiet. "You and your troops are a credit to your lord. Rarely have I seen such zeal. But then you are something of a legend in my wards . . . or what is left of them."

"It is good to be highly regarded," Faraii said with an air of confidence, snapping the two batons away from their owners.

"I did not say that, Baron. Rumors still abound since you departed my Wastes."

Faraii's eyes narrowed fractionally.

Astaroth took a deep breath and gathered himself. Eligor knew what would follow; he was familiar enough with the Ritual of Defeat. During Sargatanas' campaigns he had witnessed it many times. "I must concede defeat," Astaroth said, "and, as per the ancient Compact of Demons Major, I, Great Lord Astaroth, humbly ask you to bring me before your lord, the victorious Lord Sargatanas, that he may do with me as he will."

Faraii, Eligor saw, was looking down, weighing the

two batons in his hand. He turned and handed them to a
hulking trooper. When Faraii returned his gaze to Astaroth it was with his black sword again in hand. With a
lazy twist of his wrist he sliced Nebiros' head from his
shoulders. The breath caught in Eligor's throat as he
started forward. Giant Shock Troopers effectively
blocked his and his flyers' way. Eligor realized that even
if he and his small cohort could take wing they could do
nothing to prevent the inevitable. He could only bristle
and watch impotently.

Patting the steaming Nebiros phalera in place upon
himself, Faraii gazed for a moment at Astaroth. Faraii
tilted his head like a stonemason regarding a block, en-
visioning it in its reduced form. He was an artist, after
all.

"You have no intention of bringing me before Sargatanas, do you?"

Faraii paused. "No."

"Are you no longer loyal to him?"

"His crusade is not mine."

"Be careful, Baron. Remember what you see here at
Maraak. When you are facing him across a battlefield."

"Sound advice, indeed, from a broken, old demon. I
will be doing Hell a favor by destroying you."

Faraii backed up slowly, leaving Astaroth alone in the
circle of Shock Troopers. Faraii caught Eligor's eye,
held it for an instant, and then turned away grinning.
Whether it was upon a signal from the Baron or not
Eligor never knew, but he saw the troopers set upon the
kneeling demon with a fury. He closed his eyes. Their
ferocious snarls and the sounds of the Great Lord's demise lingered terribly in the air.

Eligor opened his eyes in time to see Astaroth's Great
Seal fade away. He saw that Faraii was nowhere to be
seen and saw, too, his lord and Valefar arrive on foot,
their gaze flashing over the scene.

"What is happening here?" Sargatanas said to Eligor over the din. "Where is Lord Astaroth?"

"He is no more, my lord. There was nothing I could do."

Sargatanas' eyes widened. "Who did this, Eligor? Who disobeyed me?"

Eligor's insides twisted. The admiration, the loyalty, and the closeness he felt for Faraii were suddenly unclear. But his fealty to Sargatanas was not.

"My lord, Baron Faraii's Shock Troopers committed the deed; the Baron did nothing to prevent it," Eligor blurted, realizing his mistake immediately. "In his defense, however, he fought heroically; your goals could not have been achieved without him."

"One of my goals, Captain, was Astaroth's survival."

"Yes, my lord."

"Where is the Baron, now?" said Sargatanas, probing the outside ranks of troopers. They had regained their feet, forming a circle once again, and stared sullenly at him, avoiding his eyes.

Sargatanas strode forward, falcata in hand, pushing brusquely, angrily, into the troopers. He was no Astaroth, weakened and old, but instead was capable of wondrous acts of carnage—a fact not lost on the assembled warriors. Not accustomed to being swept so easily aside, they reacted with baleful, hissing intakes of breath and nothing more.

Sargatanas found Faraii at the circle's center crouched, with Astaroth's disk in hand.

"Baron, what has happened here? Why have you disobeyed me?" The ominous rumble was unmistakable.

"My lord," Faraii said, rising, "it was not I but my troops. They destroyed him." He paused, shaking his head. "You did not see him . . . in the miserable condition he was in. My troops, in their overzealousness, did him . . . and you as well . . . a service by ending his life."

"You decided this? On *your* own?" Sargatanas' face-plates shifted, and even from where Eligor stood, he could see that the new configurations were threatening. Flames atop the demon's head blossomed wildly.

"I neglected to give my demons explicit orders regarding his disposition; that *is* my fault." Faraii's free hand nervously played with the hilt of his sword. "But as I said, my lord, he was a broken figure . . . pathetic. He would have asked for that end . . . a noble end . . . if he had been thinking clearly. But clearly the battle's outcome affected his—"

"So you did the thinking for him . . . and me as well."

"His demise saved everyone much trouble."

"Not yourself, however. You will return immediately to Adamantinarx, where you will consider yourself confined to your chambers. Only your exemplary past service to me is keeping you alive, Faraii." He reached out and plucked the disk from Faraii's hand.

The Baron dropped to one knee, saluted, and rose. Without a backward glance he walked stiffly through his troopers, who, in turn, filed away with him.

"Valefar," Sargatanas said, "you and Eligor are done here. Send the legions on to Askad. I must remain and go in and secure Astaroth's wards. Or what is left of them."

Valefar nodded and sent out the command.

Sargatanas regarded the Astaroth disk, holding it tightly, and sighed. And then, with reverential solemnity, he put the disk to his breast, where, with a bluish glow, it fused.

Many hours passed before Adramalik felt he could approach the place where, from afar, he had seen Astaroth destroyed. The Duke had already withdrawn and was heading back to Dis via a discreet route, and Sargatanas' legions were well into Astaroth's wards.

The Chancellor General walked with some difficulty through the turbulent darkness of the storm, its winds seeming to delight in gusting the knee-high ash up into his face. The only sound upon the once-tumultuous battlefield was that of the wind-driven grit that pelted his bony armor. He climbed the cairn that he had watched Sargatanas' troops build from the rubble of dead legionaries and stared up at the commemorative sigil that hung above it. It had been a marvelous victory, one worthy of his own lord—complete in its outcome, merciless in its devastation. Faraii's performance had been incredible; Beelzebub would have to know how adept he was. And just how brilliant a commander Sargatanas had become. *A foe to be reckoned with for sure,* Adramalik mused.

On the positive side, Adramalik reasoned, at least he did not have to shepherd that ridiculous old demon all the way back to Dis.

Again he looked up at the luminous sigil. *Maudlin sentimentality,* he thought. Perhaps that and that alone was Sargatanas' greatest weakness.

XVI

ADAMANTINARX-UPON-THE-ACHERON

It was as if the very buildings, their vaulting exuberance, their relative lightness of architecture, mirrored her exultation at arriving in Adamantinarx. This city, so unlike shadowed Dis with its flattened and oppressive vistas, was more alive in its spirit than most of Hell's inhabitants.

Seated within an inconspicuous, unadorned howdah

atop a giant Waste crosser and swathed in folds of skin, Lilith drew not even a single glance. Just, she thought, as Ardat Lili had not on her many treks to this place. And now she was gone and her mistress, for whom she had sacrificed all, was here.

With some effort Lilith reined in her deepening sadness. Ardat Lili had known the dangers and would have wanted her to be safely ensconced in Adamantinarx. Of all the cities, this had been her favorite. Lilith tended to look at the cities of Hell as organic, as immense bodies lying strewn upon the unholy ground. They had streets that flowed with the souls that were their blood and buildings that were their bones, lower demons that functioned as vital organs, and, for better or worse, the demon aristocracy that served as their minds. Most, she had concluded, were necrotic, and some quite insane. But this city was living, somehow rational, and its attempts at diversity and relative tolerance could only make it rise above its rivals.

As she passed through the mammoth Eastern Gate she saw Sargatanas' Captain of the Foot Guard, Zoray, waiting patiently with a small contingent of his demons, all clad in their fine, green-hued skins. Upon his shoulder sat the small, winged form of her familiar, which, upon seeing her, sprang into the air and flapped its way to her extended arm. Lilith smiled behind the cowl of her traveling skin. This was all like a dream. To be free of Dis and the Fly!

"My lady," Zoray said, watching her dismount. "Welcome. Your journey was not too difficult, I hope?"

"My journey has always been difficult, Lord Zoray," she said with a light laugh as she stroked the stubby-winged creature. "But I expect that will change now that I am here."

"Your chambers await you, my lady," he said, gesturing in the general direction of the central mount.

"Is Lord Sargatanas back from his campaign?" she

inquired, unfastening her cowl at the neck and letting it fall heavily to her bare shoulders.

Zoray hesitated and she could hear the breath catch in his throat as he tried not to stare at her. "He will return in a few days, my lady. Winning a battle is one thing; securing an entire province with all its wards in disarray is another."

Lilith nodded and the small party began the long ascent to the palace complex. The long, arcing avenue that sliced through the city was really an attenuated series of steps that rose so gradually Lilith only realized they were climbing when she looked behind. Outlying Adamantinarx was fairly sparsely populated, but the crowds grew the farther into the city she walked.

Whereas her former master had viewed the uselessness of Dis' incarcerated souls as an excuse to torture them, Sargatanas' attitude seemed to be one of enforced industriousness. There were no souls cast limbless to the curbsides, no lines of the damned impaled against row upon row of quivering houses, and no unpredictable roundups by unrestrained Order Knights bent on simple slaughter.

Instead, as she looked around her, she saw nothing but the ceaseless toiling of souls as they built, crafted, and enriched Adamantinarx. Creaking bone scaffolds, enormous piles of winking bricks, great mounds of rendered soul-mortar, all bore witness to Sargatanas' grand vision of his capital. Her escort pointed out many of the new landmarks that dotted the metropolis, including the monumental standing portrait of Sargatanas himself, its head ablaze in a vibrant cowl of flame. She paused when Zoray drew her attention to it.

"Was that his idea?" she said with a wry expression crossing her perfect features.

"No, my lady, it made him angry."

"Really. I can see why; it does not do him justice."

"That was not the reason, my lady. The statue was

erected upon a decree of the Prince, and my lord does not easily suffer mandates from Dis."

Lilith nodded sympathetically. She was all too familiar with the kind of orders that issued from within the Keep.

They gradually, unhurriedly, ascended toward the palace, cleaving easily the growing crowds of craftsmen, demon soldiers, and bureaucrats. A thin mist hung low over the streets, the strangely fragrant by-product of the soul-rendering process. Clots of workers, souls mostly, sat in open plazas stitching skins, carving bone for ornate entablatures, herding souls for brick transformation, and fabricating all of the many furnishings that would eventually find their way into the palace's thousand rooms.

Lilith looked at the haunted, gray faces in the crowd, the faces of those she and Ardat Lili had worked so hard to reach out to. And she was met, not surprisingly, with frequent looks of startled recognition. Some silently reached out a hand as if to touch her. She knew then that across Hell, and in as many cities as her handmaiden had visited, she was known. She knew she would have to talk with Sargatanas about them, that he, perhaps, would take the first steps toward freeing them.

The party passed through the palace gate and there, Lilith noted, the buildings took on a grander aspect, their scale broader and their surfaces more ornate. Souls were in little evidence, replaced by robed bureaucrats, elite troops, and the occasional caravan of carts bringing goods up from the city. *What is so different here? The buildings, the open plan of the city, or is it something else?* It took her some time to realize what had seeped into her unconscious. All of the demons here, and indeed in the whole of Adamantinarx, went about their business with their heads held up, in contrast to their counterparts in Dis who always seemed to be looking over their shoulders as they performed their errands. Lilith felt the weight upon her heart lighten.

Zoray led her up a series of wide staircases, and atop the final flight before the wide entrance to the palace she stopped and turned to survey, once again, her new home. Her eyes lit upon the distant Eastern Gate and beyond, toward Dis. She knew that Beelzebub would not be pleased when he discovered her absence and that once he ascertained her whereabouts there was little doubt that she would be putting this city in jeopardy. Was it nothing more than selfishness for her to put Sargatanas in this position? Or was there a deeper reason for her to have left Dis behind, something, as yet, unclear? She turned to rejoin Zoray, who waited patiently under the threshold. The sense of self-determination, of being in control, for once, was as overwhelming as the newness of her surroundings, and she vowed never to get used to either of these newfound emotions.

Eligor patted the ash from his skins and watched it sift slowly down forming a ring of ash, like the shadow of a nimbus, upon the flagstones.

The sealed chamber-doors, built tall and wide to accommodate his wings, were just as he had left them, his red seal affixed to the center, his handprint intact. As he swung the doors aside he smelled the familiar and comforting odor of his space and his possession within. Sometimes, when he was abroad, he would call up that smell from his memory, to distract himself from some of the other smells prevalent in Hell, and sometimes simply to comfort himself. Orange light, shimmering in through the leaded-obsidian windows, bled through the darkness, playing upon his many things, and he smiled.

Valefar had given him one of Astaroth's generals' axes, hand still attached, and this Eligor hung from a pair of outstretched fingers on his wall. As he lit his many small braziers he saw that all his clutter was as he had left it. Strange bits and pieces of his travels, his wars, his past, adorned nearly every flat surface visible.

There by the twin windows and seated upon a carved table were a hundred small effigies carved from various native stones by the Waste tribes, each one mute evidence of some obscure cult created to quell the fears of their fierce surroundings. Near them stood the chiseled apex of a pointed column, all that remained of the distant city of Slavark after Sargatanas had leveled it. Beyond that an entire wall-cabinet, bone framed with translucent quartzite panels, contained his collection of bizarre souls' skulls, each so outlandish that one had to look upon it very carefully to see any common marks of humanity. Next to that, his library of skin-scrolls gathered over the eons from a hundred different wards throughout Hell was neatly tucked into an alcove near his writing stand. And there, just as he had left it, was his ongoing project, his diary, open to the last entry, the precious feather quill—his sole intact quill plucked from his own wing just after the Fall—lying upon it. A beam of firelight from outside touched the inscribed vellum as if its import was greater than he felt.

Eligor perched himself, wearily, upon his stool, his tingling wings nearly touching the floor behind him. The trip from Astaroth's capital had been nonstop and tiring; the Flying Corps had flown into the hot, buffeting wind nearly the entire journey back. He closed his stinging eyes, and shreds of the events of the last few days passed through his mind. As with all campaigns, there was much to remember, much to write down. These campaigns were finally wearing upon him. Eons of fighting and all for what—endlessly shifting borders, vague alliances? Sargatanas was right to feel the way he did. Right to want an end to this way of life.

Head nodding forward, Eligor found himself drifting willingly into the state that was neither sleep nor wakefulness. He floated on the feathered wings of his past, through the smoke of his present, falling and rising and falling gently.

A soft knock roused him and he stood slowly and walked to the door. One of Valefar's messengers knelt before him and, then rising, bade him to follow him to his master's chambers. With heavy footsteps Eligor passed through the many glyph-lit corridors to the Prime Minister's anteroom, where he waited for only a moment before being ushered in.

The large, open rooms were part office, part living quarters, the abode of one whose work was an integral part of his life. Bolts of red heat lightning flickered soundlessly outside the panoramic window, momentarily negating the soft brazier-light that suffused the chambers and casting vivid light upon its familiar contents. A large and intricately vesseled heart-clock mounted on the wall beat a steady and muffled rhythm. Valefar sat in his robes, hands folded in his lap, looking every bit as weary as Eligor felt. A giant stack of vellum dispatches and orders lay ominously upon the Prime Minister's desk awaiting his attention, having grown to staggering proportions in his absence. Even as Eligor watched, one of Valefar's aides entered and placed an armload of tattered documents upon a side-desk.

"As if the workings of Adamantinarx were not enough, I now have to deal with the mess that is Askad," Valefar said, indicating the newly arrived pile and rolling his eyes. "When I am finished with these I am going to suggest that they be reused to rebuild that ruin of a capital!" The Prime Minister sighed. "You know why I called you here, Eligor?"

"I can guess."

"The Baron. Unlike you, I have never really been able to have anything but the most cursory conversations with him."

"He *is* a mannered individual."

"He is a *headstrong* individual." Valefar closed his eyes and shook his bowed head slightly.

The heavy candles guttered noticeably as the door

opened and Baron Faraii entered, still wearing his black battle-armor and Abyssal-skin field-cloak. Eligor saw something in Faraii that he had not seen before, a predatory look in his eyes, a certain insolence in his bearing. It was challenging, and Eligor did not like it.

The Baron strode purposefully up to Valefar's desk and stopped crisply. Faraii assumed a position not unlike his customary drill stance, feet apart, hands clasped behind him.

Valefar did not lift his head when he spoke.

"Faraii, we two have never been close, have we?"

"No."

"Well, we do not need to be. But we do need to agree on one thing. Our duty to our lord."

Faraii shifted slightly. "That is open to debate. Sargatanas is making choices that may not be sitting well with all of the demons, Major and Minor."

Valefar lifted his chin. "And by that I take it you mean yourself?"

Red lightning scoured the room and threw Faraii's hard features into sharp contrast for an instant.

"Interpret it as you will."

In the brief flicker of light Eligor thought he saw a tiny movement upon the far wall. It had looked like a finger or, perhaps, an ear.

Valefar rose and with a single sweep of his arm scattered the pile of documents to the floor, in a gradually settling mound. His eyes wide, his bony jaw jutting, he placed his fists on the desktop and leaned forward.

"You are evasive at best and treasonous at worst!" he hissed. "Very close to the edge, Faraii. All of this, as well as what seems to have been questionable behavior on the field of battle, suggests to me that you are not to be trusted. What do you have to say for yourself?"

"Are you going to destroy me where I stand or allow me to get back to my troops?" The mocking tone was unmistakable.

Eligor moved slowly across the room to the far wall, listening as he passed the bristling Baron. He had seen something—a thin trickle of black blood that seemed to surround a sudden protrusion. It looked like an ear.

"Ah, yes, such commendable loyalty to your troops!" Valefar said. He turned his back on the Baron, hands clenched at his sides.

"At least my troops are demons. An army of souls, indeed!"

Valefar's chin dropped in resignation.

Eligor was nearly at the wall. The soul-ear that jutted from the gray wall tilted fractionally, as if it heard him approach.

"What am I to do with you?" Valefar continued. "Our lord, while angry regarding your mistreatment of Astaroth, was pleased with your performance at the head of your troops. If it was my choice alone, Faraii, you would not leave this room alive. Your loyalty is deeply in question. Despite that, your lord has seen fit to test you, one more time, upon the battlefield. But be careful, Baron Faraii; the battlefield can be a very unpredictable place."

Without turning back to him, Valefar raised his hand in dismissal.

"Indeed it can," said Faraii plainly.

Valefar spun around, silvered eyes intense, dark wrath written upon his features. But Eligor saw him regain himself quickly.

Faraii pivoted on his heel and strode toward the door, glancing at Eligor as he passed through the threshold.

At nearly that instant, Eligor's hand darted out and, amidst a brief spray of black blood, wrenched the ear from the wall. He immediately put his own ear to the spot and heard a faint whisper from within the brick. The susurration stopped and was picked up, again and again ever more faintly, as it traveled deep into the wall.

"Who do you think arranged that?" Valefar asked, pointing at the hole.

"It could be anybody. I will try to trace it. Why does Sargatanas not simply cast him out?"

"He knows too much, Eligor; clearly somebody feels attention should be paid to him. And he is too good with his sword and his troops."

Eligor nodded.

Wiping the blood from the side of his face, Eligor held up the dripping ear for Valefar to see and shook his head. The Prime Minister looked at it, took a long, deep breath, and sat down heavily. Eligor tossed the ear into a nearby brazier, where it sizzled momentarily, and, with a nod, he left Valefar's chambers. The dullness Eligor felt within his body he knew was due, in large part, to his vast weariness, but he also felt it deeper. His regard for Faraii was irretrievably altered, and as he headed slowly back to his own chambers, he knew that he could never speak with him as freely as he once had. And that he could never trust Faraii again.

ADAMANTINARX-UPON-THE-ACHERON

Tales of the victory outside Maraak-of-the-Margins were already being passed from soul to soul in the streets as Hannibal Barca made his way through the jostling throngs. Returning troops, still covered in the battlefield's black blanket of ash, marched in tight, well-disciplined columns back to their barracks inside the city. Many among them bore the severe scars of conflict—arms hacked, heads cleft, and pole-arm piercings abounded. And many, too, proudly bore the newly acquired phalerae of their victims. From some distance, Hannibal caught a glimpse of dozens of Demons Major and Minor, the returning general staff accompanied by their guards and banners, and next to them he discerned Sargatanas and

Valefar and Eligor as they climbed the long stairs to the fortress above. It really was odd, Hannibal thought, how pleased he was beginning to feel being a part of this demons' world.

Hannibal knew that he had much more than that to be pleased about, for walking a pace behind him, flanked by their newly created demon bodyguard, was his once-dead brother, Mago. Finding him—Hannibal's only request to Sargatanas—had been a miracle wrapped in a coincidence. In a spare hour Valefar himself had pored over the Books of Gamigin, locating Hannibal's brother faster than any soul could have done even had he or she been able to read the complex angelic script. And when, tracing down the page with his clawed finger, Valefar came upon Mago's name, he closed the book and looked up at Hannibal with the slightest smile. Mago's entry had recently been updated, Valefar told the soul, with an eternal punishment for attempting to incite his fellow souls to rebellion. It was Hannibal's turn to smile. Mago had, for his troubles, been transformed into a brick and was located not too far from where they sat. The walk to him and the resurrection together probably took less time than it had to locate his name in the great book. And now Hannibal's beloved brother, Mago Barca, perhaps the only human he could truly trust, was again walking by his side, as he had done so long ago along the paths of his Life.

Hannibal looked at him, at his wiry frame, at his familiar, vigorous stride, and at the flattened face that only half-smiled back at him. Hannibal understood the less than perfect resurrection; there would always be the stamp of the brick upon Mago. That was Valefar's little reminder to both brothers.

Hannibal had spread his words like seeds upon fertile ground. A soul who had once been a general was recruiting an army to fight alongside demons. Recruits were to meet at the Plaza Napeai. At first, he had been told, the message was met, predictably, with incredulity, with disbelief. The sheer ludicrousness of it made countless souls either snort with derision or fearfully redouble their efforts at whatever tasks they were laboring over. Strange rumors were always swirling about the souls like sparks on the wind—fast traveling and equally fast dying. They never knew what was real and what was malicious trickery.

But Hannibal reasoned that he could count on many, like himself, whose awareness of the currents in Adamantinarx told them that changes were in the wind. They would serve as the foundation upon which he would build his army. And eventually others would join.

He and his party strode through the streets quickly, purposefully, their destination the aptly named Plaza Napeai—the Plaza of Swords. Clad in tattered skin robes and carrying a long, wrapped bundle, Hannibal held his chin and eyes level and looked the demons he passed directly in the eye—a luxury he would never have dreamt of before his commission. He told Mago, as well as the burly bodyguards in tow, to do the same. Attitude was everything in Hell, and Hannibal was not about to relinquish that which had been so hard-won by adopting anything less than the mien of a great general. And, ironically, the demon bodyguard, under their lord's direct orders, would defend this new right to their destruction.

A giant, fiery-headed statue of a fallen demon crouched upon a soaring stepped pedestal at the head of the plaza, and Hannibal saw this in fleeting glimpses as he approached the wide space. Its bent back was spined with dozens of angelic arrows, but its fist, clenching a broken sword, was raised heavenward. There were a hundred such statues, he was told, strewn throughout Hell, but forever afterward he would regard this one as special. Two large piles, covered with shrouds of stretched Abyssal skin, lay at its feet, guarded by souls picked by Hannibal himself.

Gray crowds were streaming in and he found himself forced to use the bodyguards to clear a way before him. They were efficient legionaries, and their mere presence and number caused enough commotion to part the shuffling souls. Mago tapped Hannibal's elbow and pointed up toward the rooftops of the surrounding buildings. There he saw the dark forms of scattered flying demons leaning on shields and lances, their attitude attentive. A precaution, he thought, nothing more. To Sargatanas, Hannibal was still someone to be watched and measured, and he knew that his demon lord would be swift in his response should any move he make be interpretable as insurrectionist.

But even the presence of heavily armed demons could not dampen Hannibal's elation. This was a watershed moment in his afterlife, a moment that he had to take the fullest advantage of, for there would surely never be another. He saw himself as a torch, one that would either ignite the cold furnaces of emotion in every soul around him or immolate them and himself as well.

At the base of the stepped pedestal Mago cupped his hands, and Hannibal used them to climb up to the next level. Reaching down, he grasped Mago's hand and pulled him up next to him. In this manner the two rose up two more levels until they were twenty feet above the massed murmuring souls. Hannibal had been mended, somewhat, by his new lord and stood tall, a surge of emotional power coursing through his body. He had addressed hosts before, hosts that had been disparate and doubtful, and his formula had always been the same: one part lie to one part hope. *This is not hypocrisy,* he thought. *An army is no different from a sword. It first needs forging and then needs to be trained with and tested in battle. Lies, hope—they are the hammer and tongs one uses to forge the blade. The better they're used, the better the blade.*

He stood with his back to them, adjusting the straps

on the bundle so that it could depend from his improvised belt. When he turned abruptly around to face them silence descended upon the plaza. It was an old trick that he had learned as a young prince on the walls of his father's city. Mago smiled.

"My name is Hannibal Barca and I remember my Life!" Hannibal began, his voice carrying clarion clear against the distant sounds of Hell. "Yesterday I was as you are now. Tomorrow you will be as I am today!

"Change has been thrust upon us. Hell is changing around us as we stand here. That I stand here before you, addressing you in this way, should be proof enough of that. I *know* who I was and what I did in my Life. And what I must do now. The path to our redemption lies before us, and it is Lord Sargatanas who will lead us.

"The Fallen are no longer of one mind! The hierarchy of demons no longer united. Some have started to question things . . . to change things. Our lord is one such demon; the White Mistress is another. Most of us know something of her; some of us have even been touched in some way by her. She has been fighting this place in the only way she could . . . by reaching out to us. It was she who led me to offer myself to her ally, our lord Sargatanas. And it was he who gave me back my past.

"You will ask why I should follow a demon master who has oppressed me. And I would answer by telling you what you already know: Sargatanas' temperance and leniency are like no other lord's in Hell. Our torments, which could have been greater by tenfold, are as nothing to that which he has endured for all these thousands of years. For, unlike us who left our earthly lives behind like corrupt vessels drained and broken, he lost a life of beatitude . . . a life at the knee of his creator. Lord Sargatanas can no longer endure the punishments and privations of Hell. As you long for an end to your torment, he longs for that which he lost so long ago . . . the tranquility of Heaven."

Hannibal heard the word "heaven" uttered from a hundred twisted mouths and for just an instant wondered what he was offering them. He, himself, was not certain. He had to be careful not to go too far.

"We are all here to be punished for our past lives, and rightly so. None of us are here unjustly. And yet which of you would not try to redeem yourselves, to prove that at your very core you can be more than you were in life?

"Your souls have been punished for what you did in your Life, and that is how it had to be. There are some among you whose heavy sins ensure that you will never leave this place. And that, too, is right. But for most of us, our torments need not be eternal. Just as the transgressions are behind us, so should be the punishments. For what is the good of the lesson if one cannot apply what one has learned?"

Hannibal began to open the tied bundle at his waist. He glanced at Mago, who was nodding encouragingly. Hannibal looked again at the mass of humanity and saw every eye upon him. With a sudden flourish he let the wrapping fall from his waist and grasped the hilt of a sword, pulling it free of its scabbard to hold it before him. He heard a gasp issue from a thousand throats. A soul with a weapon! It was unheard of! He felt their rising excitement.

"If you truly wish to make amends for your sins, then you must take up arms in this holy cause," he shouted hoarsely. "Sargatanas' Rebellion may fail and we all may be committed to oblivion or, worse yet, punishments beyond our reckoning, but at least we will have fought against those forces whose dark influences put us here in the first place. And Heaven, whose lambent Gates may never open to us, will know that good *can* come from those who seem irredeemable. They will know that even from the darkest bowels of Hell souls can reach for the Light!"

He took a deep breath and raised the sword Sargatanas had given him above his head. Some in the crowd were shouting with newfound fervor, giving voice to a dormant sense of self they had suppressed for so long.

"Will you reach for that Light and fight for my lord Sargatanas and our White Mistress? Will you fight for me? Will you fight for your eternal souls?"

An enormous cry of approval rang through the plaza and Hannibal heard "For Hannibal!" evenly mixed with "For Sargatanas!" Seeing that his words had had the desired effect, Hannibal signaled to the guards below. In an instant they pulled back the skins from the great mounds and revealed a huge pile of weapons, which the suddenly surging crowd began to take up. Hannibal looked up and saw that the demons atop the buildings were paying very close attention; this was a critical moment. The mob could turn either way, and even Hannibal worried that a thousand armed souls might march through the streets to foolishly attack the palace.

He stepped right to the edge of the plinth and shouted, "*For Sargatanas!*" It took a moment for the souls at his feet to notice him, so engrossed in their new weapons were they, but within a minute, like a tide surging away, the chant was picked up, echoing across the plaza. Abyssal flyers, which had been perched along the high ledges of the buildings in the hundreds, suddenly took wing startled by the noise. Hannibal watched them ascend, and their dwindling body-lights looked like stars climbing into the heavens, perhaps an omen. Again he looked around at the encircling demons and now, with the shouts of "For Sargatanas!" ringing in their ears, he saw that they had relaxed, satisfied. One by one they, too, took wing, vanishing into the dark sky, and Hannibal smiled, even as he continued to pump his sword in the air. He was himself again. Almost reluctantly he sheathed his sword and turned to Mago, who beamed at him and walked toward him. As they clasped hands his

gaze traveled up the crouched statue and rested upon
the ash-dusted clenched fist, its broken sword frozen
in defiance, and he wondered whether this war, already
so full of hope, might not end as that one had. He looked
high into the sky and saw the stars still climbing upward.

XVII

DIS

He fell back heavily upon his pallet and heard the thing
scrambling noisily in the darkness to get away from
him. He had pleasured himself with it for the third time,
pleasured himself until it had cried out terribly in pain,
which did not make him stop but only redouble his
fierce thrusting. He roared ferociously in his moment,
and that had only terrified the creature more. Adramalik
looked over into the corner of his sleep chamber, into
the blackness, and saw only its tiny lights, shivering,
and heard its whining, gurgling breath as it panted in its
fear of him.

   The Order Knights had conspired behind his back; of
that he was now certain. There was no other conclusion
to reach. They had had an odd look to them when he had
returned from the battle. He had spoken to each of them
to get their individual reports and each had, in his own
way, seemed less than forthright, unwilling to look him
in the eye. That had aroused his suspicions. And when,
accompanied by so many of them, he had entered his
suite of chambers they had seemed expectant and for a

moment, an irrational moment, he had thought that perhaps they were about to assassinate him. He remembered lighting the first brazier, the one by the sword stand—just in case—and remembered the enormous surprise at his first sight of the two-legged Abyssal, a young Skin-peeler. The Knights had captured it, filed down its teeth and spines, clipped its blade-hands, bound and gagged it carefully, and covered it in thick skins so that its luminous spots would not give it away in the darkened room. He could still hear their peals of laughter when, as they had pulled away the skins, he had jumped. Now that he thought about it, the room had been perfumed with the acrid aroma of the beast, a whiff of the Wastes. The Knights had honored him with this present, and he felt so much emotion toward them that his mind raced. They would have to be rewarded, not immediately and obviously, but in ways that were significant to each one. And there would be surprises. Just to make them jump, as well.

He lay in the dark, reconstituting himself, gathering himself for another assault upon the creature's quivering silver-scaled body. What would he do this round? Compel it to come to him with a potent, irresistible glyph or bludgeon it with his fists until, resigned to its fate, it surrendered? He heard it mewling, and he felt himself growing powerfully aroused again. He sat upright on his pallet, and just that movement alone caused the creature to let out an anguished shriek. *This really is too delicious,* Adramalik thought, a grin twisting his bony features.

A light suddenly appeared, casting an odd glow upon the chamber's contents, and in the farthest corner, amidst an overturned table and chairs, he could now see the beast cowering, its eyes wide, both battered mouths agape and drooling blood. The serpentine tendrils of an approaching glyph had entered the suite, finding him in its deepest recess, his sleeping chamber. It formed into a fiery, purple glyph of summoning—Agaliarept's curious handiwork—and its urgency was not to be ignored. Adramalik closed his eyes and shook his head, feeling his passions—as well as his fearsome erection—dwindling. The Skin-peeler would have to wait.

What could Agaliarept be about, summoning me to him so late? It was a thought Adramalik repeated bitterly as he swung his cloak about his shoulders, as he latched his door behind him, and as he walked the corridors toward the Conjuring Chamber. His mood further darkened as he found himself traversing the tubular, offal-strewn corridor beneath the Rotunda, a place he was never pleased to venture. At the threshold he felt the chamber's stagnant, hot air and discerned a faint and echoing twittering as from a hundred tiny throats.

He heard, too, the Conjuring Chamber's occupants before he saw them, and when he entered he saw that not only was Beelzebub present along with Agares, but they had been joined by the Prince's greatest general, Moloch. Different from a Demon Major by his former status, he was the most powerful of Those Forsaken, the Pridzarhim, a relatively small and especially feared community of sullen former seraph-turned-lesser-gods who had been forgotten or discarded by their subjects. Moloch, like his brethren, was mighty and proud and bitter. Adramalik feared him and was no stranger to the tales of his savagery both upon the battlefield and in his administration, as Imperial Mayor of Dis and as Prince of the County of Tears that ringed the city. He bore upon his scarred chest the Grand Cross of the Order of the Fly, a decoration shared only by Adramalik in his role as Grand Chancellor General Knight of the Order.

As he spoke with Moloch, part of Beelzebub's face peeled away to watch Adramalik make his way through the orbiting bricks and glyphs, toward the chamber's depressed center.

"What is it, my general? You seem distracted," the

Chancellor General heard the Prince say to Moloch. Adramalik saw their dim forms in the gloom, the broad corona of symbols, ancient and unglyphlike, slowly rotating around and lighting the old god's head. Moloch, giant in stature, shifted uneasily upon the crutchlike wing bones that twisted out of his back, spindly substitutes for his burned-away legs. Their seeming fragility, Adramalik knew, belied their strength and agility. He had seen Moloch upon the battlefield, a veritable cyclone of carnage.

"Prince, I am disgusted by the refugee demons that pour forth from Astaroth's wards into your wards . . . and, indeed, into Dis . . . by the hundreds of thousands. There are no Demons Major among them and only few Demons Minor have been seen. They were mostly petty officials and as either lower functionaries or common laborers would be useless, never having been properly trained by their incompetent lord. I think that, like a cancer, their very presence will corrupt those around them." Moloch paused, clenching his jaw. "What would you have me do with them?"

"Why, Moloch, I would have you do whatever you please with them," Beelzebub said agreeably. "Be as creative as you like; pry away any information they may have. But, in the end, I want them as part of my city. Gather what is left of them, turn them to brick, and brand them with my Seal."

"As you wish, my Prince."

Adramalik stopped before the Prince and bowed. Beelzebub nodded and solidified his face to look fully at his Grand General. The towering god's head was lowered, deep in some dark thought. Charred flakes fell away as he rubbed his jaw.

"Do you miss that place, Moloch? The Above?"

"No, my Prince, never. There was weakness there, as there was in the realm of men. Men are fearful and wretched, and watching over them when I was a seraph was . . . tedious," he snarled. "That is why I played with them . . . why I lost favor and why I," he indicated his missing legs, "was burnt. But I *do* miss their offerings . . . their children. Their hopeful, futile burnings. They had no idea how much I enjoyed the smell of that smoke! Had they but known, they would have stopped in a day. If I could get them to do that with their own children, imagine what I could have done with more time."

Adramalik felt something brush past his foot, but when he looked down he had only an impression of a small, vague shape heading toward the center of the chamber. Others, too, were converging there.

"*He* yearns for the Above," the Prince buzzed.

"Who, Prince?" asked Moloch.

"Sargatanas. I have heard that he sits on his throne staring through the hole in his dome, staring upward . . . toward the Above. He has spent all these long millennia here and yet, as dim as it must be, he can still see the Light. He is stirring the same feelings in others among the Fallen. I cannot let this continue. Minister Agares and I have been hard at work drawing up plans for ridding Hell of him, plans that you, my general, will execute. You will take up those grievous Hooks of yours and with them tear away his dreams!" The Prince's form shifted and billowed with anger. "With you victorious, I will take back Astaroth's wards and Sargatanas' as well. And I will wear him around my neck, crushed as you leave him, as a reminder to all that the line between Hell and the Above shall never be crossed!"

Adramalik had not seen Beelzebub this agitated since the early times—not since the wars of territory that had carved up Hell so long ago. He looked then at Agares, who had been silently listening. *Why was I not brought in on the earliest discussions of battle plans? Why Agares . . . why is he so favored? I will have to watch him.*

A growing commotion drew the demons' attentions

toward the center of the room, where they saw a gathering of many-legged, chittering creatures scrabbling in a flailing mound to climb atop one another. Each one's body was unique in shape and looked like an animated chunk of flesh, ragged and moist. Only a few bore single pallid eyes. In a frenzy of many-jointed legs they clawed themselves upward into a roughly demonic shape, a shape that, after a series of shudders and ripples, smoothed its form and became the Conjuror General, Agaliarept. He gave one more spasmodic twitch of his many arms—arms that had been legs moments earlier—and turned to confront the demons.

Adramalik heard his sibilant voice, a hissing like the venting of steam, issuing from the mouths of a hundred suspended bricks.

"Look," the Conjuror said, and pointed at the floor. A pattern of bricks was already in place, and when he touched the closest brick it began to whine, setting off its neighbor, until the entire line, which disappeared into a wall, was noisily active.

"While I have not yet found her, I have finally found Faraii, my Prince. His domicile lies deep within a glyph-guarded building atop the central mount of Adamantinarx. Just as you suspected. It would seem that he has been confined to his chambers after his actions at Maraak," Agaliarept added. "I summoned you because I have, just this hour, found a way in."

Even in the gloom, Adramalik could see the Prince's smile.

"That is welcome news, Agaliarept. The Baron has always been my insurance against the day that Sargatanas became difficult. With his help we will open up a second front on the Lord of Adamantinarx."

Without waiting for a signal Agaliarept's many mouths began to move, each one murmuring a different incantation until Adramalik had the sensation that a crowd of conjurors stood around him. Agaliarept's eyes rolled and bubbling foam from his lips dottled his cowl and when, in the course of his trance, he trained his wand-arms upon the floor, just behind the bricks that were already aglow, these began to arise, separating and assembling themselves with screeches and small puffs of blood.

Before a few moments had passed, a four-armed figure stood upon a single thick pillar before the assembled demons—a brick construct nearly as tall as a demon. A large soul-mouth trembled in what seemed like its round head, and its overlong arms terminated in bricks with vacant eye sockets.

"Do it . . . do it now, my Prince," Agaliarept croaked hoarsely. "We must act now or the glyphs will find us."

Beelzebub coughed loudly and protruded his long, black tongue, and upon it Adramalik saw a fly trembling. It was slick with saliva, and its back was fiery green with tiny glyphs. The Prince withdrew it slightly and stepped up to the brick figure, clasping its oversized head in his hands, distended his proboscis, thrusting the fly deep into the slack soul-mouth. Adramalik heard a barking cough and knew that it was done. They watched the dull green glow of it as it descended into the bricks, gathering speed through the opening conduit on its way toward Adamantinarx. He and the other demons immediately grasped a waving arm and placed their eyes over the empty sockets, watching as the millions of soul-brick eyes between the Conjuring Chamber and Faraii's chamber winked open and the darkness parted.

Their view through the countless eyes was less than perfect; a certain clarity was lost to the distances, the vast number of eyes needed to peer across so large a distance, and the overall gloom of the chamber.

Faraii was sitting upon the floor of a room that had been at once austere and elegant. Rage had visited that room, though, and in its wake had left a tableau of utter chaos. In the half-light it appeared that the room and its contents had been torn apart, clawed and mangled to be thrown in every corner. By turning the brick slightly, Adramalik could see once carefully worked wall hangings of stitched flesh lying in shreds, rent floor mats woven of tough Waste-veins, and fractured personal objects of every description looking like the jumbled and broken bones of so many skeletons.

But to the Chancellor General, the terrible centerpiece of the room was unquestionably the Baron himself. He was not as Adramalik remembered him, not the quiet, confident, self-contained demon who had wandered into Dis from the Wastes. Faraii sat awkwardly, still in his armor, almost as if he had been dropped upon the floor, his head canted to one side. His unblinking, glittering eyes were staring into someplace deep within himself as, with long, deliberate strokes, he slowly honed the black sword that lay across his lap. *Like a creature from the Wastes, captivity does not suit him,* thought Adramalik wryly. *Thus has the Great Lord Sargatanas rewarded him for Astaroth's overdue death.*

A mouth in a brick, a darkness within the darkness, opened behind Faraii, and Adramalik saw, somewhat indistinctly, a glow ascending from the wall's depths. The bright, emerging spark of Beelzebub's emissary paused upon the crushed lower lip and then took wing, entering the room to hover momentarily behind the oblivious seated figure. Purposefully it flew the short distance to Faraii's head and alighted, and still the Baron took no notice.

Boldly, the fly crossed Faraii's forehead, scuttling over his bony brow, and, clawing under his hard eyelid, disappeared underneath. The hand that held the whetstone paused above the blade as a faint ring of luminous green limned Faraii's trembling eye. It lingered for a few seconds and then faded. Adramalik saw the hand still poised above the black blade and then saw it slowly dip down to finish the stroke. With each following moment the strokes became quicker, firmer, more assured.

Then, unexpectedly, the mask that had been the Baron's face cracked as the thinnest smile crept over his face, a smile not dissimilar from the one that had played upon Beelzebub's face only moments before.

Adramalik thought about that smile as he left the other demons and headed back to his rooms and grinned himself. Sargatanas, together with his few misguided followers, would soon be stopped, and Adamantinarx would lie broken. And the bitter Acheron would flow around a new city and the ash would fall and the smoke of the new fires would rise and Hell could go back, without contest, without distraction, to the primacy of punishment.

As Adramalik drew nearer to his chambers he remembered the delight that awaited him and felt himself growing excited, succumbing, once again, to the powers of the flesh. As tired as he was, he would finish what he had started with the creature. But upon arriving at his doors the Chancellor General noticed them unlatched and slightly ajar, and pushing them apart, he made his way deeper into his rooms with a growing haste and sense of misgiving. Only when he arrived at his bedchambers did he find his worst suspicions confirmed. Gnawed and bloodstained sinew ties lay upon the floor. The wretched Skin-peeler had somehow escaped, chewed through its bonds and slipped away to some recess of the Keep, undoubtedly well away by now. Or, perhaps, even now, was being used by one of his Knights; Adramalik would never know. Sadly, there was no one to butcher and bleed for the mistake; he could only curse himself for not locking the doors. It did not matter now, he thought with a resigned shake of his head; pleasure was always ephemeral. He lay down upon his pallet and when he closed his eyes

he thought about Faraii, far away, sharpening his sword
in the darkness.

ADAMANTINARX-UPON-THE-ACHERON

Lilith cried out in the night and sat up drawing the
thick sleeping skins about her for comfort. She had been
with Ardat Lili again, had been held in her warm, comforting embrace once again, and the dream's realism
left Lilith panting, thinking that she was back in her
bone-paneled chambers in Dis.

The room was cold and dank and she was clammy
from her tossing about. She shucked off her covers and
rose, the warm air caressing her bare skin as she crossed
to the closed window. Unlatching it, she stood in the
room's darkness, breathing in the warmer air and gazing out into the night at Adamantinarx, reassured that
the world outside her had indeed changed.

A beautiful, ruddy fog had crept in off the Acheron to
swathe the great city in soft, nocturnal mystery. She
could not see the slow-flowing river or the distant quays
that lined it. Nor could she see the city's walls or gates
or even the barracks that were situated on the near side
of the walls. What she could see was the flickering
points of fire that sketched out the nearer streets and the
indistinct shapes of spires and towers and statues that
tentatively probed the sky, fearful in their wavering
forms, it seemed to her, of vanishing into it.

The scuff of footsteps below her window caused her
to lean forward and peer directly down at the expansive
courtyard that lay, bordered by Adamantinarx's most
important buildings, across the uppermost portion of
the citadel. It served and would serve again, she had
learned, in times of war as a gathering space and parade ground for Eligor's Flying Guard but was now

empty of demons save for the curious procession of demons that she saw emerging slowly from within her own building.

A cohort of Foot Guard led by Lord Zoray marched slowly forth from the wide door followed by two heavily robed figures whom she thought she recognized as the Lords Eligor and Valefar. And directly behind them was a larger figure, also cloaked, that could only have been Sargatanas. Back, at last, from the battlefield of Maraak. More Foot Guard brought up the rear of the line of figures, and as she watched them begin to cross the courtyard Eligor turned suddenly and looked up toward her window. Lilith pulled back reflexively, hoping the darkness hid her paleness, and, upon an impulse, decided that she would follow them.

She had packed Ardat Lili's traveling skins, more as a reminder of her great loss than as a useful garment, but now she drew them on, grateful for their concealing folds. The scent of her handmaiden, still clinging to them, mingled with that of the Wastes. Lilith was still pulling the hood around her as she ran soundlessly along the corridor and down the wide stairs to the ground floor.

Lilith cautiously pulled the door open and saw that the spectral procession had nearly crossed the courtyard. She waited until they had disappeared behind the corner of a building before she ventured out into the fog. They had turned onto the street known as the Rule, which descended, arrow straight from the mount's crest, and eventually ended at the docks on the river's edge. This bolstered her confidence; still a newcomer to Adamantinarx, she dreaded trying to find her way about the city's countless twisting streets.

As she rounded onto the Rule she saw the small demon contingent already a hundred yards ahead, their swaying forms generalized by the fog. A progression of three-story buildings, each with an overhanging jetty, lined both sides of the street, dropping gradually until she could only discern their hair-topped roofs. Dozens of receding braziers, their diffused, orange glows like soft stars, lit the relatively narrow street as it descended in long steps. Few demons trod upon its worn and fog-slicked flagstones, but many souls were performing their regular and unending tasks, taking little or no notice that it was so late at night. Their torments knew no hours.

Lilith's clawed feet left dry prints upon the warm flagstones as she made her way down the street. She kept enough distance from the small procession as she felt was safe, but all the while she wondered, as they never seemed to arrive at any destination, just how far from the citadel they would go. Doubt began to slow her steps somewhat. This quiet mission of Sargatanas', surely it was of no concern to her. What would he say if he knew that he was being shadowed by her? They had not even seen each other since her arrival.

Something drove her on nonetheless. Perhaps, she worried, a part of her mind was intoxicated with her newfound freedom and this almost inexplicable adventure was, in some way, a reflection of her clouded judgment. Or maybe it was something about Sargatanas, himself.

She passed silent crowds of souls—specters that were made solid as she drew near, some carrying mortar or wheeling brick-carts made of bone or burdened with skins or tools or metal fittings for building. Some looked at her directly, but none penetrated her disguise. She returned their gaze, studying their misshapen faces and seeing in most the unmistakable mark of evil. Only a few among many seemed out of place, confused and terrified. Those, especially, were her souls, the human beings she had spent her time in Hell caring for. As she looked from one to another she wondered whether she had placed her faith in the wrong cause and whether their redemption was unattainable.

She glanced up and recognized a pair of twisting, smoke-belching spires that rose from the Forges, a landmark that she knew marked the halfway point between the palace and the quays. Even through the mask of her skins she could smell the airborne residue of the smelters and dozens of weapon forges. The number of bone-carts carrying weapons to the barracks rose dramatically as she passed the grimy building.

Farther down the Rule, Lilith encountered the dwellings of skin stitchers, the long drying racks loaded with skins visible through their courtyards, as were the stacks of skinned souls that writhed slowly by the gutter. The low demons sat in small knots chanting in throaty whispers in time with their sewing. Two thick-set gristle-dogs suddenly bolted from one courtyard directly in front of her, grabbed the arm of one of the discarded souls, and began to noisily growl and snap at each other, their white eyes bulging. They managed to twist and tear it free, and with foam flying in arcs they disappeared back from whence they had come. The soul gurgled something and went silent.

Lilith found it difficult to watch these unfolding tableaus. After all these millennia it was still hard for her to reason through what could be done about the souls, harder with the knowledge that the activities of souls in Hell were so integral to keeping it running. She knew it would not be easy to convince any demon in Hell—even, perhaps, Sargatanas—to reform their policies toward the souls. But, she was convinced, it needed to be done, and beginnings were always hard.

Eventually, looking past the demons she was shadowing, Lilith saw the oxbow of the Acheron, shining from the fires in the skies above and looking like a ribbon of copper suspended in the fog. If she had not known that it flowed with heavy tears she might have mistaken its reflective brilliance for lava. Dim shades of cargo barges occluded the river's brightness in shifting patches, as did the very occasional passing of formations of flying demons. So beautiful was the sight that she stopped in the middle of the Rule, for a moment, and put her hand to her mouth. And for the thousandth time told herself how lucky she was to be away from Dis.

Sargatanas and his party had continued down the street and she hurried to catch up. Presently she found her surroundings shifting toward those of the docksides where great square buildings rose, their portals agape, awaiting off-loaded goods from Sargatanas' many wards. In the distant past, when the city was young, she knew these enormous warehouses had been filled to overflow and the streets around them had been virtually impassable. Now they stood, for the most part, disused and hollow, their bricks looking about sullenly.

The distant fires in the sky abruptly died away and Lilith saw the return of the river to its misty, luminous pallor. She welcomed the deepening gloom, as it made her clandestine trailing of the demons considerably easier.

Keeping to the shadows of the looming buildings, she edged closer to the demons ahead of her. They filed out of the foot of the Rule and marched toward a plain bone and iron gateway that protested loudly when it was unlocked and opened by Valefar. Lilith had never been this close to the embankment, and when Sargatanas, Valefar, and Eligor and their Guard passed through the gate and began to descend a flight of unseen stairs she had no idea what lay beyond. When the last of the Foot Guard had disappeared she cautiously made her way across a hundred yards to the gate. The sad Acheron was much louder here, she realized, its thick, opalescent waters swirling in slow eddies as it passed before her while a strong wind blew from across the river, tearing at her skins. Low, ululating wails broke the pervasive background sound of the river's sobbing, and she felt her limbs grow heavy with the burden of the tear-laden spray that touched her face. Nearly all of Hell, she knew, was built on a foundation of fury, but this river, as deceptively languid as it appeared, was every bit as powerful. It etched its meandering course through the landscape with those most bitter of waters—the waters of misery. Lilith closed her eyes tightly against the fine spray and felt her body shudder. After a few moments she forced herself to open her eyes and peer down to the river's edge, where she saw a short salt-encrusted jetty that ended somewhere beneath the opaque water.

Lined up along the near portion of the jetty were the Foot Guard, silent and motionless save for the muffled flapping of their cloaks. Farther out, flanked by Valefar and Eligor, who held his sword and robes, was Sargatanas, stripped and poised at the water's edge. His dark, powerful body, contrasting sharply against the pale waters, was more human, albeit much larger, than she would have expected, and it was quiescent—not undergoing any of the transformations of which she knew it was capable. For a full minute he stood immobile, like one of the innumerable statues that dotted the city above. The fire atop his head was growing and whipping about and he was slick from the spray, and she marveled at the control she knew he must be exercising. He was so still that she was distracted momentarily by a floating skeletal torso that bounced listlessly against the jetty and spun away. Her eyes focused back upon him as he stepped forward.

The moment Sargatanas was ankle deep in the Acheron he cried out, and the sound was like a hammer to Lilith's heart. Heard above the sounds of river and city alike, it was prolonged and raw and anguished, a disharmonic cry as from the torn throats of a lost multitude. Why was he doing this? What could this possibly answer for him?

She watched as he moved slowly, painfully, out into the water, which had begun to steam and bubble violently around him. From her distance she could just see that his body was changing, at first slowly and then with gathering rapidity. His wings grew broad and full, spreading into wide petal-shapes, finned membranes, or abstract forms held together with traceries of glyphs. His trunk and legs and arms grew luminous, expanding and contracting with an array of plates, fins, spines, and horns, some of which reached for yards around him. And all the while his head blazed like the brightest of torches, with only the shadowy suggestions visible of the changes that were taking place.

Lilith moved toward the gate. Part of her wanted to go to him, to drag him from the Acheron and its pain. She realized that this must be some ritual, some form of penance, perhaps; it was the only explanation. She placed her hand atop the unlatched, pitted gate, which whined noisily, immediately causing her to shrink down. Valefar had turned his head quickly, looking back and up toward the freely swinging gate. Did he sense her? She was hopeful that the sound's origin would seem obvious and sure that he had not seen her, but that did not keep her heart from fluttering.

She was, she knew, in serious jeopardy of being caught, and she had no idea what her punishment might be, if any, for witnessing this rite. Carefully, soundlessly, she backed away from the gate and the river's edge, reluctant to leave yet fearful to stay, and retreated into the fog and anonymity of the Rule.

Hours later, after the steady climb back up the central mount, she arrived, tired and unfulfilled, at the building that housed her chambers. What had she seen? She now had more questions than answers about Sargatanas. For the moment there was no one who could answer them. But she was confident that would change in time.

Pulling off her skins and letting them lie where they fell, Lilith climbed onto her pallet. The orange glow of sky-fire had reignited above central Adamantinarx, blossoming into a firestorm that pelted the window with tiny, tapping embers. Sweepers were already out in the courtyard below, their brooms whisking paths through the ash. The repetitive sounds lulled her tired mind, blurring the line between reality and dream. Had she really gone down to the river's edge or had she only been lying in bed? The last image that floated through her enervated mind was of Sargatanas, his glowing body changing, changing.

XVIII

ADAMANTINARX-UPON-THE-ACHERON

Eligor watched the long, curving ramp from the main doorway of the palace. From this distance he could see that most of the traffic was heading toward him and the flow of demons continued unabated as it passed him and continued into the palace. The victory on the border was drawing the disaffected from the four corners of Hell, and they had been gathering for weeks. But it was still a small number considering the numbers of the Fallen. *They are coming to him, now that he has returned from a great victory. But, for now, most remain guarded and are only sending their emissaries. It will take more than one success on the battlefield before they come themselves,* Eligor thought. *Will they leave just as eagerly if he suffers a defeat?*

Palanquins and beasts, caparisoned in heavy, ornamented blankets and elaborate trappings, all stopped at the foot of the palace stairs, where each ambassador dismounted, each having finally received some form of invitation. Escorted by Zoray's handpicked guards and

accompanied by flabella-bearers and stooped lower
demons bearing gifts, they climbed the many stairs and
entered the palace, where they were met by Sargatanas'
trusted aides, his corps of junior ministers. Passing him
with nods, Eligor noted that many were frequently seen
faces and these were greeted with solemn familiarity
while others, the newcomers, were met with all the official ceremony of court.

After a while, he grew restless and left his own Honor
Guard at the door and headed in among the ambassadors.
They were as dissimilar a collection of demons as he had
ever seen. Most were Demons Minor with enough of the
fallen angel about them as to be unremarkable. But others
had adopted the conventions of their lands or their lords,
bearing bizarre forms and countenances that he sometimes felt were borne solely for effect. Great coronets of
horn or torso spines corkscrewed into baroque patterns,
or eye-dotted flesh, trimmed and draped like layered
scales, adorned them, as did prideful and intricate reticu-
lations of embers that sizzled as he passed. He saw some
from the Lowlands who, used to the colder tempera-
tures, were wrapped in thick layers of soul-skins and
others from the craggy Uplands who favored multiple
winglets and featherlight membranes. Those demons
whose wards incorporated the Wastes saw fit to integrate
some of the fierce, visual decorations of the Salamandrine Men, combining spiky webs of incomprehensible,
glowing marks with piercings of bones from Abyssals
and sigils that hovered, slithering like worms, inches
from their bodies. Eligor heard their many dialects and
understood most; his talent for tongues was something
for which Sargatanas valued him, he knew, but now it
simply made his head hurt.

Feeling crowded in by the noisy, milling mass of
demons, he made his way to Valefar's side. The Prime
Minister was deep in quiet conversation with Lord Furcas, one of the few regents who had journeyed, himself,

to Adamantinarx. He was a stocky Demon Major, very plain in his appearance, with only a few modest hornlets and a round face bearing seven cobalt eyes of differing sizes. He made animated gestures with his hands as he spoke, gestures that reminded Eligor of the arcing flight of the Waste dart. It seemed, to Eligor, who could not hear what was being said, an almost ridiculous pantomime, but Valefar watched intently as Furcas finished his conversation. Eligor bowed to them and turned away to speak with his entourage. Distant trumpets sounded a signal causing heads to turn, and both demons fell into the current of the crowd as it began to move toward the arcades and the Audience Chamber beyond. Respecting Valefar's silence, Eligor did not speak; the Prime Minister was clearly deep in thought.

And he remained so as the demons assembled in the immense chamber. Eligor took his position at the base of the giant pyramidal dais and looked out at the fervent expressions of the hundreds of ambassadors who had journeyed across Hell to proffer allegiance to his lord. Most had never been to Adamantinarx and seen for themselves the fabled domed palace; they would surely bring impressive tales back to their lords. High above the ambassadors' heads, above their own multicolored sigils, floated Sargatanas' Great Seal, larger than Eligor had ever seen it and casting a livid light upon them.

Eligor glanced around and up at Sargatanas, whose form, now alight with fire, flickered with intensity. He had not seen Sargatanas in a week and smiled inwardly; his lord was a fiery creature of destiny now, a force that could not be stopped by anything short of his complete destruction. He stepped to the edge of the dais and spoke in the old language, the forbidden language. Its mellifluous tones echoed throughout the chamber, causing a stir among the gathered demons.

"What is it that keeps us here? Is it our love of this place and its hospitable clime? Is it because our cities are luminous and golden and the air within them fragrant and cool? Or is it our love of its benign and forgiving ruler and its fair and just governance? Are we here because we are all truly evil or were some of us misled and misdirected, carried away on the scalding winds of rhetoric? Are we not still creatures beholden to the Throne, no matter how far we have strayed from it?" Sargatanas paused. "Or is it, perhaps, our damaged pride that keeps us filled with shame and bound to this place? Are we truly condemned to stay here, resigned to our fate, never to see the Above again? Should we never attempt to go back?

"So many questions. But Lords, Ambassadors, you would not be standing here before me if the answers were not clear. You would never have made the difficult journey to Adamantinarx had you not seen the truth. It is time for sorrow to become hope and hope to become action. It is time for you to reach up out of the charred flesh and the smoldering cinders to join me."

Eligor saw the nearly immediate effect the words had on those assembled. He heard the growing murmur of assent and saw the rippling, outward-spreading wave of demons as they began to kneel. Above their heads their many glittering sigils began to disarticulate, sending attenuated tendrils of glyphs up toward Sargatanas' Great Seal. There they embraced, intertwining like luminous tentacles until they rearranged themselves into a cohesive whole. The enormous, flat seal was now surrounded by an incomplete globe of delicate symbols, and Eligor realized that his master, ever looking to the future, was waiting to fill in the spaces with more allies' sigils. Elisor looked back at the crowd, from bowed head to bowed head, and wondered if each of them bore the same thought: *Will I walk, once again, through the cities of the Above? Will I look again upon the Throne?* He suddenly remembered a moment long, long ago when another charismatic figure had stood before him and a

similar, disaffected crowd and entreated them to join
him and take up arms. Would this rebellion share the
same outcome? Was Faraii, for all his bitterness, right?
Of one thing Eligor was certain: Sargatanas was correct; there were many questions.

The greeting of each ambassador or rare lord took
many long hours, with Sargatanas, seated upon his
throne, patiently according each his due respect. Andromalius and Bifrons, already staunch allies, joined Eligor
and a contingent of his Guard behind the throne while
Valefar stood at his lord's side, amiably making intro-
ductions, identifying each demon's native land and
highlighting the outstanding qualities of each. Eligor
was, to start, watchful and interested but found his concentration flagging after the first hundred or so demons
had passed; then only the most important of the new
clients received his full attention.

"Lord Malpas has, for these long eons, studied the art
of siegecraft, my lord," Valefar said, intruding on Eligor's
thoughts. "He was instrumental in aiding Architect General Mulciber when many of the palaces were first
built—including Prince Beelzebub and Lucifer's empty
fortress. He knows their strongpoints and their funda-
mental weaknesses. Of course much has been added to
them since then . . . but still."

"Malpas, thanks to you for joining me," Sargatanas
said. "Your knowledge and your forty legions will, I am
sure, prove invaluable."

Malpas bowed so low that his long, thick beak scraped
the floor audibly.

An hour later Eligor saw an especially ornate Demon
Major stand before them, his floor-length robes alive
with dozens of souls flattened and picked for their un-
flawed pelts, each dyed, delicately stitched together, and
highlighted with golden thread and embellished with
rolling, precious stone eyes. In all, Eligor thought, a
masterpiece of foreign craftsmanship.

Valefar, too, seemed taken with the figure, smiling and nodding openly.

"This, my lord, is the honored Lord Yen Wang of the distant Eastern Wards, who brings with him the swift and powerful Legions of Behemoths. Even as we speak, the terrible creatures are being stabled in some of the abandoned storehouses along the far shore of the Acheron. Well, I might add, away from the city."

Sargatanas' eyebrows rose. "I have heard much about you and your legendary Behemoths, Yen Wang, but have never set eyes upon them myself. I would like very much to visit my new stables with you at my side. I am sure there is much for me to learn about them. Thanks to you for bringing them so far."

Yen Wang's scarred face creased in an earnest attempt at a smile. "My pleasure, Lord," he said in an oddly accented voice. "I am most proud of them and would be only too honored to offer my insights. As well as," he added with a bow, "my generalship."

"I would have them both willingly," said Sargatanas with a nod.

Eventually, Eligor saw the crowd growing thinner. Dwindling like the fading light from the oculus, those demons who had passed before his lord descended and exited the chamber. What had started as a flood of dignitaries became a trickle until only a mere handful awaited introduction. Off to either side of the throne a moundlike, glittering collection of gifts lay arrayed, some items that Eligor recognized when he had seen their bearers arriving. Life-size gold statues of demon generals from ages past stood next to giant urns filled with the precious stones found in distant mountain mines. Beautifully crafted spears and axes fashioned from brilliant minerals and metals by local Waste artisans lay piled in neat arrangements atop fine rugs, tapestries, and carefully worked Abyssal pelts. In all, it was a fabulous tribute, but Eligor knew that, apart from its symbolic nature, it was of little value to Sargatanas.

Lord Furcas was the last to approach the throne, and far from being unhappy at his position in the queue, he seemed expansive and even eager. As he stopped before Sargatanas, Valefar, who seemed tired of court pretenses, relaxed and stepped forward to clasp hands with the portly Demon Major.

"My lord," the Prime Minister said, "Lord Furcas of the high montane wards of Faragito Coraxo has amiably agreed to wait to be presented last, because he has brought us a most unique contribution that requires some demonstration. I had a chance to discuss this but briefly with his lordship, and he and I feel certain that you will be intrigued by his discoveries. Among his other qualities Lord Furcas is a Pyromancer Exalted. Lord Furcas."

Furcas knelt heavily, bowed his head, and rose upon a signal from Sargatanas.

"Ages ago, my lords, I spent much time wandering the Salbrox Mountains of my home-wards. To most, I am sure, it seemed that my solitary journeys were no more than the meanderings of an eccentric demon." Furcas paused as his silver eyes looked inward at the memories of his travels. "But I was actually prospecting, searching out the resources that I needed to make my armies strong—stronger than my neighbors'. For millennia I found nothing but the most common minerals, and because of that I suffered the kinds of defeats that gradually diminished my realm. And then one day I was sitting by a seething mountain cleft and looked down to see a small Abyssal carrying a crystal that flickered like solid fire in its armored mouth. I followed it and found an entire nest made of the rocks. I wrested one away from the creature but dropped it immediately—its heat was so tremendous. So I caught and skinned the Abyssal and carried the mineral home in its scaly skin.

After many years I unlocked its stubborn secret, extracted its essential energy, and with the addition of a few crafted glyphs I learned to control and shape the mineral. It is solid fire, my lord."

Furcas raised his clawed hands, holding them apart and at Sargatanas' eye level. A tiny mote of the glowing mineral danced upon Furcas' palm. With a glance toward Valefar he murmured a few words, and almost immediately an orange, artery-thin line began to glow between his bony palms. Thin, hairlike geysers of fire sprang forth from within the demon until his entire dark body was alight with a shimmering corona of thin fire. He then spread his hands farther apart and the straight, thickening line grew until it was twice his arm's length. A tapered, pyramidal tip appeared at one end, sharp as a fang and white-hot. He grasped the newly formed javelin in a glove of glyphs, tightly conjured to negate the insufferable heat.

"I need a target for my malpirg," said Furcas plainly, holding up the fiery javelin.

"Eligor, have your Guard place one of those upon the floor below," Sargatanas said, indicating one of the golden statuary generals he had been given. "I am sure old Field Marshal Kethias would be flattered to be used in this way."

Moments later three flying demons were, on the instructions of Furcas, positioning the life-size statue far out on the polished floor—farther, Eligor thought, than was reasonable. He looked dubiously at the portly demon who watched, confidently hefting the incandescent shaft.

Sargatanas stood and moved to Furcas' side. The short Pyromancer took a moment to gauge his throw, and with a graceful gesture that belied his bulk he pulled his arm back and cast the malpirg far up and out into the air of the dome. At the top of its arc he uttered a word and the malpirg split in two, each gaining momentum as they fell until they appeared as long glowing lines. Both hit the statue squarely in the chest, erupting in a spectacular, smoky shower of molten gold.

"This I have taught my troops," said Furcas. "I have ten legions of malpirgim ready to serve you."

A great drifting cloud of smoke retreated and Eligor saw his master's faint smile as he viewed the shattered and bubbling statue.

"Excellent, Furcas, excellent," Sargatanas said quietly. "You bring me a great gift and in return you shall ride by my side in the next engagement, commanding those same ten legions."

"Thank you, my lord." With that Furcas bowed deeply, his pleasure obvious.

"Lord, someone is moving out there in the smoke," said Eligor abruptly. His keen eyes had picked up a pale shape moving toward them. Immediately the Flying Guard rose, as one, into the air, their lances poised and ready.

"No one was left to be announced, my lord. The chamber should be empty," Valefar said quietly.

The Guard closed rapidly upon the approaching figure.

"Stay their hands, Eligor! No matter who this is, I am reasonably sure we can handle him," said Sargatanas drily.

The figure seemed to grow from the white smoke itself, becoming more solid and distinct as the clouds dissipated. Clad in pale skins, hood drawn up, it looked like little more than a common traveler.

"So *this* is my reward for my patience!" the figure said, its husky voice carrying easily. Eligor could not be sure, but he thought he recognized her accent, for surely it was a female beneath the swaths of Abyssal skin. Just as she climbed the last few steps of the pyramid and dropped her hood he remembered. Shaking out her thick, white hair, Lilith looked up at them and smiled. She dropped the skins in a twitching pile at her splayed feet. "I thought I would melt away wearing these for so long indoors."

Lilith stepped away from the robes and stood before them pale as bone. Clad simply, she exuded that same mixture of fragility and power, eroticism and fierceness, that Eligor had felt the first time he met her.

Sargatanas knelt, followed by the other demons around him. "Consort Lilith—" he began.

"Consort no longer, my lord," Lilith corrected, the words tinged with the barest trace of triumph. "Rise, Sargatanas. I no longer hold any position of rank in Hell. My being here should tell you that."

"Lilith," the Demon Major said, once more standing. The others around him rose and, with bows, began to descend the flight of steps and cross the broad floor. "I did not think you were ready yet to be out and about in Adamantinarx. When Valefar told me of your arrival I expected that you would want to remain hidden until the unrest with Dis was resolved."

"True It does not yet know of my whereabouts, though It probably suspects the truth. If I may say, there is no point to my remaining in hiding, my lord. Your power and your disregard for Beelzebub's orders have made your case plain enough to Dis; the Fly's regard for you is already deeply questionable—"

"And will surely become more so when he discovers that you, his Consort, are residing within this city's walls."

"Would you have me return, then? To Dis?"

"No, my lady, never. But I will have to impose serious, personal safeguards upon you."

"Thank you, my lord."

Eligor's eye met Valefar's; the Captain of the Flying Guard had lingered as much from the lack of his lord's orders as from his own fascination with Lilith. But now, with a meaningful nod from Valefar, Eligor turned and followed the Prime Minster as he began to descend the stairs. Valefar stooped and picked up Lilith's skins, folding them as he walked. Minutes later, at the entrance to the arcades, Eligor turned back and saw the two distant figures deep in conversation.

Lilith watched Sargatanas walk to the edge of the dais and sit down upon the pyramid's top step. His smoldering dark form contrasted sharply with the pale stones, the many ebon and red folds of his robes fanning out behind him. He seemed weary, cocking his head slightly as he looked at the distant, melted statue.

"Very impressive, that," said Lilith.

"Yes," the demon said diffidently after a pause. "Just another tool for me to use against your former lord when the need arises. Please," he said, beckoning Lilith to sit next to him. She sat and delicately arranged the folds of her long, sheathlike skirt.

Sargatanas turned away from the darkening chamber and looked at her for a moment without saying anything, studying her small movements. His carefully composed court face was expressionless, but Lilith thought she saw, implicit beneath the slowly sliding plates a mixture of emotions. *Is it melancholia?* As they regarded each other she saw his expression change, saw the plates cease moving, the tight set of his jaw lighten.

"So why *did* you leave Dis?" he said. "And then come here?"

Lilith looked away and for an instant she imagined that her vision cut through the palace's stone walls, darting across the umber landscape all the way back to the Keep and her abandoned chambers. It was so odd that she would never see them again; she had spent so long within its confines. So long a prisoner.

"It's actually very simple, my lord. . . . I cannot be . . . owned. It is how I was made."

"Cannot . . . or will not?"

"Both." The word hung in the air. "When Lucifer

passed on his scepter to Beelzebub, when I became a bargaining chip in the transaction between them, I felt hurt, disgusted, outraged. But after all those millennia with that thing, I felt scooped out, bereft of my . . . self. The Fly took away nearly everything that I was. That is Its way. And then, after so very long, the tiny part of me that I kept locked away . . . the part that could imagine the Light . . . saw a possible way: the souls. If I could give them hope and nurture it, then maybe they could become themselves again and by weight of numbers overthrow the Fly. Perhaps it was naive, but I secretly began to send out my little statues, sowing them among the damned. They became my surrogates for freedom and salvation . . . and revenge."

He nodded gravely. "That answers why. But not what made you come here."

"I . . . suffered a great loss." She paused. There would be a time to tell him about Ardat, about just how much she meant to her, but not now. "My lord, do you know what the demons in Dis call Adamantinarx? With slitted eyes and filled with hate they call it the 'City That Fell from Heaven.' Everyone there knows what it represents . . . that it is the best that one can find in Hell. Everyone, too, knows of its lord and how he rules that city."

Lilith knew well the other reason she had chosen Adamantinarx, knew that she could not yet tell him that she had seen in his infrequent visits to Dis something in him that had reminded her of another demon—her lost lord. Sargatanas bore many of the same irresistible qualities that had made Lucifer the force he was: the ambition, the idealism, the ferocity. And now she had seen yet another similar side, the self-flagellating remorse.

"From what I have heard," he rumbled, "they spit after they utter that. And not just because they say the word 'Heaven.' Everyone may know of Adamantinarx, but not everyone wants it to exist."

"True, but I do. And I would call it home. I can never see Heaven; this is as close as I can come."

"And just how did you make your journey? Valefar never told me."

"Anonymously, alone, and upon the back of a beast. Prime Minister Agares had a hand in it. He is a strange one, my lord. On the surface dutiful, but beneath he is in great turmoil, I think. Were I the Fly I would not put too much trust in his allegiances."

"Interesting. I cannot imagine being in proximity to the Fly each and every day and *not* being a willing vassal. It would destroy a lesser demon. Well, Lilith," Sargatanas said, extending his hand, "you are welcome in the City That Fell from Heaven and as long as you stay here I will protect you with my last phalangite if need be."

Lilith put her hand—so white and small compared to his—upon his upturned palm, feeling the heat of it spreading. She shuddered as an unfamiliar sensation spread throughout her, a clawing away of the fear and misery that was such a large part of her being. Trapped beneath the millennia-deep sediment of her torment and resentment lay a pearlescent sealed casket and, within it, that imagined, barely fluttering self that Lilith knew had been deeply buried since she had arrived.

She looked down, shaking her head slightly.

"What is it?" Sargatanas asked softly.

"I . . . I feel as if I am either dreaming or awakening."

The demon lord rose and, still cupping her hand in his, drew her up.

"It cannot be a dream, Lilith. *My* dreams are never this . . . engaging."

Lilith smiled, closed her eyes for a moment, and felt as if her soul, like a flock of winged night-silvers, had risen, released at last, from within that now-open box.

XIX

DIS

The Keep was more silent than Adramalik had ever remembered it. What few functionaries he saw in its corridors and rooms bore the unmistakable mark of terror upon their faces. Tales were beginning to filter up from its base, tales of what had happened out in the city's Sixtieth Ward after the Prince had finally resigned himself to the fact that his Consort was no longer in Dis. What Adramalik heard made even him shudder.

He had been present when the Prince had finally come to the dark conclusion that Lilith was gone. Adramalik and Agares and a few other principals had, at first, stood rooted to the floor with mouths agape when Beelzebub's howling rage had manifested itself. Tiny flies, growing in size, had peeled away from his body in a seemingly unending, rising spiral, horrific to behold. And their faces, faces that he knew to have once belonged to angels, were pocked and distorted, torn and twisted, sublime in their madness. Each bloated fly was different from its brother, but each bore many limbs that ended in black blades that snapped and cut the air as the creatures, enlarging as they flew, jostled toward the Rotunda's openings and flooded forth into the dark skies of Dis. Relief spread through Adramalik's shaking body as he watched them depart; for a moment he had actually wondered if Beelzebub's rage might spill over onto him and Agares and indeed everyone in the Keep. But in a few short minutes the small gathering was standing alone in the quiet Rotunda, left wide-eyed and trembling, watching the frantic swaying of the skins above. Adramalik could not remember when his master had left the Keep last.

Even now he could hear, in the fearful silence that smothered the Keep, the echo of the whir of their wings and the sound their clattering bodies made, and a part of him held his breath in awe.

A day later, after the Prince had resumed his throne, someone had ventured into the Sixtieth Ward and come back to the Keep with a tale of what he had seen there. It was a large precinct, but, even so, nothing had been spared. Souls, demons, buildings, even the very streets had been shredded, chopped, and ultimately defiled. Squashed hummocks of body parts stood in the plazas, misshapen islands in expanding lakes of blood. The stench of tens of thousands of rotting, half-consumed bodies, of buildings chewed and vomited up and stinking feces from the ensuing feast, had been overpowering even by hellish standards. And over the entire ward a fog of blood hung so thick that it made the carnage all the worse for its gradually revealed butcheries. The fog blanketed the ward for a few days and then it moved, by either command or the caprices of the infernal zephyrs, off toward the Wastes to ultimately descend, he had heard, upon Adamantinarx. Adramalik did not agree with those who rationalized it as a natural event; he knew his Prince too well and knew that he had every reason to suspect where his Consort had fled to. The fog was a warning. *But,* Adramalik pondered, *how had she so easily managed to leave Dis unseen and unquestioned?* This was something he needed to find out.

Now keeping to himself, alternately pacing and sitting at his desk in his chambers, he felt no sense of comfort, even surrounded as he was by his loyal Knights. They, too, knew that venturing forth might provoke the dark figure who sat so nearby upon his charnel throne,

wrapped in black hatred and paranoia. It was a time to
measure one's appearances, a time to be careful.

ADAMANTINARX-UPON-THE-ACHERON

Lilith entered the arcade and passed a dozen ambassadors as they exited the main chamber. She was becoming a regular visitor, and none of the guards she
stepped past challenged or even questioned her. Her
freedom, a balm to her, was that complete.

Counter to her fears, her sense of awakening had not,
in any way, diminished as she shared more and more
time with Sargatanas. When he wasn't holding councils
with Valefar and Eligor and the others he would walk
the streets of Adamantinarx with her, and gradually she
came to realize that they were both enjoying and looking forward to their meetings. Frequently their conversations centered upon the souls, and her philosophies of
tolerance toward them, and Sargatanas, to her delight,
seemed receptive. She saw him for short periods only,
as he was consumed with the affairs of his great city, but
the encounters were growing pleasantly, uncharacteristically, relaxed. The huge demon's tone was less tense,
less filled with the edge of pain that she remembered
from so long ago, which was even more exceptional
given the imminence of conflict that loomed over the
city. She had to attribute it to her presence, a fact that
made her smile when she was back in her chambers.

Lilith entered the Audience Chamber and saw that it
was suffused with a light miasma of smoke that hung
like a gently shifting veil softening the finger of ruddy
light that dropped from above. A flock of silver-black
Abyssals circled the inner dome on distance-muffled
wings, disappearing in its shadows, briefly glittering in
the light like coins thrown into the air. Looking toward

the throne, she saw Sargatanas seated and flanked by Valefar and some ambassadors, and she felt more protected than she would have ever imagined before. She had to admit that, despite her independent inner self, she liked the feeling.

Arriving at the pyramid's foot, she waited as Sargatanas disengaged himself and descended the long stairs and she wondered, not for the first time, where today's special destination, only hinted at by his messenger, would be. Just in case, she carried her traveling skins. The city's sights had been amazing: the mammoth, incandescent Forges, the vast artisans district, the seemingly endless Armory, the organized and efficient Abyssal husbandry pens. But while these had all been impressive locations, it was the enormous Library within the palace itself that sparked her imagination. She could not yet read the ornate script, but Sargatanas himself had promised to teach her and, most intriguingly, he had told her that there were a few rich texts that recounted life so long ago in the Above. These, she knew, would prey upon her imagination only until they yielded their contents. On a deeper level, she looked forward to her lessons not only for the knowledge gained but for the shared intimacy as well.

"You can leave those behind," Sargatanas said, indicating the draped skins that Lilith carried. "Eligor will have them brought back to your chambers."

"Are we staying in the palace, then?" she said, hoping for the first of her lessons.

"Actually, Lilith, we're going to be very close to where we stand at the moment."

"I am intrigued, my lord," she said, laying the garments down carefully, patting them unconsciously. It worried her only a little to leave them behind.

She and Sargatanas crossed the broad floor, wended their way through the forest of the arcade's pillars at its periphery, and exited into the great entry hall. Sargatanas led her through the crowd of functionaries that had stopped and knelt in place before their lord. He took her through a tall doorway, passing through a floating guard-glyph, and gradually Lilith became aware that they were slowly descending, corridor by corridor beneath the main floor. At each important juncture they passed through another glyph. Sargatanas led her in silence and as the many branching corridors grew darker and lessened to one, only the sounds of her clawed feet, his deep breathing, and the fires of his head broke the stillness.

Lilith did not care how long the walk through the labyrinthine halls took; it was another adventure with Sargatanas, whose proximity was becoming both reassuring and disturbingly necessary. The novelties of both feelings, the sheer improbability of them, were things she went over frequently and accepted willingly. She had been spiritually in exile for too long.

The corridor's ceiling rose, and before her she saw a doorway and a bench. Above the lintel was Sargatanas' seal wrought in flowing silver, inset into the purest white stone, and with a stab of realization Lilith knew that something secret and special lay behind the imposing door.

Sargatanas stopped just as he put his dark hand upon the door's latch. Lilith watched him pause and counted her heartbeats while he looked down at the flagstones. Some inner conflict was at work upon him, and she thought to reassure him that he did not have to show her what lay beyond. But she said nothing.

The dull thunk of the latch was loud in the otherwise tomblike silence.

A vestibule just behind the door opening led into a much brighter room beyond, and Sargatanas looked up at her, his glittering eyes intense as he carefully watched her expression. He said nothing, but somehow she knew that he wanted her to enter first, and, moving slowly, she stepped past him and over the threshold.

Into Heaven.

As she walked forward Lilith brushed her fingers unconsciously along the wall's lines of incised script, her wide eyes fixed on the lambent room so unlike anyplace else in all of Hell.

She moved from statue to frieze to mosaic as if she were dreaming, slowly, and with the feeling that she was not within herself. Occasionally, like someone who had been blind for all her existence, she would reach out and, with a delicate finger that rivaled the paleness of the stones around her, lightly trace it across the carved, perfect face of some seraph or up the smooth side of a golden spire or over the jeweled streams that flowed throughout the cities and fields.

As she made her way around the room she grew more and more exhilarated, reaching a point of near breathlessness in her eagerness to drink it all in. Sargatanas quietly whispered a running commentary and Lilith attentively listened to every word. She could not understand all of their meanings, but most served to heighten her sense of wonderment. The hosts gathered before her and she could nearly hear their silver voices raised in praise of their Throne's manifold glories. Strange tears of joy, of unfamiliar exultation, rolled down her cheeks and she felt weak and light-headed. Once, she stumbled and nearly fell, but a strong, dark hand caught her.

When she reached the final frieze the Radiance she saw reflected there, the sheer majesty and beauty of it, overwhelmed her almost as much as her hatred for it, and the room spun before her tear-filled eyes and went dark and she collapsed. She felt Sargatanas scoop her up and place her gently upon a central bier, an unadorned stone platform she was sure he used in some private ceremony.

This is where he is from. This is where he yearns to go back, she thought, staring up at the shimmering opal ceiling. And then a coldness gripped her. *This is where I can never go. Nor would I want to.* A clawing sadness like none that she had known, not even when Ardat Lili had not come back, washed powerfully through Lilith, replacing the fragile, newborn joy she had felt. *I must not let him see this.*

But it was too late. Sargatanas leaned concernedly over her, and, like smoke dissipating, she saw him for the first time for what he had been. Perhaps it was the influence of the images she had just seen or how he wanted her to see him, but looking in his eyes she saw the seraph. Not even with Lucifer had she been so sure of anyone's inner self. *There is so much pain and longing in those eyes.*

Sargatanas lifted her upright and, hesitating for a moment, ran two fingers through her hair.

Sargatanas paused and Lilith realized that, from that moment on, she would not be able to look at him without seeing that true, angelic core, no matter how awful he made himself.

"Lilith, until you came to Adamantinarx, this . . . this place was my heart."

She could not avoid looking into the glowing hole in his chest as he spoke and realized for the first time what it must mean for there to be nothing within. The loss must have been nearly impossible to bear.

"Don't," he said quietly, wiping away the tears that again welled from her eyes. "Your being here fills both places," he said, indicating the room and then his chest.

Lilith smiled through the curtain of tears and realized that she, too, felt a sense of completion. She swung her legs off the bier and stood shakily.

"Now," she said, pulling him slowly at first toward the vestibule, "tell me again, from the beginning. About Heaven."

THE FIELDS OF ADAMANTINARX–UPON–THE–ACHERON

The hot wind, hotter than any desert wind he had ever known, blew across the plain, burning his unprotected face, unnoticed. Standing upon a hillock, his back to the Acheron and the city beyond, Hannibal surveyed the massed troops—his troops—and felt drained. It seemed hopeless. The exuberance that had been building steadily within him as he had assembled his army was dissipating just as quickly as he began to realize what it would take to get them battle ready.

What was I thinking? Adamantinarx is not Qart Hadasht; its buildings are still made of souls! And I cannot have the pick of the finest mercenaries money can buy. I have these *instead.*

Twenty thousand souls stood upon the field's gray skin, the fruits of his recruitment, an army that even the term "ragtag" would elevate. Hannibal had never anticipated the problems that would arise in trying to form units when no two souls shared any apparent strengths. He had been forced to make his officers break down individuals into categories. Those whose arms were dominant or even possessed two were either handed weapons or, more often, adapted to bear them by demons specially attached to Hannibal's retinue by Sargatanas. But those adaptations were rarely completely successful.

Mago and he had been lucky in finding souls with any significant military background, and those they appointed as officers. Upon his order, he watched them begin to train the souls, and shortly he turned away from

the scene, chin down in disgust. It really was hopeless.
But other challenges had seemed hopeless before. And
he had prevailed. He turned back, and this time his keen
eyes studied the figures below, appraising and quantify-
ing them. Slowly, as he shifted his gaze from cohorts of
swordsmen to spear-bearers to mace-wielders, patterns
of movement began to appear and he saw the glimmer of
possibility emerge. It would be hard, but he would not
give up and melt away into the crowds of the city he had
sworn allegiance to. He would see it through if for nothing less than his oath to Sargatanas. Or wind up a brick,
trying.

XX

DIS

Algol rose and set seven times before Adramalik was
summoned by his Prince to join him in Moloch's tower.
He welcomed the climb to the Keep's highest point. Not
only did it finally release him from his prudent, self-
imposed exile, but it also seemed to signify that the
cloud of suspicion was lifting. He pulled closed his door
and negotiated the many twisting corridors to the foot
of the tower. The base was a hundred feet wide and
buried within the mantle of flesh that lay atop the Keep.
Only the uppermost portion of the tower protruded,
phalluslike, through the heavy tissue, but what rose free
into the sky provided the greatest unobstructed view of
Dis possible. It was a clear sign of exalted rank, a token
of Beelzebub's admiration. Whereas Agares' smaller

tower was a carefully designed piece of architecture, a dark parody of the Above's buildings, Moloch's tower was a brutal spike bearing no friezes or adornments and windows only at the very top. Adramalik thought it almost primitive by Dis' standards, a direct correlate to how he viewed Moloch. But what it lacked in refinement it made up for in sheer arrogant height. Looking up, Adramalik saw the stairs that hugged the tower's tall, tubular interior ascending hundreds of feet above and lit at uncomfortably long intervals by small, inadequate braziers. Normally, annoyed, he would conjure a glyph of light and begin his ascent with an oath, but newly freed, he took the rough steps lightly, ignoring his feelings toward the Grand General who resided at the tower's top. Still, Adramalik was in no particular hurry, savoring his freedom, and decided to take the steps rather than fly; in rare moments of blunt honesty he admitted to himself that he found Moloch difficult to predict, intimidating, another reason not to hurry. After the battle at Maraak, he was in no mood to be called to task by the general.

It had taken some getting used to, Adramalik admitted as he began to climb. The consuming of farmed or hunted Abyssals was the only real choice in the demons' new, dark homeland; their spare flesh was uncompromisingly bitter next to the memory of repasts in the Above, but eventually he, like the others, had grown grudgingly used to it. A few, however, had, from the first day, committed themselves to another more repugnant alternative—the eating of souls, a practice that former angels, no matter how angry, could never truly condone. Moloch, Adramalik knew, felt no such compunction, and that he found revolting. Too many times had he entered the general's chambers to watch him dining upon some flailing soul. So as not to be distracted, Adramalik would focus not upon the hungry general but, instead, upon the pooling blood, collecting in and oozing through the twin runnels that fed into identical troughs in the room's center.

Arriving at the tower's uppermost threshold, Adramalik opened the heavy door and was gratified to see the general already in discussion with the Prince, the joints of his recent meal tossed, trembling, in a corner while three more terrified fat souls crouched, waiting, in the shadows of the far wall. The dank smell of blood filled his nose-hole. Moloch, still licking his lips, lifted his head and fixed his many ice-blue eyes on the Chancellor General. He had to make an effort to keep the disgust from his face.

The pair was standing before one of the three wide, paneless windows that afforded the grandest unobstructed view of Dis in all of the city. As he approached, they grew silent, and the three demons stood for a moment, taking in the vastness of the world they had shaped. A sharp lightning-glyph dropped noisily from the clouds, licking the distant streets like a beast's tongue. They all saw the fragments of buildings that it had exploded rain down slowly upon the distant, narrow streets.

Adramalik waited. Beelzebub seemed in one of those contemplative moods that he knew better than to interrupt. "Adramalik, have you ever stood on the edge of Abaddon's Pit?" he asked finally with a buzzing intake of breath.

"Once, my Prince. And it was enough." Even though it had been eons ago, Adramalik remembered the overwhelming stench and the nearly irresistible inward-rushing air that had threatened to pull him into the seemingly bottomless gorge. And the fear he had never known he could feel.

"Then you have an idea what it might mean for a demon to be destroyed and be brought down there. As one of *his* Horde."

"Yes." It was Hell's hell and Abaddon was its legendary regent. Adramalik had frequently thought about the loathsome souls and the way they spent eternity. It was almost enviable to lie where you were destroyed, no matter what your condition was, aware, it was true, but not corrupted into something so far from an angel as to be unrecognizable.

"We will send him there."

"Who, my Prince?"

"Adramalik," the Prince buzzed, "I have given the order for General Moloch to begin amassing an army from the primary wards of Dis. It is my intention to rid Hell of Lord Sargatanas."

The words hung in the air, their implications powerful. This was not going to be any ordinary petty border contest for territory, thought Adramalik. No, this was revenge against a powerful Demon Major. This was to be a war of scope and breadth, a war not only to recover the Prince's Consort but also to send a message to the other Demons Major: the Crown of Hell would not tolerate disobedience.

It was a thrilling moment, Adramalik realized, one that he felt so privileged to witness that he could barely repress a savage grin. This simple order would herald a new reign of terror followed by a new era of stricter vassalage that would right some of the profound wrongs that had been steadily eroding Beelzebub's influence.

"All to the good and long overdue, my Prince," said Adramalik, believing every word.

"I knew that you would agree," the Prince said evenly. "Agaliarept has, over time, given me good reason to suspect that my Consort has fled to Adamantinarx. So far, I do not know how she managed this and with whose complicity, but I want your Knights to find her and bring her back to me. I do not care what condition she is in so long as she is still able to feel pain."

Adramalik nodded. His Knights would be grateful for the action and the opportunities, and he would personally supervise looking after Lilith when she was found.

"Chancellor General, what have your Knights uncovered in their . . . tireless investigation?"

Adramalik noted Moloch's face crease with derision as he looked away.

How we despise each other! Adramalik thought. *Just as it should be. He is* not *one of us no matter how much he tries. Once he voluntarily left the Above he stopped being one of us. A god, indeed!* He looked at the general, gauging him, and came, as he always did, to the same inevitable conclusion. With all of his upstart posturing Moloch was still so formidable that Adramalik was uncertain whether his Knights, together, could bring him down. The powers his worshipers had imbued him with were broad and potent. And even if Adramalik were to challenge the deposed god, Moloch was the Prince's champion and as such bore his unrelenting favor.

"My Knights managed to trace the Consort's movements to the Sixth Gate, but from there . . . nothing. Of course, this is really Lord Nergar's area of expertise. . . ."

Adramalik saw the Prince's head drop slightly. "Never mind, Adramalik. In truth, it does not matter. I have more than enough excuses to go to war with Sargatanas."

The general snorted with barely veiled contempt. Adramalik watched Moloch move away from the window and across the room, his surrogate legs carrying him in unnaturally long, gliding strides. He stopped before the twin troughs and without hesitating plunged his hands into them. The blood sizzled and steamed as he searched for and found two objects that he pulled out and held before him. Adramalik saw them and even he felt a ripple of fear; held aloft before him were two of the most feared weapons in Hell—*Puime-pe-Molocha,* Moloch's Hooks. Each bore ten vicious hooks, and even dripping blood as they were, Adramalik could see the fused-diamond inner edges, glistening and razor sharp, that no armor in Hell could withstand.

Moloch turned and looked straight at Adramalik, a

predatory gleam in his eyes. The threat was unambiguous. The Chancellor General met and held his gaze but, facing those Hooks, knew that his attempt to match the general's challenging mien was, at best, bravado. He was relieved when Beelzebub spoke.

"You are *both* to work together that we may be rid of him. Anything less and I will send you to give the Great Lord Abaddon my compliments personally."

Both demons nodded.

Strapping the steaming weapons to his braided soul-sinew belt, Moloch dropped down and knelt awkwardly before Beelzebub.

"My Prince, I must gather my lieutenants and their troops. There are legions to be Summoned, blades to be sharpened," he said, his voice flinty. "I would beg that I be allowed to begin at once."

"Go, Moloch, and stir the fires of the Summoning Fields. And bring me Sargatanas that I may wear him upon my chest!"

Moloch rose, swung around, and headed for the door, the Hooks swinging where his legs would have been. Without a backward glance he crossed the threshold and leaped from the uppermost landing into the yawning darkness of the tower's shaft.

A loud crack boomed through the chamber and drew the attention of Beelzebub and Adromalik back out into the ashen night. Another bolt of glyph-lightning, this time much closer, had smashed into the city, this one closer than the last. They could hear the faint dull cascading of the screaming chunks of buildings as they landed heavily upon their groaning neighbors.

"He is a weapon, Adramalik, my sharpest sword, little more," buzzed the Prince. His body was beginning to ripple and vibrate and flies were separating, heading for the open doorway. "You are my shield. It may seem as though I favor him, but it is you and your Knights that I truly need in this world."

"Thank you, my Prince," Adramalik said. It was a candid statement that he had never thought he would hear. Whether it was said merely to keep him loyal or to simply bolster him in the face of impending war he did not care. It was said and that was enough.

"Adramalik, find the Prime Minister and ask him what he remembers about Lilith's departure. I doubt that he knows anything, but any small clue might be important."

"Yes, my Prince." It would be amusing interrogating Agares. He was not the most imposing of demons.

"I have not yet decided to which of you I will award Sargatanas' wards afterward," the Prince said, only his rapidly disintegrating face remaining. "Be careful of Moloch, Chancellor General. He might well attempt to simplify my choices."

And then the few remaining flies spread apart and he was gone.

Adramalik looked around at Moloch's disagreeable chamber, thought for a moment about attempting to force the doors of the adjacent rooms, and realized the futility of it. Moloch's Arts were at least good enough to keep anyone out of them. He turned to leave and just as he reached the doorway he heard the three caged souls begin a raucous keening, clutching the bars and rattling them. Perhaps they thought he would release them. For a moment he actually toyed with the idea, relishing the anger it would elicit, but instead he closed the door, shaking his head with the pettiness of it. Or, he wondered, was it fear? For now, it did not matter; the thought of war made him open his wings, and he hurriedly dropped through the tower's darkness to tell the Order his news.

ADAMANTINARX-UPON-THE-ACHERON

"My lord, our spies have just this hour returned from Dis," Eligor said to Sargatanas upon entering the newly renovated warehouse. His lord and his bodyguard and their guides had not yet made their way through the small corridor that opened into the main stables. The pervasive salt smell of the Acheron, he noticed, was almost immediately overwhelmed, replaced by the powerful odd musk of the huge creatures he could just see in their high-walled stalls beyond. It had been no small feat getting them here. Before he had arrived, a special immense Conjuring Chamber, laced in lightning, had been constructed for Yen Wang and his Conjuror General, and it was never inactive until the dozens of his beasts had been brought forth.

Suddenly they heard loud snorts, which ended in strange, grumbling words unlike any Eligor had ever heard. Some unseen Behemoth was voicing its irritation, and soon each of them took voice, sharing their displeasure until the din in the front of the stables sent vibrations through the paved floor.

"And what have they discovered in the Fly's nest?" asked Sargatanas loudly as they walked into the open paddock. Almost as he spoke, the snorting subsided and the air was filled, instead, with the quieter sounds of the Behemoths' wheezing breathing and heavy shifting. Eligor wondered if the sound of his lord's voice had been, in some way, responsible for their sudden quiet.

"All traffic in and out of the city has been curtailed; Beelzebub wants none of what we have learned to get out. But we have been fortunate. The spies are unanimous in their reports that a great army is being summoned and gathered, and that it is marshaling just outside the walls of Dis. It is under the banner of Grand General Moloch, my lord." Eligor hoped he did not look as apprehensive as he felt.

Sargatanas did not break stride but looked gravely at his feet as he walked.

They began to pass the stalls that each held a single Behemoth, and Eligor, rather than trying to speak with his lord, examined them carefully. Each bay was constructed of elaborately carved Abyssal bone, brought on the conjured creatures' backs from the Eastern Wards and installed carefully within the foreign warehouse to make the Behemoths feel at home. Fresh slabs of yielding fatty flesh nailed to the stall sides protected them from inadvertent injury.

But as interesting as the exotic stalls were, Eligor found their inmates more so. He had found out just as much as the taciturn Yen Wang had been willing to divulge about them. In their Lives they had been great human emperors, viziers, and generals from a land known as Qin. There they had committed terrible acts upon their subjects, and so, because of their former power and ruthlessness, it had been seen fit to turn them into giant quadrupedal beasts of burden and war, at the constant disposal of their mahouts. Minus their toes and fingers, which had been removed to create flat hooflike feet, the thick-hided souls stood at least three times Sargatanas' height. Two large arms that terminated in enormous, heavy bone-hammers sprouted from their shoulders, and these, for the moment, were relaxed and resting upon the floor. Each weapon was the mass of two or three demons. Eligor's eyes took in their strange horn-crowned heads, their missing noses and upper jaws, their long, curving chinbones that served as weapon and ram, and he admitted to himself that he was eager to see them upon the battlefield. As he passed them their narrowed, suspicious eyes followed him and occasionally one would call out and laugh or mumble some indistinct utterance that the Captain was sure was an obscenity.

Sargatanas looked up occasionally but more often slowly stroked the restless bones of his jaw or pursed his hard lips in thought. Neither the foul odors of their dung and their musk nor the barks of their imagined insults seemed to affect him. Eligor knew that Sargatanas had been looking forward to visiting the stables and felt a pang that his message had been so ill timed to ruin the moment. Only when the party approached the last stall did Sargatanas look up at him.

"It would use Its greatest general to put an end to us. To this city and everything within it," the demon lord said, almost to himself. "It is sooner than I wanted; our legions have only just made camp. But that is, perhaps, the Fly's design. This battle was inevitable, Eligor. Make haste to Valefar and tell him this: He must gather our new allied Demons Major and Minor in council and have them brief their junior officers. Tell him that they must then begin the deployment of their legions immediately, as I will do with my own. And have Hannibal called back from his recruiting with whatever army he has managed to amass. The battle with Astaroth was but a skirmish compared to what we will face at the hands of Moloch and his legions."

"I understand, my lord," said Eligor grimly.

"I am finished here," Sargatanas said peremptorily to Yen Wang's guides. "Ask your lord to prepare the Behemoths for combat, as well. I may find it necessary to deploy them." Turning back to Eligor, he said, "I am returning to the palace immediately. If you need me I will be in the Conjuring Hall. There is an invocation that I must perfect."

"My lord." Eligor nodded and when he stepped out upon the street it was with a sense of urgency that he ascended to find Valefar.

The Prime Minister stood hunched over a table, his angular body backlit and red limned against the wide windows of his study. Before him lay an open coffer that had disgorged two dozen odd objects—found bits and pieces both natural and soul made—flotsam from the Wastes that the demon had collected on his last foray. Eligor knew that Valefar had a creative bent, that many of the assemblages that adorned his walls and those of his fellow demons were the product of days of consideration and labor. The pieces were deceptive in their simplicity, intentionally imperfect, even, some chided, deliberately obscure in their meaning. Eligor's chambers, like many palace dwellers', bore its own Valefar-crafted creation, which the Captain proudly showed to his visitors. It was a dark frieze composed of translucent layers of Abyssal scales and spiny plates, some of which still glowed or shone silver-black, and though Eligor readily admitted he did not understand its meaning, he did find it in some way evocative.

He crossed the chamber, noting the ever-present, ever-shifting drifts of documents, and waited patiently behind Valefar, not eager to break the demon's stream of thought. The low pulsing of the heart-clock, more felt than heard from the next room, measured the slow minutes.

"What is it, Eligor, that has your wings twitching even while you stand there?" he said finally without taking his eyes off the carefully arrayed items.

"It is war, my lord," said the demon, frowning at just how easily he was read.

Valefar shifted a bent splinter of Abyssal bone until it juxtaposed with a rippled piece of dry skin. The demon then fused them together with a word and stood back.

"Is it what Sargatanas wants?"

"So it would seem."

Valefar appeared to weigh the answer. Eligor saw him tilt his smoke-shrouded head, still apparently evaluating his work, and then with a curt nod to himself he swept aside the fragments, pushing them to the far edge of the table and clearing the surface. He turned and, without meeting Eligor's eyes, stood for a short period slowly taking in his surroundings, his smoky-silver eyes focusing on nothing in particular. He frowned and then proceeded to make his way through the organized jumble of vellums until he stood before a tall, open cabinet containing innumerable rolled manuscripts. Taking them down carefully in twos and threes, he began to empty the shelves until the bare wall was revealed behind. Once Valefar was finished, Eligor saw a nearly imperceptible line tracing a narrow, vertical rectangle almost his own height upon the age-dusted wall.

Valefar removed the shelves and, springing an unseen latch, opened the once-hidden door. More dust billowed forth, and Valefar pulled back, waiting until it had settled. When it had he reached into the dark compartment with both hands and withdrew a long, metal box that Eligor had seen only once, when Valefar had first appeared, so long ago, upon the crag that was to become the palace's home.

Solemnly, the Prime Minister carried the box to the cleared table, placing it, with apparent reverence, in the center. With head bowed, he whispered something that Eligor could not hear, and with a hiss and the angelic word *gemeganza* issuing from within, the box sprang open. Eligor's eyes grew wide as they lit upon an *ialpor napta*—one of the flaming swords of the War. *But all had been lost in the Fall!* he thought. *Yet one is here, in Hell!* He could not take his disbelieving eyes from the blade.

It lay, lightly, in its cushioned box, a thing so thin that it seemed little more than a memory of a sword. Shaped like a long, slim primary feather, it hardly seemed substantial enough to cut vellum. But he knew what the angry seraphim could do with such a blade; he shuddered when he remembered how many angels on both sides had fallen under such weapons.

Valefar slowly picked the sword off its gossamer-gold bed and held it aloft. A single ominous point of fire traveled from the hilt to the tip.

"Let me tell you a small story, Eligor," said Valefar, studying the blade. "It took place long ago, on another eve of war. But I can remember it as if it was two days ago. I sat upon a hill near the Tree basking in the Light and enjoying the rainbow-purple chalkadri as they swooped and played in the burnished azure sky, their calls echoing like glass pipes. The air was cloudless and crisp and smelled like . . . well, you remember. How I *miss* that air." Valefar paused, dropping the point of the sword only a little as his memory flew backward.

"Sargatanas came to me that brilliant afternoon, as I sat, and before he spoke I could feel the anger that seethed beneath the surface in him. It had been Lucifer's anger, but now it was his as well. I shared it, too, Eligor, as did you, but not with the fervor he did. Sargatanas' resentment was palpable. He stood next to me, just as you do now, and told me what had been said in the last meeting with Lucifer. And I felt myself growing sadder with each word. Not angry, not then, but unhappy knowing that nothing would be the same again once the War began. With his hand trembling upon his sword's hilt . . . for he wore it always at that point . . . he repeated Lucifer's unfortunate rhetoric. I asked him then, as I just asked you, if war was what he wanted. Just at that moment, just as he vehemently said, 'Yes!,' a young chalkad flew down, landed upon the ground, and paused, cocking its head as if listening to us. Sargatanas, blinded by his rage and frustration, drew his sword and, in a move as swift as a dark thought, cleaved the creature's serpent-body in two. Perhaps he feared the Throne was listening to him through the innocent creature; I do not know. But upon seeing what he had done to one of the Throne's own he knelt down, tears streaming from his eyes, and gave me his sword. This sword."

Valefar turned the great blade in a quick shadow-parry. Heat waves from a sudden burst of blue flames caused the air around it to shimmer. "He told me that he did not want it, any more than he wanted war. But, he said, the anger had taken root and would never go away, and that war was inevitable. I took the sword from him and because he was my great friend followed him into war and, not wishing to waste such an important weapon, I wielded it in the Great Battle. Of course he had another *ialpor napta,* but like all the other Fallen save myself, he lost that one eventually in the Fall."

"Why did you get to keep it?" asked Eligor with genuine curiosity.

"I do not know. It lay there next to me in the crater when I awoke. At the time I thought nothing of it; I imagined that all demons had retained their weapons."

"It is odd."

"Yes, odd." Valefar spun around cleaving the sizzling air with a practiced flourish, grinned fiercely, and then, quickly placing the sword back in its box, closed the lid and sealed it with a word. "And so we have another great war at hand, Captain, a war unlike the incessant wars we have been fighting since we were sent here. Again, Sargatanas chooses to go to war, but this time, I believe, for the right reason."

Eligor looked at Valefar and knew, more then than ever, that Sargatanas had chosen his most trusted friend well.

"As do I," Eligor said. Both demons turned toward the door.

Valefar paused. "We *will* need him, Eligor."

"Who?"

"The Baron. As potentially dangerous as his troops are to us, we are going to have to put our trust in them and use them. And keep a very watchful eye on their fractious leader. If we keep the Baron and them in line, they will do grievous work upon the armies of the Fly."

"I understand. I will go to him now and see how his newfound solitude has affected his disposition."

Valefar began to create a series of command-glyphs in midair and then enfolded them into a hovering pyramid of light, which he sent off to Faraii. "Are you prepared for what will come?"

"Yes, Prime Minister. And yourself?"

"For Abaddon's Pit, if that is how it ends," he said with a half grin.

Valefar then turned away and Eligor opened the door. Something made him look back at the demon, who was again standing before the window, back to him, his steaming hands upon the long box. His head was bowed, his jaw seemed to be moving, and for a moment Eligor thought he might be silently praying. It was such an improbable notion that, as Eligor pulled the door quietly behind him, he shook his head slightly and then, as he started toward Faraii's quarters, began to focus on the difficult conversation that undoubtedly lay ahead.

When he arrived outside Faraii's chambers Eligor knocked upon the door, and when he heard no response he pressed his ear against its cold surface. He heard a faint rasping from within and, puzzled, pulled the knob-latch on the door. With some difficulty he pushed his way into the darkened room, smelling the tang of blood, stumbling over some unseen obstacles on the floor, and then, reflexively, invoking a glyph-of-illumination to better see his surroundings. The room and its objects were as he remembered them from his last visit, but only when he entered farther did he see the damage wrought. Every bit of furnishing, every square foot of floor and wall, was hacked and sliced as by a very sharp blade until the flesh of the bricks hung in long, bloody tatters, the floor was uneven, and the sparse furniture teetered on sword-chiseled, bony legs. And punctuating his examination was the ever-present rasping of what sounded like metal upon stone.

Eligor's eyes narrowed as he put his hand upon his sword hilt and walked slowly in the direction of the continuous sound. *There is madness here.* But when he actually set eyes upon the Baron, seated upon an untouched chair, Eligor was no longer certain. Faraii appeared composed, even serene, and were it not for the conditions of the surroundings and the whetting of his black sword, performed with ominous deliberateness, Eligor would have thought nothing amiss.

"Faraii, are you . . . ?"

"I am fine . . . Eligor."

"These chambers are not fine."

Faraii shrugged. "I was angry."

Eligor's hand stayed upon his sword hilt.

"And are you still?"

"Of course I am. I was sealed in my quarters for doing my job too efficiently. I think that would bother you as well."

Eligor saw the other demon's eyelid flutter.

"But," continued Faraii, "does that mean that I am unable to perform my sworn duty to Sargatanas?" The words hung for a moment, accompanied by the measured sound of the sword.

"Will you stop that while we talk?"

The whetting stopped.

"I just received word of the coming war along with my orders," the Baron said matter-of-factly. "My incarceration, it would seem, has ended as of your arrival. Imagine that, Eligor; my lord suddenly has need of my services and I am free."

"He does. We all do."

"So, am I to be released simply to fight? Only to be put back in my cage afterward?"

"No, Faraii, that is not Sargatanas' intent. He is offering you a chance not only to regain your former status but also to win his trust back, a second chance," Eligor said with an edge to his voice, "and I am reasonably certain there will not be a third."

"There will not need to be." The Baron stood suddenly, as if a string had pulled him up from his chair. He sheathed the sword with an abrupt and perfect flick of his hand. His eyes gleamed with fervor. "I *will* serve my lord, Eligor. I have truly *grown,* both wiser and stronger, as a result of my punishment."

In the half-light of the glyph Eligor saw, again, the nervous eyelid-flutter.

"Of that I have no doubt, Faraii," said Eligor, but his suspicions and doubts were many and strong. Something ineffable about the Waste-wanderer had clearly changed. *But,* Eligor could not help wondering, *why has he changed? Why has he gone from that outsider I found so admirable, quiet and self-assured, to this blatantly arrogant, defiant demon? What is eating at him?* Even though Eligor knew that Sargatanas needed his leadership in battle, he personally would keep a watchful eye on the demon. Faraii's ferocity was not something he wanted turned toward Sargatanas.

"All this," Eligor said, indicating the ravaged rooms as he walked to the door, "will have to be addressed. For the moment, I will keep it between us and have it taken care of."

Faraii stood amidst the chaos, arms folded and looking at his feet, his only thanks a curt grunt.

Troubled, Eligor ascended into the skies above Adamantinarx. He peered down, taking in the absolute dark magnificence of it, its broad avenues and great domes, its thousands of fire-lit buildings teeming with demons and souls, its many-colored, blazing glyphs, its frozen army of monumental statues, and wondered how it would be changed by the events that were to unfold in a war with the greatest forces of Hell. And then his gaze fell upon the slow-flowing Acheron, the River of Tears, and the unwelcome thought entered his mind that it was perhaps, after all, an unfortunate landmark, an uncomfortable omen for a city whose future was now, at best, ill defined.

XXI

ADAMANTINARX–UPON–THE–ACHERON

It was a dream that had begun when he regained himself, a dream that echoed his life before Hell. He knew that he was dreaming, but it did not help; his legs and arms, so heavy bearing the light, squirming burden, moved as if they were made of bronze. But when he looked down into the infant's eyes so bright, something he always did to find succor in the innocence he saw there, his heart raced and the hatred he felt swelled. Not for her. Never. But for *him* up there. And his gaze, as cold as the blue heavens themselves, reached skyward. *How can I do this thing? It goes against everything: humanity, fatherhood . . . nature. They, the hated people of Roma, do not even do this.* The privations those people had imposed on his city after the war, that was why he was here today. That and the merciless summer.

The acrid smell of smoke wafted into his nose, and hatred filled his mouth.

His daughter made that gurgling, cooing noise he loved so much, and he faltered and thought of breaking and running but could not. His feet kept moving and the rows of people on either side, somber and quiet, nodded as he passed them. As he drew near the smoldering Tophet, the warring emotions of hate and love, so powerful in their strength and opposition, twisted something primal deep inside him and he knew, someday, many would suffer because he did this on this day. Now, today, he, a noble Barca, would set the example and they, like the stupid, believing sheep that they were, would follow with their own firstborns.

The cooing had stopped, and after a brief silence it was replaced by her crying, softly at first and then louder.

Shreds of smoke stung his eyes, and the tears it created mingled with those that had formed as he walked. Around him the air began to waver with the intense heat. *This is Hell.*

He stepped to the edge of the burning pit, taking in the pointed pillars, the mounds of ash, the tiny charred and broken bones and heat-split urns, and the sudden din of drums and sistrums made him flinch imperceptibly. He had to forcibly will his arms to extend, the crying, flailing bundle now, oddly, unheard against the riot of sound. He was a powerful man and she was light and when, upon a signal from the priest, he threw her she went farther than he expected. And as he did, through his uncontrollable tears and the overwhelming hatred, he cursed the god who had given his people this ritual of death, who had convinced them that only the most precious of all gifts would expiate their sins. As the clammy fingers of the dream released him he was still cursing the hungry god named Moloch.

With half-closed, tingling eyes he smelled the salt of the Acheron caught on the wind, mixed with the brimstone-scent of the city's far-off fires. Wrapped in an Abyssal-skin cloak, Hannibal, Soul-General of the Souls' Army of Hell, lay alongside his new army and thought, not for the first time, of Imilce. It was the usual pattern—first the dream about their daughter and then Imilce. In his half-slumbering mind's eye he saw her strong, beautiful face as it had looked perhaps thousands of years earlier, and he hoped that she was not somewhere in Hell. *Not her, not in this place,* he thought. But he could never be sure; she had been born of warriors after all.

The sound of distant horns from the city caused him to open his eyes. He stood, pulling the ash-covered hood down, adjusting the darkly iridescent cloak about himself, and smiled faintly. It was almost funny, he thought, how the demons had not understood, at first, why he would not, himself, have a soul-skin cloak or allow anyone in his army to wear one. They had laughed in his face, uncomprehending, but when he had remained firm they had simply shrugged and given the souls the scaled cloaks. Imilce would have liked his steadfastness; it was so like her own. But the cloak he wore now, tough and protective, could hardly have been better than the tear-dampened one she had given him before he left her life forever.

Looking toward Adamantinarx, Hannibal watched its domes and towers growing indistinct, vanishing altogether save for their fires, and reappearing with the passing waves of clouds that surrounded it. Tiny, distant sparks that he knew to be flying demons rose and fell between the buildings, some gathering into cubelike formations, some into flying pyramids. It was odd, he reflected, that he could regard such a place as home and yet his brief years in Qart Hadasht were as nothing compared to his stay in Sargatanas' city. Hannibal saw the approaching herald, his head aflame, long before he heard his slow wing beats. Dropping down to stand before the Soul-General, he tucked his long horn under one arm and bowed his fiery head.

"The Great Lord Sargatanas bids you and your army greeting. Lord Sargatanas wishes you to assemble just before the Fifth Gate, where he and his staff will meet you. He issues to you this baton as an official symbol of your commission in his Great Army of the Ascension."

The herald proffered a military baton, heavy and sculpted with a horizontal crescent and a disk, symbols of Hannibal's long-past empire. Thin, shivering snakes of lightning played upon its upper surfaces. This was a significant gesture that spoke of acknowledgment and even respect, and it filled Hannibal with emotion.

Taking his cue from the herald, Hannibal signaled to one of the demon cornicens that had been attached to his army, and soon the air for some distance was filled with the hollow braying of war horns.

By the time he made his way to the front ranks of the soul army, the whisper of the rumor of war that had begun upon the arrival of the herald had grown into an excited murmur.

Eagerly the souls took up their arms and quickly formed ranks and files. Hannibal turned to his brother and together they gave the order to march. An hour later the well-ordered formation surged around the last corner of the ten-span-high city walls to the not-too-distant gate where, already emerging, Hannibal saw the demon general staff. He looked at the distant gate and remembered the spikes that adorned it. *They call it the Fifth Gate, but we have always called it something very different . . . Gate of a Million Hearts.* He shook his head with the memory of its hooked decorations and with the irony of it.

Marching in a tight wedge with Sargatanas at its point, the generals were the crest of a black wave of soldiers, fifteen columns of resplendent standard-bearers followed closely by heavily armored legionaries. Above them flew two full squadrons of Eligor's Guard trailing long gonfalons from their lances, each emblazoned with their lord's fiery seal. The splendor of the scene, the sheer visual weight of it, crushed Hannibal, who stood transfixed, trying as best as he could not to show his awe.

He had never been this close to Demons Major in all of their battle panoply and realized, then and there, that he would never get used to the impossible inhumanity of them. As they drew closer, their giant, anthropomorphic forms seemed to create an organic wall that loomed fiery and dark and wreathed in smoke. Fortunately, the debilitating influence of their proximity that he so vividly recalled when he had nearly been converted no longer seemed to influence him; he had concluded that they could exert that effect if they chose. Their thick armor, pitted and hot, was annealed into their bodies, embedded for war and impossible to remove except by uttered invocation or prying blade. Between the plates were areas of umber flesh that writhed and clawed and snapped with innumerable fanged mouths and taloned fingers and bloodshot eyes. No two demons were alike, and yet there were similarities enough to suggest their kinship. No matter the form their casquelike head-armor took, the demons' eyes all shone silver upon black, all with equal intensity, and Hannibal found that looking into those eyes served as a touchstone, a grounding for him to avoid what must be happening upon the surface of their restless bodies.

All of the principal Demons Major and Minor were there at Sargatanas' side: there were Andromalius and Bifrons and Minister Valefar carrying a ten-foot-long sword that Hannibal had never seen the like of, and there was Zoray, his shield emblazoned with the glowing symbol of the Foot Guard, and the gaunt and ferocious Baron Faraii, whose spare manner and differing armor bore the stamp of the Wastes, and a heavily robed demon who could only be Yen Wang strode a pace behind with fireballs circling his head and fabulous glyphs orbiting his body. Other demons, too, followed behind, some of whom Hannibal had not yet met but seemed to him to be of very high stature. Eligor, who Hannibal had heard from rumors was somehow more accessible than the rest, flew overhead at the front of his troops and dropped down to the ground as the demon lord and his retinue drew close.

Hannibal had been warned that his souls, now mobilized as an army, were not to be permitted within the walls of Adamantinarx, and so he dutifully drew them up some distance from the towering gate. There they re-formed into parade squares facing the legions of demons that poured out of the city and the Soul-General had to applaud their discipline for not breaking and running at the sight of it.

Sargatanas stepped up to Hannibal and looked up and down the front ranks of soldiers, nodding approvingly.

"So what I have heard is true, Hannibal," he said. "It appears that you have done a fine job of assembling and organizing your army. Their numbers are far greater than I would have expected. Many said it could not be done."

"Thank you, Lord," Hannibal said, bowing his head. He was proud of his ability to levy such an enormous host.

"It is time now, perhaps prematurely, to test them against an enemy who is both strong and bold. But I have been giving their usefulness some thought, and this I will discuss with you as we march."

"March, my lord?"

Looking up at the demon's shifting countenance, at his spark-nimbused head, Hannibal could feel the radiating contagious mixture of determination and excitement. "At this moment the formidable Grand General Moloch, the Imperial Mayor of Dis, is himself headed toward us with a handpicked host whose sole purpose is the destruction of me, my court, and Adamantinarx. I will not meet him here in the shadow of my city so that he may divert our efforts with his siegecraft. It is my hope to pick where and when we will meet him."

Hannibal's chin dropped suddenly.

"My lord . . . ," he said with eyes closed, a quaver in his voice, "the general's name? What did you say his name was?"

"It is Moloch."

The Soul-General remained still and Sargatanas looked intently at him, reading him.

"The same, Hannibal," Sargatanas said softly. "This battle will be important for both of us."

For a moment the demon and the soul stood facing each other, the unspoken emotions passing between them.

"We *will* prevail, Hannibal," Sargatanas said. "Everything must change eventually. You, me . . . even Hell."

As he spoke, Hannibal saw the legions part and a column of light mounted soul-beasts emerge from the city, padding quickly toward them. Watching the Spirits approach in precise formation, Hannibal felt a twinge of envy; leading his beloved Numidian cavalry had been a special thrill for him, and he knew that there would be no such similar joys for him in Hell. And yet as he watched the first of the cavalry pull up he saw a decurion put the reins of a smaller mount—an Abyssal—into the hands of the Spirits' commander.

Sargatanas raised his hand acknowledging the approaching mounted demon. "Lord Karcefuge has had this mount prepared for you; he had it captured recently, thinking it inappropriate for a general not to have a proper mount in battle. I agreed."

Tribune Karcefuge sat nearly fifteen feet above Hannibal upon a saddle of ornately carved bone that had been impaled into the huge soul's back. He leaned down and offered Hannibal the reins.

The creature, unlike any he had seen, was half the height of the other steeds but still towered over the demon foot soldiers; Hannibal looked forward to it affording him a superior view of the battle to come.

"Thank you, my lords," Hannibal said, beaming. "It is an unbelievable gift, a gift beyond my hopes. But what kind of creature is it?"

"We call them *qirial-pe-latha* . . . skin skippers to the Waste dwellers. It has been trained to answer to 'Gaha.' Its name means 'Cub of the Wastes' in our tongue."

Unlike the tough-hided soul-beasts, its body was encased in the broad, almost gaudy silver-black scales characteristic of so many Infernal species, scales that Hannibal knew were both flexible and tough. Low spines adorned most of the plates' edges, growing into a short, spiky mane around its shoulder girdle. Its front legs, more like thin arms, were considerably shorter than its rear pair but nonetheless gave it a lithe and quick look. Arching away from its narrow shoulders, its neck supported a vertically flattened, heavily beaked head equipped with two yard-long daggers, which curved downward dangerously from its bottom jaw. Four tiny red eyes stared at him, watching him warily, and when he extended his hand and said, "Gaha," it pulled back, emitting an odd hissing chatter.

Encouraged by a nod from Sargatanas, Hannibal walked to its side, grasped the thick stirrup strap, and took hold of one of two strangely placed projections on the newly made saddle and climbed atop the creature's back. His knees fit perfectly in front of two strangely placed projections, and he guessed that he would sit very securely if the beast reared. With a grin, Karcefuge handed him a sparking crop. Tapping the beast's plated haunch with it, Hannibal brought Gaha around to face the demons. The smile was unmistakable upon his face; it had been so long since he had ridden. The demons were right; a general should be mounted.

"Ride him with care, Soul-General," Karcefuge said. "Gaha may have a few surprises for you on the battle-field."

"For now, have your brother assume command of your army, Hannibal," said Sargatanas. A command-glyph blossomed above his head like a fiery flower, split apart, and sped off to ten different unit commanders. "We have much to discuss, and I want you by my side for the first leg of our march." Whereupon the Lord of Adamantinarx wheeled his huge beast and, unsheathing the sword *Lukiftias,* signaled his fellow demons to mount and, amidst the shrill blaring of war horns and the hollow, rhythmic beat of kettledrums, set his army out to face the advancing legions of Moloch. The exultation that Hannibal felt at that moment was in no way dampened by his awareness that he might not return to the city he had sworn to defend. He was, and it would appear always would be, a warrior, and warriors by trade had to be pragmatists; the risks were no different in Hell than they had been during his life. He simply hoped, as he had so many times before, that if Oblivion took him it would find him with a sword in his hand. It was a simple hope, an age-old warrior's hope.

Lilith woke suddenly to the sounds of horns and the deafening flapping of countless wings and banners mingled with shouted orders. She reached the window just in time to see Sargatanas and his lords pass beneath at the head of a large contingent of Foot Guard. They continued down the Rule and then took a turn marching out of sight toward, she guessed, the Fifth Gate. She looked up and saw the gathering formations of flying demons begin to stream in the same direction, following their lord's command like migratory Abyssals answering the imperative of instinct. She watched this gathering of forces for some time, until something made her peer out farther into the darkness beyond the walls. There she could just discern a gathering clot of infinitely tiny figures that she knew must be another army, and she realized that this must be the Soul-General Hannibal's army. Seeing them forming up, she was suddenly overcome with emotion; she realized that this was the army she had always envisioned, the army she had begun with her little statues, the army for which Ardat Lili had been flayed. But notwithstanding that bitter memory, Lilith recognized that she, with Sargatanas, had given the souls something they could never have had in Hell otherwise, something she valued beyond almost everything—a semblance of free will. It was the beginning of their Infernal emancipation, and no matter whether they won or lost their battles, they were now more than they could ever have been without her efforts.

THE WASTES

The march lasted two full days, during which Hannibal had watched his army carefully, measuring their spirits as they trekked through the umbral landscape. Yen Wang and his Behemoths had been left behind; Sargatanas deemed them too precious to use in this encounter. Well into the second day, winged scouts brought word that a suitable location for their camp had been found, the shallow valley between two long ridges that smoldered with perpetual flames known as the Flaming Cut. When Sargatanas and his staff arrived at the scouts' favored location the demon lord appeared satisfied that the lay of the surrounding terrain favored him.

In his Life Hannibal had seen many eves of battle but only one eve of war. That war had lasted sixteen long years. Here, in Hell, it was no different; this eve of war was as pregnant with possibility, both fearful and glorious, as that one had been in his Life. He knew that conflicts had raged for eons, since Hell had been colonized, tearing away at the uneasy borders of every established feudal kingdom. But while those borders had constantly shifted no demon had ever gained anything that might threaten the hegemony; war, true war that feeds hungrily upon entire kingdoms, had not been permitted. But, Hannibal reflected, all that was about to change.

"Mago," he said, approaching his brother, who was seated, quietly sharpening his blade. "Gather the generals. There is something I must tell them."

Mago hesitated but, seeing that Hannibal would not offer any explanation, set about his task. The Soul-General waited, impatiently. Sargatanas' plan came at a

price, and Hannibal was almost as reluctant to relay its
details as he was to disobey his new lord.

One by one the souls appeared and stood before Hannibal, anxiously awaiting word of what their roles would
be in the coming battle. When he was satisfied that all
were present, Hannibal cleared his dry throat.

"Generals, I will be brief. What I am about to ask of
you on behalf of Lord Sargatanas will shock you and
truly put to the test our mettle as leaders. Our role . . .
that of the souls . . . will be essential to the outcome of
this battle, but it will be seen by our soldiers as nothing
short of treachery on the part of our demon allies. I ask
you to listen and then go back to your officers and units
and make them understand the gravity of the situation. I
ask you to trust me as I trust Sargatanas. I believe in him
and this plan for battle."

Hannibal looked as his handpicked generals and remembered other reluctant generals and other difficult
times and knew then that he could be convincing, that
he could lay out his lord's plan effectively. It was Hannibal's talent to be able to persuade those around him to
die for him.

XXII

DIS

The two hundred Knights stood around him drenched in
the steaming blood of sinners. Behind them, hung by
their heels on sturdy racks, gagged and flailing, were
hundreds of skinned souls, unwilling participants in a

pre-battle tradition that went back to Dis' distant origins. Fresh skin cloaks hung about the warriors' shoulders still rippling and twitching, parted from the souls only moments earlier. A number of orbs lay in a cluster to one side awaiting dissolution. Dripping in glistening rivulets from scarlet-hued breastplates, cloaks, and weapons alike, red-black blood pooled slowly at their heavily shod feet, leaving the assembled Knights deeply stained. Adramalik, leaning on a long, barbed pike, noted with pride the perfectly aligned star-shaped pattern of their parade formation, the precise angles of unsheathed swords, and the fierce, toothy grins that each of his protégés bore. It had been a long period of relative inactivity for them, a period filled with restless activity, of controlled violence and uncontrolled perversion. But even knowing this, it was apparent to the Chancellor General, reviewing them in tight-lipped silence, that their loyalty and discipline were total, that they had not lost anything of their edge.

A soul was brought forth, dragged by two large Knights-in-training to the center of the formation before Adramalik. Selected for the unusual barbarity of his life, he was a large individual, in Hell a chief mason perhaps, with oversized hands and a sloping, furrowed head. He was trussed in deep-cutting, crisscrossing ceremonial cords of gold, and from each intersection depended an amulet, an inscribed, fly-shaped talisman that the Knighthood had been awarded for every hard-fought victory. As they dragged the soul the golden flies jingled against the wires, an odd, light sound that was disharmonious with the muffled, throaty moaning that issued from his gagged mouth.

Adramalik lowered the barbed shaft until it was chest high, pointing it at the kneeling soul. Seeing this, the Knights began, in low whispers, to intone their credo, a series of short obeisances first to Lucifer the Lost and then to Beelzebub. Each Knight in turn stepped forward and with his drawn sword, and with only one thrust, pierced the soul in a different space between the golden cords. The chanting grew louder with each recapitulation, and when it was nearly shouted the Knights-in-training grasped the soul under his arms, raising him above their heads and then dropping him with gurgling screams upon the upraised pike. There, vertically impaled, he slumped, and all eyes watched what was left of his blood flow down the pike's shaft until it reached Adramalik's hands.

Silence descended like a hammer.

Capping the pike with Beelzebub's crest—a great, golden fly—Adramalik raised the newly created standard high overhead, and the Knights responded by breaking formation, each moving to his steed at the head of a full mounted battalion that stretched out and down the broad, torch-lit Avenue of War. Barracks along its length were still emptying their legions onto the avenue behind the cavalry. Fiery unit sigils stood out in the haze of ash, dwindling as they progressed down the avenue to pinpoints of light in the far distance, lights that reminded the Chancellor General of the specks upon an Abyssal serpent's back.

A sound of cries and crunching caused him to turn in time to see Moloch looming huge upon his soul-steed, trampling a few luckless demon foot soldiers underfoot as he took the forward position. His wheeling mount was an immense Melding—a many-legged, headless steed fashioned of souls compressed into a form from which sprouted a dozen weapon-wielding arms. With a snarl and an annoyed flick of one of his Hooks, Moloch set the army in motion. It was a small gesture, Adramalik noted, but a gesture heavy with significance. War was at hand, a war that Adramalik was certain would have but a single outcome. And when it was over, tired as he was of the ceaseless politics, he thought that he might take up residence far from Dis, perhaps somewhere in the newly conquered territory where he could indulge himself away from the ever-watchful eyes of Beelzebub's court. It was a fantasy that caught Adrama-lik off guard, one that he had never considered before but which brought him some pleasure. As he made his way out of the capital, he found himself looking at the passing succession of familiar landmarks as one who was, at long last, bidding them farewell, a conflicting mixture of euphoria and melancholia washing through him.

THE WASTES

The ground screamed behind them as the army headed toward Adamantinarx, making its way through terrain that had grown rougher and more difficult the farther from Dis it marched. The ancient trackway to Adamantinarx had been disused for a very long time and had become overgrown, the sliced flesh of the old roadbed cuts having filled in considerably in the millennia. But, Adrama-lik could see, it was essentially still there, the roads remaining clearer in most cases than the tunnels, which were frequently tangled with heavy-branched, arterial trees and tangles of intertwined, venous growth. Small obstructions had been chopped away by the pioneers in the vanguard, but eventually the enormous ribbon that was the army reached the first foothills, low and rolling and grown higher since the road had been cut. Adrama-lik had watched as the blunt-headed Maws—faster and more precise than the lumbering Demolishers—had been brought forth and had been set upon the landscape amidst a chorus of gnashing teeth and screaming groundswells. Enlarged and attenuated into long tubular shapes and then bound tightly together by the hundreds, the soul-bundles chewed through the fleshy landscape, clearing the straight trek so characteristic of Dis' relentless generals—the arrow-straight path that almost symbolically allowed for no obstacles. Adramalik knew the fields would heal, that the capricious slashings of the soldiers' weapons and the gnawed roadway would scab over eventually, but for the moment, as they made their way through the frontier, he would enjoy the choir of shrill screams that the ground gave voice to.

On the third week of their march the army came upon a wide, gurgling river of blood, which had, long ago, been spanned by a thick-pillared bridge, but while the pillars remained erect, the broad roadway had fallen, forcing the soldiers to ford through the fast-moving currents. The mounted battalions had no difficulty negotiating the river, but the legions were momentarily thrown into disarray as the currents churned and shifted. Stained a glistening, deep red, they climbed the far banks and veered back onto the old road. Here the ground aflame and the black smoke billowed in huge sheets. Peering into the gloom, Adramalik saw shapes, gigantic Abyssals that concealed themselves the smoke and dogged the columns, watching hopefully for any small scout detachment to stray too far from the protection of the army. Theirs would be a swift end, signaled only by the sudden flare of lights in the darkness. The Chancellor General knew that few, if any, of the mounted scouts would be foolhardy enough to lose sight of the column.

Without rest the army marched, straight through the wilds of the frontier, through the noisy fields of indifferent Sag-hrim and their Psychemancers, past the towering and floating stelae bearing gigantic sculpted fly heads that marked the border of Beelzebub's realm. Beyond them, through the wide Wastes and past Astaroth's broken realm, lay the wards of Sargatanas' kingdom, a rich prize that the Prince would easily wrest from the upstart Demon Major. *If I am careful they could be-*

come mine, thought Adramalik. *Careful and ruthless. A kingdom of my own with the best of my Knights would be powerful indeed.* It had become a frequent thought that brought a cold ghost of a smile to the Chancellor General's hard face as he plodded along atop his mount.

THE FLAMING CUT

The outpost, a low, jagged silhouette of broken buildings, was situated between two long, flaming ridges. It was not on any map that Adramalik had seen back in the chart-rooms of Dis, but that, he knew, meant nothing; those floating maps had been drawn and redrawn dozens of centuries ago, and with relations growing strained between the two cities surveyors had not been sent out since. The ridges may not have even been aflame back then. Or, he thought, perhaps this was simply a convenient roosting spot for the abandoned buildings that had been cut from the city and had floated into the wilds.

Adramalik followed as Moloch and the staff entered the empty town. Old weapons, swords, long spears, and hatchets lay about everywhere, some in piles, others strewn randomly amidst the rubble. How old they were or why they had been left behind Adramalik could not begin to guess.

The light wind that had been easy to ignore picked up and grew turbulent, blowing ash in thick swirls that seemed alive in their determination to attack the warriors; some thought they saw the telltale tendrils of glyphs woven into the shifting fabric of the clouds. Aware that the winds whipping in from over his wards might be an artifice of Sargatanas', Moloch's legions took a full day, under the slitted, watchful eyes of their leaders, to pass cautiously through and around the town, flowing down into the valley between the ridges like a dark and viscous liquid. There, as they built their fortified camp,

each of them saw the distant lights of Sargatanas' encamped army, a broad and incandescent swath of fires
and picket-sigils that stretched into the distant gloom.
Flanked by his two Knight-Brigadiers, Melphagor the
Primus and Salabrus, Adramalik stared into the carpet
of light and tried to gauge the strength of the opposing
force but found that it was impossible due to the obscuring clouds.

"They have no idea what they face, Chancellor General," Melphagor said in his hoarse voice, relishing the
thought. Wisps of fire flicked at the burned corners of
his mouth. "Sargatanas is as misguided as he is indeci-
sive."

"I have *seen* otherwise, Brigadier. Sargatanas is no
mere upstart to be ridiculed and easily shunted aside."

"Yes, and Moloch is no mere general. Are you doubtful of our coming success, Adramalik?"

Adramalik's eyes narrowed. This was no time for the
shadow of suspicion to fall upon him. Not with the prize
so close. His trust for the Brigadier was significant, born
in battle and in the Keep. But trust, in Hell, went only so
far, and Adramalik's was a coveted position.

"Not in the least," he said smoothly. "I am simply
saying, Melphagor, that while we may have greater losses
than the Prince or Moloch expect, the battle's outcome
has *never* been in question."

Melphagor smiled, seemingly satisfied.

A squadron of pinpoint lights, winged scouts keeping
watch, banked across the sky over the enemy encamp-
ment. *What is he planning? Clearly he did not want us
near his precious city.*

He turned back to the growing camp and was rewarded with the sight of dozens of their own protective
picket-sigils blazing to life with a loud hiss. They would
not withstand Sargatanas himself but would, at least,
slow him down were he to be foolish enough to attack
them where they were encamped. Adramalik looked at

in the opening battle of what may be a long and terrible campaign. If we lose we will not be given any quarter. But if we win, as I know we will, it will shape our existences forever. Each and every one of you bears within him the past we once cherished. When we unsheathe our weapons let us remember the angels we once were but fight like the demons we are.

"Heaven awaits!"

XXIII

THE FLAMING CUT

The furnace-breath of stinging cinders blew forcefully into the determined faces of Moloch's legions as they streamed from their camp. Even with that and the vicious winds, Adramalik could not help but reflect on how much he thrilled at the unforgiving world he lived in. Kneeling next to his giant soul-steed, Adramalik washed his dusty hands in the red blood of an artery broken besides a fallen tree. *This day,* he thought, *this day, to me, is what it means to live in Hell. The ash, the blood, the fires,* and *this battle—I am truly in my element!*

As he savored the moment, he heard an enthusiastic shout go up from the front lines and carry back through the legions to his position; the summoned sulfurous wind had suddenly faded and ceased altogether; slowly the blackened veil lifted from the landscape. Adramalik saw more clearly now the two sheets of fire that extended on either side nearly to Sargatanas' camp shimmering into the sky for hundreds of feet. *A natural wonder,* he thought, *so beautiful.* It seemed almost like a punctuation to complete his contentment, an ironic gift from his enemy. *Moloch's battlefield conjurors must have found a way to counter Sargatanas' invocation. We can match anything he has to offer. We* will *crush him and his misguided army. And when we have finished him we will punish the wards of his allies.*

For some minutes the two armies faced each other and the only sound was of the breathing of demons.

Drawing his saber from its scabbard, Adramalik swung lightly up into his saddle and pulled the reins until he was facing Moloch. *You will be the instrument of my goals,* Pridzarhim *general,* he thought, raising his sword in a perfunctory salute to the mounted general. Moloch, barely acknowledging him, cast a command-glyph in his direction and set off at a trot toward the head of the decamping army.

Absorbing the glyph, Adramalik closed his eyes, visualizing its meaning. The battle plan was relatively simple. Massed heavy cavalry, followed by the legions, would punch its way through the middle of Sargatanas' lines, flank them, and return to split them into smaller and smaller blocks. The legions would then engage those pockets of disorganized infantry that fought on as he was certain they would. Having borne witness to Sargatanas' battle with Astaroth, Adramalik had little doubt that the fighting would be fierce.

Around him he heard the thunder of a million footfalls as the heavy cavalry formed up and began to gain speed. He saw the innumerable banners of Dis, surmounted by the Prince's fly-and-sigil device and attached to long lances, lower in anticipation of the final contact. With a word eagerly uttered, glyphs appeared along his sword's tempered length, giving way to white-hot flames. While not even close in power to the swords of the Above, it was still more than most demons could

withstand. Adramalik pulled his battalion alongside that
of Moloch and off to his left, a few hundred yards away,
he could just see that the general had lit his baton and
was issuing commands, tightening the formation. He
held both Hooks in one massive hand, at the ready.

Looking far ahead between the two camps, the Chancellor General saw what appeared to be a distant wall,
low and long, and, he imagined, hastily thrown up. Behind it troops of some kind could be seen scurrying
back and forth. Even though they were faintly illuminated by the suspended sheets of flame, he could not tell
what kind of infantry they would be meeting shortly.

Moloch cast out the command to pick up speed and
suddenly, at his urging, Adramalik's soul-steed was gal-
loping, racing over the ground-skin in huge, bounding
bursts. Exhilarated, he watched as the distances between the armies rapidly closed. He could now plainly
see the small figures, cowering in fear, he was sure, behind the wall, and to his complete astonishment he realized they were souls. *By Abaddon's Pit, this is unheard
of! Bringing in dirty larvae to fight against demons!* Directly behind them Adramalik thought he could discern
a motley array of legions, including a few composed of
pike-wielding demons—most likely Sargatanas' phalangites. *Is this all that he has brought to face us? The
battle with Astaroth and the occupation of his wards
must have stretched his resources more than I thought.
The phalangites are tough veterans . . . but souls? How
desperate is he?*

As Adramalik and the speeding cavalry drew closer
he began to see more and more legions waiting in the
wings. Distant and without any demon's sigil of possession, they were concealed within summoned smoke, he
imagined with some dismay, so as not to alarm the onrushing forces of Moloch. Obscured by clouds in the far
gloom, high above Sargatanas' lines, Adramalik even
thought he saw airborne troops, but he could not discern

their numbers. And suddenly it seemed to him as if the
day might not be won so handily.

With Metaphrax Argastos in command of his Flying
Guard, circling overhead, Eligor felt at some ease accompanying Sargatanas to the front. There Eligor's flyers would stay, concealed in the clouds, ready to pounce
if and when needed.

His eyes fell upon the dark shapes of Baron Faraii's
Shock Troopers as they lumbered in a purposeful, ominous wedge ahead, parting the massed legions by their
mere presence and making easy transit for his lord,
Lord Valefar, and himself. The generals—Demons Major mostly—followed behind, and Eligor examined
them in all their occult martial splendor, bedecked in
their hardened armor and every manner of physical or-
namentation. He paid particular attention to Lords
Bifrons and Andromalius and finally to Lord Furcas,
who hung closely by Sargatanas, looking concerned
and somewhat uncertain. Eligor had not been privy to
all of the intricacies of his lord's plans but had enough
of an awareness of the broad strokes to know the importance of the corpulent demon's role.

Arriving at the front and protected by the Baron's
iron-eyed forces, the general staff saw the growing line
of Moloch's cavalry begin its advance, gathering speed
in the distance. Above them tiny sigils flared to life and
command-glyphs began to dart from officers to soldiers. As they passed silently along the length of the
bordering walls of flame they caught the light in such a
way, Eligor noted, as to make them look like a glowing,
onrushing flow of lava—an illusion enhanced by the va-
porous cloud of steam that trailed off them. It was an
amazing spectacle and he decided that if he survived
this battle, he would write down his impressions back in
his chambers in Adamantinarx. Just to remember the
day eons hence.

Eligor's gaze moved down to the few hundred small figures crouched behind the newly erected wall. None had a weapon in hand, and because of this he imagined that their nervous tension regarding the onrushing cavalry must have been extreme. Yet they held still, each one a soul-centurion, each one awaiting the proper moment when he would be called upon to issue their all-important orders. That moment was not far off, the Captain reflected, as he just began to hear the rumble of footfalls across the plain. His keen eyes, the eyes of a flying demon, picked out the many scarlet-clad figures that he knew, from his trips to Dis, to be Knights of the Fly. And then his eyes fell upon the general at the head of the flowing carpet of cavalry. Reflexively, Eligor tightened his grip upon his lance.

A roar of raw hatred shattered the air, easily audible to all in the front ranks of the charging cavalry. Eager for battle, Moloch gave voice as he slowly drew ahead upon his leaping Melding. Adramalik saw long streamers of flame trailing from his head and saw, too, that his field-baton was no longer in his hand; the commands were already firmly in place. Instead he rode with both arms extended outward at his sides, the two Hooks twirling in his hands; he would welcome his enemy with an embrace of shearing oblivion.

Reluctantly acknowledging the general's charisma, Adramalik began to feel the battle-ecstasy warm his own body, urging him to put the spurs to his charger. The battlefield around him became a blurred hurricane of sound and movement and fire with only the enemy ahead standing out in the sharpest detail. He focused on the olive-brown wall that now, oddly, appeared taller than he had first thought, but, undaunted, he galloped on.

The soul-steeds were howling wildly, a sound designed to wither the resolve of any enemy foolish enough to stand their ground. With a final rush, the cavalry closed

the gap to the wall, and Adramalik saw an unusual and
brilliant glyph flash upward from just behind Sargatanas'
front lines and thought, peripherally, that it was issued by
either a Lord Bifrons or Furcas. Splitting, its duplicates
dropped like stones into the small souls and impacted
with a roar atop the wall. To Adramalik's amazement, the
wall rippled, began to geyser wisps of flame, and suddenly hundreds upon hundreds of arms extended from
along its length. An instant later the upstretched hands of
souls and bricks alike came alive with the glow of some
kind of glyph-glove from which then blossomed what
looked like fiery javelins. Adramalik could almost feel
the collective disbelief of his fellow riders, a momentary
wave of hesitation—more imagined than real—to which
it was too late to pay attention.

For just the briefest moment, before the front rank of
Dis' heavy cavalry crashed against the wall, the Chancellor General had the impression that he was leaping into
the hot-breathed mouth of some enormous prone Abyssal,
its awful gums lined with long, fiery teeth. And then he
saw that terrible beast's teeth loose themselves and launch
in short, fast arcs directly into the riders, aimed, it seemed,
at the soul-beasts they rode. And as soon as the hands had
released one incandescent javelin another appeared. Some
immediately found their mark, penetrating deep into the
breasts of the oncoming souls, disappearing with a brilliant, orange glow within their bodies, and cleaving them
from within. Their bubbling screams of pain rose above
the sounds of the battlefield as they turned and twisted in
agony. The soul-centurions were barking orders inces-
santly, guiding the blind weapon-wielding hands to their
targets. Adramalik clenched his jaws as he wheeled his
mount. *This was not* meant *to have happened; we were*
meant *to have breached the wall and streamed into the enemy forces.* He felt an uncontrollable mixture of anger and
disappointment rising within him and found himself beat-

ing his moaning steed upon the head with the hilt of his
saber in frustration. *Furcas! It has to be Furcas the Pyromancer's doing!*

The heavy cavalry was in complete disarray. With
their forward momentum checked there was no chance
of them bounding over the wall and into the ranks of
troops beyond. Instead their bodies crashed into one another and the buckling wall and made turning extraordinarily difficult. But turn they eventually did, amidst a
deadly rain of fiery missiles that took a heavy toll upon
them. And from the corner of his eye the Chancellor
General saw that even though it had suffered minor
damage, the wall still stood firm.

A red command-glyph soared skyward and split into
a dozen smaller replicas of itself. The command to retreat and regroup!

Within the tangle of demons and soul-steeds he
looked for the order's source. He found Moloch by his
size and brilliant sigil-corona, some distance away and
visible in his own maelstrom of pivoting cavalry, spinning away as well, and Adramalik could only imagine
the blinding rage that must have been filling the general.
That the general, for all his boldness and ferocity, had
been brushed so easily aside by a simple subterfuge
spoke volumes about both him and Sargatanas. Adramalik's hatred for Moloch cut so deep that even as the
cavalry began to regain a semblance of order he found
this inglorious retreat an ironic, bitter pleasure. Favorite
or not, Moloch would hear much about it from his
Prince.

The javelins were now arcing higher, whistling up
over Adramalik's head and landing among the rearmost
mounted demons. Without waiting for orders, they were
breaking and heading back toward their camp, forming
up into ragged, surging groups, which suddenly found
themselves heading directly into their own oncoming

legions. Adramalik saw javelins hitting his demons, blasting their heads from their shoulders, sinking deep within their chests, and blowing them asunder, the shattered chunks of their bodies falling all around him. The din of destruction seemed ceaseless, the missiles limitless, until Adramalik had finally drawn out of range. Decimated as the cavalry was, he knew, as he plunged ahead, that those legions marching directly in their path were about to experience the unchecked impact of the panicked battalions. He saw his Knights issue hasty orders and thought he saw the great formations begin to turn. But he knew it would be too late.

A thousand steps back from the wall the two forces collided and, just as he had anticipated, the foot soldiers suffered beyond measure. Trying desperately to evade the cavalry, Moloch's legions' orderly ranks were torn apart, dragged under the hands and feet of the frantic mounts, and crushed into rubble. Adramalik's own soul-steed leaped and dodged wildly and he dug his horn-shod heels in to stay atop it. Growling, he shook his head angrily.

The destruction lasted just as long, the Chancellor General guessed, as it took Moloch to realize that a complete disaster would ensue if he did nothing. Adramalik was waiting for the order, and when it did rise into the sky he raised his saber high overhead, pointed it downward at the back of his steed's head, and plunged its fire-hot length deep into the beast's skull. As it crumpled to the ground with a whining exhalation of breath, he felt no remorse, no sense of loss. These were souls, *skin-sacks;* they were meant to be used and destroyed. *Let the Abyssals pick at it,* he thought as he extricated himself from the saddle and walked away.

Looking across the field, Adramalik saw the other cavalrydemons dismounting from their now largely inert soul-steeds. Some demons were hacking angrily at their twitching bodies in a rage of frustration.

With the destruction of the mounts, the havoc within the beleaguered legions of Dis ended abruptly and for a few moments the only sounds were those of the seriously crushed soldiers crumbling away. Adramalik and the other cavalrydemons found themselves standing among the barely controllable legionaries whose fury had been aroused by the frenzy of annihilation that had swept over them. But so cowed were they by the presence of the scarlet-armored Knights of the Fly that they dared not act on their rage.

Adramalik ordered his Knights to integrate themselves and the remaining dismounted cavalry into the legions and to assume command. Thus bolstered, the legions would come closer to their original strength and under the leadership of his Knights, resented as they were, might regain their confidence. Or so he hoped.

The Chancellor General saw the cohesion of the legions returning and then saw Moloch approaching, baton in hand, striding easily upon his wing-stilts over the rubble and towering above the infantry. The anger was written upon his blood-dark face and his eyes bore something aside from the normal film of resentment. *Is it disappointment?* Adramalik could barely repress his satisfaction.

"*What,* Chancellor General? Have you something to say?"

"Not I, Grand General. But our Prince *surely* will."

Moloch snorted.

And then, almost to himself, the ex-god said, "Even without the cavalry we have sufficient numbers to absorb casualties. We will overwhelm them and finish this . . . in the name of the Prince."

For a moment the two demons' eyes locked. *Would it be so hard, right here and now, to order this legion to destroy him—to send him to the Pit where he belongs? They would obey me . . .* and *follow me into battle.* But, Adramalik reasoned, there would be too many questions from the Prince regarding his champion, too much suspicion. There were easier ways.

"This does not end here," Moloch rumbled, thrusting the top of his baton into the Chancellor General's chest. Adramalik reflexively grasped its end and shoved it aside.

Perhaps not here, General, but soon.

A shrill cry came from high above them and both demons looked up simultaneously. Barely visible against the shadowed clouds was the large silhouette, lit along the sinuous length of its body by tiny glow-spots, of a cinderfly. They were rare, Adramalik knew, and portended great events. A hissing flight of black arrows reached up from somewhere nearby and a moment later the Abyssal's winged body disappeared amidst the troops. Adramalik heard a cheer go up—the omens were good—and shook his head when he saw Moloch's fierce grin.

Pulling his Hooks from his belt, Moloch gave Adramalik one last look—smugness and disdain mixed—and shouldered past him on his way to the front of the legions. The Chancellor General heard him grate out, "Keep your legion close, Knight."

Moments later the braying of war horns echoed across the field, followed by Moloch's command-glyphs, and the hundred legions of Dis began to move slowly forward. Beneath them, in response to their relentless tramping, the ground flexed and rippled, making the footing for the marching troops less certain. But even with what was, undoubtedly, this further evidence of the enemy's battlefield-influencing invocations, the troops pushed forward and soon found themselves at the farthest limits of the range of the fiery javelins.

The wall was gone, dissolved into a broad line of souls, each holding the new weapon.

There simply had not been enough time for the battlefield conjurors to create counterspells for the new weapons; Adramalik saw, once again, the devastating effect the missiles had on relatively unprotected troops. But he also saw Moloch, in quick response, order all the many cohorts of his archers to race ahead, and despite large numbers of their ranks being destroyed, Adramalik saw sappers dig low, protective trenches, enabling the legions' archers to begin to let fly their arrows. Such was the discipline of the army of Dis!

Much to his surprise, the Chancellor General realized the sheets of arrows were finding their marks and the javelins' numbers were gradually decreasing. Such a simple solution! The cavalry had been a terrible mistake—a blunder of reconnaissance—but the unclean *Pridzarhim* had redeemed himself. Tangled piles of souls lay where they fell, pierced—a sight Adramalik thought odd. Souls—resource that they were—were rarely left unheeded when the life went out of them. But there they lay, and he had the strange errant thought that they were being wasted.

Behind them and barely diminished by the arrows stood a long, unwavering line of Sargatanas' veterans, heavily armored and not nearly as vulnerable as the souls had been. They were the phalangites of Adamantinarx under the collective command, Adramalik knew, of the Demon Minor Aetar Set. In count they numbered a full twenty-six legions, and each of their ranks bore a long pike that was leveled at the oncoming demons.

Moloch commanded the middle of his line—three legions of heavy halberdiers—to form up behind him into a thick wedge. Recognizing that there could never be an effective flanking maneuver with a defensive line as long and deep as Sargatanas', the general was clearly determined to reach the demon lord by ramming his way through the bristling wall of pikes.

Adramalik felt a sudden wave of envy for the general's bravery. As he watched the two armies converge, he knew that Moloch was going to do everything possible to shatter the enemy and that that was why he was so favored by the Prince. Moloch's unhesitating loyalty was at once naive and invaluable. And, Adramalik grudgingly admitted, admirable.

From a short distance the Chancellor General could see Moloch standing within a group of standard-bearing demonifers. Suddenly he rose up, tall upon his flightless wings, encircled in glowing bands of protective glyphs, and all the troops of the surrounding legions could hear him roar, *"Legions, for the Prince of Hell!"*

Twirling his terrible Hooks, the ex-god leaped fearlessly into the wall of pikes, chopping them down with blindingly fast swipes of his hands. Raised up by his wing-stilts and twisting away from the pike thrusts, he was a whirlwind of movement. His height and agility made him a very difficult target for the stationary phalangites and their awkward pike-hands, and Adramalik, fighting not too far behind, saw that steady progress was being made. The tip of the wedge was now well buried within the deep line of pike demons, and it was forcing a broad and ever-widening gap.

As there was no art to an avalanche, there was no art to Moloch's unceasing destruction. And wherever he created an opening Adramalik and the legionaries would rush in, exploiting the opportunity. In a last-ditch effort to hold the line, Adramalik saw that the phalangites had been ordered to snap their pikes and use the new shorter weapons' rough, pointed ends as close-fighting spears. But it was to no avail; the gap was too large and their cohesion was diminishing by the moment. Clouds of dust rose where the phalangites were being broken.

The phalangite commander Aetar Set, whom Adramalik found easily by his Demon Minor's sigil, strode forward, impressive with his glyph-lit antlers, a long fire-tipped lance in hand. He raised it in preparation for the combat with the approaching ex-god, but as its white-hot head leveled with Moloch's chest the grapple-like Hooks came up in a blurred, prismatic flash of diamond that was so fast Adramalik's jaw opened. Aetar Set dropped the broken lance, a look of shock upon his face. And then his body, ripping apart in six diagonal sections, imploded.

The Chancellor General saw Moloch laugh, snatch up the demon's disk without breaking stride, and move past the reeling enemy, springing over steaming mounds of their still-crumbling rubble, and on into the body of Sargatanas' army. While Moloch's hands moved with a fluid rhythm of their own, wielding the Hooks with an almost casual savagery, it was clear that his focus never strayed from the Seal of Sargatanas that hung some hundreds of yards ahead.

Eligor watched with some uncertainty the advance of the legions of Dis and, in particular, the steady, relentless approach of the *Pridzarhim* champion amidst the fray. He had recognized the personal sigil from afar and knew its significance. And he watched Aetar Set's sigil go out abruptly. In single combat Eligor knew of few, if any, under the station of Demon Major who could match Moloch, and even those of high rank would be challenged. Eligor looked down toward the Baron and his hulking Shock Troopers, as yet untested in this battle, and wondered how they might fare. Perhaps collectively they would stop Moloch. But if not, would it only be his lord or Valefar who could finish Moloch, and at what cost? The Guards' Captain looked up into the clouds toward where he knew his troops to be but saw nothing.

Turning around, he saw his lord standing motionless, observing the battle without any sign of emotion. Even the layered plates of his face, usually so expressive, were hard and unreadable. Perhaps it made sense, given the ebb and flow of battle.

Beside him, Valefar stood fingering the hilt of the huge sword that rested lightly upon his shoulder. He saw Eligor looking at him and nodded, as if to reassure him, but Valefar's concern was clear.

Eligor heard a raucous outcry and spun around in time to see the flood of enemy troops surging behind the phalangites, cutting them down at their unprotected flanks. The wound Moloch had ripped into Sargatanas' phalangite legions was quickly hemorrhaging. Clouds of steam and dust were rising thickly from the battle-field, but Eligor could still see the unmistakable sigils of the legion commanders winking out as they were destroyed.

"My lord, my Guard . . ."

"Would be shredded, Eligor," Sargatanas said evenly. "This is not a fight for them to take up. Better that they stay out of sight and deal with any scouts Moloch may send up."

Eligor's disappointment was profound, but he could not responsibly disagree with his lord's appraisal; this was not a battle where precision would prevail.

Moloch and his broad wedge of soldiers were chewing into Sargatanas' secondary line of legions, a force that combined the new allies and legions from Adamantinarx and was comprised primarily of thousands of sword-wielders and hatchet-armed demons. These were slowing the enemies' advance, blunting the sharp edge of their attack, but Eligor saw that, no matter how the legions of Dis fared, Moloch and those Knights and standard-bearers around him never slowed their approach. So much latent energy was being released from the furious fighting that short tendrils of lightning played along the grinding edge where the two armies noisily clashed.

Sargatanas flared a complicated command-glyph that Eligor noted was created for Tribune Karcefuge and his Spirits. Whisking through the air, the glyph set the cavalry into motion, splitting their battalions so as to enter the gap between the decimated front line and the rear from both sides, converging upon the enemy in the middle. By now, other breaches in the phalangite line were beginning to appear, and the Spirits might have to deal with them before engaging the main force, but the hope, Eligor surmised, was that Moloch's forces, so intent upon the destruction ahead, would become aware of Karcefuge's arrival only too late.

The sword in Adramalik's hand rose and fell so swiftly that he ceased feeling as if he were actually in control of it. Demon after demon fell before him, melted and shattered and split to rubble by its sizzling blade. And through it all, panting and snorting with the effort, he wore a savage, tooth-baring grin, a mask of ferocious, unrestrained, prideful delight. It had been so long ago that he had been a participant upon the battlefield that he had forgotten just how much he missed the carnage. Holed up in the Keep and preoccupied with the endless stultifying minutiae of the Prince's paranoid court, Adramalik had lost touch with what it was to be purely physical. To be a demon. He thrilled to reawaken the presence that he was upon the battlefield.

Through his exhilaration Adramalik began to sense that perhaps his plans for the future were not to be so easily attained after all. As much as he reveled in his own prowess, the Chancellor General recognized what his rival was accomplishing; the army of Dis would not have gotten so far without him. Moloch seemed all but unvanquishable, and Adramalik watched with growing unrest the ease with which the *Pridzarhim* dispatched the enemy. Was there none, Adramalik wondered, among them capable of facing him—no newly allied, renegade Demon Major willing to match blades? Something would have to be done, and between sword falls the Chancellor General scanned the field for his Knights' sigils.

A plume of dust to one side and behind him caught Adramalik's eye, but before he could fully grasp its meaning Sargatanas' cavalry was crashing into the legions with full force. He realized, as he spitted yet another enemy legionary, that this was exactly the opportunity for which he had been waiting. He would be taking a supreme risk, a risk that threatened his very existence, but in the balance he knew he would always regret passing it up if he did not act.

Without hesitation and even as he fought, he issued the command-glyph to his Knights to pull back the legions and protect their flanks.

Almost immediately Moloch responded with a counterorder, but the Knights, well aware of their Order Chancellor General's intent, continued to regroup. Forward movement ceased, and because of the suddenness of the order the ex-god, Adramalik reasoned, would find himself quite alone within a deep pocket of the enemy.

On the surface it is not an unreasonable order, Adramalik thought. And then suddenly he realized that, in fact, there was great cause for concern. Sargatanas' attack had been a coordinated blow coming from both sides, its design to neutralize the archers, and now Adramalik watched the Spirit-lancers of Adamantinarx carving away at his legions with a fury that his own troops could not match. He ordered the Knights to leave their positions at the head of the legions and concentrate along the line directly confronting the cavalry. Perhaps, he thought, that would slow them.

He watched Sargatanas' roaring legions surge forward, encouraged by the apparent ground being gained. Circling the embattled ex-god, the demon soldiers managed, through weight of numbers, to halt his progress. Most continued on to attack the regrouping legions of Dis, but two full legions were ordered to contend with Moloch.

Adramalik pulled back and took a moment to scan the battlefield. Was he not now, after all, the self-appointed commander of the army of Dis? Through the clouds of dust and flickering lightning he saw that the repositioned Order Knights were fighting magnificently, taking a heavy toll on the rebel Karcefuge's Spirits, and that the legions behind them were now fully regrouped. The lightly armored archers on their former flanks were no more, having borne the worst of the attack. Adramalik turned, hoping to see that the ex-god had finally fallen, but to his dismay and amazement, Moloch was still fighting, his Hooks catching and rending the enemy without pause. He shook his head, marveling at the pile of rubble that was accumulating around the spinning figure, but in moments it became apparent that while the fighting remained furious, the two sides were becoming stalemated.

"Lord, I *could* go down there and confront him myself," Valefar ventured. Eligor saw his silvered eyes glittering with anticipation.

"It is time for the Baron to make amends," Sargatanas rumbled, shaking his head slightly. "If he and his troops can finish him, and quickly, I will fully reinstate him. Otherwise . . . otherwise it *will* be left to us alone."

Valefar nodded.

Eligor felt a wave of relief. He was uncertain that any single Demon Major could dispatch Moloch and was not eager to see Valefar test himself. It was a thought, Eligor suspected, that had crossed his lord's mind as well. Valefar was far too valuable a friend to risk.

A violet command-glyph streaked away from Sargatanas and dove into Baron Faraii's position, not too far from them, where it was absorbed. Almost immediately Eligor saw the Baron issue the order to advance and he and his troops began to move forward.

Something deep within Eligor made him want Faraii
to succeed, to regain his status so that the two of them
could go back to their old ways. He sorely missed the
endless tales the normally taciturn Baron had unreeled
for him in their countless meetings and missed, too, entering the tales into his chronicles.

He watched Faraii's back as he and his bulky troops
parted the legions and came within yards of Moloch. As
they drew near Eligor even saw the flying rubble of destruction, cast into the air by the *Pridzarhim,* rebound-
ing off the Baron's armor. Faraii did not duck or flinch
as the debris hit him but moved like a figure in a dream,
impassive and without hesitation. Despite himself, Eligor
could not suppress his feelings of admiration. And then, as
Baron Faraii's troops moved out in broad wings around
him, with black sword in hand, he turned and faced Sargatanas.

*By all that Lucifer stood for, the Prince will not be de-
nied! Faraii has finally awakened!* Adramalik thought.
He roared in exultation, a cry picked up by a thousand
legionaries around him when they, too, realized how
events were unfolding.

He saw Faraii issue a green glyph that only Beelzebub could have created and watched it spread like fire to
the troopers, each of whom spun on his heel in turn until a solid wall of them faced back toward the rise upon
which Sargatanas and his staff stood.

Moloch, seeing this, redoubled his efforts to push forward. Some moments later, he was swinging his weapons
so close to Faraii that he might have reached out a Hook-
wielding hand and touched him. The Baron raised his
sword-hand and with incredible deftness began to cut his
way back toward Sargatanas.

Adramalik saw many things happen at once. A Demon Minor, the Flying Guard Captain Eligor, he thought,
shot up into the sky and vanished into the clouds. Lord

Valefar began to move hurriedly toward them, parting his legions with a steady stream of glyphs, and then, sprouting four great fanlike wings, took to the air. And an enormous glyph, unlike any Adramalik had ever seen, billowed out from the rise, soaring high over the battle-field and then moving over and behind the legions of Dis to explode into a million fragments that stabbed downward, scratching a curtain of harsh light into the dark sky, somewhere in the vicinity of the abandoned town. *But why? Was Sargatanas blocking their way back if they were forced to retreat?*

The Chancellor General managed to make his way closer to what he now felt was the center of the battle. In his mind, as well as the enemy's, he was sure, Moloch's fearsome presence was the fulcrum upon which the battle seemed to balance. This moment, this sudden un-leashing of all of Sargatanas' troops, could only reveal his desperation; it would not be too long now before the battle was won and the Prince was rid of him. And, Adramalik hoped, the *Pridzarhim* as well.

Leaping over the piles of shifting rock that had once been legionaries of both sides, Adramalik clambered to within a dozen yards of the ex-god. Here, atop an ash-blown mound of rubble, Adramalik began to work at the attacking legionaries, keeping an eye always on the back of Moloch but meeting easily the ferocity of the legionaries he was felling.

Faraii, too, was busy leading his troopers deep into the heart of the enemy. No common legionary could stand before them, and the Chancellor saw that the Baron was leading them in a direct path toward the en-emy field-camp. Ever the artist with a sword, he was creating yet another masterpiece of destruction by his own hand as well as with the chopping ax-hands of his troops.

In the short time that he was in close proximity, Moloch dispatched a full cohort of Bifrons' legion; only

its centurion remained, and he was surviving only by
his remarkable agility. But his fate was inevitable and
the centurion stumbled and was swept up by one of the
Hooks. Before he could be shattered, something, Adramalik saw, distracted the ex-god.

A silver-blue sigil heralded the approach of Lord
Valefar, and when he stopped a yard above the ground
just before Moloch the carnage in the immediate area
all but ceased in anticipation of the fight to come. Adramalik hardly recognized the Prime Minister, not just for
the many horns, small wings, and embers that had formed
a living crown about his head but more for the terrible
wrath he saw upon Valefar's face. Resting lightly in the
Demon Major's hands was an unusually long sheathed
sword.

The demon lord looked from side to side, taking in
the half-dozen scarlet-armored Knights who flanked the
ex-god. With wings rippling, Valefar pulled his sword
from its sheath and in one fluid, unanswerable move
lopped the heads of the Knights cleanly off. Adramalik's jaw opened in disbelief as he stared at the featherlight blue-flame sword from the Above—an ancient
ialpor napta! He could not begin to imagine how it had
come to be in Hell, but the sight of it sent a ripple of
fear through him.

Adramalik looked at Moloch and saw that he was
grinning, his eyes fixed balefully upon Valefar. As if in
answer to Valefar, the ex-god tore the struggling centurion in half, treading upon his smoking remains as they
fell to the ground and crumbled into rock. Moloch then
squared his shoulders and held his Hooks out in a beckoning gesture of defiance, the same gesture with which
he had baited Adramalik, the same purely predatory
look in his glittering icy-blue eyes. Covered in black
ash, panting, he appeared primal, savage.

The fires of Valefar's corona flashed for an instant
and he lunged and the blue flames of his sword arced in

a half-circle of violet and purple. Moloch spun to one side, but not quickly enough, and Adramalik saw the long and terrible cut the ancient sword had sliced into his upper arm. A sound like the screeching blast of a dozen fumaroles split the air as the enraged ex-god countered with a clawing combination of strokes that pushed the demon backward with their ferocity into his own troops.

The harsh sound of weapons beating upon shields arose from the legions of Dis as they watched their champion and general stalk forward. The Chancellor General had never seen him so angered. Short bolts of lightning wavered in sinuous tendrils from within his body, sheathing him in a crackling net of energy.

Valefar was quick to recover, charging forward with a powerful thrust of his wings, and again the two combatants faced each other, lashing out in great sweeping attacks. Lunging, parrying, and counterattacking, they twisted around each other, the ex-god spinning nimbly upon his wing-stalks, the Demon Major diving and dodging with a constant whirring of wing beats. Evenly matched, they circled, wary at one moment and bold at the next, each inflicting small wounds upon the other, the speed of Valefar's sword matched by that of the two flashing Hooks.

A growing cry of dismay suddenly swept through the battlefield, coming, Adramalik realized, from well behind his own lines. He turned and his eyes widened as he saw the town far to the rear of his legions appearing to melt away, the buildings bending and crashing forward like the slow cresting of a wave of cooling lava. And between all of them, in the center of the town's widest avenue, Adramalik could just make out a solitary figure—a soul, it would seem—seated motionless atop a war-caparisoned Abyssal. Where the cascading bricks fell souls suddenly arose, and Adramalik could see them running purposefully to and fro, snatching up the weapons that he had seen so carelessly strewn about. He could also see that they were assuming formations and that the lone mounted figure was directing them. The Chancellor General could already see, to his dismay, that they easily equaled his remaining legionaries in numbers and not even half of the buildings had broken apart.

Shouts brought Adramalik's attention back to the duel. Moloch's focus had not wavered, but apparently Valefar had, for the briefest instant, taken his eyes from his crouching opponent. The Hooks whipped out simultaneously and one caught Valefar, raking through his left wing, shearing through the bone, and rippling membrane, and dropping the demon to the ground. Down on one knee, his wing in long tatters, Valefar counterparried another blow and slipped his sword under Moloch's guard and into the ex-god's shoulder. Both combatants pulled back, the pain unmistakable upon their faces.

Valefar rose to his feet and, seeing that Moloch could no longer wield his right-hand Hook, began to concentrate his efforts on the ex-god's weaker side.

At the periphery of his awareness, Adramalik began to sense the legions of Dis pulling back, melting away from the duel that had only moments before seemed so important to them. Now their own existence was in jeopardy as the first wave of souls attacked their flanks. The Chancellor General, himself, felt the tug of both battles but remained in place, unable to pry himself away from the unfolding duel. Valefar's wondrous, awful sword was, more and more, finding its mark, and every grunt from Moloch revealed his diminishing strength. With grim satisfaction, Adramalik watched events unfolding just as he had hoped.

Streaking down through the murky clouds, Eligor burst into clear air only to see his lord and the staff generals beset on all sides by Faraii's Shock Troops. With lances extended, Eligor's Flying Guard hit the black-armored soldiers from above, catching them unaware as their ax-hands rose and fell. He could not immediately see the Baron and so moved deftly from one trooper to the next, penetrating their heavy armor from above wherever possible. Sargatanas had been right to suggest that Eligor's lightly armed Guard would be relatively ineffectual against Faraii's soldiers. The best Eligor could hope for was to slow them and wound them enough to make his lord's work easier.

For their part, Sargatanas and the other Demons Major were taking a heavy, relentless toll, felling the enemy one by one, but not as quickly as Eligor would have hoped. Brief, intense fountains of sparks arose where *Lukiftias* shattered another of Faraii's elite warriors. Too often, though, the Shock Troopers' axes found their mark, and to his dismay, Eligor saw Bifrons fall amidst a brilliant flash, cleft completely across his waist.

Gradually, amazingly, Eligor saw the combination of his Guards' and the embattled Demon Majors' bladework take effect; the dark, hulking Troopers began to give ground, falling one at a time as they grudgingly moved backward. Finally he spotted Faraii, untouched, flicking his blade skyward to deflect the new aerial onslaught. Eligor looked at the lean figure, so masterful in his attacks, so poised, and hated him more than he could have imagined. As he watched he saw the Baron suddenly break ranks and fall back, Eligor guessed, to lead his now-beleaguered troops in a reluctant retreat. Pulling up, Eligor saw the souls under Hannibal's generalship crash into the enemy legions' flanks, causing great confusion. Faced by an enemy at both their head and tail, the legions of Dis began to flee from either side. But where was Valefar?

Moloch was clearly weakening; that much was obvious to Adramalik. While the *Pridzarhim* still swept out with his remaining Hook, the conviction, the snap to his wrist, was missing from his attempts. Valefar, seriously injured himself, was taking his time, measuring, picking the targets carefully upon the ex-god's body and then flicking his sword with precision. Each wound caused a new flow of black blood, a new degradation of Moloch's considerable power, a near stumble, a tiny hesitation.

The Chancellor General began to sense the shifting tides around him, the dwindling of his own forces to his back, and the sudden influx of soldiers as they began to retreat from the wavering front. With little effort he now saw Shock Troopers, and perhaps Baron Faraii himself, backing away from the vortex of destruction that emanated from Sargatanas and his fellow generals. And, hearing the tumult from the souls attacking behind him, he began to wonder whether it was fast growing time to withdraw.

Valefar flicked his sword and a terrible scream rent the air as Moloch's already-disabled hand fell to the ground severed. Blood streamed thickly from the wound, black and thick, clotting upon the fleshy ground and making the *Pridzarhim's* footing uncertain.

Adramalik suddenly saw souls hacking at his legionaries, much closer than he had realized. Turning fully around, he saw the same soul—their general, he guessed—leap into the fray upon the back of his Abyssal mount. The soul was clearly an expert rider, raising his mount upon two feet to avoid the more concentrated knots of fighting soldiers. Swinging a heavy sword, the general leaned far out of his saddle, chopping fiercely at Adramalik's demons, even destroying one of his Knights not thirty paces from him. The battle had turned, and now, Adramalik thought, *now* would be the time to leave the field. He glanced back at Moloch. No need to stay; the duel's outcome was all but certain.

Shock Troopers and demons from Adamantinarx fought just behind Valefar, but seeming not to notice, he

raised his sword once again and as it plunged deep into
the ex-god's chest a strange look came over the demon
lord's face—a look of shock and puzzlement mixed. For
just an instant Adramalik thought he saw the thin point
of a black sword protruding from just beneath Valefar's
chin. The blade worked from side to side, deftly slicing
a long arc, and then was gone. *Did I really see it?* Adramalik wondered. Without waiting he turned and ran,
finding a dozen or so of his Knights who had banded together for protection against the overwhelming numbers of souls who now flooded across the field. Escape
was uppermost in their minds.

It was a total failure. *Somehow,* he thought, *somehow
Sargatanas has done it again!*

Dis was a long way off; with them hunted continually
by Sargatanas' troops, theirs would be a difficult journey home. And, Adramalik realized with a pang of terror, at the end of that journey the Prince, without his
Consort and now his champion as well, would welcome
him from this day with little less than total contempt
and all of the pain that it would bring.

Eligor dove down toward where Valefar had been standing, the sense of urgency pounding in his head, the hot
air screaming beneath his wings as he tried to gain
speed. He had finally spotted the demon lord amidst a
carpet of retreating demons, found him by the fire of his
blue-flame sword. Moloch, Eligor had also seen. The
ex-god was struggling to stand, propped up by his broken wing-stilts and burned by a hundred cuts. Valefar
stood before him, legs apart and sword-arm outstretched,
but something was not right, because as Eligor descended he had seen the sword leave the demon lord's
hand and fall to the ground. And then, to Eligor's horror,
he had seen a brilliant flash followed by a gathering
whirlwind that began to obscure the field in a funnel of

ash that grew in intensity, making his and his fellow Guardsdemons' rapid descent extremely difficult.

When he alighted he knew that what he had feared, what in the back of his mind he had tried to deny, was true. Valefar was nowhere to be seen and Moloch was still alive, panting heavily, blood streaming in a hundred rivulets, single Hook raised defiantly. At bay and swiping at the Flying Guard who were harrying him with their lances, he was dangerous yet.

The Guard Captain, momentarily in shock, saw his lord's sigil through the wavering sheets of wind-driven ash and the countless fleeing enemies; Sargatanas was nearly at hand, and Eligor knew that his lord would be all too eager to confront Moloch. But as that thought crossed his mind, Hannibal's steed leaped upon two legs into view, the general pulling hard upon the reins, making the creature drop quickly down on all fours. Without hesitating, Hannibal sprang down from the saddle and attacked the ex-god, swinging the sword that Sargatanas had given him with a fury that Eligor had never conceived possible in a soul.

Moloch, spent as he was, was no faster than Hannibal in his defensive moves. They traded blows and parries and then one long, raking attack caught Hannibal on his shoulder, twisting him around and tearing a gash that peeled the soul's left arm to his knee and lodged the Hooks in his ribs. Moloch tried, futilely, to disengage the weapon from the soul's body for a killing blow but in the effort brought Hannibal to within striking distance. Caught on the weapon and grimacing with pain, he leaned in even closer to the bent form of the ex-god and with a single vicious one-handed chop severed the snarling head from its neck. Immediately the ground began to shake, knocking Hannibal and those demons around him off their feet, and Eligor, some paces away, took wing and watched Moloch's body collapse inward in a red flare of light and disappear.

When the shaking of the ground had subsided, Eligor rushed to the Soul-General's side, pulling him to one knee. Carefully Eligor pulled the giant Hook from the terrible wound. Hannibal held himself up by his sword and raised his eyes to Eligor's.

"So you see," Hannibal said weakly, "it is not so hard to kill one's god, after all." His eyes closed and he slumped against the demon's leg.

Eligor nodded respectfully; he knew what Moloch had been to Hannibal and understood what the soul had achieved. Eligor waved some of his Guard over to surround Hannibal and instructed them to bind his wounds. The Soul-General was still alive, and Eligor carefully watched glyphs-of-healing being created to keep him that way until they returned to Adamantinarx. Eligor was uncertain about the soul's ability to heal himself; these awful wounds had been inflicted by a weapon with unimaginable properties. When he looked up he saw the welcome form of Sargatanas standing before him. Apart from a fist-sized, oozing hole in his armored side, the Lord of Adamantinarx was unharmed. Eligor watched him move slowly to where Valefar had stood and saw Sargatanas reach down to pick up the demon's sword. The fires of its blade grew, spreading briefly over the hilt and onto Sargatanas' shaking hand. The strong blue light etched the profound sadness of his face forever upon Eligor's mind.

Eligor began to search through the rubble and ash for Moloch's disk. When he found it, a dark, heavy, and tarnished thing, he brought it to his lord, who regarded it for a moment.

"Keep it with him," he said quietly, indicating Hannibal. "I am sure he will want it."

Eligor's eyes began to search the ground where they stood. Steam began to form in their corners, hindering his efforts.

"I . . . I do not see *his* disk, my lord."

Sargatanas scanned the ground as well, finding nothing.

Turning away, the demon lord looked up at the curling zephyrs of ash that rose high into the olive sky. Eligor could almost feel the enormous grief that was taking hold of him.

"Perhaps, the winds have taken it."

XXIV

ADAMANTINARX-UPON-THE-ACHERON

Valefar's empty chambers seemed like another world altogether to Eligor as he sat glumly at the Prime Minister's enormous bone desk. The absolute silence, the transparent wisps of smoke that drifted in the slowest of curling eddies from the tiny crack in one of the windows, the dull sound of the heart-clock, all contributed to the overwhelming sense of absence.

It had been weeks since Eligor's return to Adamantinarx, and the sense of loss at the passing of Valefar was keener than ever. Before he had locked himself away in his chambers, Sargatanas had told Eligor to go and sort through the Prime Minister's belongings and papers, to gather the important documents of state and anything Eligor might want as a keepsake. Sargatanas had asked for nothing himself; the chambers were to be sealed, and their contents were to be left as they were. With that imparted he had turned and headed to his chambers, a dark and somber figure in a now-emptier realm.

Eligor shifted a heavy stack of vellum documents to one side of the desktop. He had chosen one of Valefar's aides, a Demon Minor named Fyrmiax, to assist him in what he knew would be a difficult task, and he could hear the demon in one of the far rooms rummaging about. Sargatanas had yet to appoint a new prime minister, and Eligor knew that it would not be this demon. The position had been equal parts administrative and honorary; Eligor suspected that it might be some time before the position would be filled.

He pushed himself up from the desk and, with a sigh, began to make piles of the documents, stacking them by the door so that Fyrmiax could load them onto the small bone pull-carts that waited in the corridor. As Eligor went from one chamber to another, he saw innumerable poignant signs of Valefar's presence, objects or arrangements of objects that gave the impression of just having been used. The case his sword had been kept in lay open upon his pallet, the imprint of its light form still visible upon its cushioned interior.

Moving farther into Valefar's private world, Eligor caught sight of the cabinet behind which he knew the hidden compartment lay. Inexplicably, he felt a compulsion to open it and look within it for one last time. Its existence was a secret only he, now, knew of, and he saw no reason to mention it; it was, after all, only an empty space.

Closing the door to the brazier-lit inner room, he went back to the cabinet and began to pull the scrolled vellums down, careful not to crush any. He removed the shelves and then spent some time feeling around for the hidden latch that Valefar had so easily found. Eligor felt a slight thud beneath his hand from somewhere behind the wall, and the panel opened and again the dust of time sifted upward.

Eligor knelt and peered into the dark, rectangular space, not really sure what, if anything, he expected to find. It looked just as he had remembered it, featureless and simple. But when he ran his hand against the rough back wall he discovered a ledge and upon it something that moved slightly when he made contact. Reaching farther in, he found a small, footed casket, which he carefully pulled out. It was carved of bone, dyed, and inlaid with precisely cut chips of obsidian of differing colors.

Eligor found a low bench to sit on and, unfastening its simple latch, opened the box. Within it were two objects carefully wrapped in thin, finely dressed soul-skin, one larger than the other. He picked up the two bundles and weighed them in his hands, debating whether opening them represented an act of posthumous betrayal, an uncontestable intrusion into the Prime Minister's privacy. Ultimately, Eligor remembered Sargatanas' offer—that he could take anything he wanted—and this provided enough justification that he began to slowly unwrap the larger object. In seconds a small bone statue, exquisite in its every detail, rested upon the skin spread upon his lap. It was Lilith, carved, he now knew, by her own hand. Bits of what Eligor guessed were the charred remains of Valefar's own feathers, presumably gathered like sad reliquaries from the Fall, lay in dark flakes around it. *How could he have gotten this statue? They were given only to souls by Lilith. Valefar had been present when his lord had taken the female soul's statue that fateful day so long ago. Perhaps he had acquired this one in a similar way. But if so, would he not have mentioned it? Or . . . or did* she *give it to him?*

Scooping up the statue and the precious bits of feather, Eligor placed them on a small table. Taking up the second small burden, he noted how heavy it was comparatively. If he was surprised by the first object, he was positively astonished by the second. Lying upon its dark wrappings, simple in its design but ominous by its very significance, was an Order of the Fly medallion. *Valefar . . . an Order Knight? Impossible!* Beneath the dully gleaming Fly, Eligor saw the corner of a folded

piece of vellum, and smoothing it open, he began to
read the crabbed script of Dis:

> Valefar,
>
>   I have taken the liberty of secreting this among
> your personal effects. This commission was well
> earned; the services you performed as Primus of the
> Order to our Prince, if performed unhappily, were ex-
> emplary. It was your sad misfortune to have Fallen in
> the immediate proximity of this city and thus to have
> to serve it and its master; I know you will be more at
> ease wherever else you choose to settle. And I know
> that, in departing, you will leave behind the one for
> whom you care most. She will be safer for your deci-
> sion. I will see to it.
>
>   For now and always remember me as your friend
> in Dis.
>
>   Agares

Was this possible? thought Eligor, his mind racing.
The conclusions he was inferring went beyond anything
he could have guessed. The statue and the medallion,
together in a casket hidden away, both precious, painful
reminders of a time past in Dis. Did they signify a relationship between Valefar and Lilith? The more Eligor
pondered it, the more certain he grew. But did Sargatanas know of it? Eligor sat stunned, the medal growing heavy in his enervated hand.

Frowning, Eligor regarded the opening in the wall,
considering his choices. He would not take these things
as reminders of his friend, would not run the risk of
their ever being found. Instead Eligor carefully separated
the feathers from the skin around the statue and put
them on a table. He then rewrapped the statue and the
medallion and placed them back inside the casket, latch-
ing it shut. He put it back into the wall compartment,
sealed the opening, and reorganized the bookcase, leaving

it exactly as he had found it. Returning to the small pile of feathers, he carefully scooped them into a clean blood-ink vial, a fitting symbol, he felt, for the demon who had been Prime Minister of Adamantinarx for so long.

Eligor cast a final look around the innermost room and then closed the door behind him, sealing it with a glyph. Its secret was safe. He navigated through the rooms, passing Fyrmiax as he quietly went about collecting scrolls and vellums. Eligor's eyes fell upon a volume from the Library, something that Valefar had apparently been in the midst of reading—a collection of reminiscences of the Above. He picked it up wondering whether the Prime Minister had been reminiscing himself or had been questioning his lord's decision. Eligor would never know. He put the book aside unsure whether he would read it himself or simply return it to the Library.

As the two demons filled the small carts, the rooms' clutter melted away, revealing, one by one, the bare surfaces of their many desktops. Eligor could not help but think the rooms looked, if possible, even sadder relieved of their friendly clutter. It was as if the demons were erasing the hand of Valefar.

After nearly a day of sorting and stacking, the carts were filled to overflow and Eligor and Fyrmiax, leaning against the corridor wall exhausted, watched as six demons trundled them off. Tired and dispirited but glad that the job was done, Eligor wordlessly clapped Fyrmiax on the shoulder, and the other Demon Minor nodded and began down the corridor.

There was only one act left, and that was to seal the chambers. Eligor took a final look at the familiar, once-inviting rooms, picked up the large volume, and closed the door behind him. He produced the red seal that Sargatanas had given him and, with a wave of his hand, floated it directly over the door's lintel. When the seal was in place he uttered a command and watched the complex glyph replicate itself dozens of times until a hundred identical copies had slowly outlined the door frame. He then extended his hand to touch the door and a hundred swift glyph-arrows converged to prevent him from making contact; had he persisted he would have been destroyed. He pulled his stinging hand back. It was done.

The tome tucked under his arm, Eligor took a deep breath and headed back to his chambers. He would try to forget this day but knew that, like so many other dark days, he probably never would.

DIS

"Will you be able to do this, Chancellor General?"

Nergar's voice, which seemed to come from somewhere far off, sounded concerned, but Adramalik knew better than that. The Chief of Security was sure to be enjoying Adramalik's profound misery.

"Of course, Lord Nergar," he said with little conviction. Adramalik felt as if he were not really there in the Keep's Basilica of Security, not really sitting in the small, featureless, brick-walled room with the despicable Nergar awaiting the arrival of Prime Minister Agares.

Adramalik closed his eyes again and, this time, thought of the pain as some kind of a parasite, something recently acquired that now lived within him, feeding off his body with a blind hunger. He had seen such creatures far out in the Wastes, attached by the dozens to Abyssals that could barely move for the collective weight of them. Then he could hardly imagine the host's pain. But now he could.

The ragtag survivors of the Battle of the Flaming Cut had filtered back to Dis, exhausted and miserable, and

most had been greeted with summary destruction. Beelzebub's manifold anger had spared no one, and to his
shame, Adramalik bore the unenviable distinction of being the highest-ranking demon to return. Knowing that
he could not afford to be without his personal bodyguard, the Prince had determined to inflict as much pain
upon his Knights as they could endure before they were
entirely broken. The ceaseless moaning in the Knights'
quarters was unending testimony to their Prince's patience. Adramalik, himself, had not been exempt, and
now, some weeks later, he still wondered if it might
have been better to destroy himself on the field of battle.
As the unpredictable waves of searing pain ebbed and
flowed throughout him he still toyed with the idea.
Beelzebub's Invocation of Atonement would only stop
when the Prince chose to lift it. And he was not known
for his forgiveness.

Adramalik opened his eyes and looked across the
room into the shadowed corner where Nergar sat. A single light-glyph cast a partial radiance upon the room,
but even in the gloom Adramalik could see the demon's
chiseled features, features that many believed were not
his own. There was something too perfect, too angelic,
about them to have survived the Fall so minimally affected.

"He is late," Nergar said.

"Would *you* be eager to sit down and be questioned
by us?"

"If I was blameless . . ."

Adramalik heard footsteps and turned to see the tall
demon enter the room. He could see Nergar's escort
taking up position behind the door. The Prime Minister,
usually so proper in his mien as well as his dress, looked
ruffled and slightly unkempt, as if he had been just
awakened; open concern was written upon his tight, severe features.

"It is late and I was resting. Why have you had me

roused and brought here?" His creaky, indignant voice was muffled somewhat by interrupted rest, further indication of his having been brought to the Basilica hastily.

"You do not know?" Adramalik asked.

"No," Agares said flatly.

"You were telling . . . who was it, Lord Nergar . . . ?"

"Baphomeres."

"You were telling Baphomeres that you felt Lilith was better off wherever she was. That is what you said, is this not so?"

"What of it, Adramalik? She is. No one could doubt that, not even you."

"Baphomeres is one of Nergar's demons . . . a lowly, covert Security functionary, actually." He saw Agares wince slightly. "As for me, it is not *my* place in the court of Beelzebub to judge him and his relationship with his Consort. Is it *yours*?"

Agares stared at the Chancellor General. He was now attentive and on guard, the gravity of the interview obvious to him. His silvered eyes glittered intensely.

"Perhaps not."

Nergar cleared his throat. "Can you tell us anything regarding the disappearance of the Consort?"

Agares looked down.

"I can only tell you what you know already, that she departed, incognito, from the Sixth Gate. No one knows where she went from there."

"Had you seen her shortly before her departure?" Adramalik asked.

"Yes."

"How did she seem?"

"She was understandably distraught. Her handmaiden had just been—"

"We know," said Adramalik without feeling. That one had gotten what she deserved. "Did you comfort the Consort?"

Agares looked at him angrily, small flames licking

from his flared nostrils. "Remember to whom you are speaking, Chancellor General. I *am* the Prime Minister of Dis, the capital of Hell. I resent your collective implications, I resent your having brought me here at this time of night, and . . . and I resent you."

"That is as it may be, Duke Agares, but your behavior is now an open question."

Agares looked from one demon to the other and, after a long moment, said evenly, "As Prime Minister it is my duty to look after the well-being of the Prince's interests. That includes, by my understanding, his Consort."

Adramalik considered this. "There is a difference between looking after his interests and countering whatever the Prince has implemented as his personal policy. By comforting the Consort you chose to counter his punishment of her through her handmaiden."

"The very real question for you to ponder," Nergar interjected, sounding very reasonable, "is just how is the Prince going to feel about your role in all of this? Especially now that his Consort has not been brought back to him."

"*My* role?" Agares sputtered. He jerked his thumb at Adramalik. "Ask *him* why Lilith has not been returned."

Adramalik clenched his jaw. The pain was back with teeth, and Agares' bluntness was almost too much to suffer.

"The Prince already has," said Nergar, "and the Chancellor General is paying, in his own small way, for it. It is now time for your master, through us, to turn to you."

"I have told you what little there is to say. Do I feel that Lilith is better off now? I have already said as much. Did I help her leave Dis? No. And you will never prove otherwise. Now," Agares said, rising, wavering slightly, "may I retire to my chambers?"

Adramalik stood as well; he felt fractionally better on his feet. "You may, Prime Minister, but I would not expect too much rest, if I were you. We are, after this interview, bound for the Rotunda and must deliver our conclusions to the Prince. You will be sure to hear his response before the night is over."

Agares' hand balled into a fist even as he swallowed hard. Focusing on neither of them, he turned brusquely and, without another word, strode stiffly from the room, followed by his unwelcome escort.

"What do you suppose he will do?" muttered Adramalik, looking at the Prime Minister's retreating form.

"What any demon would in his circumstances. Attempt to destroy himself." Nergar looked pleased at the prospect.

"Better Abaddon's Pit than Beelzebub's wrath, eh?"

Nergar nodded as he rose. "Well, yes, actually."

Adramalik steadied himself as another clawing wave of agony shot through his body. As he passed through the threshold on his way to his chambers, he caught sight of Nergar smirking at his obvious discomfort from the corner, but the pain was so intense he ignored him. As Adramalik lurched into the corridor, he promised himself he would not forget Nergar when the time was right.

ADAMANTINARX-UPON-THE-ACHERON

As soon as what was left of the victorious Great Army of the Ascension had returned, Lilith excitedly left her chambers to seek out Sargatanas. Apart from the lines of returning soldiers, the streets as well as the landings leading up to the palace steps were relatively open. Once before the huge doorway she saw that her progress was not going to be so easy; small groups of demons gathering down on the plaza below had formed into larger crowds and were waiting to enter. Once inside, she found traversing the palace corridors difficult; the milling about of demon clerks eager to hear of the battle slowed her progress to a crawl but also allowed her to hear snippets of battlefield news. Sargatanas had, she gathered, been brilliant against the worst Dis could marshal. He had been wounded. And some of his generals, along with their armies, had been destroyed.

Lilith made her way toward the Audience Chamber, but she soon found that she was far from alone in that goal. When she arrived at the outlying arcades she could see that a huge crowd had gathered around the base of the dais; it seemed as if Adamantinarx had emptied its streets and avenues into the great circular chamber.

Tales of the passing of Valefar found their way to Lilith in incomplete fragments, shreds of conversation caught as sad whispers in halting Angelic from the murmuring crowd. She had taught herself the language from books but never heard it spoken and wondered why now it was; when she had pieced the words together she had to stop and, supporting herself by a column, catch her breath. It had been hard not to let slip anything about their shared past in Dis; it would be harder still not to let her grief show. *He had been an extraordinary demon,* she thought, *wise and undeniably noble. And now he was gone, leaving that other noble demon Sargatanas to fight his noble war without him.*

As she moved toward the foot of the dais the crowd parted for her, but, still, she heard quite a bit. The battle had been won, but by all accounts the price had been heavy. The complete destruction of Adamantinarx's military backbone—the phalangites—the end of Earl Bifrons, and the resultant chaos within his legions that had led to their massive casualties all had left the city weakened. *At least the same or worse can be said for the state in which Dis must find itself. The Fly must be enraged! How happy that makes me!*

Lilith climbed the steps noting that more demons were coming down than going up. All who passed her saluted in some manner or another, each according her

the honor as was their custom in their own wards. She
spotted Zoray, deep in conversation with three other officials, and went to him. He disengaged from the demons
and greeted her warmly as she gained the top of the
dais, but she could sense immediately that something
was wrong. Clusters of conversing demons obscured her
view of Sargatanas, but Zoray navigated through them
until both he and Lilith stood before the throne.

Bathed in the red light of the oculus, it stood empty,
flanked dutifully by Eligor's Guard.

"I thought you should see for yourself, my lady," Zoray said softly. "He has not been seen since the first day
of his arrival in Adamantinarx. He ordered that the
court language be changed to Angelic in Valefar's honor
and then he was gone."

"Is he injured?"

"Yes, but it did not seem to cause him too great discomfort. It was but a flesh-wound, deep but not debilitating. He would not let anyone minister to it, though.
And there is something else."

"Yes?"

"I saw him the day he returned. His appearance was
shifting so rapidly, so awfully, that were it not for his
sigil I would have scarcely recognized him. The seraph
has never been further from him."

Lilith looked at the throne and shook her head
slightly. His misery at Valefar's loss must have been
consuming him.

"Is he in his chambers?"

"We think so, but there is no way to be sure. Perhaps
you . . ."

"If he wishes to be alone then it would not be my
place to intrude," she heard herself say with apparent
conviction. But Lilith knew what she would do. And she
knew where she would look first.

"Tell me of the Soul-General, Zoray."

"He is terribly wounded; Moloch's Hooks dug too

deep; he cannot possibly heal himself. On the battlefield he was patched up, but we have not been able to do much more. We have purged and safeguarded the traitorous Baron's quarters and Hannibal now lies within. But he is not well. My lady," Zoray said gravely, "we are not accustomed to *healing* souls and we are not certain he will survive."

"Then I must go and see what I can do; I have some knowledge of them and may be able to help him." She pressed Zoray's arm and turned away. And then, so as not to arouse any undue suspicion, she said over her shoulder, "Zoray, if he *should* venture out . . ."

"If he should venture out, my lady, you will be among the first to know."

"Thank you, Zoray."

Zoray bowed and she continued down the steps, her bird-feet clicking lightly against the stone. *First,* she thought, *first I must see to Hannibal. But then I will go to* him.

Lilith was relieved and pleased to see Captain Eligor outside Hannibal's chambers. Eligor was a levelheaded demon and someone whom she trusted. And better than that, he was a relative expert in the ways of souls. She knew quite a bit about them herself but welcomed his bolstering presence as she entered the chambers.

The room that Hannibal occupied was dark and warm, and as she approached she saw that he lay upon a soft pallet, unconscious and still. Even though Faraii's chambers had been purged and the walls sealed, complex glyphs-of-protection circled at ceiling height, designed to raise an alarm if the Fly in any way attempted to reenter this particular chamber. Lilith passed a solemn Mago on her way to his brother's side. Leaning over the Soul-General, she examined the wound that had him so close to destruction. His entire shoulder and arm, attached to his torso only by the crude field-glyphs, had been peeled down in thick strips, the result of the multiple prongs of the Hook, which lay by his side. It was huge and she picked it up by its thick handle with difficulty, turning it in both hands and noting how the moving light of the glyphs overhead played upon its diamond recurved prongs. As she placed it back upon the table with a loud scrape she noticed, lying in shadow, the large, round disk that had been Moloch. She ran a finger over its blotchy surface and withdrew it quickly. She knew that it was inanimate but somehow, whether real or imagined, she felt a malevolent energy emanating from within. She hastily turned to Hannibal. The soul's torso was open and she could easily see the very large black scab that ran from his neck to his hip. That was good, she thought. It had probably been the only thing that had kept his fluids within him. She would have to remove that and clean the wound beneath, but she knew that whatever she did, he would lose his arm completely; the glyphs apparently healed demons but were not effective on souls. The Arts Curative were not very highly developed among demons, but as she was careful to distinguish, she was no ordinary demon. She had known human beings from their own beginnings.

The arm was already shriveled and useless, the black, slow-moving blood having entirely drained away. She imagined that the organs within his chest must still be vital enough for him not to have been destroyed on the spot. The viscous blood in souls she knew was present only to keep the body flexible; it had no other properties that any demon had ever been able to discern.

"Mago," she said haltingly, "he will lose his arm and a part of his shoulder as well." She did not easily speak the common language of the souls, and it always sounded harsh and percussive to her ears.

Mago rose and stood by her, watching her pulling

gently on Hannibal's skin, gauging just how she would
stitch him up. She unrolled her little kit of tools and selected a sharp little knife—her favorite carver. With this
she deftly sliced the few remaining ropes of skin that
had kept the arm attached to the torso.

"Eligor, if you would," she said, pointing to another
larger knife with a blackened finger.

Silently, they worked off the scab and immediately
saw the black fluid begin to seep quickly, dangerously,
from Hannibal. Lilith put the knife down and picked up
a needle she had also brought from her chambers and
quickly threaded the thinnest sinew into it. As Eligor
pulled the gray skin taut, she began to carefully stitch
the two flaps together. She knew that this was less than
an ideal solution and that she would have to seek out
someone with more knowledge of soul anatomy and the
Arts Curative than herself.

Her stitches were very fine, close, and tight, and it
took longer than she wanted to work her way up to Hannibal's neck. As she worked she realized just how much
she had invested in this soul; not only was he a capable
general, but he also had a profound potential to govern
his kind. In fact, she would do whatever she could to
help him do just that.

Eligor was told that as she closed the gaping wound
he could gradually release Hannibal's skin. When Eligor
could completely let go he stood back and admired
Lilith's deft finger-work; he commented that her stitches
were so precise that he could barely see the sinew, and
when she finally tied the tiny knot at the soul's neck and
straightened to look at her handiwork she was smiling
faintly. No fluids seeped from any point, but just to be
sure she uttered a single word and traced her finger
lightly over the seam. It vanished completely.

"Now, that should do. I can do nothing for the damaged organs. We shall have to see how they affect him."

Eligor nodded and turned and saw Mago, the hope written upon his face.

"He will mend, Mago," Eligor said fluently and convincingly in the soul's tongue. "The loss of his arm will be a problem only for a short time. Considering what souls are used to here, his problems will seem insignificant."

Lilith was looking at Eligor with a raised eyebrow. "That is a skill I did not know you had, Eligor."

"What? Lying?"

"No, Eligor," she said gently. "From what I could tell, you were reassuring. I meant speaking their tongue. It is very difficult."

Eligor looked pleased. "I have made them a focus of study, my lady."

"So I have heard. Once again it is clear to me that Lord Sargatanas has chosen his staff with great care." Lilith replaced her knives and rolled her tool-blanket, carefully tying the skin ribbons that held it together. She looked once more at the soul. His features were as strong as his will. *He must have been quite a force to reckon with in his Life,* she thought. And then, in an odd way, she realized that she was proud of him. In Hell, he was her finest creation.

Lilith turned to Eligor and looked up at him. For a moment she looked deep into his silvered eyes.

"I want to go to Sargatanas, but I am sure that I cannot find the way. Will you take me?"

There was the briefest of hesitations.

"But, my lady, he is certainly in his chambers."

Whether Eligor knew his lord's whereabouts and was simply protecting him as was his duty or truly did not know Lilith could not be sure.

"No, Eligor, he most certainly is not."

Eligor's chin went up a fraction. Again she could not tell if he was being intractable or was merely found out. *Does he know where Sargatanas is or am I revealing*

something to him that he had not considered? The demon's wings twitched slightly as he slowly looked down
at his feet, either considering the situation he was in or
realizing just what she was suggesting. Both paths led to
the same door, and either way, she knew that he would
have to obey her; she was Lilith and there was no way to
deny her.

When he looked up again he said, "I know the way."

"I knew you would."

She dreamt of green trees heavy with scent and brightly
colored fruits and streams of diamond-glittering water
and yielding, fertile earth beneath her feet, and those
feet were like the feet of souls. And she dreamt, too, of
a sun's golden light upon her naked body, bathing it in
sensual warmth, as she wandered the Garden heaven
she had once known. In her dream she knew she was
dreaming, but it did not make the turquoise sky any less
blue.

The distant soft scuffing of Eligor's approaching footsteps drew her away from her lost, short-lived heaven,
pulling her back down into the darkness of reality. She
awoke fully, and as frequently happened when she had
this dream, the bitterness washed away from her any
pleasure she might have derived. She missed that place
and the freedom that had gone with it, missed it even
more than her equally short life with Lucifer. But it was
gone forever and she had vowed that even if all of the
seraphim of the Above came on bended knees to beg
her to join them she would refuse. The Throne had cast
her away and here she would stay. She knew this was
nothing more than an idle fantasy; her anger, wreaked
quite purposefully on the souls, had lasted a dozen of
their generations—a moment really in the Above, but it
had been enough.

Lilith rose from the hard bench, her skin robes falling
in some disarray, and stretched unselfconsciously. But

as he came closer she could see Eligor's eyes avert, and she quickly covered herself. She often forgot the effect she had on those around her.

A sound from behind the thick door of Sargatanas' shrine caught her attention and she nodded to Eligor, who, apparently, had not heard it; his eyesight, so keen when he was airborne, was far better than his average hearing. Lilith watched him step close to the door and press his ear to it. She smiled, for each tiny sound from within confirmed her certitude that he was within.

Eligor pulled away from the door and shrugged.

"My lady, I beg your forgiveness that I did not tell you immediately that he was here. You were wise to understand him so well."

"He doubts himself, Eligor," Lilith said. "And now he has lost his one true friend. This is where he would have to come."

"Only a handful of us know of the Shrine. I should have—"

Lilith put a sharp-nailed finger to her lips.

"He is repeating the same phrases over and over," she whispered. "He has been doing that since you left me here. I cannot make out what he is saying, but it is as if he were praying. In the old language, no less."

"No, you must be mistaken. It is forbidden. Even he would not . . ."

"He, especially, would."

Eligor smiled and then said, "We are, indeed, in a new world."

A low keening moan could be heard, loud enough even for Eligor to discern. The pain, more like something that might spring from the throat of an animal, was unmistakable.

Lilith sucked in her breath.

And then the floor trembled.

Eligor and Lilith looked at the heavy stones beneath their feet and then at each other and the bewilderment was clearly written upon their faces, but before they could speak they felt another, heavier tremor vibrate under their feet.

A sudden deafening blast like the crashing together of a thousand crystal cymbals accompanied a brilliant flash of purest white light that limned the door of the Shrine from within. Lilith fell to her knees and Eligor staggered, holding himself up with both hands upon the bench. Where the sound abated, the light persisted, and suddenly the broad door, once locked but now seemingly loosened by the tremors, parted slightly, shedding the moving light from within upon the two figures.

Lilith found herself trembling uncontrollably. Shakily she rose to her feet. Something was terribly wrong; a strange light still lingered in the glowing, living embers that danced upon the floor of the Shrine, even as the clangorous echoes of that fantastically powerful peal rang in her ears. Springing forward, concerned only for the well-being of his lord, Eligor pushed the door open and entered the Shrine. As they made their way hurriedly deeper into the chamber the only sound that met their ears was the now-diminishing sizzle of the embers. Both gasped as they came upon the inert form of Sargatanas lying beneath the frieze of the Throne, dotted in hundreds of dissolving specks of light.

Eligor and Lilith stood over him, dumbstruck, for he was entirely white, from spiked head to shod toe. Every detail of his demonic form, every spine, every armored scute, every fold of his flesh, and even his robes stood out in pale relief, all of him the white of bone, the white of fangs—the white of a seraph from Above. And when they called his name and he did not move they both knelt and turned him over and saw, each with a shiver, that his open and pleading eyes were no longer smoked silver from the Fall but had gained their former rich copper hue.

Sargatanas' body jerked spasmodically. He blinked and then reached out slowly, clutching at Eligor's robes.

With his eyes unfocused and his voice echoing of bells, he said, "They answered me."

XXV

ADAMANTINARX–UPON–THE–ACHERON

As she walked its streets, Lilith sensed that the once-ordered streets of Adamantinarx were awash in a tide of rumor and unease. The slow-flowing Acheron seemed to mock the city with its steady, unchanging currents, sharp contrast to the endless hasty stream of newfound allies that now threatened to overwhelm the palace.

Algol had risen and set many times since Sargatanas' change. In that time, Zoray and Eligor had had their hands full balancing the affairs of a growing court while dispelling the incredible rumors that began to circulate about Lord Sargatanas. As if the truth, with all of its implications, were not miraculous enough. Nonetheless, tales of apparitions, of giant flaming swords pointing toward Dis, of almost-seen hosts of Seraphim or Cherubim flying downward, of masses of Abyssals congregating in the Wastes, of souls becoming demons, even of Lucifer's imminent return, floated through the streets on currents of excited gossip. All these rumors, she knew, were false, the product of times that were changing too rapidly.

A great caravan was arriving just as she ascended the palace steps, and she recognized the elegant, blue sigil as belonging to Put Satanachia, that most refined and charismatic of demons arrived from his cold, outer realm. With him were his three subordinates, the Demons Minor Aamon, Pruslas, and Barbatos, each as commanding a presence as many Demons Major. Lilith knew enough about Satanachia and his court to be amazed at his apparent new alliance with Sargatanas; there were few demon sovereigns more powerful in Hell, and in some ways he outranked the Lord of Adamantinarx. As Eligor had said, it was, indeed, a new world.

As she negotiated the corridors farther into the palace she wondered, for the thousandth time, about just what had happened to Sargatanas. It had taken them hours to get him back, weak as he was, to his chambers so far above the Shrine. They had wanted to get him there without being seen, but in a palace this active they realized soon enough that this would be an impossibility. Others, the curious and concerned, had gathered around and lent their support, and despite themselves, Eligor and she had been grateful for their help. Once inside Sargatanas' darkened chambers, she had stayed with him for days, but they had not spoken except in the most cursory way. He was distant and seemed to be in enormous discomfort, and she knew better than to press him. Gradually, the apparent physical difficulties subsided and she had left him for longer and longer periods. However, even with his returning strength, he was no more forthcoming.

Today would be different. Enough time had passed that she felt reasonably confident that she could get him to tell her what had happened.

When she approached his chambers, Lilith saw the dozens of the Foot Guard, arranged in a square formation that completely blocked the corridor and barred anyone, save herself, Eligor, and Zoray, from entering. Saluting, they opened the door, and she stepped into Sargatanas' private world.

He had pulled up a heavy chair before his wide opened window and was seated, looking out over Adamanti-narx, a pale shape against a dark background. His city was now a nexus for the disenfranchised of Hell, and even from this height he could not have failed to see the steady flow that entered it.

"There is little or no difference," he said without turning, "between my rebellion and his."

"My lord?"

"Lucifer. His rebellion. And mine. We are both responsible for what we started."

"Yes. But surely you can see the differences."

"What if they're not so clear?" He took a deep breath. "What I *can* see is the destruction of those around me because of my own selfish goals."

She looked at him and felt the radiance of sadness that seemed to emanate from him. "This *isn't* a selfish cause. His was."

Sargatanas remained still. An ash-laden wind was whipping up, and the banners below were beginning to flap.

Lilith stood next to him, watching the city as it grew less distinct for the encroaching ash.

"It's Valefar. His loss is making you question all that you're attempting; that much is clear. He wouldn't want that."

The demon pursed his lips, the agitation clearly written upon his face. She suddenly realized—amazed after all these weeks that she had not seen it—that he was no longer shifting his form. While he was still very much a demon, his whitened body was as stable as the chair he sat upon. *How could I have missed something so obvious? What else has changed within him?*

"What was it like?"

"What?"

"In the Shrine."

His mouth opened as if to speak and he hesitated. She

saw him take his eyes away from the window and look down.

"I was . . . upon my knees praying." He shook his head slowly. "Lilith, I prayed *so* hard, first for him . . . for Valefar . . . and then for me. And it was then that the floor shook. I thought it was a response to such selfishness."

"Eligor and I felt *that*. I think the entire palace did as well," she said, immediately sorry she had interrupted him.

"Then there was a brilliance, a living whiteness, that seemed to descend like the furious fall of a sword blade. It hit me so hard, Lilith. And when it did, I thought it the purest anger I've ever known. Directed solely at me. It only touched me for an instant, but even in that span I felt it change . . . to the purest imaginable balm. Suddenly my mind was flooded with the Above; I could smell it, see it, hear it . . . even taste it. It was like awakening after dreaming of blackness and decay and seeing . . . my home." He paused. "I'm sorry, I can't truly tell you."

Lilith smiled. He was right; she could only imagine.

The ash cloud was rising, making its inevitable way up to the lofty heights of the palace towers, and Lilith moved to close the open windows. There were a dozen casements to latch, and as she began she heard Sargatanas rise from his seat and start to close them at the far end of the room.

She glanced at him surreptitiously and saw him pausing, holding his wounded side. Without thinking she went to him, and for a moment, a long, silent moment, they looked into each other's eyes. She had never seen eyes like his, made angelic by the change; past the bony brows and white lids they were deep wells of liquid copper flecked with tiny specks of azure—quite beautiful, she thought. But, more than that, it was the sadness, the inward-reaching longing, she saw within them that she had never seen before. Even the eyes of Lucifer, which she had fallen into, had held more anger than anything else.

Impulsively, keeping her eyes on Sargatanas', she reached out and touched him, running her pale fingers down his steaming forearm and feeling the heat of his flesh and bone. The touch burned but in a way that sent a thrill through her. She saw his eyes widen fractionally, but he did not pull away, and she put her other hand upon the hand that covered his wound and slowly, purposefully, pulled him to her. She heard a release of breath, deep and hollow, and suddenly, with a fervor that surprised her, he crushed her to him, closing his eyes and wrapping his heavy arms around her.

They stood motionless, holding on to each other in Hell's first embrace of love, for what Lilith deemed the most wonderful eternity she had spent. They were both unique yet alike, alone yet together. And Lilith knew that, for her, Hell was forever changed.

I am, indeed, in a new world.

They lingered upon Sargatanas' disheveled pallet, in a room made hazy by the steam of their lovemaking. Lilith lay partially atop him like a dismounting rider, her nude body looking like highly polished ivory, slick with perspiration. He drowsed beneath her, his huge hand playing unconsciously with her sweat-tangled hair, his words few but endearing. The heat of him that was still spreading upward from between her legs suffused her entire body, warming her. Lilith had never felt more content. Her mind, enervated by the intensity of him, ranged back to those most ancient of memories, of the Man for whom she was created and of lost Lucifer, and she knew that neither could compare. Sargatanas' yearning hunger had been obvious and his skill amazing; she had found him nothing less than sublime in his passion. She had exhilarated in his power.

It was odd, she thought distantly, how so much about

her existence seemed to center upon sex. The intent of her very creation had been about it. Her own Fall had indirectly been because of it. Her millennia of imprisonment had been to exploit it. With Lucifer it had always been about Lucifer. But with Sargatanas it seemed different; there was an equality about it, a give-and-take, a sense that she was *someone,* in how attentive he had been. She ascribed this parity, in part, to her having reached out to *him*. And that, she thought smiling faintly, she would never regret.

She watched his scarred and broken chest rise and fall, saw the fire that lay within his torn breast—where his heart should have been—fade and glow, fanned with each breath. And she closed her eyes, thinking of the possibilities. She thought about what Hell would be like for her if he succeeded in his dream, with him absent forever. Or—and this was a pleasantly guilty thought— if he failed, what it might be like if he were not to leave.

DIS

A single week in a thousand-mouthed screaming-room at the mercy of a pack of Scourges had wrought changes upon Agares that would never be erased. When Adramalik saw him he straightened, tightening his jaw, for the former Prime Minister, once so proper and refined, could no longer stand as he once had. Nor would he breathe or speak as he once had. In fact, the Chancellor General was not sure, looking at him, whether on a cursory glance he could really even be mistaken for a demon anymore. Which had been exactly what Adramalik had recommended his peer's punishment be. Adramalik now thought his own punishment, as severe as it was, was nothing in comparison to Agares' suffering. Of one thing he was certain: Agares would never be Prime Minister again.

Naked, he shuffled sometimes upright, sometimes on all fours, ahead of Adramalik, trailing a bloody train of flayed skin as he moved into Beelzebub's Rotunda. Agares had difficulty traversing the floor; pattering through its ankle-deep pools of blood and chunks of half-consumed meat made him strain and contort his twisted body so much that he occasionally let out wincing shrieks of pain. Apart from the very apparent re-arrangement of his joints, every internal organ, feathered in exposed capillaries, protruded through innumerable holes in his body in a way that Adramalik could only think of as decorative. The whips and tongs and hooks had been very creatively applied.

The Rotunda contained only a single demon in attendance to the Prince. Sitting cross-legged in the blood before the flesh-throne was Faraii, and as Adramalik approached him he could see that something was not quite right about the Baron. Motionless, still clad in the dark and tattered garments he had worn on the battlefield, he made no move to indicate that he was aware of the arrival of the Chancellor General and the ex–Prime Minister. Adramalik narrowed his eyes as he looked at the seemingly oblivious figure, as he began to more fully appreciate the extent of the Prince's plans for Faraii. *The fly that invaded him . . . it has hollowed him out. Now he is nothing more than a vessel. A fighting husk. Husk Faraii!*

Adramalik stepped closer to the throne and knelt down on one knee while Agares squatted nearby in what had to be an uncomfortable position. The Battle of the Flaming Cut had changed things; a degree of sub-servience was now demanded of him that had never been necessary before. He was unsure whether this new requirement would remain in place even after his ongoing punishment subsided. As the thought crossed his mind a jolt of withering pain sliced through; they were fewer these days but no less intense. When it subsided he looked up and saw the headless body of Prince Beelzebub seated atop the rotting pile.

A muffled howl arose from deep beneath the bowels of the Keep. The Watcher had been unusually restless these past few weeks, Adramalik thought. Was it a portent, some sign of impending disaster? The dying sound reverberated through the Rotunda, creating myriad concentric ripples in the puddles.

He looked back at Husk Faraii, who gave no evidence of having heard the sound; instead a familiar buzzing now seemed to be emanating from within him. Adramalik noticed a large pool of saliva gathering inside the gray-blue Husk's slackly opened mouth. Due to a slight tilt in his gaunt head, the saliva began to drop in a slowly lengthening rivulet from his mouth until it touched his thigh.

As Adramalik watched, he saw a few flies appear inside Husk Faraii's mouth. Emerging from within, they perched for a moment upon his lips and teeth and then took wing, rising higher and higher until they were directly over the shoulders of Beelzebub's waiting form. An improbable number of them began to issue forth, a steady stream adding layers of solidity to the featureless head that was forming and then, once the last of them was in place, refining itself into the Prince's countenance.

Without preamble, as the last flies were settling themselves, the Prince asked, "What is noble here in Hell?"

"Nothing, my Prince," Adramalik said. "Nothing can be noble in such a place. You have always said that nobility has the stink of the Above."

"And yet . . . and yet somehow Sargatanas can create the illusion, through his actions and aspirations, of nobility?"

"No, my Prince."

"How else can you explain, then, the sudden flocking of allies . . . important allies . . . to his side?"

Adramalik paused. Whatever he thought, he must tell Beelzebub what he needed to hear.

"They are weak and stupid," Adramalik ventured. "They are cleaving to him because they think that aligning themselves with a new, defiant power in Hell will bring about a chance to topple your court. They do not care at all about his 'cause.'"

"Well, Adramalik, there *is* a chance. This court now stands upon shaky feet. I, Beelzebub, the Prince Regent of Hell since its founding, must accept the fact that there is now a rising power that threatens my sovereignty. A demon has come to shake me from my throne!"

The words hung in the air. Adramalik looked over at Husk Faraii and saw that the saliva had pooled upon his thigh and was now slowly dribbling downward. Agares, too, was staring at him.

"Dis is now deprived of Moloch's standing army; it is ash upon the winds as we speak. My Great Summoning Pits are, for the moment, impotent . . . my conjurors sit idle at their edges, waiting for them to bestir themselves. But I am sure the same can be said for him; it will take some time for his allies to gather their armies. It was nothing short of genius for him to use his souls."

"It was *disgusting,* my Prince," said Adramalik vehemently, forgetting himself. "An army of skin-sacks! It was an abomination worthy of no demon; imagine, demons . . . no, angels Fallen . . . destroyed by that filth!"

"You speak of 'angels' and 'abominations.' Just where do you think you are?" asked Beelzebub.

"But to use them as he does is to become as dirty inside as they are."

"To use them, you fool, was to annihilate my army!" Beelzebub roared, the buzzing making the Chancellor General's painful head throb. Agares splashed backward as the Prince rose in a roiling cloud from the throne and rematerialized seconds later below, before Faraii. High above, the hanging skins flapped agitatedly. Slowly and

with apparent affection Beelzebub reached out a hand and began to caress the seated demon's face, wiping the drool from him with the fluttering wings of a hundred flies. The act seemed to soothe the Prince. He turned to the Chancellor, who had bowed so low that his upper robes hung well into the crimson puddles.

"I was *there*," the Prince said. "I was at the Flaming Cut. At least, *part* of me was there. Look and understand, fool." He extended his left arm; it ended in a stump of angry, milling flies. "I wanted to see Sargatanas for myself, see his 'brilliance' with my own eyes, and so my Hand, formed into a simple legionary, marched just behind you . . . no farther than I am to you now . . . all the way to the Cut and into battle. Did you think Faraii chose his own moment to betray his lord?"

Adramalik shook his head. He had truly never guessed.

"In the chaos of Moloch's destruction I changed sides, I became one of them and returned with them to their city, and even now, even as we speak, I search the streets of Adamantinarx. Do you know why?"

Adramalik knew what was coming.

"Because you failed to bring *her* back to me!"

Adramalik staggered. In the haze of pain that suddenly swept through him he wondered if he was going to walk from the Rotunda or finally be destroyed.

But the moment passed. Beelzebub continued to stroke Husk Faraii's face.

"What have I done . . . ruling in Lucifer's stead . . . to deserve this . . . but what Lucifer himself would have done?"

"It is as you say," the Chancellor General uttered through clenched teeth. "You *have* ruled just as Lucifer would have done. With firmness and steady resolve."

"And so I shall continue. I fought at Lucifer's side against the armies of the Above. If I cannot destroy the rebel Sargatanas I do not deserve to rule in this place. I will *not* use the souls of Dis to fight a demon . . . their lot is punishment, not empowerment. But I, too, can call upon allies."

He would risk everything to compete with Sargatanas! He will bring Dis to its knees!

But Adramalik glanced over at Agares and held his tongue.

"Allies, my Prince?"

"Lucifuge Rofocale, Lords Berith, Carnefiel, and Malgaras, all have pledged their support; their legions are forming at this moment. Together they will form an alliance that will bring my army back to full strength and more."

"And who will coordinate them, my Prince?"

Adramalik sensed the answer and felt his spirits sink lower than he could have imagined. This responsibility would surely take him down the path to his destruction.

Beelzebub looked sharply at Agares and then back at the Chancellor General. "I thought that would have been obvious . . . Prime Minister."

XXVI

ADAMANTINARX-UPON-THE-ACHERON

Hannibal woke with a start.

Taking a deep breath, he opened his eyes; he knew immediately that he was not as he had been, not whole. Weakly he tried to sit up, but he heard Mago quietly tell him to lie still. He was in an unfamiliar room somewhere, he guessed, in Adamantinarx. Which was a relief, because it told him that the battle had been won.

His entire left arm was gone, traded, he saw, for the immense hooked weapon that lay ominously on the table nearby. It was as long as his arm had been. *Strange that it is here, the instrument of my loss.*

But stranger still was the tarnished and pitted disk that lay next to it. It was Moloch—or what was left of him. A spoil of war, a prize beyond measure, and, clearly, left for him as an honor. But what, if anything, could he, a soul, do with it: wear it around his neck? He would have to ask Lilith or Eligor.

"Tell me, Mago. Tell me what I missed."

"You are fortunate, my brother," Mago said plainly. "Fortunate to have survived Moloch and more so still to have had the First Consort, herself, attend your wounds."

He thought about the battle and about his confrontation with his ex-god. As blurred in Hannibal's mind as was the duel itself, equally sharp was the memory of that furious face.

"And Lord Sargatanas?"

"He lives . . . but he is not as he was."

Hannibal looked down for the first time at his vacant shoulder and said, "Nor am I."

"No, Hannibal, it isn't like that . . . he was wounded, true, but that isn't the change I meant. He is now bone-white from head to toe."

"A miracle?"

"Or a curse. The city is full of rumors, not all good. Some see it as an omen of catastrophe. Lord Yen Wang, in particular, seems uneasy; some of his minions are spreading doubts among the other demons."

"Doubts?"

Mago rubbed his chin. Hannibal could not tell which side of the argument his brother favored.

"The city is in a state that you and I remember well

enough from our own fair city . . . war preparations. While most believe the officially disseminated story, only a few truly know what happened to him to change him as he now is. Some say it is Lucifer's doing and that he has marked Sargatanas. Or the First Consort's ensorcellment, which, in my opinion, holds a grain of plausibility. Cynics say that he is delusional, mad, and that somehow this has transformed him inside as well as outside. They are in the minority. And the newer allies . . . Put Satanachia, whom you haven't met, aside . . . seem like little more than opportunists. I might be wrong; that's my impression, though. But all of this creates an aura of uncertainty that runs through the streets like effluvia."

Hannibal knew that variety of poison. During wartime it could be as deadly as a well-aimed arrow. He had done everything in his life to avoid it.

Mago looked down. Hannibal saw his brother's gray hands working at the folds of his Abyssal-skin robes.

"What is it, Brother?"

Mago frowned. "This is not the time."

"Ask."

"Does it not trouble you, this alliance of ours? Demons and souls?"

Hannibal closed his eyes. How could he explain his need to pursue power no matter where he was? Would Mago understand?

"Yes, it does trouble me. If it were any other demon but Sargatanas I would never have had the courage to get involved. Nor would I have had a chance. I'm sure you've noticed that they're not at ease having us as allies, either. Sargatanas isn't like the rest of them. He has a single-minded purity of purpose . . . something like my own."

"And just what is your . . . purpose?"

"You spoke of opportunists. That would be what we are, Mago. For us, this is a rebellion of convenience. At first, I was swept up by the goal that he held out . . . that shining chance to go to Heaven. But now . . . especially after the battle . . . I just don't know.

"When we were fighting, and the souls around me were being cut down, it didn't seem to me that they were anything but dead, not the living death of being turned into a brick, either. I wondered, 'Will that ever change?' To me, Mago, it's still very much an open question as to whether we will ever have that chance."

Mago stood and turned toward a stone-sheathed wall. He looked up at the glyphs-of-protection that circled the ceiling.

"Does that change anything . . . I mean for you as our general?"

"No. You know me, Mago; I'm no dreamer. I'm a realist. I am in Hell and I deserve to be here for what I've done. As do you and all the others. If we cannot go to Heaven, I, for one, won't be surprised. I hope that we can. But, with that said, I will lead the souls with the same vigor I'd have if I did truly believe."

"Hannibal, your entire life was about pursuing dreams."

Hannibal laughed and then winced, clutching his painful shoulder.

"The power I have in the here and now," he said after a few moments, "that's what's important. Could you have imagined, during all those long, torture-filled centuries, that I . . . we . . . would be in the position we're in now? If I can better our lot here, then that is reason enough to lead."

Mago turned back to the pallet and looked down at his brother. "For you, this is about power?"

"Everything is about power."

"Not everything. Not for Sargatanas."

"That's why he may fail."

He saw her face again and could not believe, with all that he had seen in Hell, that it was still the most affecting image his dream-mind could produce. Funny, a part of him reflected, that the Hell inside his head was more potent than the one outside, that no matter what horrors he saw, it was her shining, trusting infant eyes that cut him to the marrow.

The child spoke his name and it felt like an arrow flying into his breast, but as it was repeated its sound changed, growing huskier and assuming a strange accent until, after a moment, he realized that she was not uttering it. As he awoke he recognized the voice to be that of Lilith, and when he opened his eyes he was looking up into her perfect oval face.

"Hannibal?"

"Yes, my lady."

"How are you?"

"Mending, my lady. With thanks to you."

"Are you feeling 'mended' enough for an answer to your questions about this?" another voice asked. Sargatanas appeared behind Lilith, the disk of Moloch held in his hand.

"My lord!" It had seemed so long since he had seen Sargatanas. *He is transformed!* Hannibal swung his legs over the side of the pallet and tried to step down, but Lilith put a restraining hand on his chest.

"He seems strong enough, my lord," Lilith said, smiling.

"He will have to be," Sargatanas said. "I need him at the head of his legions."

Sargatanas turned the ugly disk in his hand. Its edges were sharp and jagged, and Hannibal heard them scrape on the demon's hard palm as he regarded it. He seemed apprehensive about the object, almost cautious in the way he handled it.

"Hannibal, there are many things that I can do in this world, but giving you your arm back . . . to undo the dismemberment . . . is not among them. There are ways, though, that you can, once again, have a living limb, but to do this I would need, simply put, a catalyst . . . an object of power that would add the necessary new elements to my abilities. This," he said, holding the Moloch disk up between his thumb and forefinger, "is one such object."

"And how would that be done?"

"I would have to place this inside your shoulder."

A ripple of fear spread through Hannibal as he unconsciously reached for his shoulder. To enfold the exgod within himself was a detestable idea, an act that would embrace the very entity that had caused him so much grief. He shook his head.

"You can, of course, elect to not use the disk. It will be otherwise useless to you . . . a simple trophy, well won, to put upon a shelf," Lilith said. "There is no shame in choosing that alternative, Hannibal."

"I have no other such items at hand," Sargatanas said. "I am sure one will turn up eventually, but not in time for the upcoming battle."

Hannibal looked down, considering the possibilities.

"This is *our* way . . . the demons' way," Sargatanas said plainly, putting a hand to the countless layered phalerae that were embedded in his chest. "There is no telling how it may affect you. I have never heard of this being done with a soul, and so there is no precedent. In all likelihood you will benefit by simply growing a new arm . . . that is the invocation I would be using. It would be too unpredictable to attempt to augment your abilities in any way."

"We can give you a short time to decide," Lilith said, "but the allies' armies are arriving and very soon Sargatanas will be departing." She looked toward the demon and Hannibal saw the concern flash across her features. "You will have to decide before then."

Hannibal closed his eyes for a moment and saw the fleeting image of his daughter's face, still fresh from his dream. It would feel like another betrayal of her to accept the Moloch disk. But would it really be one? What would

Imilce say? He did not relish the idea of fighting with only one arm, nor could he be the kind of general who stayed behind the front ranks, ordering others to fight. He was in Hell, and to survive he needed every advantage.

"There is no need to wait, my lord and lady. I will accept this." The ashen taste of fear, an unfamiliar taste, tightened his throat.

Lilith put a hand on his shoulder.

"You need not worry, Hannibal. Sargatanas has no doubts regarding the outcome of this invocation."

"Then let's get it over with."

Sargatanas set himself, took a deep breath, and began to intone four phrases four times in a voice comprised of four harmonics:

"Ogiodi Azdra . . . Tplabc Zibra . . . Rnoizr Nrzfm . . . Rplalen Bbemo . . . Yolcam Abzien!"

Four large glyphs, simple in form but different in color, appeared and began to circle the Demon Major's head and by the fourth revolution they spread out, two on either side.

Lilith squeezed Hannibal's hand as Sargatanas used the disk's sharp edge to slice open her careful stitches. With a powerful thrust he pushed it deep within the shoulder until it was lodged beneath the soul's collarbone. Immediately the demon spoke one of the four paired words and the corresponding glyph dropped down into Hannibal's open wound, causing a terrible burning that spread throughout his body. The next glyphs brought, in rapid succession, the sensations of drowning in some engulfing, cloying liquid followed by a sudden cracking coldness and finally parching dryness. He saw Sargatanas' lips moving but could hear nothing. Shocked and nauseated, Hannibal retched until his stomach ached. When he was finished he looked weakly at his wound and was dimly amazed that, without stitches, it had sealed itself.

"I chose you well, Hannibal Barca," Lilith said softly. "Your strength is matched only by your courage. Rest now and we will send Mago in to be with you."

She turned to leave, but Sargatanas lingered.

"There is one small thing more." He extended his hand and with his index finger described a flowing pattern in the air above the soul's shoulder, an arcing, actinic line of blue flame that looked, to Hannibal, like a charging animal. The glyph did not fade, and with every slight movement the soul made it moved with him.

"You are the first soul in Hell's long, dark history to have earned his own sigil. It will be a mark of distinction . . . of power and protection . . . upon the battlefield," the demon said with a touch of pride. And then, as he stood, he added, "You *will* be needing it in the next days!"

Exhausted as he was, Hannibal managed a faint grin.

Lilith glanced at Sargatanas and thought he had never seemed more preoccupied. He was at once attentive and loving but consumed, as well, with the minutiae of state. He had an army to create—even greater than before— and time was running short. Accompanied by Zoray and a cohort of his Foot Guard, he and Lilith, after reviewing the remaining legions just outside the gates, ascended along the Rule from the tangle of the Acheron's bank-side streets up toward the distant palace. On either side of the avenue, souls and demons alike knelt silently, staring at the two white figures in wonderment.

These were the days that she would long for, Lilith knew, even as, like jewels falling one by one from a broken necklace, they fell away. Though Adamantinarx was in a bustling state of mobilization, she and Sargatanas managed to keep constant company, to go from site to site and watch the mustering city at its finest. Part of her sensed that he was bringing her along not only out of love but also to familiarize her with the workings of the great city. In some place in her mind she wondered if he was grooming her for some role in the city.

Walking next to the demon lord, Lilith found it difficult not to descend into melancholia; the thought of his possible impending loss—through either the attainment of his goal or his destruction on the battlefield—was so daunting. And the third alternative—a hollow victory wherein he simply returned to his city, unfulfilled—worried her nearly as much. She did not want to feel dependent upon him, but that possibility was becoming truth. The pushing and pulling of her conflicting desires—her own admittedly selfish hunger for him against her urge to help him attain his goal—confused her. Perhaps it was just the vapors blowing off the Acheron that had made her so low spirited.

As they entered the palace precincts, a messenger approached Zoray, saluted, and spoke briefly as they walked. When he departed, the Demon Minor turned to Sargatanas.

"My lord, we are still coming up short on the numbers of souls. Mago and his commanders have informed me that they are able to field only nineteen full legions . . . not even close to what you had hoped for."

Sargatanas looked up at the sky and sighed. "We need to be ready to march the moment our allies' armies arrive. Begin to take down the buildings."

"My lord . . . ?"

"And conscript the workers as well. Mago will know how to integrate them into the soul army. Every soul who survived the Flaming Cut should be put in charge of a new cohort."

"But, my lord, the city's buildings . . . ?"

"Are a resource to be used. Start with the domiciles, destroying those within, then the shops, then the bigger buildings, and so on until we have the numbers we need. And, Zoray, use the palace as well."

They resumed walking. Zoray looked confounded.

"My lord . . . you are sacrificing Adamantinarx?"

"The city can be rebuilt . . . but not with souls. There is plenty of native stone out there to be quarried."

"And the number of souls is to remain as high as you had first said?"

"Yes. We are marching on the capital of Hell, Zoray, not some insignificant ward of Astaroth's."

Zoray nodded and then saluted. Breaking away from the procession, he hurried ahead and disappeared amidst the streams of legionaries that were heading down to join the gathering legions.

Lilith, who had overheard the exchange, moved closer to Sargatanas and placed her hand on his forearm.

"What's to become of the souls who return?"

"They can do as they please . . . within limits. Limits that I'll leave up to you. They can build their own cities out in the Wastes or live in what's left of this one."

"Why not decide their future yourself?"

"Because I don't love them the way you do, Lilith," he said simply.

"Not even Hannibal?"

"Perhaps Hannibal," he admitted with a grin.

The party entered the palace, splitting apart, with the Foot Guard and other functionaries leaving Sargatanas and Lilith to head up the giant staircase to his chambers on their own. Without a word they took each other's hands and the gentle, reassuring squeeze that he gave her brought a smile to her lips. The day's great meal was being prepared, but she looked forward to feeding their other hungers beforehand.

Something was subtly different; that much was clear. Whether it was the pall of the deconstruction that gripped the city, her sadness over Valefar's absence, her own un-ease at the prospect of losing Sargatanas, or something more ineffable, she could not positively say. Sitting at the ancient, long table amidst the many noisy demons of

Sargatanas' court, Lilith watched the enormous joints of Abyssal meat slowly turning over a wide pit-fire and felt only the weight of change. But beyond that, she could not shake the sense that something *physical* was different. And so she sat quietly, listening but not adding much to the demons' conversation that flowed around her.

Sargatanas' feasting hall was aglow in the copper light of a dozen tall four-legged braziers that were placed evenly around the central table. A running mural framed the wide room, depicting continuous scenes of ancient hunts with Sargatanas himself wielding famous weapons and joined by equally famous demons. Normally Lilith's gaze would travel upward to that mural, but this evening she focused on her plate, only glancing up to look at someone when she was addressed.

Seated across from her and Sargatanas and next to Andromalius were Put Satanachia and his Prime Minister, Pruslas. The Demon Major was, in this time of unrest, a welcome guest and easily the most powerful of her lord's allies. Satanachia was, she thought, extraordinarily refined, robed in layers of thin, nacreous flesh and delicate spines, his moving features fine and ascetic, reflecting what Sargatanas had once described as the "nobility of the Highest Order of Seraphim." The timing of his arrival could not have been better; not surprisingly, Lilith had learned that Sargatanas, Satanachia, and Valefar had known one another in the Above and had been regarded as inseparable. Satanachia was an engaging demon, exuberant in his storytelling, effortlessly pouring forth tales of his many hunting expeditions into the Wastes. Lilith had met him in Dis about as frequently as she had Sargatanas, and her impression of him was not dissimilar from that of her lord's with one exception: where Sargatanas was appealingly earnest, even serious, Satanachia's nature bordered on self-absorption. But because he was a true friend of her lord's she recognized

Satanachia's importance to him and had, so far, been especially attentive. However, as her sadness deepened she listened only halfheartedly.

". . . and once we got past the volcanoes that border the western edge of my realm," Satanachia continued, his voice mellow, "we were suddenly confronted by the Salamandrines who had been gathering in great numbers in hopes of streaming down toward my outlying cities. We slaughtered them all easily enough and then skinned their scrawny bodies for the hides. One of my tribunes knew enough of their tongue and was inventive enough to suggest that we leave them on the flesh-fields splayed out to spell a warning in the creatures' own language. They have not troubled us since." He paused for a moment, then added wryly, "Apparently they *can* read!"

A murmur of approval ran up and down the table and Lilith smiled perfunctorily. At her side, Sargatanas grinned without looking up while slicing his silvery meat with his clawed fingers.

"Satanachia, you must have spoken with Eligor by now," he said, indicating his Captain. "He is the scholar among us and is actually quite well versed in the Waste primitives. He finds them . . ."

"Fascinating, actually," Eligor said with genuine enthusiasm, remembering Faraii's many stories. "They were here for eons before us, surviving in the harshest environments, almost, it would seem, preferring them to the more moderate ones. They believe . . . or so I have been told . . . that this toughens them and that if they can make do with Hell's worst then the other areas become effortless. It seems to work . . . they are very nearly as tough as the Abyssals they live among."

"Not so tough as to dull a skinning blade," Pruslas remarked archly.

Eligor persisted. "True, I suppose. But I have been

considering the idea of capturing a few of them alive
and bringing them back here to study. They are much
brighter than we give them credit for. We all might learn
something from them."

"Just how primitive they are is my guess," added Satanachia.

An enormous bowl of blackened, chopped finger-fan
was placed before Lilith, and she looked at it dubiously.
She squeezed Sargatanas' arm and then rose from the
table. For a moment all eyes were upon her; she supposed that they thought she was preparing to make
some kind of speech, but instead she turned and headed
for the balcony just off the feasting hall.

As she approached the leaded doors she could hear
the sound of innumerable tiny taps upon their thick, obsidian panes; frequent gusts laden with hot cinders almost made her regret her decision to come outside.
Stepping out onto the balcony, she drew her whipping
robes about her. Brushing away the coating of cinders,
she put her elbows upon the balustrade and squinted out
into the smoky-brown night of Hell. As cinder-storms
went, this was a mild one, but even so, she frequently
had to close her eyes.

*This place is all that I will ever know. It's Lucifer all
over again. Sargatanas will go on and I will be left here.
How can I have found him only to lose him after so
short a time? How can I love him so much and yet not
wish him to attain what he wants?*

Lilith saw, through the curling currents of ash and
cinders, the broad carpet of lights outside the walls that
were the joined fires and sigils of the legions' and souls'
encampments and imagined the legionaries preparing
for war, yet again. *His war. They must be numbering in
the millions by now. And he commands them all. Such
power! All of which he is so willing to give up—and me
as well. For a dream.*

From below, the tiny, distant screams of buildings coming apart reached her ears, almost inaudible against the noise of the feasting hall and the wind. Eventually, as the demons retired, the sounds from inside diminished and she heard only the soughing of the hot wind through the sculpted eaves above her. The cinder-storm was passing. And just as she thought to go back inside, she felt a hand placed gently upon her back and she turned and looked up into Sargatanas' face. Compassion was written upon his even features, and she almost could not bear to look at him. He returned her gaze, staring deeply, probingly, into her eyes. She knew what he was doing, what he was capable of.

He took a deep breath and said, "I know."

"Can you?"

"Yes. I know what you're feeling. . . . I feel it as well. I know how unfair this all seems. The irony of finding you after all those millennia, only to . . ."

He looked out toward the legions.

"Only . . . what?"

"Only to lose you because of a . . . vision."

She said nothing.

"Lilith, my heart," he said softly, "my mind was made up long before you came here. I'm too far along in this to stop now."

"I know." She was neither bitter nor angry. "Yours is the greatest vision anyone in Hell could have. I could never ask you to betray it, Sargatanas. Never. Especially not for me."

"You are the only reason I *would* consider giving it up. And knowing that you would never want to go to Heaven . . . it's one of the hardest truths I've had to accept. I know how much resentment you have inside you . . . it's understandable . . . but will you not reconsider?"

If anyone other than Sargatanas had asked, anger would have been her first response. But she knew just

how serious he was and responded with equal serious-
ness, as firm in her mind as he was in his.

"Hell is where I will stay, my love."

"Would that I could give you Heaven instead."

"You have."

She reached up and pulled him down and they kissed,
their emotions fanned by their awareness that now all
things between them were, in all likelihood, transitory.
*How tightly must I hold him to make this a memory that
will never fade?* Some time in the solitary and distant
future—perhaps millennia from now—she would remember this moment and almost disbelieve that it, like
all the others they had shared, had happened.

When they separated she looked into his eyes and for
once knew without question what lay behind them: no
matter where he was, his love for her would never cease.

"What will you do if—*when* you are back?"

Sargatanas looked away, almost as if the prospect of
returning were now, somehow, something he could not
talk about. After a moment he said, "I will bathe for a
small eternity in the river called the Source to wash
away *this* place. After that, I suppose, I will wait to be
brought before the Throne. And you . . . when this is
over?"

"I don't know; wander, I'm guessing. But I won't be
staying here."

He nodded, clearly understanding; staying in Adamantinarx would be a constant wounding reminder of their
separation. The all-too-short time spent with this demon, in this city, was, she thought, so unlike her time in
Dis, and yet both were proving to be sad beyond measure, for very different reasons.

Without a word, he turned and beckoned her to come
inside with him. Lilith held back for just a moment, the
bitter memories of her past colliding with her unachiev-
able, fleeting dreams of the future. And from them came
inspiration.

"Promise me one thing, Sargatanas," she said. "Promise me that you will not let the Black Dome stand when you are done with the Fly."

He looked into her eyes, again finding what he needed to know, and said, "I will. For you . . . and Ardat."

XXVII

DIS

"I summoned you because something appears to be happening across Adamantinarx," the newly appointed Prime Minister heard Agaliarept hiss. Pointing abruptly and in a revelatory manner with five of his arms, the Conjuror General continued, "Pockets of weakness are opening. . . . Look at these configurations. Here and here and . . . there! See how they fade?"

Adramalik had to admit that the map of Adamantinarx that floated before them was, indeed, changing significantly. The intricate multilayered latticework of glyphs that represented individual buildings and streets and tunnels, even certain personages, seemed to blister and pop like the bubbles upon the surface of a shifting flow of magma. Some of Agaliarept's many mouths made sucking noises of pleasure, sounds that seemed appropriate for the bursting of the glyphs, as the carefully constructed defenses mutated, affording him perceived opportunities that had not been there before.

"We should inform the Prince if the palace itself begins to degrade," said Adramalik. Most of the activity, for the moment, involved what appeared to be domiciles

and storehouses. "I am now convinced she *is* somewhere within it and not being kept outside its walls as a
foil. The Prince's Hand has searched the city ceaselessly and come away with nothing."

Agaliarept appeared not to be listening but, instead,
to be in some kind of trance state, his finer manipulators
dexterously separating and plucking away at the newly
configured glyphs, his minds digging, prying, calculating. Adramalik stepped back as disinterested portions
of the Conjuror began to peel away and fall off, chittering and fading away in the darkness of the chamber, setting about on other unknown tasks. Seeing them, he
moved farther away and then left the Conjuring Chamber altogether, careful to observe whether the smaller
parts of Agaliarept were on their own mission. He knew
he must hurry.

A smirk twisted across his face; he would not wait to
tell his Prince as he had advised Agaliarept. Beelzebub
would be pleased with the news, and he very much
wanted to be the bearer of it; he did not want to risk
lessening his punishment by diluting the message. Sargatanas' strategy should have been predictable, he
thought reproachfully, that in his hour of need he would
tap the only resource he had left to him—the souls—
and that this would benefit the Prince. And, more important, himself.

ADAMANTINARX-UPON-THE-ACHERON

When Eligor finally brought Hannibal out of his
darkened chamber the soul found himself squinting at a
very different Adamantinarx, a heavy blanket of dust
hanging over the city, evidence of the ongoing demolition that was reshaping it. Supported by the Guard Captain, Hannibal walked weakly at first, trying to regain a
sense of balance and poise that was hampered by his

lingering pain and the loss of his arm. Mago was not far behind, and when Hannibal seemed comfortable enough to stand on his own, Eligor let go of the general and allowed his brother to offer his help. Looking at the soul's uncomplicated sigil, Eligor admitted to himself that it would take some getting used to. He also had to acknowledge that Hannibal was more than deserving of the honor.

Like Sargatanas, Eligor had grown to admire the resourceful soul. Hannibal, Eligor had learned in speaking with Mago, was what souls regarded as a military man, born of what they thought of as nobility, and perhaps because of these factors he seemed unfazed by the company he now found himself in. Not the fact that he was among demons, not the reality that only a short time ago they had been his zealous wardens, not even the sheer comparative size of them—none of this seemed to impinge upon his ability to remain focused.

Eligor kept a concerned eye on Hannibal as the trio descended toward the waiting armies. The Soul-General had elected to wear a heavy cloak that mostly concealed his asymmetrical shoulders and would probably continue to do so until his new arm was fully regrown. Despite his recent trials, he seemed strong and only stumbled once. He was silent as they traversed the Rule, taking in the changes that had been wrought in his absence. Groans and cries carried from distant quarters as structures came down, the sounds of Sargatanas' city in agony.

Nearly at the river's edge, Eligor saw that in contrast to the city-center, here virtually no buildings were left standing; only those essential to the waging of war had withstood the tide of destruction. Adamantinarx's demolition had progressed efficiently and, Eligor thought, somewhat ruthlessly. Walking through the palace had reminded him of its construction rather than any imminent razing, whereas the city's aspect was one of pending morbidity. His dismay was profound. More than

most, he understood Sargatanas' pressing need, but Eligor
was saddened by the wanton destruction of what he knew
would surely take centuries to rebuild. Where buildings
had stood there remained little but geometric depressions
upon the ground. Only the massive internal gate remained, a smaller cousin of the cyclopean checkpoint
gates that still ringed the city, a stark sight still attached to
the adjacent walls but standing free of its once-plentiful
surrounding buildings.

The sound of trumpets and drums reached their ears
as they crossed the Acheron's largest bridge, the *Kufa-
vors Eophan,* and Eligor lengthened his stride. The encampments were far enough away from the river not to
be influenced by its sorrowful effects, and once they arrived at the encampments' outskirts it took some time to
negotiate the improvised streets that crisscrossed the
military tent-city. The allied armies that had been promised by their lords and ambassadors had finally arrived,
and the Guard Captain knew there was no reason to
linger another day. The time for his or any other demons'
doubts had vanished long ago, and now that the decision
to attack Dis had been made by his lord, Eligor simply
wanted to send his troops aloft.

A small army of demons numbering, Eligor guessed,
in the few thousands knelt over their sheathed swords in
close ranks before a newly erected rostrum. As he ascended the steps toward Sargatanas and his generals,
Eligor saw that those waiting before the rostrum were an
assembly of all of the lesser-ranked field commanders—
Demons Minor mostly—who would lead the immense
host into battle. Each army in itself was so large that it
required its own major general and his staff to coordinate movements.

Hannibal excused himself and moved to speak with
Mago and the other gathered soul field marshals. He
had much to work out with them, and once again Eligor
admired Hannibal's calm under such pressure.

As Eligor approached, he saw the pale form of Sargatanas with Put Satanachia—a five-pointed starburst of flame above his head—standing just to one side. The two were so similar in their height and bearing, the stamp of their rank, Eligor knew, but Sargatanas' intensity was nothing at all like Satanachia's more open nature, the latter's personality more closely resembling Valefar's. Certainly, Eligor realized with self-reproach, Sargatanas had changed within most recent memory, gone from being more composed to being more closed, a creature of deeper introspection. Such were the enormous pressures he had created for himself; such was the burden of the decision he had made. But even sympathetic to that, Eligor had to admit that he missed the Sargatanas of old, the attentive mentor of millennia past.

Eligor saw Satanachia's Glyph-caster, the flamboyant Demon Major Azazel, in deep conversation with the two principal demons. Like most Glyph-casters, he was an especially ornate demon, crested and frilled in thin spines and stretchy membranes and like Eligor hued a brilliant scarlet. Until Satanachia's arrival, Sargatanas had never used a Glyph-caster, choosing to issue orders himself upon the field, but given the vast size of this army he had bowed to his new ally when he had offered him the specialized and exalted talents of Azazel. Eligor, knowing the value of such a generous gift, was more than content to defer some of the responsibilities of messenger in favor of one so well equipped.

Satanachia acknowledged him with a lifted hand as he stepped closer. All three saluted in response and then turned to look out at the dark swath of sigil-crowned officer demons.

Upon a signal from Sargatanas, Azazel flared to life, covering his body in a hundred Demon Majors' sigils and raising his new lord's in a fiery vertical column high above him. The newly reinforced, newly dubbed Second Army of the Ascension, massed behind their commanders, rose thunderously as one and lit their countless unit-glyphs. Eligor's eyes widened at the sheer number of them, at the legions nearly beyond count that extended into the darkness of the night.

"Was there ever so magnificent a sight in Hell . . . or the Above, for that matter?" Satanachia remarked.

"It *is* impressive," agreed Sargatanas.

"Impressive? This," Satanachia said, waving his hand at the expanse of soldiers, "this is power beyond anyone's wildest imaginings. Only the Fly commands numbers like these. I envy you, Sargatanas, envy you because I did not think to do this myself millennia ago." He paused, smiled to himself, and said, "You know, I actually think Lucifer would approve."

"Do you?" Sargatanas' voice lowered, but Eligor was close enough to hear him nonetheless. "The idea of going against his delegated proxy . . . it felt as if I were going against him. I am *still* his loyal warrior no matter where he is."

"As am I, old friend," Satanachia said with conviction. "I would not have joined you in this if I had thought otherwise."

Sargatanas turned and took in what was left of his city. His eyes settled, Eligor saw, in the direction of the enormous fire-topped statue of himself. Now, with so many varied structures no longer standing, it, as well as all of the other giant statues that dotted Adamantinarx, stood out oddly, seeming somehow naked without their covering of buildings.

"Amazing how this all could have started because of the souls," he said almost to himself.

"The War in Heaven?"

"And the War in Hell."

"They are ceaselessly difficult." Satanachia stared at the fields where the souls waited. "I think they have much to answer for."

"Yes, and so do we regarding them," Sargatanas said.

"When Lucifer rebelled I do not think there was one among the Seraphim who dreamt that we would find ourselves so enthusiastically meting out their punishment."

Sargatanas grew silent. Was he thinking of the past, of the life from which he was trying so hard to extricate himself, of his own treatment of the souls—of Lilith? Eligor could not guess.

Sargatanas turned abruptly and said to Azazel, "Your first order, Glyph-caster: we march at Algol's zenith."

Azazel bowed ceremoniously and immediately the sigils that hovered inches above his body began to transform, each quickly growing an attached order-glyph, which peeled away from him and sped into the night air.

"That is not too long from now," Satanachia said, looking at the angry star.

"My Conjuring of Concealment was successful. . . . Eligor's Flying Guard, as well as your own, will not be visible to the Fly or his defensive glyphs. At least not for the initial assault over Dis."

Eligor's head turned at that and he caught Sargatanas' knowing grin. He had been foolish to think that he could eavesdrop if his lord had wanted it otherwise. And Eligor felt privileged to know that it did not trouble Sargatanas that he had heard.

"There is little for me to do now other than roam the empty halls of my palace," Sargatanas went on with a disingenuous sigh.

"Oh, the tragic demon!" said Satanachia gravely.

Sargatanas' grin broadened. It was, Eligor realized, an exchange such as his lord would have had with Valefar, and it gladdened him. It seemed that, now that the weighty decisions had been made and the day of departure was now upon them, Sargatanas had reverted to his former self. None but Satanachia—or Valefar himself—could have brought him back.

The demons turned as one as a low, incongruous peal

of laughter came from the souls surrounding Hannibal, who clapped his only hand upon the back of one of his generals. Hannibal looked past his staff and saw the demons' reaction and, as if to make amends, without hesitation knelt and withdrew his sword and saluted. The gesture was taken up by each of his generals. In answer, the demons spontaneously unsheathed their own weapons and saluted, eliciting a deafening roar of approval from the army at their feet. It was an unrehearsed moment, a moment of undeniable potency, precipitated by the Soul-General, and Eligor immediately recognized its value. It was the kind of moment every general dreamt of.

"Hannibal is an inspired general," Eligor heard Satanachia say as the din died down. He sheathed his sword. "You chose him well."

"I did not choose him; he chose me. With Lilith's help. And you are right. He leads the souls as if this were his own rebellion."

Satanachia looked again toward where the still-clamoring, sigil-less soul army stood.

"What will become of them?"

"Truly, Satanachia, I do not know. Their fate is no clearer than my own. And they know it."

"Given that, their bravery is commendable."

"Their bravery is a measure of their hope and desperation," Sargatanas said. "Again, not unlike my own."

"And what of Lilith's future?"

"Lilith is more than capable of deciding that for herself. It is what she wants more than anything."

"Not more than you."

Sargatanas took a deep breath and Eligor saw his head tilt skyward, his eyes reach into the clouds above.

Hannibal found it odd that he could feel so at peace with Hell that he could laugh and relax with his troops and even look forward to the battle ahead. It was almost as if the dark clouds had parted and the golden sun of his life was shining upon him, not the cold, dispassionate rays of Algol's bloodshot disk. Whatever had caused his shift in mood, it barely troubled him; he had come so far that even if he was destroyed attacking Dis, his would be a name demon and soul alike would remember. It was more than he could ever have hoped for and, in the end, all that he had truly received in his life.

Breaking away from his staff, he descended from the rostrum and walked alone amidst the quiet, orderly lines of soul infantry, watching as they touched weapons, passing simple spell-glyphs the demons had given them from one to another. Traced in every fiery hue imaginable, the glyphs would make their swords and pikes and axes only fractionally more powerful, but, he thought, what little advantage they could take from their former masters could make the difference. When they looked up at him passing, seeing his blue sigil for the first time, they bowed their heads in respectful, silent salute. They were tarred with the brush of evil, many much worse than himself, but they would fight, whatever their reasons, for him and the mere chance of redemption, and that was enough for him.

Eventually growing tired, he returned to Mago and the other generals, all of whom were huddled and asleep, trying to get as much rest as possible before the long march. As Hannibal settled in and pulled his heavy cloak around him, he looked out toward Adamantinarx, the city he, like all of the other souls, had helped build, and saw a beauty there that he had never seen before. Ruddy from the light of the ascending star, its few remaining buildings, mostly huddled on the central mount, were, he realized, aesthetic wonders. Even though the streets were now devoid of the smaller dwellings and mostly barren of the larger edifices, he could see the city, in his mind's eye, for what it had been—a noble, and some might say naive, attempt by Sargatanas to bring something of Heaven to

Hell. The dark grandeur of it had been unlike anything
that had ever existed, and Hannibal was saddened by its
precipitous razing. The great and gleaming domed palace,
intact only from the outside, rose through the enveloping
shroud of dust, the broken heart of a stricken city. And
within it, somewhere well inside its hollowed interior, he
knew Sargatanas and Lilith abided. For now.

Hannibal's lids grew heavy and he slipped into his
Tophet dream again. Only now, as he descended deeper
and deeper into the familiar smoke-filled world of his
great guilt, it seemed, as he faded away, that he saw himself through new, more accepting eyes. Less pained eyes.
And very dimly, though he could not question why, he
felt grateful that, after so much time, he could be at peace
with himself.

XXVIII

DIS

The arrival of Lucifuge Rofocale went, as far as Adramalik could tell, unheralded. As important a figure as he
was, he and his Ice Legions entered the First City with
little fanfare. The Prime Minister was certain that Lucifuge, as an old ally of the Prince and near equal in
abilities, would have been welcomed in a more obvious
fashion, but he had been instructed to meet the demon
himself at the gate and bring him up to Beelzebub.

Lucifuge was an unusually mannered and proper demon, as rigid in his behavior as he was in his overly
elaborate appearance. Glowing blue from his exclusive

diet of a rare flying Abyssal's flesh, he was extremely conscious of every detail of his form, manifesting a staggering array of low horns and trailing finlets and fiery tendrils. Around him orbited a dozen small abstract objects of dark and unknown purpose. Having retreated to the frigid region surrounding the Pit and viewing himself as its guardian, he seemed to have become as cold as the black fire, ice, and frozen brick of his capital, Pygon Az. His arrogance was as legendary as his reclusiveness. Barely acknowledging Adramalik, Lucifuge dismounted his huge Shuffler, leaving his army under his field marshal Uricus' command as it entered Dis, and merely jerked his head to indicate he wanted his audience with the Prince.

The ascent into the uppermost levels of the Keep was achieved without a word passing between them. Adramalik, uncomfortable with the silence, could feel the irritation that the Demon Major exuded, irritation, he imagined, at being wrenched from his isolated wards to support the Prince against an upstart demon. The relative warmth and humidity of the Keep's bowels must have made the journey upward unpleasant for Lucifuge, used to the cold, and this alone was solace for Adramalik. And now that his punishment was over, thanks to his carefully calculated tidings, nothing could trouble him. For hours they climbed the myriad stairs and wended their way through the convoluted maze of tunnel-corridors until they finally arrived at the Rotunda. Adramalik hung back as the door sphinctered open, allowing Lucifuge his moment, ostensibly as a sign of respect.

The ubiquitous buzzing was barely audible above the sighing of the hanging skins. Beelzebub, distant atop his carrion throne, was feeding as Lucifuge approached, and Adramalik thought, only briefly, to dissuade Lucifuge from interrupting him, but the part of him that delighted in seeing his fellow demons in discomfort was curious about the Prince's reaction. And so as Lucifuge strode stiffly toward the throne, Adramalik held his breath, the unpredictability of his master both terrifying and exhilarating.

As always, Husk Faraii sat at his Prince's feet and the Prime Minister took little notice of him; he neither spoke nor moved in all of his past audiences, and there was no reason to expect more of him. He looked more emaciated than ever, and the bluish gray of his face had visibly blackened around its flaking plates' edges. Not surprisingly, the Baron was not faring well on his new-found diet of leavings from the throne.

When he and Lucifuge drew near, Adramalik noticed that what had appeared to be the Prince's fully round torso was, in fact, only half-finished, its shoulder and left arm completely missing. The other half had dissolved into a thick layer of flies that contentedly rasped at the large, unidentifiable chunk of offal that lay in its lap. The partial body of Beelzebub turned disconcertingly toward them.

"Prince-in-Exile Lucifuge," he buzzed, the trace of mockery unmistakable, "how was your journey?"

"My journey was long and tiresome, Beelzebub. And," he added, "disturbingly necessary."

"It has been a long time since you retreated to your frozen wards, an equally long time since you visited us here in Dis."

"Retreated? No, 'distanced myself' would be more accurate. It is no secret between us that when Lucifer handed his scepter over to you I felt . . . slighted. What he was thinking I cannot guess, but we are now bearing witness to the consequences of that ill-chosen act."

Adramalik could not believe Lucifuge's brevity. No one spoke to the Prince with such candor, and suddenly Adramalik could feel the swirling of some momentous event about to take place. Lucifuge would be an invaluable ally; few so far had answered Beelzebub's call. But, even so, there were limits to his tolerance.

"Perhaps if I had stayed by your side as Lucifer had wanted . . . ," Lucifuge continued. "Ah, but that was never really a possibility, was it?"

The flies stirred for a moment and then settled back onto the glistening meat.

"So, what is it I hear about our old friend Sargatanas? I understand he is no longer happy here in Hell. Why not simply let him see if he can find a way to go?"

"Because free will has no place in Hell. Not for him or anyone else who might be inspired by him."

"You never questioned Lucifer's free will."

"Sargatanas is *not* Lucifer."

"Nor are you. Do we have Lucifer's Seal on this? According to the First Infernal Bull, 'no Demon Major may set out against another with the express goal of destroying that Demon Major himself.' "

"We do not need it. The Heretic Sargatanas is coming here."

"Then, if you succeed in fending him off, he can be taken prisoner and exiled. Not destroyed. Only Lucifer's Seal can mandate that. As I just said, no Demon—"

"I am not a Demon Major."

"But *I* am."

"*You,* Rofocale, are out of touch with the pulse of Hell. And, simply put, I need your legions. If you agree, you may have half of the Heretic's wards when this is over."

"You may have the twenty Ice Legions that I brought with me and no more," Lucifuge said plainly. "And I will remain in command. I will not have any of your generals determining the fate of my legions."

The flies took wing with an agitated whirring and began to stream down toward Adramalik and Lucifuge. The Prime Minister swallowed hard.

"You will have your command," said Beelzebub quietly. "Or so it will seem."

Without a word and with incredible speed, Husk Faraii leaped up and, oblivious to the myriad horns that covered Lucifuge's glowing body, grasped him around the arms and torso so tightly that for a moment the shocked demon did not even struggle. Lucifuge's stunned immobility instantly turned to anger and then desperation as he realized that he could not move even if he chose to. The flies formed an ominous circle over his head and dropped down, creating a black, roiling collar around his neck.

Adramalik's eyes widened as a protective series of glyphs rose above the demon only to be easily dissipated by Beelzebub's own glyphs. Lucifuge's head began to transform involuntarily, his rage—the only visible constant—etched in every incarnation. But that anger was short-lived when it was suddenly replaced by an expression of agony as the yoke of flies began to gnaw down into his shoulders, rasping apart the layered plates of bones to burrow deep into the underlying flesh. An instant later the life went out of his eyes and something twisted inside the demon's torso.

Adramalik watched the head slowly cant to one side, mouth still writhing, and then tumble to the floor with a loud splash. And with the Husk still holding the shaking torso upright, a new head began to appear, forming quickly up from the ragged neck and made of milling flies. When, with a glyph cast by Beelzebub, its thousand parts had changed texture and color and was completed, it was indistinguishable from the original. The head blinked spasmodically and then turned to look at its master. To anyone who might have seen him, Lucifuge had entered the Rotunda and exited it a short while later.

"Prime Minister," Beelzebub said. He had re-formed, but now his left forearm, already minus its hand, was somewhat shorter. "Go with him back to his legions and see to it that his field marshal understands the need to have *all* of the remaining Ice Legions dispatched to Dis immediately. It would arouse less suspicion if he sends his own courier."

Husk Faraii let go of his captive and resumed his place squatting at the foot of the throne. Jerkily he reached for the head of Lucifuge, which lay facedown in a puddle of blood.

Adramalik bowed, fear making his legs stiff. "Yes, my Prince."

Head still bowed, Adramalik began to move away, but from the corner of his eye he saw Husk Faraii pull a stubborn piece of flesh from inside the demon's skull, put it in his mouth, and begin to slowly chew.

Revolted, Adramalik turned away and, followed by what had once been Lucifuge Rofocale, exited the Rotunda to begin the long descent through the Keep to the legions waiting outside. As much as Adramalik had enjoyed the predicament that Lucifuge had found himself in, as much as he felt the demon had as much as precipitated his own demise, the episode had begun a cascade of thoughts that had only one conclusion: Beelzebub was desperate and Sargatanas, wily, powerful opponent that he was, might actually destroy him.

Mulciber's Tower no longer bore the many-pointed and tiered spire with which it had originally been built. Piercing the Keep's mantle directly in its center, the tower's spire had been demolished to afford Architect General Mulciber, and anyone who chose to make the difficult ascent, an incredible view of the shadowed city. But Adramalik had not taken the time to climb the tower to admire the city; there was more of Beelzebub's bidding to do before Sargatanas arrived at the seven gates of Dis. After fulfilling his mission with Lucifuge's unsuspecting field·marshal, Adramalik had had to make

the lengthy ascent through the Keep yet again. Had
there not been a sudden gale coming almost portentously
from the direction of Sargatanas' wards, he would have
taken wing to rise to the tower's top, avoiding altogether
the massive structure's labyrinth-like halls, but it was not
to be.

Adramalik had rarely visited the Architect General,
had rarely had any need of his services since the founding of the capital so many eons ago. And even then
Adramalik's needs had only been to convey those re-
quirements of the Knights and their Order Priory.

Sequestered by choice in his tower atop the Keep,
Mulciber was no longer recognizable as one of the
Fallen. So thoroughly had the demon given himself over
to his ever-growing masterwork that eventually he had
decided to become one with it, to meld with the thick,
phallic tower, to integrate his own body into the supine
archiorganism that was Dis.

The Prime Minister had, during his infrequent visits,
seen the slow transformation over the millennia and
now, uncertain as to the demon's current state, strained
to locate Mulciber amidst the eccentric brickwork of
the open turret-top. If the architecture of Dis could be
accused of anything, it was not of being overly ornate,
however, Mulciber had been uncharacteristically self-
indulgent in his treatment of his own abode. Perhaps,
Adramalik thought, it said something deeper about the
demon, about his self-image, but he had always been
disinclined to pursue the question. Using the demon's
sigil as a guide, Adramalik walked around the dozen or
so raised brick pedestals that sprouted from the floor,
many providing platforms for the demon's self-
eviscerated organs, which had been married to thick arteries and in turn joined with the Keep's own organs.
Squinting through the particle-laden wind and carefully
avoiding the fleshy conduits that led down into the

Keep, Adramalik threaded his way toward an assemblage of bricks, heavily carved and filled with niches within which, like reliquaries, were small remnants of Mulciber's empty demonic body. Were it not for the floating sigil, Adramalik might have missed Mulciber altogether; only a flattened face remained barely emerging from a tall freestanding column, a column dotted with brilliant yellow eyes that enabled the architect to view his creation around and beneath him.

"Chancellor General Adramalik," said Mulciber, his voice dry and hollow, like two stones rubbing together.

"Prime Minister."

"I am so out of touch up here. Forgive me."

Adramalik waved a hand dismissively.

"Architect General, I am here on behalf of the Prince. He is in need of your talents. A wall needs to be built."

"What kind of a wall?"

"A wall to protect your Prince."

"Does our Prince *need* a wall to protect him?"

"You do not know?"

Mulciber closed some of his many eyes.

"It is quiet up here, Adramalik. Quiet and removed."

Adramalik pivoted and took in the sprawling panorama. The wind had blown away the last tatters of clouds and he was able to see quite far, almost to the horizon. The sky, red from Algol's slow rising, brushed the livid rooftops below, making the city look as if it had been daubed with blood.

"All of this . . . all of this is about to change, Mulciber. Whether you know it or not."

"I am not really sure I care."

Adramalik considered this. Why should Mulciber care whom he built for? Without loyalty, there really was no true incentive. Or was there?

"How would you like to spend whatever of Eternity is left in the Pit, Mulciber? Away from all of this. Forever. Do you suppose Abaddon has any need of your services?"

Mulciber was unreadable in his expression, but his silence spoke for itself.

"What does the Fly need?"

"A little more respect, Mulciber." Adramalik enjoyed negotiating from strength with Demons Major.

"What does the Prince need of me?"

"The Prince, as I said before, requires a wall . . . a wall around the Keep so imposing and featureless that it will prevent the Heretic from entering. My spies in Adamantinarx tell me he is marshaling a vast army the size of which has never been seen in Hell. This Keep and the Prince's palace are clearly his goals."

"And how much time do I have to build this 'imposing and featureless' wall?"

"A week. Perhaps two. No more."

Mulciber's eyes widened.

"Just where am I to get the raw materials for such a project? As impossible as it is."

"You have at your disposal every soul in the capital. Every brick in every building, every paving-soul, every single soul who walks the streets of Dis . . . they are all to be used either to build it or to be built into it. All the Maws and Demolishers in the armies of Dis are at your disposal as well. After construction is completed you are expected to layer atop it the most potent of guardian-glyphs you can formulate.

"And one thing more, Mulciber. You are to supervise the construction yourself."

"But *look* at me. . . ."

Adramalik did not need to look at the pedestals and the walls where the demon's body parts were strewn to know what he was asking. "Your first task clearly is to become ambulatory. I could not care less how well formed you turn out or how uncomfortable you will be. I—the Prince expects you to be present on the wall to deal with any problems, not up here, quiet and removed, as you put it."

Mulciber's eyes closed in resignation. Adramalik thought he saw small puffs of steam start to obscure them.

"As you will, Prime Minister."

Adramalik turned and left Mulciber, content in the knowledge that the one demon in Hell who had found relative peace was about to become the busiest.

XXIX

THE FIELDS OF ADAMANTINARX

Algol had finally risen.

The din of ten thousand war trumpets and drums, of uncounted sigils flaring to light, of a million impatient, armored bodies rising to their feet, was beyond anything in war Hannibal had known or could have imagined. The ground beneath his feet trembled in response and he clenched his toes just to remain standing. He knew that if he had had a heart it would have been thundering in his chest.

Algol had climbed to its zenith and with it the great Second Army of the Ascension had taken up arms to begin its long march toward Dis. As they left their front ranks to join Satanachia for the beginning of the march, Hannibal and Mago exchanged grins, but each knew what was in the other's mind: would they ever see Adamantinarx again? The Soul-General looked behind him toward the city and saw, still standing on the distant rostrum, the white form of Sargatanas and the less distinct shapes of Eligor and all of the others who were to stay behind until their moment came.

There had been no grand speeches, no ceremonious invocations, nothing in the host's departure that could be construed as anything but necessary. What had been said in the past was enough for the present.

The briefing had been short and direct, with Sargatanas and Satanachia doing most of the talking. The assault on Dis was to be something of a ruse, as Hannibal understood it. The massive ground attack would ultimately prove to be a diversion from the more covert aerial attack to follow. Eligor and Satanachia's Flying Corps commander, Barbatos, would combine their forces and train until they were sent to Dis. The generals under Satanachia's command had been given their orders and departed for the field, leaving the two Demons Major and the Soul-General to linger with Sargatanas.

Walking slowly before each of them, Sargatanas had said, "Demons, Hannibal, I cannot tell you what we will find waiting for us in Dis or how this will come out. But I can tell you that even though we live in shadow, we fight for light. Go now, and spread that light where none has ever shone!"

Each of them had bowed and then returned to the head of the waiting army. When Hannibal found his brother he remained silent for some time, his mind swimming with the tactics and possibilities of the impending siege. His and the other ground armies, no matter how huge, were effectively a delaying force. And that meant staggering attrition. From what he knew of the Prince and his spies, the armies of Dis would know well in advance of the size and nature of the opposing legions. Little was known in Adamantinarx of the demons who might have allied with the Fly. But such was the nature of war, and after explaining what he knew of Sargatanas' plan to Mago, he felt somehow better. Talking it through with his brother, as he had before so many campaigns so long ago, relaxed him for the time being. But he knew, as their host drew near Dis, his apprehensions would surface anew. Some said it was a sign of a good general to fret; soldiers should not have to worry, only fight. With his world of experience, he agreed.

Attendants brought up Gaha, and he had difficulty mounting the Abyssal. He could not have been more impatient for his new arm to grow in but knew that it would not be in time for the upcoming battle. He smiled inwardly; he certainly did not need more incentives to want to survive. Once he was in the saddle he swung around and made for Put Satanachia's position. The beast was light on its feet and moved quickly across the crowded field, never misstepping. Hannibal passed rank upon rank of troops, both demon and soul, and even he, accustomed as he was to multicultural mercenary armies, was impressed with their variety. The demons that had arrived from every corner of Hell, formed and tempered and improved in the crucibles of their unending border-wars, were equipped with a dizzying array of weapons. His gaze shifted from demons who bore everything from integrated axes, maces, halberds of every shape, and pikes to more exotic legionaries from distant realms whose arms were the separated blades of great scissors or ended in huge, sharp-toothed, gaping mouths or giant claws. There seemed to be no restrictions on the ingenuity that the demons had exercised in growing implements to cleave, cut, rend, and smash one another. Such was the way of Hell; any exploitable advantage over neighboring demons could prove decisive upon the battlefield and garner a ward or two from a rival. The souls, not benefiting from the creative energies of their masters, had been equipped as best as the demons could manage with an abundance of improvised weaponry. Many, he saw, wielded the sawn-off weapons of demons who had fallen on both sides in the last battle while the rest gripped crude, but effective, weapons that had been hastily manufactured in Adamantinarx before the Forges themselves had been dismantled.

Satanachia, resplendent in his newly formed opalescent armor and standing at the very tip of the gathered legions, was waiting for him. Flattered, Hannibal realized that it was a measure of their esteem for him that the demon second in prestige to his lord would only give the signal to advance when he was present. As the enormous blue glyph, visible for many hundreds of spans, billowed up into the ashen sky Hannibal felt the vortex of fate pulling him toward Hell's capital. As the army slowly surged forward, uncertainty flooded his mind. Whichever way the battle went, the outcome in Dis would prove to be the end of the rebellion. Of one thing he was certain: Sargatanas would not sell himself cheaply and, even if the Fly somehow managed to survive, the shape of Hell would forever be changed.

The wind whipped fiercely over Eligor's straining body, snapping at his folded wings, as he clung, one-handed, to the gently rounded exterior of Sargatanas' dome. The heavy, bifurcated prongs of Eligor's newly issued climbing-staff were firmly lodged in the crack between two massive roofing stones and had, regrettably, damaged the surface where they had been inserted. He had been dismayed when Sargatanas had outlined his planned training regimen, knowing that the final exercise was going to do extensive damage to the once-majestic dome. But Adamantinarx was no longer the city it had been, and the Captain was gradually growing accustomed to the unfortunate changes the city was undergoing.

Looking through the shifting clouds at the gray curve of the dome, Eligor saw the generalized shapes of his flying troops, hammers in hand, begin the mock-assault for the tenth time. They, like Barbatos and his flyers performing the same exercise on the dome's opposite side, would only be ordered to actually strike the building when their tactical maneuverings were satisfactory, an achievement that Eligor guessed would be about a week hence. While the breaching of Sargatanas' dome would only be executed once, for obvious structural reasons, the Guard Captain wanted to feel completely confident that the hundreds of flyers were able to move about comfortably in a high wind on a curved and polished surface. He saw the other flyers trying to hover above where the giant hole would be opened, and even as he watched, chaos erupted as a particularly strong gust buffeted them and sent hundreds of them crashing into one another. And then, to worsen matters, Eligor felt a few drops of blood hit him and soon a steady light rain began to fall, spattering the already treacherously smooth dome, slickening it dangerously. Truly, he thought, this was a good and difficult test. Within moments the rain had streaked the dome shiny and red and, almost mesmerized, he watched myriad thin rivulets winding their way like fast, thick worms downward. He saw how his demons scrabbled and slipped and suddenly one lost his handhold and slid down into another and then another and, before he could warn them, more than twenty of the flyers were tumbling, trying to disentangle from one another and open their wings. But, to his mixed disappointment and anger, they did not succeed and plunged headlong to their destruction upon the cloud-shrouded pavement far below. *A good and difficult test indeed,* Eligor reflected.

He watched the remainder of the exercise with a decidedly disagreeable attitude. The planning and subsequent training for the assault on the Fly's palace was proving to be about as difficult as Eligor had envisioned; he had known all along that the whims of Hell's weather would play havoc with any aerial assaults. Finally the thousand-odd demons were in their stations, some bearing hammers and focused on breaking through the stone, some ringing about where the hole would be smashed, and the remainder, lances in hand, hovering as best as they could in formation above and awaiting a command to drop through into the palace beneath. A dense cloud passed in front of him and, for a few moments, he could only see the tiny lights of their unit-glyphs through the patchy haze. He held them there for some time; it would be good for them to wait, to lock into their minds their respective roles. Then, satisfied only that they had finally reached the exercise's end, he raised his free hand and issued the command to withdraw and return to their camps. He saw his glyph circle the dome once and vanish and then watched the blood-wet demons break away and drop into the clouds.

Eligor sent a signal to Barbatos at the opposite side of the dome and wondered if his demons had fared any better. He unhooked himself from the dome and spread his wings, descending in a slow, controlled drop through the reddish curtain of clouds. When his feet scraped the flagstones of the plaza it was just in time to see the last of his Flying Guard entering their barracks. And he also saw the crumpled forms of three of his demons lying in twisted piles, their broken wings reaching up like slender fingers. Already he could hear the creaking wheels of an approaching bone-cart sent to remove them.

Limbs stiff and trembling from the exercise, Eligor made his way up the palace stairs and entered the empty entrance hall. Usually, after newcomers entered the palace from a downpour, there would have been attendants ready and waiting to towel them down, but now there was no such courtesy. Instead the metallic tang of the blood and the uncomfortable feeling of it drying upon him only heightened his growing sense that all was not well. When he was back in his chambers he would have to spend much time cleaning himself. Only the distilled and still-irritating saline waters of the

Acheron would remove the stain, a ritual that, considering his exhaustion, he did not look forward to.

For some reason only a relative few of the palace's many braziers were lit, and the shadowed areas that Eligor passed through seemed to him like ominous lakes of darkness. Trudging through the halls, past the infrequent distracted functionary or brick-laden worker, Eligor noted again with now-familiar sadness that the entire geography of the immense building had been altered. The mandated removal of any and all soul-bricks, a process that was still under way, had caused the complete rearrangement and, in some cases, structural weakening of the interior, leaving great holes, collapsed ceilings, or crudely supported walls. The dust of deconstruction was everywhere. And more than once he saw it kicked up by winds that, in the past, would never have been possible in the building when its integrity had been sound.

But even with conditions as they were, the palace retained some echoes of its grandeur, and the closer to its Audience Chamber he walked the more the great building resembled its former self. On his way to the stairs leading to his chambers, he peered through the columns of the arcade into the great space beyond and looked to the top of the pyramidal dais half-expecting to see Sargatanas seated on his throne. But only the shadows and emptiness greeted him. Algol's beam, almost always visible, was absent, occluded by the heavy weather above—something that he tried hard not to view as an omen. He imagined that Sargatanas was in his Shrine or his chambers, perhaps with Lilith. It was a thought that only served to deepen Eligor's melancholia; their time together, whether his lord got his wish or was destroyed trying, was drawing to a close.

And then the realization hit him like a hammer-blow. He understood, for the first time, just how much he

would miss Sargatanas. Since the rebellion had begun
every act, every word, had been about Beelzebub, his
defenses, his armies, his cities, his tactics. Eligor had
been so preoccupied with his office that he had not really had a moment to envision his world without his
lord. Sargatanas had been a mentor and a paragon, a focal point and a guide, and now that Eligor saw a glimpse
of what it might be like, of the emptiness he would feel,
he did not like it.

He continued to his chambers, up the long, curving
staircase and down the wide hall, past Valefar's sealed
chambers and then to his own. As he entered and lit his
braziers with a cast flurry of glyphs, he questioned if
Sargatanas' vision was worth all of the incredible
changes that had been wrought upon Hell. If the rebellion did not succeed would it have been the greatest act
of selfishness imaginable to have plunged them all into
this war? The question hung in his mind as he dipped a
soft capillary-knot from the Wastes in the water and began to sponge himself as best as he could. The dull burn
of the Acheron upon his exposed flesh and bone almost
felt like welcome penance for the guilt he felt in doubt-
ing Sargatanas.

They left the Shrine together for the last time, and as they
exited, Lilith could not help but wonder if Sargatanas had
not brought her there as a last effort to get her to change
her mind. He pulled the thick door shut and then turned to
her and her suspicions were confirmed.

"You can change your mind, Lilith. If I do go back, it
will mean that the way is clear for others. You could—"

She reached up and put a finger to his mouth.

"My love, this is the way it must be. As much as it
will pain both of us."

He nodded and, as she watched, the beginnings of his
armor blossomed forth in the manner of demons and

angels alike, coming up from his skin like rising white magma, smoothing and shaping itself to conform to his body.

He shook his head and took her hands.

"Why, *why* do I reach for Heaven when it's already in my grasp?"

"Because the Heaven you reach for will give you that which you desire . . . a world of sublime tranquility. Beatitude. That I cannot offer you."

Lilith paused to see his reaction. The pale armor continued to exude from within him, encasing his head and shoulders. He did not say a word but looked at her, the inner turmoil obvious. She almost felt that a single word from her could dissuade him from his path, halt the assault on Dis, and keep him in his city, in Hell. But she did not utter it.

"You are a seraph, Sargatanas. The highest of angels. You can never be anything else, no matter what shape you take. No matter where you are. You'll never be content unless you are back where you belong."

He let her hands slip out of his and she knew, then, that there was no turning back for him.

His new armor was nearly fully formed, its congealing surface swirling and blending and smoothing. When Lilith stepped back to look at him she saw a mountainous figure of power and intensity, unquestionably heroic yet almost physically unrecognizable to her save for his unchanged face. His sigils suddenly flared to life upon his breast, flanking the dark hole where his heart should have been, piercing the shimmering steam that wafted in curling sheets that were denser than normal from the armor's formation.

"We must go," he said. "Zoray awaits his Elevation. And then . . ." The demon's voice trailed off and Lilith tried not to think about the future.

"Yes, and then."

As they walked the darkened palace corridors toward

the Hall of Rituals, Lilith realized that, even with her
sadness at Sargatanas' imminent departure, she was actually eager to see the ceremony in which he raised the
Demon Minor to the status of a Demon Major. An Infernal mirror of angelic Risings, it was not a commonplace
event, and while she had heard about the ancient rite,
she had never witnessed it in either Dis or Adamantinarx. The city was to be left in his hands and Sargatanas
wanted his former Foot Guard commander as well
equipped for the job as possible. She was relieved that
Sargatanas had not chosen her; while she felt capable of
governing Adamantinarx, it was a task best left to someone who had been in the city since its founding. He and
Andromalius, the new provisional General-in-Chief of
Adamantinarx, would be able officers of their posts.

Lord Zoray was, as Sargatanas had predicted, awaiting their arrival clad in the ornate symbolic six-winged
trappings of the occasion and surrounded by his staff.
Some of them would, as a result of his Elevation, be
carried upward in station as well, and they fidgeted and
shifted in anticipation. Zoray's eagerness, too, was undeniable, and when Sargatanas strode ahead of her
Lilith watched the soon-to-be governor kneel and pros-
trate himself. This was to be Sargatanas' last official
duty and, as she watched the heavily armored figure begin to fill the air around and over Zoray's form with line
after line of fiery glyph-script, she began to formulate
plans for the time when she would be alone.

BEELZEBUB'S INNER WARDS

For two weeks the Second Army of the Ascension
swept across the gray fields of Hell with all of the incandescent savagery of a surging sheet of lava. Opposition during the long march had been minimal, but when
small armies of the Fly had been chanced upon Hannibal

had watched as Sargatanas' legions had flowed over the enemy, the encounters barely slowing the advancing souls and demons. He had no time for the niceties of negotiation, nor did the enemy seek it. It was a time of change, and the Soul-General felt proud and honored to be a part of it. Finally, his eternity had some meaning.

The landscape outside of Adamantinarx was something largely unfamiliar to those souls who had not been in the first great battle, and even those veterans who had grown quiet when they passed the limits of familiar territories. Their march took them past the Flaming Cut, where they saw the great cairn, and on into the wards of the enemy, and Hannibal saw that the closer they drew to Dis the more hostile the terrain became. It seemed as if Beelzebub, creating a first line of defense, had imbued the very ground and peaks and blood-rivers with his own anger. No town or outpost had been left standing, a curious fact, Satanachia had remarked, in light of the Fly's historical reluctance to let go of his territorial possessions.

Whenever the vanguard of the army approached the blasted remains of happened-upon outlying settlements, demon sappers were called forward and the rubble was immediately demolished. Any freed souls who were whole enough to spring unaided from the resulting piles of brick and who were not immediately amenable to joining the army were destroyed on the spot, but, Hannibal always noted, with little surprise and a thin smile, they were few.

When, eventually, there were more of Beelzebub's wards behind them than in front, demons and souls alike saw the air ahead, heavy with haze, suffused with a red-gold lambency, and Satanachia informed his generals that, due to its location, the source of this effulgence was most probably the Keep.

A scouting party was sent forward and after a day came back to the gathered general staff with news of the city ahead. Or, more properly, with news that the capi-

tal, in its familiar form, was no longer and that most of
its buildings, like those of Adamantinarx, were gone. In
the brief weeks since the battle of the Flaming Cut,
Beelzebub and his Architect General had not been idle.
The Keep still stood, surrounded by its ring of lava, but
its mountainous form was now encased in an immense
and featureless wall. And waiting at its base was an
army nearly equal in size to that of Sargatanas.

None of this was comforting news, and the generals'
silence reflected their inner misgivings. Hannibal, too,
struggled to find something in the report that might
point to a weakness in the Prince's stratagem. Every advantage seemed to lie with the Fly. Only Satanachia
seemed unaffected by the circumstances, and he did his
best to bolster his staff.

On a high escarpment just outside Dis' immediate
outskirts, Put Satanachia sent the order aloft for Yen
Wang's Behemoths to form up in multiple wedges in the
host's front ranks. With this first battle order the Second
Army of the Ascension would descend upon the vast
plain that had once been Dis and, however the battle
went, the fate of Hell itself would be decided.

ADAMANTINARX-UPON-THE-ACHERON

She saw him from afar, from a window in the tallest
turret left in his palace. Standing upon the high parade
ground, he was a white figure in a sea of ranked deep-
olive flyers. Eligor strode at his side, as did Barbatos,
each, she imagined, receiving his last orders. The wind,
furious and steady, whipped at them almost as if they
were already aloft, and Sargatanas' ivory flight skins
flowed around him, billowing dramatically. The time had
come and in moments he would be gone. Gone from
Adamantinarx, gone from her existence. And soon, in all
probability, gone from Hell.

Lilith turned away and walked back into her chamber, heading toward the area she had devoted to her sculpting. From the open window the sound of rank after rank of flying demons taking to the air suddenly filled the room, a loud roar of wings accompanied by a steady wind that rattled her sculpting tools on their small table. She would not stand by the window and watch him ascend into the clouds. She did not want the sight of him disappearing into the dark clouds to be burned into her memory.

Instead, she sat holding the large block of compressed Abyssal bone in her cold hands, turning it stiffly as if she were actually considering what to transform it into. She even picked up a tool just to convince herself that she was actually intent upon her new project. But as she lingered, scraper poised, she caught sight of the traveling skins, Ardat Lili's skins, a corner of which peeked from beneath the flat, carved lid of a long chest. All of the possessions Lilith could carry from her life in Dis and her long journey away from the capital were within that chest, and she thought, with some pleasure, that, with the exception of her cherished tools, she had had no need of them since she had arrived in Adamantinarx; she had only to have hinted about any need and Sargatanas had provided it. Now she was not so sure that some of those items within the chest—the skins, the masks, the long dagger Agares had secreted in her bags—might not be useful yet again.

Lilith listened to the wind of the wings and when, after a very long time, it had subsided she placed the scraper and the untouched block back down on the table and rose. At the window again, she saw that the parade ground was empty, a dark and heavy cloud lowering to make it indistinct. As dark and indistinct, she thought, as her future now seemed.

XXX

BEELZEBUB'S WARDS

He had never flown so easily, so quickly, and with such a sense of purpose. The hot wind that Sargatanas had summoned weeks ago with characteristic forethought sped the multitude of winged demons toward Dis in half the time Eligor would have estimated. In only two days, and with only one mass landing, the combined flying forces of Sargatanas and Satanachia had covered nearly all of the ground between Adamantinarx and Dis.

As one of the two force commanders, Eligor flew well above the main flights. In an effort to remain unseen no sigil was lit, making the formations hard to see even for the sharp-eyed Captain. Sargatanas, his pale wings spread like fans, soared just above him issuing unobtrusive command-glyphs that the Guard Captain and Barbatos had to pass on with equal stealth to the lesser officers.

Looking down between the dense pyramidal flights of flyers, Eligor saw landmarks that he knew from his infrequent land journeys to the capital. Even from this altitude, he could see the myriad roads and paths that were obviously converging on the sprawling city from all points in the Prince's empire. Along one of these, Eligor finally saw the rear guard of his lord's army.

Sargatanas had waited until the two great land armies were engaged before leaving the palace with his flying troops. Far below, Eligor now began to see the orderly battle formations at the rear edge of the Second Army of the Ascension wheeling into position according to their generals' needs. He knew that they were still very far from the front lines and he looked forward and, not seeing the distant battlefield, saw only the great glow that surrounded the Keep. As high as he was, the Black Dome atop the Keep reared higher and, for all of its size, he only saw it in fragmentary glimpses far ahead and behind the luminous clouds. *Is this not a truly mad plan? How can such a mountain of a building possibly be breached and then occupied? We will all be destroyed before our feet touch the dome, let alone the Rotunda floor!* And then, as he shifted his lance uneasily in his hands, the echoes of tales of Abaddon's realm and eternities of ice and darkness and shredding claws filled his mind and he clamped his jaws a little tighter. He had rarely thought of those stories before and especially not during his countless battles, but now, as he approached Dis, they seemed more threatening, more of a fearsome possibility.

Sargatanas sent down a glyph ordering them to gain even more altitude. Strangely, the wind seemed to be dying down, and Eligor noticed that the air was not only thicker but also foul smelling. Whether by his lord's presence or his design or by some protective counterinvocation of the Fly's, the gale's lessening would more easily facilitate their landing. They rose quickly on well-rested wings, entering a thick bank of red-tinged clouds and steering through the heavy, disorienting mists only on the strength of Sargatanas' certainty.

As Eligor soared upward, he tried to picture the chaos of the battlefield far beneath them, wondering about the fortunes, good or bad, of Satanachia, of Yen Wang, and of that resourceful soul Hannibal. For all Eligor or any of the other demons flying with him knew, the battle had turned one way or the other and glorious victory or utter defeat was already written upon the rubble-strewn fields of Dis.

On he flew with a diminishing sense of time and distance. The cloud-bank was an enervating environment, its passing billows slow and hypnotic. The sere wind-current they had sailed upon had left him and the flyers more than enough strength for this final dash to the dome. Over the sound of his own now-moistened wings, he could hear the cloud-muffled flapping of the nearest demons below him, their breaths coming in short but unstrained huffs that matched their wing beats. Above, Sargatanas flew silently, and Eligor could only imagine what must be going through his lord's mind. Not only did the Demon Major have the innumerable concerns of the battlefield to address but also the fraught possibilities stemming from his army's success or failure. Eligor found himself actually grateful that his only concerns were his duties as the commander of many hundreds of demons.

Closer to the Black Dome the flights began to encounter luckless patrols of demons patrolling the night sky. These were easily overwhelmed, their ash dissipating on the wind, erasing any trace of their presence and any evidence of their demise.

The huge formation leveled off at an altitude high enough to allow Sargatanas to issue command-glyphs without fear of being detected. This, Eligor knew, was essential to the final approach to the dome. Many of his lord's spies had been destroyed ascertaining even the smallest structural weaknesses in the Black Dome. It would remain to be seen whether they had been sacrificed for naught.

ADAMANTINARX-UPON-THE-ACHERON

The Library no longer had the familiar, comforting smell of dust and ancient volumes. Too many holes had been opened in the palace, allowing the winds from outside to purge it of its characteristic musty scent. Lilith watched the corner of the page she was holding quiver in the steady current of air that made its way to where she sat from a demolished corridor wall to her side.

Since her arrival in Adamantinarx, Lilith had found herself drawn toward the Library and its hitherto unimaginable wealth of learning, striving to come back every day for, at least, a short time. In Dis she had been so cloistered that her only source of learning was from demons she had met at court and on those rare occasions when they had been accessible they had never been terribly forthcoming. She had lived in a world of enforced ignorance.

She looked over at Librarian Eintsaras as he transcribed yet another of the Library's volumes. This was the one place where Sargatanas had realized freeing the souls would be a detriment to the demons. To lose the Library was to lose the collected knowledge of eons. Because each book was fashioned around soul-vellum, they had to be transcribed to Abyssal-skin pages before they could be converted. Giving Eintsaras the glyph-of-transmutation, Sargatanas had known just how long it would take to change over the Library. The small army of librarians had barely made a dent.

Even as she watched, Eintsaras finished another page and, with the suddenly conjured glyph, set its narrator free. The soul, a female, looked around in utter confusion, holding herself up by the solid table in front of her. One of the librarians rose from his seat and escorted her away. Her life in Hell was her own again.

Lilith touched the tiny glyph on the page that initiated the narration. She had chosen a major work on the Wastes, a book that Eligor had heard and recommended, which detailed the findings of the most far traveled of the ancient mapping expeditions. The party had included many souls and the pages had been fashioned from them, lending the book a firsthand immediacy. But, as fascinating as it was, she found herself distracted. Zoray had promised to meet her in the Library to discuss her future in the city and just what her role might be, and she had been giving that question considerable thought since Sargatanas had departed. She knew she was going to disappoint him.

The newly appointed governor of Sargatanas' wards arrived alone. To Lilith's eyes, though he was now a Demon Major with all of the newly acquired physical attributes that went with his Elevation, he looked fatigued, and it was little wonder. Since Sargatanas had begun to free the souls this was a new world, and with its beginning came new challenges. Working out just how the wards would function in their present condition was taxing, involving the creation of new economies and new ways of meeting challenges without the enforced use of souls. She could only imagine, with a bit of wryness, Zoray's boredom as he listened to Sargatanas' army of advisors.

Lilith touched the glyph again and the page's ancient soul went silent.

Zoray moved around the table and stood, peering over her shoulder at the open book.

"Should I read anything into your choice of books, Lilith?"

"Perhaps. I have always wanted to see more of this world of ours. There are many mysteries out there, Zoray. Things I would like to see."

"Really? Well, perhaps you might start with the surrounding wards. And the mystery of how we will get them to run smoothly."

Lilith smiled, but then a look of bewilderment suddenly crossed her face. Looking past Zoray, she saw the dark figure of a soldier approaching, apparently having entered the Library from the wall that had been broken open. As he came closer she saw that the right side of the demon's torso was missing, giving the appearance of having been cleft away in battle. This was not unusual in itself, but something about the way the demon moved was not right.

And then Lilith heard the buzzing and knew.

With deliberate and quick steps it walked up the main aisle, and as it passed each working librarian something that Lilith could not see from her distance cleanly sliced their heads from their shoulders, causing their lifeless bodies to gout blood and collapse in upon themselves. Its appearance was so sudden that there was no time for the librarians to react, and in only brief moments the floor was littered with their disks.

Zoray spun around, pulling his sword from its sheath, and Lilith heard him quietly invoke a protective glyph. Not expecting combat, he had no armor upon him, and summoning it up would take too long.

The Hand of Beelzebub paused. Lilith knew that virtually every part of it could see, and yet, unnervingly, its gaze seemed fixed upon her. For a heart-pounding instant, as she was paralyzed and staring into its expressionless face, the world of the Fly spread darkly through her mind, filling her with dread and revulsion.

She cried out when a thin tendril of flies whipped forth, beheading Eintsaras where he had risen.

With sword extended, Zoray moved forward and said "Leave, my lady! *Run!*"

But Lilith knew that it was futile. With the palace opened up like a worm-bored body there was no place to which she could flee that would keep this monstrosity from her now that she had been uncovered. Even so, she found herself moving backward, toward the doors.

Zoray did not wait for the Hand to strike out at him. Closing swiftly with the dark figure, he lashed out at its head, its chest, its arm, but watched, with widening eyes, as the flies parted and his sword passed ineffectually through. Lilith heard the whipping wind of his sword-work as swing after swing met with only air. He turned his blade flat-on but succeeded in only batting the flies away in larger groups. She saw the Demon Major's mounting frustration boil over as he upended a heavy table and shoved it, scraping noisily, across the floor at his opponent. The Hand simply dissipated into a shapeless cloud and then, just as quickly, resolved into its original form.

Like a demonic whirlwind, Zoray swept chairs and tables aside, treading upon the fallen books and circling around in an effort to draw the Hand away from her. But as he tore through the room, the desperation clear upon his face, the reality of the moment washed through her and suddenly she felt an overwhelming pity for him. As powerful as he had become, he was going to be destroyed protecting her, and there was nothing she could do to save him.

With a roar of frustration, Zoray dropped his useless sword and grasped a flaming wrought-iron brazier that momentarily caused the dark figure to billow and pull back. Lilith heard the buzzing crescendo, the flies' anger clear to her ears, as the demon fanned its outrage with the guttering fire. Without warning, the Hand leaped forward, parting around the extended brazier and colliding with Zoray. The brazier clanged to the stone floor as the demon suddenly froze in place, his entire front blackened with noisy, writhing flies. And then, to Lilith's horror, they disappeared into Zoray, boring their way through bone and then flesh and then bone again until she saw them emerge in blotchy patches from the back of his head and torso. When the flies left his perforated body it fell lightly to the Library floor, barely making a sound. She hardly noticed as Zoray drew inward, becoming a glowing disk. Rising up from the destroyed demon, the Hand of Beelzebub turned and regarded her with its thousand eyes.

"*What* is mine?" it grated in that all-too-familiar voice.

Lilith did not answer.

"*Hell* is mine."

Lilith could not control her trembling.

"Hell's *minions* are mine."

It took a step toward her.

"Hell's *souls* are mine."

She closed her eyes.

"*You* are mine."

She felt the coldness of them as they slammed upon her body with so much force that she tumbled backward, landing flat upon her back. As the room dimmed and her mouth was pried open, as the sound of them drowned out even her own terror and she felt them moving down her throat and into her belly, she heard one word repeated until she heard nothing more.

"*Mine!*"

XXXI

DIS

To Hannibal's eyes, the capital of Hell looked as if giants' hands had swept the inner wards of its buildings, leaving only the gouge-marks of their colossal nails— its former twisted alleys and streets and avenues—upon the ground.

After the hard march through the Wastes, progress toward the Keep had been easy. Dis was a shattered city, the shards of its buildings few and scattered, the obstacles to a marching army nearly nonexistent. What few buildings had been found stood shaking on the fractured edges of its outermost wards. These had been summarily razed, their souls liberated.

Dense with the still-lingering, eddying dust and ash

of destruction, the air grew brighter with the red-gold glow that emanated from the direction of the Keep. The terrain between Hannibal and the mountainous edifice was so barren and relatively smooth that it acted as a dark reflector of the dim fires of the Fly's abode, making the ground look like the surface of a frozen lake. Only the swath of the great army that waited near the base of the new wall, now growing visible in the thick atmosphere, bespoke of any life upon the otherwise deserted plain. He turned in his saddle and looked into the red-tinged carpet of souls that was his army. Receding until they were tiny specks, the souls' countless weapons, reflecting the fires of the Keep, sparkled like embers in the hanging ash. *Breathtaking,* he thought, *a sight of unexpected beauty.*

The plodding footsteps of the enormous Behemoths ahead shook the ground continuously, causing those waves of jostling souls closest to them to move forward in irregular clumps, but somehow Hannibal's nimble steed managed to maintain its footing among them. The Soul-General was close—some thought too close—to the flanks of the advancing Behemoth line, but he felt that his troops should leave little open ground between them in the unlikely event that the giant creatures' line was breached. And he knew that their bone-masked mahouts, in the unlikely event that the Behemoths panicked, would be quick to react. Protruding from each mammoth soul's skull was the head of a long spike that ended inches from the soul's brain; a sharp blow with the mahout's hammer and the spike would be driven home, destroying the soul instantly.

Before him the new Keep Wall rose up, still distant but immense, ascending until it nearly obscured the Keep itself. Bathed in red, it was a sheer, solid expanse covered in an ever-changing net of glyphs that played upon the flat soul-brick surface like firelight through waves of blood. It was the product, he had been told, of

Mulciber's genius, and it was a marvel, built, Hannibal guessed, with such haste that it could only have been achieved with the use of every soul's hand and body in Dis. He stared for long minutes as he moved forward, the layer of glyphs mesmerizing in its shifting patterns. Behind that floating shield, the wall was unbroken save for their goal—the single huge gate that lay behind a titanic raised drawbridge a thousand feet above the Keep's base and no longer accessible by its wide bridge, which had been destroyed. Lying between the gate and the Second Army of the Ascension were not only the massed legions of the army of Dis but also the wide, bottomless moat of Lucifer's Belt. Too hot and broad to traverse with any improvised barges, it would, unquestionably, prove a formidable barrier—a barrier that somehow needed to be crossed. Satanachia had already pointed to the gate as their objective, but the distance between the moat-edge and the gate above was too great to cast ropes. And no flyers in any great enough numbers accompanied them, all of their squadrons having been already committed to Sargatanas' maneuver. For the moment, Hannibal could see no physical way of gaining their objective.

Even as Hannibal watched the advancing lines of demons ahead, an enormous bolt of red glyph-lightning, a curse he thought from the ground below, exploded into the ranks of Satanachia's demons, pulverizing scores of them into a thick cloud of black dust that fell back down slowly. *Was it sent by the Fly high above in his Rotunda? Was it just the beginning? Or am I letting my misgivings get the better of me?* Hannibal had never been this skittish before a battle. Another bolt of lightning, this time closer, jarred him and made Gaha flinch and then more discharges began to burst upward and Hannibal knew for certain that they were not natural. The Fly had created a defensive perimeter and they were edging all too slowly into it. Hannibal would lose many troops to the lightning before they had a chance to engage the waiting army, but there was nothing he could do.

The ground, which looked so uniform from a distance, had become irregular with wide, bubbling fields of dark, cooling lava, making their progress difficult. The Soul-General had not heard of these lakes in his briefing and wondered if they had been churned up by Dis' rampant demolition. He became even more suspicious when he thought he heard dull sounds issuing from within them. Through the shimmer of heat and steam he thought he saw strange shapes in the slowly swirling crust but reasoned that it was nothing more than his imagination fed by the tension of the moment.

Above, the cloud-cover over central Dis was dense, and Hannibal knew that Eligor and his lord must be well on their way, perhaps closer than he expected. The thought comforted him, but he knew that even while their efforts would shorten the battle to come, many souls would be destroyed and many demons would find out how much truth lay in the dread tales of Abaddon.

Suddenly, with a brilliant flash and a great rushing sound, a huge, circular glyph materialized before the Keep Wall hanging many hundreds of feet over Lucifer's Belt. Surrounding its central sigil—Beelzebub's pale green mark—were myriad smaller devices, each, Hannibal recognized from their forms, the sigil of one of Dis' field commanders. He heard a collective hissing intake of breath from the surrounding troops of the soul army as the small sigils detached themselves and flew, arrow straight, into the pools of lava that lay at their feet in front, to the sides, and behind them. It was a Summoning!

Hannibal's ill-defined suspicions had been justified. The bubbling pools he and his souls had so carefully been avoiding rippled and came to life as the gray crust burst apart, sending shards of cooled lava into the troops and revealing the super-heated magma beneath. There, kneeling, were rank upon rank of concealed incandescent figures that rose and began to surge forward, their steaming armor dulling to red and darkening, hardening in the air. Springing with halberds and swords at the ready onto the ledges of firmer ground before them, wave after wave poured forth, rushing to meet the surprised enemy. Hannibal watched as many of his stunned troops were cut down before they could react, some tumbling forward into the yellow-orange lava that had given birth to the demons who now struck them down.

Farther ahead, Hannibal saw that the fighting had spread to his demon allies and that the legions of Put Satanachia were as beleaguered as his own. A dozen massive gates—unseen for the radiance of the lava—opened out onto the Belt from the base of the Keep Wall, and from them wide barges carefully fashioned of pumice and loaded with more legionaries floated into view. They were ugly but effective vessels, and Hannibal watched with envy as the Belt was crossed quickly. Very shortly, the Fly's unopposed legionaries were clambering up the bank, charging onto the battlefield to reinforce the legions that were already fighting.

The clamor of battle, the roaring of legionaries and the clashing of weapons, rose in Hannibal's ears as the Behemoths in the front ranks crashed into the heavily armored troops of Dis' Urban Legions. Great spumes of ash blackened the air as the troops of both sides impacted and were destroyed. The advance ground to a halt and Hannibal watched the cohesion of his and Satanachia's legions disintegrate as they fell into a patchwork of enormous formations that attempted to hold off the still-gathering legions of Dis behind them as well as the already-engaged enemy legions from the front. Hannibal's plans for a battle fought in any way resembling his past exploits were over; this day would be won only by the accumulated victories of each pocket of his and Satanachia's troops—a reality that went counter to his instincts. Even with his misgivings, he knew that when a battle plan deteriorated, as this one had, the troops needed, more than ever, to see him in the fray, and with a roar he spurred his mount on into the thick of the fighting.

The sound of the two armies crashing together had been loud enough to take the breath out of Hannibal's mouth, while the souls around him had looked at one another with wide eyes and shocked grins of amazement. Most had never before seen battle—in Hell or in their lives—and the newness of it was, to the majority of them, emotionally exhilarating. But that was fated to change.

Hannibal urged Gaha on toward the denser clots of fighting. He wondered why, other than the Spirits, there were no cavalry regiments in Hell; the mobility and ferocity they would bring to the battlefield would be spectacular. Perhaps breeding Abyssals was too difficult; perhaps flyers took their place. It was a shame. The creature he rode was as fierce and well trained a battlemount as he could have asked for, far more potent a war beast than any horse could have been. Rising off its shorter front limbs to its more bipedal fighting stance, Gaha needed only to be pointed at the enemy to create havoc. With raking sweeps of its taloned paws the nimble Abyssal cleared wide swaths, allowing its master to swing his sword and move easily from one salient of imminent disaster to another. In this way, and with shouts of encouragement, the Soul-General kept his troops' morale high and his own confidence from flagging.

Chaos had been created upon the battlefield, but Hannibal knew that it was a chaos deliberately orchestrated by Beelzebub. The organization of its seemingly random elements followed a logic, Hannibal recognized, that most likely only the Fly could comprehend and control.

Far off in the haze of mist and ash, during a short lull, Hannibal saw the silhouetted forms of the giant soul-beasts seemingly motionless, gaining ground one difficult footstep at a time. The Urban Legions were tough, hardened troops, he had been told, accustomed to living in a harsh city formerly under that severest of generals, Moloch; they would not be an easy obstacle to pass over.

As Hannibal resumed fighting he occasionally stole a glance toward Satanachia's position, and as time wore on he saw that the Demon Major's forces were suffering considerable losses. A large salient of Rofocale's troops was bulging deep within Satanachia's lines, and try as the Behemoths might to stop the enemy from pushing forward, they seemed too few against the seemingly limitless waves of steaming legionaries that issued from beneath the Keep. Time and again Hannibal saw their massive hammers come down amidst the carpet of enemy demons only to see the pulverized foe immediately replaced by clots of aggressive halberdiers climbing atop the rubble.

The ten nearest legions, arranged in close formation, entered the fray, packed tightly so that they seemed a solid wall. The rubble from the destroyed demons of both sides was so extensive that both armies found their legionaries climbing up steep, irregular inclines to engage each other. With the ceaseless, mounting destruction the footing was becoming extremely unstable, and he saw as much damage incurred because of masses of falling soldiers as there was from actual combat wounds.

Slowly, the Behemoths began to gain ground and what had been a standstill turned into a rout. The Summoning of legionaries from the Belt finally abated and Satanachia's legions fell upon the fleeing demons, leaving a field strewn with smoking rubble.

Briefly, Hannibal thought he saw Satanachia's sigil floating against the brightness of the Belt just where he would expect it—over the line's center. A swift flash of white might just have been his brilliant two-handed sword, but Hannibal could not be certain. A giant green glyph emerged unexpectedly from the summit of the Black Dome and with a terrible scream of energy the wall came alive. Enormous bolts sprang from it, each one targeting a different Behemoth and enveloping it in a fireball of destruction. In short, disastrous moments, only fiery pits remained where the Behemoths had stood and the crackling wall had resumed its shifting glow. And a new wave of demons seemed to be forming upon the Belt. The battle had turned for the worse, and Hannibal's spirits sank.

He looked again to the Demon Major for any commands or for Azazel, and as Hannibal picked the standard-bearer's gaudy form out of the milling legionaries a glyph rose into the sky from that embattled position and he knew without doubt that Satanachia was there. The fiery command streaked toward Hannibal, and when he had taken a moment to interpret its filigreed complexities the realization of what the Demon Major was asking of him nearly made him drop his sword.

Beelzebub was, Adramalik noted with some relief, in a state of rare and unexpected calm as he observed the progress of his legions. The Prime Minister, face burning from surveying the windswept battlements, stepped closer to the throne and saw something new in his Prince's hand. Stripped of its flesh undoubtedly by Husk Faraii, Lucifuge Rofocale's head had been ingeniously adapted by the Prince's own hand to serve as a lens to focus upon the events far below him on Dis' field of battle. Mounted on a short, gold staff, the once-defiant, proud head had been picked clean, broken apart, splayed out, and transformed into a dark contrivance, all inscribed bone with inlaid, functional gems and spinning glyphlets that covered its blackened length and breadth up to its gold-rimmed, circular eye sockets. Watching his Prince peering through Rofocale's empty eyes, Adramalik had to marvel at the things his master could do, things that he found at once revolting and, despite himself, inspiring.

A noise caught his attention from the throne's base. Adramalik noticed Agares for the first time, as the distorted demon tried in vain to suppress a bubbling cough. His appearance had so worsened that he seemed no longer a demon but now, wasted and raw, a detached part of the shadowed throne of flesh that he sat beneath.

"*He* is coming," the Prince buzzed.

"Sargatanas, my Prince?"

"The *Heretic*!"

"Where is he, my Prince?"

"I cannot tell," he said, never taking his many eyes from the skull. "He is clever, Adramalik. I only know that he is close."

Adramalik looked up, past the Prince atop his throne. The dangling skins were in a constant state of agitation, creating a palpable breeze within the Rotunda and stirring the rank smells of its contents. The battle in the city below must have been affecting them.

"All is in readiness for him. We have fielded every last legion, and the Keep Wall is fully alive."

"I think it will not be enough, Prime Minister. He is a determined heretic."

Adramalik said nothing; there was little more that could be said or done than what his master had already implemented.

Adramalik never dreamt—that was for souls and beasts. But when he had returned to his chambers and laid down upon his pallet after his impossible exertions supervising the demolition of Dis, he had come close. Perhaps, he thought, what he had seen was more of a vision. Whatever it had been, it was brief and disquieting.

It had begun with him standing upon the wall, watching as countless gangs of souls hastily labored to finish its construction. He watched, too, how methodical their demon Overseers were as they efficiently prodded the shuffling, whimpering souls—most only recently able to move about again—into place while the soul-masons positioned them with precision. And he saw them transformed, course after gray course of them, into the heavy bricks that comprised the great, soaring structure. He looked down in his dream and saw their many thousand black, protruding orbs dotting the wall's flat, curving surface and was amazed and pleased.

When he turned, it was with the expectation of seeing the Black Dome rising skyward just as he knew it, but it was not there and a clenching fear gripped him. In its place, when he peered in astonishment at where the Keep should have been, there was instead a gaping hole, frost edged and impenetrable in its darkness. He knew what the hole was; he had seen it for himself. The unforgettable stench of it filled his nose as he stared once again into the entrance to Abaddon's realm, and now fear gave way to panic. From within that maw he could hear the distant sounds of moving bodies beyond count scuffling and scraping and also, most disconcertingly, their faint echoing chittering cries. Suddenly an inward rush of air began to suck at the foot of the wall, breaking it apart and dragging chunks toward the Pit, and in seconds a spiraling maelstrom of soul-bricks was disappearing into the darkness. Adramalik took wing but to no avail. His wings could only claw futilely at the cold air as he was dragged down. Just when he was even with the icy lip of the Pit did he jolt awake, jittery and panting.

Only with some effort could he get the image of the Pit from his mind, and when he realized that he was not at its blasted, icy-rimmed edge but, instead, in the Rotunda, inattentive to his Prince, Adramalik swallowed hard.

". . . is this *not* so, Prime Minister?"

"Yes. My Prince," he said, and had no idea what he was so readily agreeing to.

The buzzing paused.

"And what of the Keep itself and its defenses?"

"Mulciber is locked away and embedded, maintaining the wall just as you instructed, my Prince. The four legions of Keep Janissaries are in position awaiting any potential breach of the gate."

From the corner of his eye, Adramalik saw Agares shuffling slowly away from the foot of the throne and toward the sphincterlike threshold. Beelzebub seemed to take no notice. *Probably on his way to his miserable chambers. And why not? He is of no use anymore.*

"The Husk?" the Prince asked.

"He is one level below us with Knight-Brigadier Melphagor and as many of my Knights as I felt I could spare from the battlefield."

All this to defend our Hell, Prince, the Hell that you kept in line for so long. The Hell that, indeed, Sargatanas and his followers helped build and would now destroy. For what? His delusional aspirations? He is no heretic; that is where you are wrong, my Prince; he is simply a fool!

Adramalik looked up at the Prince and, not for the first time in recent memory, wondered what it might be like to be Regent of Hell. As this rebellion had grown Adramalik had, in the darkness of his chambers, considered the many ramifications of overthrowing his master. He had never gotten far in his speculations; the impossibility of the act caught him up short every time. Beelzebub was far too strange and unpredictable and powerful to attempt anything against, even as distracted as he was. And so Adramalik had never taken the time to seriously consider a period after the Prince's destruction. But now, with Sargatanas banging upon the Keep's gate, anything seemed possible and Adramalik frequently wondered what he and his Knights could do.

"Yen Wang's Behemoths are being destroyed, Adramalik. They are falling, one by one."

"Yes, my Prince, your design of the wall was flawless," Adramalik said without conviction. "It will take more than a few lumbering siege-beasts to take this Keep."

He saw Beelzebub's finger trace the contour of Rofocale's eye socket. "Leave me, Adramalik, before your patronizing words make me angry."

Adramalik bowed as low as he could, and, with eyes wide, he backed away and out of the Rotunda, relieved that he was still afforded the opportunity. His mind raced as he walked quickly back to the parapets. Was he just that close to being destroyed for so inconsequential a reason? Was it time to go down to his Knights and throw caution to the winds? Time to reach for the throne and either win or suffer the consequences?

But a wave of true fear washed through him and, worse, the acrid, recalled smell of the Pit. And he knew with a sinking, bitter sensation of self-recrimination that, whatever his fate, it would not be linked to any attempted assassination of Beelzebub.

A jagged constellation of lights appeared faintly behind the lambent curtain of clouds that hung about the palace high atop the Keep. Eligor looked down as he flew and saw the new wall and the shimmering glow that it cast upon everything but the darkened, mantle-shrouded Keep within its confines. *It is ever dark in there—but that will change. We will let in some light.* He was finally growing fatigued and saw that the others around him were wavering as well, having difficulty maintaining the once-tight formations.

Sargatanas' command, the briefest of flashing glyphs,

came as no surprise as Eligor neared the dome. He immediately angled downward, followed by the hundreds of Flying Guard behind, lances, hooks, and hammers at the ready. Sargatanas did not actually expect any resistance on the Black Dome's exterior but had made Barbatos and Eligor drill his demons in that possibility nonetheless.

As the dome drew nearer, Eligor saw nothing to indicate that any of the Fly's troops were positioned to defend the regent's palace. The great structure and its countless adjacent minarets were empty, and only a strong, buffeting wind seemed in place to defend the gigantic building.

Eligor's hooks found the spaces between the yielding flesh-tiles and bit deeply in. Feet firmly planted on the dome's hot surface, he folded his trembling, weary wings and turned to watch the dark clouds of his descending troops as a thousand hooks reached out and they landed without mishap. A vertical wind like a hot vortex was rising from around the Keep, and Eligor and the myriad other demons' garments flapped violently, but the hooks remained in place and soon the heavy siege hammers and prying claws were brought to bear. Their sound deadened by the wind and the softer flesh-tiles, the demons' tools worked at the dark swell of the dome for what seemed like an eternity to Eligor. Hammers rose and fell in a fury of activity—activity that he knew was echoed around the dome by Barbatos' demons—but even after many minutes there seemed to be hardly any damage done. There was little Eligor could do but watch and wait for the thick vault to be breached.

Through the billowing ash of battle, Mago, who never strayed too far from Hannibal, saw the dark expression fall upon his face and did his best to fight his way on foot to his brother's side. Mago was a deft swordsman and in short time he had cut a path to the center of the line. The souls' losses were heavy, or perhaps it seemed that way to Mago—the demons left no bodies and he saw only the hacked and broken forms of Hannibal's soldiers lying in deep ash and rubble. They were many.

Hannibal saw Mago approaching but, at first, did not recognize him. Caked in sweat and ash and the black blood of his fallen comrades, he looked like all the other souls save for his distinctive weapon and demon-forged armor. To Hannibal's eyes Mago looked tired, but his spirits seemed high. His sword was welcome; a bristling wall of Rofocale's legionaries faced them and Hannibal had no time for greetings.

Gaha was down on all fours, swiping with its huge front feet and swinging its heavy head to part the solid line of infantry just ahead. Hannibal parried a jabbing halberd and split its owner's head from crown to chin, and even before his blade was withdrawn the demon was crumbling into lifeless rubble. Another halberd immediately took its place, and another, and the two brothers silently chopped at the enemy demons, leading their troops as they had done so long ago, until the line finally buckled and the enemy fell back.

Breathing heavily, Mago said, "Brother, what is it?"

"My last order from Satanachia," he said, leaning from the saddle and wiping his face. "It weighs heavily upon me."

Mago pointed with his sword to another wave of gathering demons and Hannibal nodded.

"No one considered that the Fly would destroy his own city and the ancient bridge to the Keep. Foolish . . . it is what I would have done! Satanachia has asked me . . . not ordered, Mago, *asked* . . . to bridge the Belt with a ramp."

"But what are we to *use* for this undertaking? We

have brought no native stone to even attempt to ford the Belt!'"

"*Think* about it, Mago. What *have* we got in abundance?" Hannibal paused. The word was not going to come easily. "Souls," he said hoarsely.

Had this been part of Sargatanas' plan all along—to take advantage of the souls' presence, once again, as walking resources? To use *him*? Or, because the ground battle was always considered a diversion, did Sargatanas not care about its outcome? Hannibal would never know if the battle ended as his lord hoped.

"No." Mago's drawn face was now a reflection, Hannibal imagined, of his own. "A promise was made."

"It is the only way . . . the old way."

"You cannot give that order, Brother," Mago said flatly.

"But I must. There is no other choice for me." Hannibal's gut twisted. For a moment, he remembered a fearful day long ago on the work-gang, a day when he had come altogether too close, himself, to becoming part of a ramp not unlike this one. Could he really order others to voluntarily do what he had been so afraid to do?

"Hannibal, after the Flaming Cut you promised us that you would not let them use us in this manner again, that we would fight as souls and not be sacrificed as bricks. This battle hinges upon Sargatanas, not us. You've said it yourself . . . we will probably never see Heaven. It is *his* rebellion; let *him* make the sacrifices."

"If I—*we* want a voice here in Hell we have to earn it, Mago."

"When we are done with this, who will be *left* to speak with this voice, Hannibal?" Mago said accusingly.

Hannibal turned to his first standard-bearer to issue the order and hesitated. How could he possibly explain how he was changing, what he was feeling, that sense that the mantle of destiny was his to don? But how could he betray their trust in him? Was he being selfish or realistic? And he suddenly realized that he did not care what happened to his souls so long as *he* was fulfilled, an emotion that had never been present in all his years as a commander in his Life.

He stared at the oncoming line of enemy demons, and as he watched, he saw Satanachia's right wing of legionaries shift position preparing to fill the gap that his souls would leave on the field after he issued his order. *Satanachia knows me better than I know myself. He knows I will do it. He knows ambition.*

Hannibal looked back into his brother's eyes and saw only the past—the past of his ancient human failures, the past of the Tophet fires and his eternal remorse. Mago, the brother who now served as a constant reminder of age-old pain, seemed to be pleading, hoping that Hannibal would do the human thing. Hoping he would cling to that despicable creature of the past.

He motioned to his first standard-bearer and crisply barked the order for his army to disengage and make their way to the Belt's edge, to the bank where the soul-ramp's construction would begin. He would not look back again at the life that once belonged to Hannibal Barca.

XXXII

DIS

Two of Satanachia's battlefield Conjurors were waiting at the Belt's edge when Hannibal and Mago arrived at the head of their army. Without ceremony they created their glyphs-of-conversion and proceeded to transform the front ranks of souls and almost instantly a cry went up from the surrounding multitude that was near. The demon legionaries on either side of the ramp's foot had been given orders to act as both a screen and a funnel, keeping the vast majority of the soul army oblivious to the construction that was under way. When suspicions grew, Hannibal reassured his officers that the souls being used would be converted back at the end of the battle. But he knew that it was a hollow promise; much depended upon who would be victorious, and the souls that were converted were losing any chance they might have had to flee if the battle went to the army of Dis. Shouts of anger filled his ears.

Forced at spear point, the souls that had been impressed dropped their weapons in a long running pile that followed the construction. The relationship between souls and demons had changed in mere moments; allies in battle had reverted to oppressors and victims.

Mago's expression was disbelieving, sour. Clearly, Hannibal saw, his brother disapproved of the treatment of the souls, of the reversion to their Infernal use, of his promise broken. But if there was one thing Hannibal knew, it was that once his mind had been made up there was no turning back. And now that it had, he marveled at how what had initially seemed a treacherous act against the souls now seemed to him like the greatest of opportunities. A twinge of terrific pain lanced through his shoulder, and as he saw the ramp's foundation being laid he reached under his cloak and massaged the growing, tingling stump of his arm.

The cry went up, barely audible over the wind, from one of the six hammer-gangs attempting to breach the Dome, ending Eligor's ineffectual attempts to see the battlefield below. Waist-deep in the heavily bleeding hole they had excavated, they were shouting that they were nearly through the dense, howling soul-brick exterior. Eligor flew to them and landed inside the shallow, inclined crater, his excitement mixed with a numbing sense of dread. To enter the Dome was to see Sargatanas' vision through, to either lose him forever or watch him be crushed. Neither prospect appealed to the demon.

He was hovering overhead with his picked assault team when the inevitable hammer-strike bit through the Black Dome's roof. Strong hands held on to the heavy, protesting brick, lifting it out of the way, careful not to let it fall into the vast chamber below. Behind them, a hundred lance points directed at the hole awaited anything that might emerge from within, but only a dismal gloom, barely lighter than the surrounding dome, was visible. Even with the fierce winds he could smell the raw odor of the building's interior, a heavy stink of decay that made him curl his lips.

It seemed that no sooner had he sent his glyph off to alert Sargatanas than the Demon Major appeared in a flurry of sigils, glyphs, and spreading white wings. The intensity in his eyes was unmistakable as he peered into the hole and Eligor saw him reach down and, along with the Flying Guard, begin to pry away the heavy bricks at the rim of the hole. After an hour, the opening was enlarged sufficiently that three demons with wings extended could pass through at once—wide enough that the attack could begin.

Eligor looked away from the hole, and by chance, for an instant, his eyes met Sargatanas'. No words were spoken, but the bond that had existed between them for so long, the tie between teacher and apprentice, the tie between ancient friends, held them. The wind suddenly grew stiffer and there was no chance either could have heard the other, but Eligor saw Sargatanas smile, pull his sword—the sword Valefar had kept for him—from its sheath, and mouth the words, *Heaven awaits.* He raised his hand, sending a glyph skyward, and, with a deafening flapping of wings Eligor's Flying Guard and Barbatos' Flying Corps assembled three abreast in a long and precise column that stretched far up and away behind Sargatanas. Without another word, the Demon Major plunged headlong into the Black Dome with Eligor just behind.

The moment he passed through the opening and began to drop he, like Sargatanas ahead of him, began to chop away at the myriad obstructing skins that hung from the cavernous dome-ceiling and clearing a vertical path for the flyers behind. The skins twisted and curled, agitated from either fright or the distant awareness of the battle far below, and each time Eligor slashed a rafter away he heard them cry out. They fell by the fluttering dozens, but not as fast as the demons' diving descent, and when Eligor saw Sargatanas break free of the hangings, the blue-flame sword—his old sword—was pointing straight and true at the throne beneath them.

Eligor looked down past his lord's broad wings at the approaching Rotunda's floor and clenched his jaw; the Fly's troops were tearing wide the sphincter-threshold and streaming in from the one main corridor. *How could Sargatanas have hoped to breach the dome's ceiling and not alert its occupants?* But the Guard's Captain was distressed not only by the number of Keep Janissaries already assembled but also by Adramalik and the scarlet-clad Order Knights who led them. He recognized many of them, had fought against their brethren in the past, knew how dangerous they could be, and wondered, for just a chilling instant, if Sargatanas' assault force would be capable of withstanding the collective fury of their glyph-flamed scimitars.

Sargatanas pulled up just short of the top of the throne, but as Eligor sailed past him, followed by his Guard, he could not tell what his lord found atop the stinking mound. Eligor and his Guard slammed into the assembled legionaries with enough force to drive most of the standing demons to their knees. Ranks of the demons sprawled momentarily in the soup of blood and meat that filled the floor of the Rotunda. The Knights, however, managed to remain standing, having powerful, protective glyphs floating above, and with booming voices they rallied the Janissaries. A clot of them, flaming swords at the ready, surrounded something or someone, and when they parted Eligor saw, with dismay, that which had once been Baron Faraii. He stood with black blade bared and ebony armored as always, but his formerly gaunt body was now perforated in a thousand spots, hollowed as if there was nothing within. Tiny Abyssal worms played upon and through him, and these revolted Eligor. Faraii turned his pitted head, his one remaining eye glaring, and raised his sword toward Eligor and the onrushing demons.

Eligor and Barbatos knew that to alight was to lose the one advantage they had over their numerically superior opponents; this lesson had been learned many ages ago. They and their troops would fly until they had destroyed the enemy or were forced down. Both Demons Minor led their flyers in broad, sweeping passes that enabled their flights to thrust with their lances in well-practiced maneuvers.

Through the still-falling skins and the jabbing spears from below, Eligor stole as many glances at the throne as he could safely manage. At first, it seemed as if his lord was only hovering above the vacant seat looking about for the Fly, but in a fleeting glimpse Eligor saw the Demon Major wrenching away his flight skins and preparing himself in ways he had never seen before. No longer fully winged, Sargatanas' body was exuding an intricate interlocking armor that glistened pure white in the ruddy haze of the Rotunda. But Eligor was not able to see the transformation through; the hooked spears of the Keep's Janissaries were bringing down more of his flyers than he liked and he could not linger to watch his lord. With their growing experience against the Flying Guards' tactics, the Knights were now lashing out with powerful glyph-bolts that were nearly impossible for the tightly packed flyers to dodge. Eligor's fear that they would have to engage the enemy on the ground seemed to be coming to pass.

Eligor worked his lance calmly; oddly, the battle-Passion had not overtaken him yet. Perhaps, he thought, it was some of Faraii's training finally having effect. The Janissaries were formidable but predictable warriors, and unlike his flyers, he found dispatching them not nearly as difficult as he might have feared. He knew his presence bolstered his Guard and knew, too, that as they flew and fought they were watching his composure, the very way he was fighting. Only when he saw Faraii in the center of a maelstrom of lances did he grow concerned. The Baron was more than capable of changing the balance of a melee, and Eligor slowly moved toward him, sucked in by the vortex of destruction that the former Waste-wanderer was creating.

From the dark, newly exposed recesses of the dome a buzzing began, low but loud enough to be heard and felt over the clamor of battle. It was insistent, and something in its vibrating tone shook Eligor. *It is anger sublime.*

He saw what he thought was the briefest pause in the fighting, as if all of the combatants in the giant Rotunda felt the tremor of pure rage.

A sudden flash caused him to look past the throne and he realized, to his profound dismay, that Barbatos had fallen. A cluster of moving Order sigils hung over the spot. Apparently Adramalik and five of his Knights, bolstered by the imminent arrival of their Prince, had surrounded the Demon Minor and felled him. Eligor knew they would focus upon him next. He soared upward followed by a hundred of his best flyers, vowing to do what he could to even the loss. A bold stroke was called for, and seeking one sigil out of the many, he focused upon the dark form of Faraii.

When the ramp had reached halfway across Lucifer's Belt, the wall's defenses came alive again with a sound like the sharp snapping of a giant's back. Hannibal looked up from the edge of the ramp. Beneath him the lava flowed and swirled, and its heat reached up and threatened to choke him. Though he stood much closer to the wall, Hannibal had not reacted as had many of the souls around him, flinching or calling out, frightened by its sudden reactivation. Through narrowed eyes he watched the carnage begin anew as the wall's incandescent bolts leaped forth and decimated souls and demons alike. *What can I do? This is exactly why we must hurry.* His eyes lifted to the heavy gate, now much more distinct, and he saw the carvings on its face that he had not seen from the battlefield. *Grand curses, no doubt. Will Satanachia be able to nullify them? And if we do manage to complete the ramp, break down the gate, and enter the Keep just how many of us will there be left to fight whatever we meet up with inside?*

Another layer of souls was laid down and Hannibal moved forward a few yards with the Conjurors and Satanachia's Overseers. Progress was steady and Hannibal estimated that if they did not suffer a direct hit, it would take only a few hours before the project was completed. He saw that the next file of souls was moving quickly into place, pushed and prodded savagely by their former demon allies. *At least they are not being driven by Scourges.* He looked away, searching the faces of the souls around him—none would meet his gaze—for Mago, but knew that he was nowhere nearby. *Gone. Just as well, with the wall's bombardment wreaking such destruction.* As if to punctuate the thought, a bolt shot through the air and crashed into the massed fighting demons a few hundred feet from the ramp's base, sending up a dark plume of ash and broken legionaries. *Indiscriminate—the Fly does not care whose demons he destroys!*

Another few layers of souls were laid down, and if anything, the wall's defenses increased. The many bolts grew in frequency and in strength and Hannibal was reluctant to look back toward the blasted landscape where so many were perishing. He marveled at the puzzling fact that not a single bolt had been directed at the ramp but felt that it was just a matter of time.

Hannibal looked closely at the wall and, in particular, the countless orbs that were embedded in its surface, each one protruding from the crushed body of a soul. They seemed to somehow collect and focus the energies the architect Mulciber was using as a weapon. When Hannibal had possessed an orb himself he would never have guessed they could have been used in such a way. He nodded in silent approval of the Architect General's genius.

Hannibal saw yet another massive bolt forming, a coalescing of bright motes that would, in seconds, discharge outward in a mighty clap of thunder. He braced himself for the sound, but without warning the entire wall suddenly went dark. And then, after a long silence in which he was sure the bolts would resume, he heard a distant roar of elation start from somewhere behind his lines, a cheer that was taken up all around. Something had happened to shut down the wall.

He saw the Conjurors redouble their efforts, fearful, he guessed, that the lull might end, the wall might reactivate itself, and their opportunity to finish the ramp unhindered and gain the gate would suddenly pass. But the wall remained inactive, its only illumination from the Belt beneath, its only sound that of the howling wind that clawed at its rounded sides.

A command-glyph rose from Azazel at Satanachia's position, racing away too fast for Hannibal to read. Moments later a relatively small, bright glyph darted out from Sargatanas' army heading straight for the wall. It impacted toward the top of the battlements and the Soul-General saw a burst of soul-bricks explode away and drop the vast distance down to splash into the lava below. It was just a test, just the beginning. Destructive glyphs, greater in size and numbers, were soon speeding toward the now-vulnerable wall, pocking its sides in showers of exploding debris. Experts in the art of demolition, the demons pounded at the wall in patterns designed to shear off the largest sections with the least effort. Frequent bursts of spurting fluids cascaded down from some ruptured artery or conduit from the archiorganic buildings behind. Enormous flat chunks came free and tumbled slowly from the wall, peeled away as if by equally enormous fingers, and landed in prodigious fountains of lava that threatened to immolate the demons on the far bank. Eventually, Hannibal saw that the debris was actually creating bridges of rubble across the Belt to the wall's foot. Once the destruction was halted he knew these unexpected causeways would be exploited.

A long, muffled howl rose and fell from deep within the demon-made mountain, the voice of Semjaza the Watcher, Hannibal knew, but it seemed to him more like the Keep's primal utterance of a deeply felt wound.

What would befall that never-seen creature of legend, he wondered, if the Prince and his abode were destroyed?

Hannibal returned his attention to the ramp, which had gotten far ahead of him. The demons had been careful not to destroy the wall too close to the ramp's construction site, and now he could see that it would not be long before it reached up to the gate. Looking back down the steep causeway, he could already see the very few remaining Behemoths being brought to the fore. He knew Satanachia would use them to batter down the drawbridge, whether there were curses embedded in them or not; nothing Dis or Hell, for that matter, could offer would keep him from rejoining Sargatanas.

The battle-Passion had finally risen through Eligor's body, inflaming him with the ecstasy of destruction. Oddly, it had not accounted for the quick demise of the Knight-Brigadier Melphagor. That, Eligor had to admit to himself, had been pure luck.

With every demon destroyed, Melphagor had, as was the wont of the Knights during battle, grown a bit larger, and it was this extra height that had sealed his fate. As Eligor had dropped toward Faraii, the giant Knight had turned directly into his outstretched lance. The long point had cleft the demon's exposed head straight down to his neck, cleanly cutting through the shocked expression that froze upon Melphagor's face. The Knight imploded with a flash and Eligor, never even pausing his descent, landed and retrieved the demon's disk. It was the fortune of the battlefield, a chance stroke of such importance that it made Eligor grin even as the fighting raged around him. Melphagor's disk melted onto his breastplate, and he felt a surge of power.

As quick as the absorption of the Knight's powers was, it gave Eligor no time to prepare for his chosen opponent. Weaving agilely between the thrashing combatants with sword outstretched, Faraii advanced upon him, his single eye glittering intensely, flames licking from his breastplate's vents. Prudently, Eligor passed off supervision of the Guard to Metaphrax with a streaking glyph.

From the first moment their weapons clashed, Eligor felt an odd sympathy for Faraii. He had expected to hate the Baron, to simply want him destroyed by either his hand or another's, but his feelings were, at worst, ambivalent. Faraii's destruction was necessary; that much Eligor knew. But looking at the gutted and tattered figure he felt that if there was any part of the old Faraii left within, taking him away from the Fly would almost certainly be a favor.

As Faraii's blade sank a short way into Eligor's thigh, he winced and realized that he was a long way from performing that favor. Flapping quickly upward, he flexed his leg, feeling the pain damped by the Passion; it would blossom after the battle. The wound was deep but not debilitating, a timely reminder that he was facing a great warrior whose skills—perhaps enhanced by the Fly—would have been well beyond his if he had not just absorbed an Order Knight's abilities.

Eligor used his lance with an adroitness that he could never have hoped for before this battle; Melphagor had been quite accomplished because of either his many conquests or his own innate skill. Every perfect thrust of Faraii's was countered by an equally perfect parry. Eligor spun and jabbed, twirled and sliced, with amazing speed and accuracy. He used forms that he had only heard about, techniques that he had known to exist but had never witnessed, and employed them with the inspired creativity of an artisan. He was as exhilarated by his own newfound skills as he was experiencing his former companion's.

Faraii said nothing; the whistling point of his sword spoke for him. Whether he even recognized Eligor the demon could not tell. His sword moves were as precise as always, but underlying them was a distinct and uncharacteristic lack of imagination. Gone was the improvisational bravura that had so infused his very personal style with genius. In its place was a methodical display of brilliant swordsmanship that most who faced him would never have been able to overcome. Time and again Eligor tried to see something of his old friend's personality, but Faraii seemed wholly devoid of spirit, even of awareness. As he fought he stared through his opponent, the eaten-away eye a worm-filled hollow, the green ember that was not his eye an unblinking thing of mad hatred.

The black blade wove in and out of Eligor's guard but never actually found him. The Guard Captain, for his part, maneuvered his opponent so that he could better see his lord high atop the throne. Eligor could hear Beelzebub coming together in a noisy, furious cloud of gyrating flies and blazing sigils and it was all he could do not to stop and watch, but Faraii was persistent, his blade thirsty.

Eligor grasped his lance at its end and, extending it with a fierce snap of his hand to its fullest length, swept it in and under Faraii's arm, slicing a neat crescent from his side. The Baron neither cried out nor flinched, and for a moment Eligor was not actually certain the hollowed figure that kept doggedly advancing upon him had been injured at all. Forced backward, he worked his weapon, as Faraii had once taught him, like the darting tongue of an Abyssal and caught the Baron yet again. This time the wound, which was broad and had penetrated directly into the center of his bone-shod foot, seemed to impede him and his footwork became, Eligor saw, slower and more deliberate.

The fighting demons around them began to close in, and Faraii, never taking his eye from Eligor, reached out with his free hand and grasped the wrist of a hovering Flying Guard lancer. With a twist and a pop that Eligor could just hear over the insistent buzzing, the Baron effortlessly wrenched the wrist and the lance that grew from it free of its owner, easily speared him through the chest, and proceeded to wield it along with his sword. Two green glyphs, potent with magic, appeared and began to snake around the tips of the two weapons.

Eligor's calm, the strange confidence he had been feeling that was so different from his usual Passion, began to fade, receding into a place where he could no longer look.

What skills did Melphagor harbor that can help me with this?

It was an Art Martial, Eligor thought in something close to panic, that must come from the Fly, acquired from some nameless demon who had probably ended up rotting on the very floor upon which they stood. Certainly it was nothing the Baron had ever spoken of or shown Eligor in their time together. In Faraii's hands the two weapons became as one and then split to go their separate ways only to converge again, with lightning speed, at Eligor's throat or chest or wrist. Or conversely, they never met, moving independently in whistling arcs so intricately interwoven that it seemed to him as if they were being directed by two different individuals. Eligor could only dodge and parry and try to get back and away from the two glyph-tipped points without any consideration to landing his own blows. Fatigue was beginning to show in his own moves, to slow him just enough to be a danger, and he realized that he could not sustain this kind of defense for too much longer. His wings, especially, felt leaden.

There are *two individuals! Faraii and Beelzebub. They are fighting me separately and together.*

More and more, as Eligor twisted and jabbed, he began to focus on the unwavering green eye of Beelzebub. It became an irritant, a hated symbol, and finally a yearned-for target.

From somewhere, buried deep within Melphagor's acquired, collected knowledge, came a glyph to give Eligor hope. It was not a difficult casting, but its potency was in its timing. Because it was a glyph-of-transpiercing it had to precede his weapon's tip by the minutest distance to be effective and not be blocked, and as tired as he was growing, Eligor was not at all certain he could perform both the casting of his lance and the glyph at once. He reared back, floating momentarily up and away from the duel to gather himself, and then, with a great rushing of wings, he dove down and threw the glyph and his lance as swiftly and surely as he could. Faraii's weapons came up to meet Eligor, and their glowing tips came so close to his eyes that they momentarily blinded him. He thought his casting was true, but the dazzling green light made any certainty impossible.

When the weapons fell away he saw that the lance had caught Faraii precisely in the eye, jolting his head back and fusing instantly into the bony tissue. The eye split, radiating a shiver of searing energy downward that blew his body apart, its already worm-eaten limbs disintegrating into clotted masses of desiccated flesh and bone. His head, still mostly intact but smoking and cracked from the intense heat, fell heavily atop the breastplate, bounced once, and stuck into the floor by the protruding lance point.

While the battle in the dome continued, the fighting just surrounding Eligor ceased, combatants lowering their weapons as the impact of the moment sank in. Hearing the cheers from his troops above, he alighted, favoring his wounded leg and folding his aching wings. The charred remains of Faraii lay before Eligor, and as he looked down he felt only relief. It was done. As much as Eligor had once admired the demon, the Baron had been too great a threat to his lord; Faraii's destruction was a necessity, as much as or more than the destruction of the Knights, but it was not something in which he would take any pleasure.

He saw no disk—the intense discharge of energy had seemingly precluded that—but he did see the black sword lying amidst the remains and he bent down and picked it up, feeling its lightness and balance. All eyes were trained upon him and he thought to say something, something stirring for his appreciative Guards, but a thunderous roar from the throne brought his and all the other demons' heads around.

Beelzebub had finally materialized.

XXXIII

DIS

The ramp trembled as the two Behemoths, goaded by their mahouts, beat upon the gate with their massive hammers. Any signs of their fatigue vanished as their drivers tapped lightly, suggestively, upon the spikes driven deep within the bases of their skulls. With their heads bowed and their chinbones dug into the ramp, Hannibal saw the raw, physical power of their heavily muscled, sweating bodies, saw how they strained and flexed as they put all of their weight into each blow. The gate was broken in a dozen different places, held together only by the wide bands of metal that spread across them like veins, and while the tendrils of its curse-glyphs wound, briefly, around the giant souls and then spiraled away into the sky, it seemed that it would split apart at any moment.

A siege commander, standing between the Behemoths, guided their strikes, placing target-glyphs upon those sections of the reinforced portal that appeared weakest. Hannibal could see light from within peeking out of the long cracks.

He peered into the relative darkness of the battlefield behind him; since the wall had failed Dis had been plunged back into the unilluminated gloom of Hell. There was no longer any fighting in the front lines; Beelzebub's legions had been either destroyed in combat or crushed in the rain of gargantuan debris that had filled in large sections of the Belt. Even now, far from the ramp, Hannibal felt the dull concussion of giant slabs slamming into the lava as they continued to be chiseled away by the bombardment of glyphs.

And the rain of destruction had not been limited to the wall alone. Glyphs arced high into the air to land amidst the towers and minarets within its confines, jarring some of them loose. These rose, Hannibal saw, into the black sky, turning and cartwheeling slowly, and began to float away from the Keep.

Put Satanachia's sigil appeared at the ramp's base and Hannibal saw that its owner was mounting the incline and heading toward his position, his staff in tow. His presence was welcome; the Soul-General found himself feeling more loyalty to the Demon Major than toward his own kind. The cold glances Hannibal received even from his trusted souls holding Gaha's reins were distancing, something he was not accustomed to as a general. Something in Hell he would have to get used to if he was to maintain his position with his demon lords.

Satanachia stopped before Hannibal and patted away some imaginary ash from his immaculate armor. The splendid multicolored sigils that floated over his breastplate shone upon three new disks, talismans of hard fighting against hard foes. Hannibal wondered how the looming demon could appear so composed and, in contrast to Field Marshal Orus and the rest of his retinue, so clear of ash and blood.

"Well done, Hannibal. We are close now, eh?"

"Close enough for me to smell the rot from inside."

"We will cleanse it with sword and fire; of that you can be sure."

"And then?"

The gate sagged with a terrific groan. More blows revealed more of the dimly lit interior of the vestibule beyond. Weapons could be seen glittering in the hands of barely seen legionaries.

"And then we will take it down . . . the whole Keep . . . and start anew. It is Sargatanas' wish."

"That will take centuries."

"Time is something, with luck, we will have."

Four simultaneous deafening hammer-blows knocked the immense gate inward and the Behemoths lurched forward and over the twisted hinges, entering the vestibule and grinding the front ranks of enemy legionaries underfoot. A reverberating cheer went up from all who could see the portal's collapse. A rain of attacking glyphs met the Behemoths, stopping them for the moment; they would not be able to go too far into the Keep anyway, Hannibal knew. The corridors leading up to the palace were intentionally cramped for just that purpose.

Satanachia, a pale mountain of fury, leaped past Hannibal and disappeared between the pillarlike legs of the huge souls, followed by Orus and a steady stream of legionaries. Hannibal saw his souls far below being passed by the demon legionaries and saw, too, their indecision. If he was to have sway over them it would come from this moment. He raised his sword.

"*Follow me,*" he shouted hoarsely in the souls' language, "*or forever be their slaves!*" He turned and sprinted for the entrance.

As he jumped over the wreckage of the hinge he stole a

glance backward. Those souls who had been able to hear him—souls who had been earmarked to be converted—were taking up weapons from the long pile and running after him. *What real choice did they have?* he thought. They could fight and take their chances, either being destroyed or sharing in the victory, or they could resist and suffer the fate of insurrectionists. Or they could run and take their chances with the hungry Abyssals. Hannibal knew which alternative he would choose.

Just behind Satanachia, Hannibal was able to witness the whirlwind of destruction the Demon Major had become. Common legionaries could not stand before him and were obliterated by the dozens as they progressed through the narrow confines of the vestibule. Hannibal heard Satanachia's breathing, deep and echoing, as he worked his sword from side to side. It would be a long trek upward through the Keep's innumerable halls and corridors, but watching the fallen angel before him, he felt little doubt they would make it. He was dubious that they would arrive at the Rotunda in time to aid Sargatanas and Eligor, but at least they would divert enough of the Fly's troops away from that battle to make a difference.

Hannibal threw himself into the fighting with renewed energy. Satanachia inspired him and he unconsciously began to emulate some of the Demon Major's sword moves. After a few halls had been cleared, Hannibal's confidence had grown along with his identification with the demon. No matter what the outcome in the Rotunda many levels above, Hannibal would be sure to be at Satanachia's side when it unfolded.

"It has been too long since we last held counsel, Demon Major. What has made you so . . . restless?"

Deliberate in his movements, Beelzebub calmly stood atop his throne, adjusting the long cloak that hung from his lean form. He had adopted the mien of a regal and aloof being, thin and armored in his customary carapace, his multieyed head disturbingly flylike. Four enormous iridescent wings, unlike any others in Hell, projected behind his cloak. Churning within the angry masses of flies in his torso like an ever-moving luminous skeleton were ill-seen skeins of glyphs and sigils, the accumulated wisdom and horror that defined the Regent of Hell.

"I could not let go of my past as easily as some," Eligor heard Sargatanas answer in the language of the Above.

"That may be," Beelzebub said, "but you know *They* do not want you back. And *I* certainly do not want you *here,* so what will you do?"

The heavy armor that Eligor had seen forming when Sargatanas first arrived at the Black Dome was fully congealed upon his body, armor so similar to that from Above, painfully white and strangely reflective. But the demon's protection was not yet complete. Another layer, a mail of glyphs, was beginning to emerge as tiny, growing embers.

"I will do what I must to gain the Throne's acceptance. I will show the demons of Hell that they can be forgiven, that they can, if they choose, go back."

Beelzebub nodded slowly as if in resignation and then Eligor saw a sudden torrent of glyphs pour forth from the figure of flies with such force that Sargatanas was lifted and driven backward, his fanlike wings clawing at the air. Eligor saw his lord flinching and grimacing and could only think that it had been sublime madness for the Demon Major to presume that he could confront the Prince. His were powers unthinkable to demons.

Ever so slowly under the stress of the relentless onslaught, Sargatanas' glyph-mail finally came together. Hundreds of the protective glyphs merged across his entire body to cover him in a continuous interwoven blanket, a blanket that deflected the majority of the lethal projectiles. And equally slowly the demon descended, flaming sword outstretched, until he was nearly within arm's reach of the Fly.

Sargatanas suddenly leaned in and swept his fiery blade out and through Beelzebub's writhing neck and Eligor saw how those flies it touched flared briefly into blue-green flame and were extinguished. But the neck had parted of its own volition and when it came back together it appeared to be unharmed. The seraph sword had cleaved nothing. Time and again Sargatanas arced his blade through the body of shifting flies, weaving it through the black, buzzing motes and pulling it back, only to see a small number destroyed and the remainder rearranging themselves as they had been. Beelzebub's stance remained unchanged.

Eligor, unable to take his eyes from the unfolding duel, began, unsurprisingly, to hear the battle on the floor slowly, fitfully, resume. The dull sound of tens, hundreds, then thousands of weapons clashing rose in his ears like the beginnings of an avalanche, slow and gathering, until, once again, it filled the Rotunda. He cast a command-glyph to Metaphrax and watched a squadron of his Guard detach themselves from the hovering squadrons of demons and bank away to attack the Knight Chancellor General Adramalik and those around him. So eager was his lieutenant to fight the guardians of the Keep that Eligor knew he would have happily spearheaded the diving attack on twice their numbers. And this delegation of duty, Eligor thought a bit selfishly, would allow him, for the moment at least, to watch his lord.

Sargatanas drew back and Eligor saw a complicated glyph-weapon form in his free hand, a barbed device the color of which shifted like a crystal-prism. It was, he guessed, a gift of the destroyed Pyromancer Furcas, but as Sargatanas pulled his hand back to cast it, Beelzebub struck out with a stream of dark flies and engulfed it, smothering the burning weapon before the Demon Major even had a chance to throw it. The Fly hissed in unmistakable disgust and turned his back. Eligor knew this made no difference whatsoever in Beelzebub's defense, knew that his eyes were everywhere on his person, but saw how the gesture of arrogant diffidence, the symbolism of casual superiority, confounded Sargatanas, who flailed his sword in impotent rage.

Eligor felt his lord's frustration and sensed that his worst fears were now proven. *There is no weapon that can finish him. The rebellion will end here and the Fly will destroy us all.* In what seemed a final attempt to prevail, the Demon Major's Great Seal began to glow more brilliantly and the sigils of all of those Demons Major who had joined him in his rebellion began to flare. One by one and with a scraping sound like claws on flint, they separated from the burning disk and then arrowed straight into Beelzebub's turned back. With each terrible impact the flies broke apart, some igniting into flames and vanishing, others scattering in clouds of fiery sparks. The Prince's figure billowed, appearing at turns to disintegrate and re-form in shapeless disarray, and this made Eligor smile fiercely. He could see that every fiber of Sargatanas' being was focused on the attack and that it was having an effect. Dozens of the sigils penetrated the agitated mass of flies, and each took its toll in numbers. And when it was over and Sargatanas' sigil was no more than just his own, Beelzebub had turned back to face him and a wavering uncertainty seemed to have entered the Fly's demeanor. There was no immediate response, and for a moment it seemed to be reevaluating the demon that faced it. It had suffered considerably; half of its head was missing as well as both wings and its remaining arm. But Eligor sensed that there was enough of the Fly left to be more than dangerous.

To Eligor, at that moment, it seemed a perfect stand-off. Neither opponent had seemed capable of destroying the other, but Eligor feared that that balance might have changed, that without the many demons' sigils that had so helped his lord get to this point, Sargatanas could be vulnerable, even to a very much weaker Beelzebub.

With a gesture that Eligor thought at first was more petulant than effective, the Fly threw a glyph down to the floor that suddenly swept the demons directly around Sargatanas up, tossing them forcefully at the Demon Major. Destroying them with his flashing sword and deflecting them with his free hand, Sargatanas was engulfed in an ashy tornado of crumbling, shouting bodies, his brilliant white form nearly obscured by the sheer mass of them. Eligor saw his troops, legionaries of Dis, and Order Knights alike, indiscriminately uplifted into the air and catapulted toward Sargatanas until the floor hundreds of feet around him was empty. And as he smashed his way clear, Beelzebub cast down seven archaic red glyphs that touched the floor and disappeared, melting into the rubble and blood and flesh and leaving behind pillars of smoke.

Sargatanas freed himself from the diminishing storm of demons and saw the glyphs' trajectory and swiftly rose up well above the throne. Somehow he had read the glyphs and knew what was coming.

No one, Adramalik mused, could help but marvel at the ferocious beauty of his Prince's foe, nor could they help but admire the demon's bravery. Adramalik looked from side to side and saw that his remaining Knights, flaming scimitars flashing, were engaged in furious combat with the Demon Minor Metaphrax and his flying lancers.

Adramalik looked from that fight to the glowing disks of his Knights unfortunate enough to have been caught up in Beelzebub's petulant rage. Sargatanas' convictions had made him truly transcendent among demons.

Adramalik remembered his many punishments over the millennia and the pain of each and, setting his jaw, turned away from the Prince. *Beelzebub does not deserve my loyalty,* he thought with disgust, and in that moment, the path he had always wanted to travel upon opened for him. He raised his hand and shot a command-glyph out to his Knights to sheathe their weapons and form up around him. He would withdraw and leave the Prince and Dis itself, taking his Order with him. Wounded and distracted, Beelzebub would not be able to stop them.

Hannibal felt the sound in his bones before he heard it. Beneath his feet he felt the floor of the Keep vibrate, felt it yield slightly as if it were shifting. At the present, they were climbing steadily upward and Satanachia informed him that they were roughly halfway to the Rotunda. At first he thought the dull sound was diminishing, but suddenly it gathered into a deep rushing sound and then the floor beneath his feet cracked. Braziers tumbled to the ground, spreading pools of flame.

Satanachia turned and looked at him with knit brows, listening.

"What is it?" Hannibal asked.

But realization suddenly cleared Satanachia's face and, wide-eyed, he shouted "*Back, back the way we came!*"

As one, the vanguard turned, and the command went back down the unending stairs. The hundreds of confused troops squeezed into the narrow passage tried to maintain some form of order, but were too slow to respond. The rushing sound from below became the din of crashing bone-supports and bricks, and the Keep shuddered like a wounded animal. The floor heaved and buckled and Hannibal saw the long, dim staircase ahead thrown upward, completely broken apart by some titanic force.

As he fell, through the dust and broken bricks and tiles that flew toward him, he had a brief impression of something enormous, something vaguely human in form, rising irresistibly up through the ruptured floor on powerful wings. And as it passed, it gave voice, a deafening cry of release, pained and hoarse but also unmistakably triumphant. Hannibal recognized it as the voice of Semjaza.

The Rotunda floor buckled from the lack of support beneath it and formed a fractured and deepening bowl into which slid hundreds of Beelzebub's legionaries. The ugly mass of flesh that was the Fly's throne sank into a soup of ashy blood, rubble, and flailing demons and then suddenly erupted as the entire floor split open.

Eligor's mouth opened in silent shock.

For eons, the few scattered Watchers, buried and nearly forgotten, had been thought of almost as forces of Infernal nature. They had been in Hell before the demons arrived and, it was speculated, would be there after time ended. No demon had ever dreamt of actually seeing one.

Once Semjaza the Watcher had been beautiful, but that was very long ago. Incarcerated, it had grown immense and mad feeding upon the blackness that lay beneath all of Hell. A rank odor of age and decay filled Eligor's nostrils.

So tall that it was nearly a tenth the height of the Black Dome, the Watcher floated on six slowly beating wings that, fully extended, seemed as if they might span the Rotunda. It had fared poorly in its captivity, Eligor saw. Blind and with its nose eaten away by worms, its face was a tortured landscape of pits and wrinkles, the chiseled contours of its skull prominent. Its skin, once golden and miraculous for its magical markings, was a sickly pale gray and was dotted with holes and covered in sores. Visible, too, was the ancient, Throne-mandated punishment, the great scarred wound where its genitals had been ritually, wrathfully, excised for its sins. Upon its wrists and ankles were the burned-in scars of the elaborate glyphs that Those from the Above had used to cast it down and shackle it—glyphs that somehow Beelzebub had managed to neutralize.

Eligor saw it turn its huge horned and winged head to and fro, trying blindly to sense its surroundings. Beneath it, the remains of the floor cracked and began to slowly slide down, sinking of its own broken weight, lower and lower until it separated and dropped, taking with it those screaming demons that had been clinging to the bricks. When the dust had cleared, Eligor could see well down into the burning heart of the Keep. When he looked up he saw the hundreds of his flying demons who had retreated; there were fewer of them left than he had expected.

Once the sounds of the floor's sinking had subsided, a strange quiet settled throughout the Rotunda. Only the cavernous sound of Semjaza's breathing could be heard, as well as the slow flapping of its wings.

And then a soft buzzing arose and a green command-glyph sprang to life from the deformed figure that was Beelzebub. It sped up toward Semjaza and, without pause, sank into its head. The milky eyes closed and the six wings beat faster as the message was revealed. Eligor was sure that the Fly's weapon was gathering itself.

From the heights of the dome a white form descended and hovered before the withered face of the Watcher. Sargatanas, head ablaze and blue *ialpor napta* held before him, hung on gently beating wings so close to the titan that he might have reached out and touched it with the sword point.

Fearing for his lord, Eligor felt his breath catch in his throat. He could not see whether Sargatanas was speaking to Semjaza or simply showing himself, allowing the sightless Watcher to become aware of him. Whatever the case, the effect was immediate and startling. Semjaza reared backward as if it had been struck, fear unmistakable upon its face. *The Watcher remembers its old captors! It hears the language of the Above and the sizzle of the flaming sword and is afraid!*

A roar of outraged buzzing rent the air and Beelzebub ascended, spreading and engulfing Sargatanas within himself. In the briefest instant Eligor saw his lord transformed from a thing of potent beauty to a figure ablaze in the center of a fiery maelstrom of flies. Eligor saw, too, the layer of glyph-mail eaten away and the flies beginning to penetrate the white armor. Without thinking, Eligor found himself in a steep dive heading directly toward Sargatanas. But as Eligor drew near and the flaming green flies pulled away, their lethal work done, he saw that there was nothing that could undo the damage that had been inflicted upon the demon. Barely able to stay aloft, Sargatanas began a long, slow descent and would have plunged into the smoke-filled darkness of the open floor below had Eligor not caught him.

As he dragged his lord away from the great hole, Eligor looked up and saw Semjaza, guided by the buzzing, moving purposefully toward the coalescing figure of the Fly. The Watcher said something in its own tongue, a language Eligor was unfamiliar with, and, opening its mouth, began to inhale deeply. The Fly tried to pull away, but it was in vain. An uncontrollable, continuous stream of blazing flies was pulled from the shifting form of the Prince and began to flow into the Watcher's mouth, sucked into its glowing throat. The being that was Beelzebub began to waver and fade and Eligor heard a terrible scream emanate from the shredding cloud of flies. It lingered and echoed in his ears even after the Watcher had finished devouring the last of the Prince of Hell. And Eligor would never be sure, but it sounded to him as if that final, anguished cry was the name "Lilith."

Seeing their master gone, the remainder of the Fly's troops broke and ran, making their way as best they could over the shattered floor. Most met their destruction at the end of a lance.

Cradling his lord, Eligor landed with the help of Metaphrax, who, following the Guard Captain, had endeavored to save Sargatanas. The two Demons Minor laid him upon a broken plinth that rose from the rubble and the fallen skins and then turned as one when they heard the Watcher suddenly gather itself and shoot up toward the ceiling. Without losing a wing beat, Semjaza shattered the thick dome-tiles and, amidst a rain of debris, vanished with a final howl into the darkness of the Infernal night.

He did not care what the outcome of the duel between Beelzebub and Sargatanas was; either way, he knew his fate would, more than likely, be unpleasant, and so he backed away, followed and guarded by his Knights.

It had been easy, in the chaos of the Watcher's arrival, to exit the Rotunda. Easier still, given the Knights' prowess, to destroy the few demons who took notice and foolishly thought to pursue him.

Determining where my Knights and I will be well received, that *will be a challenge. It will be hard to gauge the loyalties of so many far-flung Demons Major. Sargatanas' call to arms left few of the undecided demons untapped. And he gained many silent allies. Surely, the farther out toward the Margins the more indifferent the demons will be and the greater my chances of success.*

Adramalik had been nothing if not prudent. Hell was a place of ceaseless change, but one thing had been constant; Beelzebub had been capricious in his madness and, because of that, Adramalik's preparations had been especially thorough. Millennia past, he had prepared for a time when he might have reason to flee Dis, but he had never envisioned it as a result of a successful rebellion. In a city as timeworn and fearful as the First City had been there were tunnels beyond count that, like a worm-chewed hide, pierced the ground and led away from the great citadel. He had investigated them himself and had

chosen an obscure one that led circuitously into the
Deep Warrens. There, in some ancient and unnamed lava
cavern, he had imagined his Order could wait out any
pursuers indefinitely. Only when he was certain they had
not been trailed would they emerge and hurry through
the Wastes to the Margins. After they escaped Dis he
could be more leisurely deciding their destination. Perhaps, now that Rofocale was no longer its governor, he
would head for Pygon Az; its proximity to the Pit was
unquestionably worrisome to him but also useful. No
one ventured voluntarily into those frozen wards.

His Knights were silent as they made their way
through the series of anterooms that led to the now-
shattered Rotunda. All were empty, but because he had
already decided that he would destroy whoever crossed
his path as he escaped, he carried his Order dagger. As
he swept through the last small chamber, he saw a
hunched figure approaching through the shadows. It was
Agares and he seemed completely oblivious to the oncoming Knights.

Whether it was out of some weary sense of nostalgia
or the odd feeling that destroying the ex–Prime Minister
was beneath him, Adramalik hesitated. He lowered his
blade and shook his head, a signal to Salabrus and the
trailing Knights, and then, as he passed, looked more
carefully at the twisted figure. Agares rolled his eyes up
in surprise as he regarded the hurrying scarlet-clad
demons, a strange smile crossing his ruined face. He
was carrying a short, ash-dusted battle-cleaver in one
hand and caressing a round, flat object in the other.
Adramalik's eyes opened wide as he recognized the ornate disk of the Architect-General Mulciber. *He always
had been the wall's weakest brick.*

Agares cackled as they passed; at this point Adramalik could not have cared less what happened to him. As
far as Adramalik was concerned, Mulciber had been an
intractable fool and received what he had deserved and,

as for Agares, his tortured existence was punishment enough. For now, navigating the broken and burning Keep would more than occupy Adramalik's and his Knights' attention. Freedom would come eventually, he knew, but it would surely be only after much blood and ash had been spilled. That in itself was exciting, but the prospect of being away from Dis was even more exhilarating. Far from regarding this as a shameful retreat, Adramalik saw it as the new beginning he had hoped for so long.

The Keep heaved beneath his feet and he broke into a trot. *Best to be free of the place, whatever was coming. Free of its miserable confines and, best of all, free of the Prince.*

ADAMANTINARX-UPON-THE-ACHERON

Lilith opened her eyes in Heaven.

The sky above danced with fiery colors, pure and beautiful, before her heavy-lidded, unfocused eyes just as she had always imagined it. Turning her head, she saw fabulously attired hosts of Seraphim standing under golden and crimson trees and peering from lofting bridges into the sparkling azure streams below. Many were staring at her.

She felt a coating falling away from her skin, a layer of small objects that pattered on the surface she was lying upon. Without moving, she looked for Sargatanas to ask him how he could have brought her with him, but her vision was too blurred to distinguish the features of the unmoving Seraphim.

She raised herself up on one elbow and felt light-headed, nauseated. Looking down slowly, she saw her skin mottled bluish-gray, its texture puckered and dry. She closed her eyes and tried to remember but was rewarded only with still air and silence.

Where is the perfumed breeze? she wondered. *Where*

are the musical calls of the chalkadri? And where,
where *is Sargatanas?*

She felt the smooth, hard stone beneath her and then
something else. Her shaky hands met with hundreds of
tiny, brittle objects that crushed easily beneath her fingertips. When she opened her eyes again she knew.

Lilith felt as if she could not breathe; her lungs
seemed congested and heavy. She dropped one clawed
foot to the cold floor, then the other, and stood for a moment in the hope that being upright would clear her
head. More of the tiny objects cascaded to the floor.

The Library . . . poor Zoray . . . the Fly's emissary!

She remembered and then stiffened suddenly, her
nausea sharpened, and she heaved. A terrible stream of
black, dead flies came up and corrupted the floor. She
did not stop gagging for minutes; the thought of those
unclean flies deep within her so repelled her that she
welcomed the retching. When she was finally finished,
the stained floor was like a sacrilege to her and she
wiped her trembling mouth, feeling ashamed.

But who had brought her here? Who could have
known about the Shrine? And she realized that of all the
demons left in Adamantinarx only Andromalius knew
of its existence. He had, undoubtedly, thought it to be
the safest place in the city. It was a sad choice.

She turned and looked at the bier, covered in the
small bodies of the flies that had nearly taken her life.
She regarded them, studying their contorted, differing
faces, a cold rage flaring to life deep within her. She
reached out with clawed hands and scooped up two
handfuls of the dead creatures, clenching them between
her fingers until a dusting of their shells lay before her.
From somewhere she heard herself screaming and saw
herself grabbing handful after handful, crushing and
pounding the brittle flies until not a single one was left
intact. Those in her puddled vomit she flattened into

black slime beneath her feet, sliding and slipping after each one, her screams of vengeance echoing throughout the Shrine.

When she had finally exhausted herself, panting and still trembling, she made her way from the center of the Shrine through its vestibule and out into the corridor beyond. Tears of gratitude streamed down her cheeks, for she knew that, somehow, Sargatanas had prevailed and the Prince was no more.

DIS

It was a dying. Not the sudden, implosive destruction that was the all-too-common termination of life in Hell, but then again, Eligor thought, his had not been commonplace mortal wounds. Sargatanas was passing and there was nothing he or any demon could do to prevent it.

The Guard had landed, gathering at a respectful distance, while he and Metaphrax Argastos tried to make the stricken demon as comfortable as they could.

Eligor wished that Satanachia could have been there. He felt there was little comfort in the presence of Demons Minor to a fallen seraph. Eligor regretted not knowing whether Satanachia had even survived the Battle of the Keep, let alone where he was. *And,* he wondered, *what has befallen Hannibal and his souls?*

Eligor looked down at Sargatanas, whose bony lids were fluttering open. It was so difficult to see him as Beelzebub had left him. His entire body and head looked as if it had been drilled through in a thousand places and the once-resplendent white plates of his armor showed tiny cracks throughout. When he moved, Eligor could hear the faintest of crackling sounds as bits flaked off.

"Eligor . . . Eligor, it is over," he said in a voice like the whispering ether of the Wastes. Small, almost invisible puffs of ash appeared with each word. "Did you ever . . . believe?"

"Always, my lord."

Sargatanas lifted his hand to place it upon Eligor's arm, but a piece fell away, shattering on the plinth. Metaphrax looked away, but Eligor gently took the once-heavy hand and placed it upon his own. The once-beautiful copper eyes were clouding over, patinated in a muddy greenish film.

How he loved his lord!

"It had to end like this," Sargatanas said painfully. "Like Lucifer, I, too, was selfish. And like him I have failed my followers. I had hopes it would be otherwise. I had . . . hopes."

"And dreams, my lord. You once said that it was time to *do* instead of dream. But I knew you never stopped dreaming. That *is* what this rebellion was all about. The Dream."

"You did understand, Eligor."

A thin dusting of ash was forming upon Sargatanas as the tiny cracks grew ever so slightly wider. His lids closed with each significant piece that fell away.

Eligor heard a soft, harmonic sound; he saw his lord's chest barely rising and falling and knew it had not issued from him. He looked up at Metaphrax, who shrugged, and then heard the faintest of tinkling sounds, like distant bells. Eligor looked up past the shattered dome and at the sky beyond. He thought it looked odd, lighter and cooler in hue, and would, he thought, be seen as a sign, spoken of millennia hence in tales of Sargatanas' Passing. It pleased him enormously.

He looked back at his lord, whose eyes were closed.

An earsplitting peal, as from some enormous bell, suddenly rang throughout the dome and simultaneously the floor around them rippled, sending rubble tumbling in all directions. A thick pillar of silent blue lightning streaked

GOD'S DEMON   405

down from Above, piercing the clouds, entering the
dome, and splitting into six separate, blazing columns directly before them. And then Eligor, whose breath had
caught in his throat, inhaled and the unmistakable, intox-
icating scent of blossoms filled his nostrils. It was a smell
that he had nearly forgotten, and he closed his eyes, em-
bracing it with every fiber of his soul. It was the celestial
fragrance of Heaven.

The columns collapsed into six coruscating oval
shapes, heavenly glyphs spinning within, and then, with
a burst of purest, supernal light that momentarily
blinded Eligor and the other demons, the shapes became
luminous six-winged Seraphim of the First Order.

Sargatanas' hand tightened upon Eligor's arm.

One of the Seraphim separated himself from the rest
and moved forward on barely wavering wings. His armor, fabulously chased and jeweled, shone fiercely with
the Light and was almost painful to regard. Eligor looked
at him and, at first, did not recognize him, so radiant was
his face, but as the angel drew nearer Eligor almost
leaped up, his joy was so profound.

Floating before him was Valefar.

"Is that you, Valefar?" Sargatanas said, his eyes closed
again. Thin wisps of steam could just be seen at their
corners.

"It is, my brother," Valefar said, his voice musical
again. "I am here for you."

Sargatanas tried to raise his hand from Eligor's arm
but could not. "What is it like?"

"You will soon see. It is as it was before. So full of
Light."

"And the Throne . . . ?"

". . . can always forgive those who strive against
Darkness. Whether it's from outside or from within."

Sargatanas' chest rose and he sighed. Eligor saw him
laboring to breathe, saw even more of him dissipating
into ash and bone shards.

"But I've failed them all, Valefar." His voice was almost inaudible. "Only Beelzebub is gone."

"No, dear friend, no. You've given them hope where there was none. The Gates are now opened and it is for them to find their own way back."

Valefar came toward the three demons. He knelt and took Sargatanas' hand from Eligor's arm. He leaned in close to Sargatanas' ear.

"Rise, Sargatanas," he whispered. "Rise and reawaken."

Eligor felt a gathering wind begin to swirl around his lord and watched it focus upon and erode his body until only the vaguest shape of the Demon Major lay outlined on the cracked and windswept plinth. An enormous pulse of energy exploded from the plinth, expanding outward until it hit the far walls of the Rotunda. The countless skins that had hung for so long from the dome's ceiling and were now draped about and under the rubble began to stir, to fill out and take shape as the souls they had once been.

The wind subsided. Of Sargatanas' body very little was left. In its place a radiance formed and became a brilliance that, in turn, became substance, and Eligor saw Sargatanas as he had been from before the Fall. Gone were the trappings of Hell, the flesh-robes and bone-plates and flames above his head, replaced now by the supple, golden flesh, wings, and pearlescent raiments of Heaven. Slowly, the Seraph sat upright and rose to his feet. He bent and picked up his flaming sword.

"Leave it behind, Sargatanas," Valefar said. "You will not be needing it."

Sargatanas nodded, regarding the blade, and then held it out to Eligor. The demon took it and held it closely, reverently. He dropped to one knee and Sargatanas put his hand on Eligor's shoulder.

"Follow me, Eligor. Heaven will shine brighter for your presence."

"I will, my lord. I promise."

Sargatanas turned away and Eligor heard Valefar say to him, "Come, my friend; it is time to go home."

One by one, the seven Seraphim extended their wings and launched themselves into the air. Before they reached halfway to the dome's broken opening they had each flared into a dazzling concentration of light and, like wayward stars returning to the firmament, shot up through the clouds.

Clutching the sword, Eligor stared up into the dark sky of Hell for some time, waiting until the lambency of his lord's passage had faded. But, to Eligor's amazement, a blue-white spot remained, fixed and brilliant, visible between the scudding clouds. A new star! To Eligor, it was the perfect symbol of the hope that now lay before them.

When he brought his gaze down, the Flying Guard was dispersing, undoubtedly to pursue the remnants of the Fly's legions, and only Metaphrax remained. He, like Eligor, was silent, affected. He turned with a stunned, halfhearted wave and followed the troops out of the Rotunda.

Eligor looked at the plinth, at the spot where his lord had lain. A handful of light, clumped ash remained roughly where his hand had been—and something else. Reaching down, Eligor pushed the ashes gently, reverently, aside and pulled from them a small, white figurine. Lilith. It had been in Sargatanas' closed hand all the while.

XXXIV

DIS

The Keep would be razed. That much the soul knew as he made his way up flight after flight of its dank steps.

The fighting had been over for some time—long enough for Hannibal to send back to Adamantinarx for some of his personal possessions. Swinging upon his back was a large Abyssal-hide pack, filled with everything he would need for a prolonged stay.

His souls had suffered great losses but had, too, attained a stature among the demons that they could have never hoped for before the rebellion. With Beelzebub gone, the souls were in a good position to reach for freedoms unheard of since Hell had been founded. And Hannibal was in a position to ask for power he could never have dreamt of. He would ask for, and take, it all.

His feet led him steadily upward along a path he had never before traveled but which seemed impossibly, disturbingly familiar. The stairs were proportioned for the stride of demons, and he stopped more frequently than he would have desired. Occasionally, as he wended his way up through the Keep, he saw open areas still supported only by beams of splintered bone, empty spaces that were evidence of the Watcher's explosive passage up through the massive structure. There was no point repairing the damage and so it would stay as it was for hundreds of years, until, bit by bit, the entire structure was torn down.

After hours of ascent, Hannibal found himself at the base of the unadorned tower. It was a foreboding sight. The windowless, tubelike interior shot up into an oppressive darkness lit by very few braziers, the staircase barely seen winding its way toward the top. He sat down on the tall first step and caught his breath, wondering what he would find when he made it to the chamber high above. And for the thousandth time wondering what drove him to this spot. Part of him was grateful for the time alone; many of the souls he had encountered since the battle still eyed him suspiciously for his broken promise, for his acts upon the ramp. He had hoped that with victory would come an understanding among them of his motives. But how could they understand something of which he, himself, was uncertain?

He tightened his pack's straps, straightened his cloak, and continued the climb. Periodically, the steps disappeared into the shadows and he had to feel his way up the curving stairs, cautious not to come too close to the edge and risk slipping and plunging hundreds of feet to his destruction. After a few hours, sweating and breathing hard, he reached the top landing. A huge door, dimly lit by a single small brazier, stood before him, its surface laced with bone designs. He worriedly looked for a keyhole, fearing that he might have made the arduous journey for naught had the door been locked, but fortune or destiny was on his side. When he twisted the oversized latch, the door reluctantly gave way. He gave it an extra shove with his newly grown arm and it moved easily inward. *Foolish to think one would need a lock here. No demon would have made this climb without having been Summoned.*

When he entered the wide, round room a hot, sulphurous wind whipped at him, drying the sweat upon his skin and ruffling his cloak. Three wide windows opened out onto a vast panorama of the region surrounding the Keep; it would have been an amazing view of Dis in the days when the capital still stood.

The room's interior was proportioned for a demon; the spare furnishings—ledges mostly—were too high for Hannibal to sit upon. He placed his pack down and removed his cape, rubbing his shoulders from the strap's chafing. His new arm—now nearly the proper length—ached less and less and felt very different from his original limb. Its muscles were heavier, denser, and he put this down to its newness and his improved health. Whatever the reason, it seemed almost like a reward for his loss and it pleased him.

Strangely restless, he spotted a pair of rectangular stone structures that rose up, side by side, in the center of the circular room. He moved toward them and noticed the twin runnels that, incised into the darkly stained floor, ran from one side of the chamber and disappeared beneath their bases, clearly some ingenious mechanism for bringing liquid into the troughs. Cages seemed to be visible in the deep shadows. *What were they for?* he wondered. *And* whose *chambers had these been?* He would have to ask some of the imprisoned demons.

He searched the room for clues and found some closed doors. Something kept him from opening them and he moved on, continuing his superficial investigation. There would be time for a more detailed examination, for he had already decided that these would be his quarters while he stayed in the Keep and searched for Imilce. With the Keep coming down his chances of finding her were, at best, fair. But he would try, if for no other reason than to tell her what he had done here in Hell. Between the unparalleled view and the welcome isolation he would endure the climb to occupy them. And anyone who had important news could make the climb themselves to convey it.

His eyes fell upon his pack and he went to it and, kneeling, emptied it out upon the floor. A large object, heavily wrapped, tumbled out with a dull thud and he began to tug at its wrappings until it came free. He started to reach for it with his old hand but changed his mind in midstream. It was too heavy to pick up with that weaker limb and he corrected himself, grasping it with his new hand by its thick handle and lifting it easily to eye level. The Hook looked right in this place, its ten diamond-edged points gleaming menacingly in the low light. Catching a glimpse of the troughs, Hannibal nodded to himself and carried the weapon to them. With some difficulty, he placed it into one of the deep troughs and stood back. It fit perfectly, but something was wrong. He looked at the runnels and frowned; that was a mystery he would have to work out.

Exhaustion finally overtook him and he reclined upon a ledge. As he closed his eyes he thought about Div and La and the other souls he had once known in his existence as a slave and reflected on his amazing rise. It had all been his doing; no one else had been ambitious enough to attempt what he had done; he owed no one. But best of all, in his new chambers, he knew he was where he should be. And he was, for the time being, content.

The little tools were much too delicate and easily lost to be brought in her packs; they would have to be left behind for when she returned. *When I return. That is a very odd thought. How many millennia will I be away? I have no idea, nor do I have any true notion of where I'm going.* She put the tiny chisel down on the table, alongside its fellow tools. Lilith wondered, as she had for weeks, whether her departure from Adamantinarx was madness, whether her goals were as unclear as they seemed. She only knew that, with Sargatanas gone, she had no real reason to remain in a half-destroyed city. As the region's new governor, Satanachia, was more than capable of administering to the rebuilding process. Someday, when she returned, she would find a beautiful city where souls and demons lived together in some form of equality. That was the dream. Her dream.

She would head out toward the Margins, bringing her tenets of hope to those souls in the smaller, remote cities who knew nothing of the rebellion. She knew that it was a dangerous mission, but she thought that, for the time being, it would take her mind off recent events. She was not bitter, simply tired, and the traveling might rehabilitate her. Hell was an unpredictable place, and as resourceful as she was, she would face its many hazards as a challenge. But she would not be completely unprepared.

She slid the long lid from a plain silver case that Eligor had brought to her and saw, lying upon the finest, iridescent Abyssal skin, Sargatanas' sword, *Lukiftias-pe-Ripesol*. The tempering that had brought its souls together was impossible to break, and so a sword it would stay. In Sargatanas' hand it had been light and deadly, but in hers it would be a two-handed weapon. While she was not so proficient in the Art Martial—what little she knew she had learned had been with Sargatanas—Lilith was comforted just knowing that it was coming with her. And she suspected there would be more than ample opportunity to work on the craft in the Wastes. She kept the sword wrapped in its skins and tied it to the outside of her pack, easily accessible but not obvious.

A rustling in the next room brought a smile to her face. The miracle of Sargatanas' Passage had brought Ardat back to Lilith, and there was nothing short of destruction that would separate them ever again. Ardat appeared in the doorway wearing the skins Lilith had once worn, and her heart was filled with warmth for the handmaiden. It seemed Lilith's world never stopped changing around her.

"Mistress, I have prepared your skins. Are you finished here?"

Lilith looked around her chambers, making sure everything was in order; she did not want to unseal them when she returned and find them in disarray. Her eyes fell back upon her small worktable and the two figures that stood upon it. One was the small bone figurine of herself, taken from the dome by Eligor. It was relatively crude—an example of her earliest work, executed before she had found her voice as a sculptor. Next to it was a piece she had only just finished, a representation of Sargatanas fashioned of many pieces of the purest white Abyssal bone that she had begun back in Dis. It was intricate and yet strong, a work of subtlety, grace, and power reflecting, she thought, all of his attributes, and she regarded it as her very best sculpture. Originally, she had planned to keep them together, but on impulse she picked them up, carefully wound a scrap of skin around them, and placed them in an outside pocket of her pack. She hoped Eligor would like them.

"Yes, Ardat, I am."

EPILOGUE

When he put his quill down it was atop a large stack of neatly arranged leaves of parchment. It had taken him over two full cycles of Algol's transit to complete his reminiscences, two cycles in which he had wandered far to collect the fullest accounts of the events surrounding Sargatanas' Rebellion.

In that time, the palace, the city's focal point and arguably most unharmed building in Adamantinarx, had been tirelessly repaired. No longer was it open to the tempests of Hell; no longer could he so easily hear the murmurings of passing demons through holes in the walls. He could hear the hammers of artisans—demon and soul alike—as they brought the wounded friezes back to life. Even now, he could see the barges heavy with native stone as they docked, manned by souls who wanted to work rather than had to. It was a new time in Hell.

The Rebellion was over and yet it continued on in its new reforms. While he was aware of the changes in those wards and cities that had been closest to the battles and survived, he also knew that there were many regions as yet unaffected. This, he thought, would take time. Already there were some who did not fully understand Sargatanas' gift, who thought to simply take up arms and indiscriminately rid Hell of their own concept of evil. Theirs would be a long path.

As he thought of these changes, he also thought of Lilith and wondered where she might be. Somewhere, wandering the distant Wastes, undoubtedly. He had watched her leave the city, watched her as she and her hand-maiden had boarded a barge on the Acheron, and watched, too, as the ship had disappeared into the ashy distance. And on his ascent up the Rule and back to his chambers he had thought about his lord, Sargatanas. It had all begun, the discontent and the dream, at the massive statue that still stood not too far from where he climbed.

Eligor sighed and straightened the stack of parchment leaves, placing the beautiful statuette of Sargatanas and the cruder one of Lilith atop them and donning his cloaks, and left his chambers to descend through the palace and out onto the Rule. The avenue was growing more crowded each day with a steady flow of workers and artisans, but it was not yet as bustling as it had once been. While there were very few buildings left, he walked the Rule out of habit, not necessity; only the sidewalks remained and he could have easily walked a more direct route, but he liked to see the city's progress. He stopped a few times to observe the foundations of some new buildings being laid by souls and demons alike, but, distracted, he focused on the giant cruciform statue and headed toward it. When the city was at its height there would have been no chance of seeing its relatively low base, but now, with few buildings standing, he could see it still survived, an anomalous soul-brick structure in a city now growing only with native stone. Why, he wondered, had it not been taken down?

He walked steadily until he arrived at the foot of the stepped plinth. For just a moment he thought of that other plinth, the one from the Black Dome that he had had brought back to Adamantinarx and enshrined.

Slowly, he paced the base's periphery until he came upon that which he had hoped to find. He put his hand upon the rugose brick and felt its warmth and then, suddenly, it opened a piercingly blue eye and stared up at him. For a moment their gaze met and then he sighed and stood up. He looked into the heavens and saw the equally blue star—the star they called Zimiah, the Gate—and knew what he would have to do. The statue would have to come down and the bricks of its base—this brick in particular—would have to be resurrected. That much, he knew, he owed his lord.